THE NAZI HUNTER

ALSO BY ALAN ELSNER

GUARDED BY ANGELS:
How My Father and Uncle Survived Hitler and Cheated Stalin

GATES OF INJUSTICE:
The Crisis in America's Prisons

A NOVEL

THE NAZI HUNTER

ALAN ELSNER

ARCADE PUBLISHING
NEW YORK

FIRST EDITION

This is a work of fiction. Names, characters, places, and incidents are either the work of the author's imagination or are used fictitiously.

Library of Congress Cataloging-in-Publication Data

Elsner, Alan.
  The Nazi hunter : a novel / Alan Elsner. —1st ed.
    p. cm.
  ISBN-13: 978-1-55970-839-5 (alk. paper)
  ISBN-10: 1-55970-839-5 (alk. paper)
  1. United States. Dept. of Justice. Office of Special Investigations—Officials and employees—Fiction. 2. Nazi hunters—Fiction. 3. Ex-Nazis—United States—Fiction. 4. War criminals—United States—Fiction. 5. Germans—United States—Fiction. 6. Belzec (Concentration camp)—Fiction. 7. Militia movements—United States—Fiction. I. Title.

  PS3605.L76N39 2007
  813'.6—dc22   2006101357

Published in the United States by Arcade Publishing, Inc., New York
Distributed by Hachette Book Group USA

Visit our Web site at www.arcadepub.com

10 9 8 7 6 5 4 3 2 1

Designed by API

EB

PRINTED IN THE UNITED STATES OF AMERICA

To my mother, Helen, who gave me music

THE NAZI HUNTER

1

*Why do I pass the highways by
That other travelers take?*

— "THE SIGNPOST" BY WILHELM MÜLLER, MUSIC BY FRANZ SCHUBERT

NOVEMBER, NOT APRIL, is the cruelest month. At least, it is in Washington, D.C., in an election year.

This year, 1994, was especially cruel for Democrats. The Republicans had won control of both houses of Congress, and now the halls of the Capitol and the federal government were quaking. You couldn't turn on the TV without seeing the pudgy, self-satisfied face of Mitch Conroy, newly elected speaker of the House, promising to shake things up. His nasal Texas twang filled the airwaves. Big government was in retreat. Heads were about to roll. You could hear the reverberations even on the fifth floor of the Department of Justice, where I worked.

It was one of those late Novembers, just after Thanksgiving, when the rain is pouring down outside your window and it's getting dark and the office becomes more and more stuffy until you feel your eyelids drooping and you catch yourself reading the same phrase three times without taking it in. I was looking forward to hitting the treadmill at the health club and cleaning out the cobwebs.

It had been a typical day, punctuated by at least five cups of coffee. Nine o'clock staff meeting, ten o'clock budget meeting, noon briefing with lawyers, twelve thirty homemade sandwich at my desk (tuna with lettuce and tomato), and then two hours reviewing files for a deposition the following week. My mouth tasted like the inside of a coffeepot. I was thinking of going for a sixth cup.

There was a knock on the door. A middle-aged woman poked her head in. She wore a tattered raincoat and carried a sopping umbrella in one hand and a large, battered old pocketbook bulging at the seams in the other.

"Is this the Office of Special Investigations?" she asked in a heavy German accent.

The security guards in the lobby and the receptionist were supposed to protect me from members of the public wandering in from the street, but the receptionist had left early because her kid had strep. "Can I help you? Who are you looking for?" I asked.

This woman looked harmless — tired, with gray hair escaping from beneath a faded scarf — but you never know; she had snuck past the guards. I reached for the phone, ready to call security.

"I am looking for Marek Cain, the Nazi hunter," she said. "I have information."

To this day, I still get a kick out of those words. Nazi hunter! They summon images of fearless adventurers tracking down ruthless Gestapo torturers to fortified jungle hideouts in South America. If only it were even a little like that. The truth is much less glamorous. I'm an attorney, not an adventurer, not a secret agent, not even a private investigator. I wear dark suits and sober ties. I spend my days in archives going through microfilm, and in meetings, and occasionally in courtrooms. The Nazis I deal with — far from being dangerous warlords — usually turn out to be gray little men in their seventies or eighties leading dull, anonymous lives in the suburbs of Cleveland or Detroit, tens of years and thousands of miles away from the horrors they committed as young men. But there was no need to tell her any of this. If she wanted a Nazi hunter, I was her man.

"I am Marek Cain, the deputy director. How can I help you?"

She scrutinized me through watery eyes and seemed reassured by what she saw. Her eyes jumped to my knitted black *kippah* — the yarmulke I wear on my head — lingered there for a microsecond, and then met mine again.

"I have important information, Mr. Cain. And there are documents, many documents." Her hands were trembling. She looked at the chair in front of me, silently asking permission to sit down. I nodded, and she dropped into it, unbuttoning her coat. Stale steam rose from her clothes as they began to dry out.

"Before you tell me about the documents, perhaps you should tell me who you are," I said, picking up a legal pad to take notes.

"Why are you writing?" she asked.

"I always take notes during meetings. It helps me remember."

She hesitated, wheezing, and removed her scarf, revealing more gray, unkempt hair, damp around the edges from the rain. I'd say about forty-five, maybe a little older. She wore no makeup; her eyes were puffy and bloodshot, and I noticed how yellow her teeth were. Her fingers were stained almost brown with nicotine, a rare sight these days. She wore a deep ruby-red brooch pinned to her sweater, her one decorative touch.

"Do you speak German? It's more easy for me. You know German, *ja?*" she asked.

"*Naturlich*," I said, switching to her language. "What is your name?"

She took a deep breath. "My name is Sophie Reiner." It meant nothing to me.

"Tell me something about yourself, Frau Reiner. Where are you from? What do you do?"

"Ach, there isn't so much to tell. I'm from Germany, as you see. A tourist in your country. As for what I do, call me a lover of German songs."

A strange reply, but I didn't pursue it. I wanted her to feel comfortable before I started grilling her. "How did you find out about me, Frau Reiner?"

"It's Fraulein Reiner. You have been interviewed by our German newspapers," she said. Again I let it pass. The *New York Times* had run a profile of me a month earlier, but I had been quoted overseas only rarely. My boss, Eric Rosen, a self-made man who worshipped his creator, usually insisted on handling interviews himself.

"Mr. Cain, these documents are important," the woman said. "I hope you will not turn me away before you have seen them." Her voice trailed off. She looked at me like a shaggy dog hoping for a biscuit.

"I wasn't going to turn you away. What is the nature of these documents?"

A pause, then she wheezed, "They have to do with Belzec. Have you heard of Belzec?"

Asking someone who deals with the Holocaust about Belzec is like asking an opera buff if he knows where La Scala is. Belzec was an extermination camp in eastern Poland where the Nazis murdered half a million Jews in 1942 alone. My own grandparents were among its victims.

"I've heard about it," I said, keeping my voice level.

"This concerns Belzec and someone who was there. The truth has been buried very deeply for many years. It has been well hidden. I can no longer stand aside and let this continue. You will surely understand what I am talking about when you see the material."

She mispronounced the name of the camp. In Polish, the word sounds like "Beljetz." This made me wary.

"Please tell me more," I said. Despite its notoriety, scholars know less about the inner workings of Belzec than those of any other Nazi death camp. Few of the Germans and Ukrainians who served there were ever identified. Even fewer were brought to trial. If there were new documents, I wanted them. And she knew that.

"This is difficult for me to explain," she said. "I have not known what to do. I thought perhaps there was another way. But there is not. The world must know."

As I listened and scribbled notes, it occurred to me that maybe she was a kook. But I'm not a judge or psychotherapist. Strange people sometimes know strange things. I looked up at her. "Truth is indeed of the highest importance, Fraulein Reiner," I said, matching her formal tone. "Perhaps if you show me one of these documents, I could examine it and offer you an opinion." A brief glance would probably be enough to see if there was anything to them.

"I didn't bring them. I wanted to meet you first."

"I see. And may one ask, where are they?"

"They are safe. I didn't know if I could trust you. Now I think maybe I can. I could bring them tomorrow."

As the Book of Proverbs tells us, "Let the wise man hear and increase his understanding." I smiled and stood up. "Very well, Fraulein, it shall be as you say." I glanced at my appointment book and saw that the morning was taken up with meetings. "Tomorrow afternoon would be best for me, shall we say at four? Come back with these documents, and I will be happy to examine them." I extended my hand, but she just nodded, picked up her umbrella, and strode out of the room, leaving a damp patch on the seat.

I thought about her on and off the next morning, wondering what she might bring. But she never showed up. My work is full of false trails and clues leading nowhere. I figured this was just one more.

I was wrong.

So this is Washington, D.C.; I thought it would be bigger. While I was waiting to get paid, I started walking around, checking out targets. This city disgusts me. Five blocks from the White House or the Capitol, and you find yourself in creepy alleyways strewn with syringes, baggies, cast-off condoms. The city teems with druggies and panhandlers—the dregs of the dregs. They're everywhere, sleeping over grates, curled up on park benches, slumped in doorways, pushing supermarket carts piled with junk, feeding on the city like maggots on rotting flesh. "Alas, alas, that great city Babylon, that mighty city! For in one hour is thy judgment come."

They approach you with hands outstretched and demand money; you look into their faces; you see their rheumy eyes and rotting teeth and you smell them—stench of piss, booze, and vomit. This one tells you he's hungry. He looks like a guy I used to know in jail, Dwayne Robertson, except scrawnier. How sweet it would be to shove a knife between his ribs and twist. I'd be doing him and the world a favor.

Last night, I dreamed of Dwayne and woke up in a cold sweat. I must have been yelling in my sleep, because someone in the next room was banging on the wall, shouting at me to shut the fuck up.

Half the city is looking for me. I strike and melt away, another face in the crowd. To them, I'm nothing. Shorty, Squirt, Shrimp, Tiny, Runt, Midget — I've been all of them. Nobody gives me a second look. I wrapped the knife in her scarf, stuffed it in her pocketbook, and left it on top of a trashcan for one of the lowlifes to find.

Each night in my hotel room, I read. Apart from the Bible, my favorite is The Turner Diaries, especially when they blow up the FBI. I must have read it a thousand times, wondering if it really could be done. Yesterday, I scouted the building out. It's huge, spread over three blocks. You could never get close enough with a truck to do much damage. That's the difference between fact and fiction. Half the buildings around here belong to the federal government. It's just a question of finding the right one.

I have begun writing my Statement to the American People. I want everyone to understand why I did it.

2

The first graves were dug by around 100 Jews brought to Belzec from nearby towns. After the graves were dug, these Jewish workers were shot.

— TESTIMONY OF EDWARD LUCZYNSKI

THE OFFICE OF SPECIAL INVESTIGATIONS was created in the late 1970s when America finally woke up to the fact that thousands of Nazi war criminals were living quiet, respectable lives here. My job was to identify them, gather evidence of their crimes, bring them to court, strip them of their U.S. citizenship, and send them back to wherever they came from.

By 1994, I'd been doing this for ten years. I first wandered in for a summer internship after my second year of law school, but now the work was getting to me. At first, I was excited by the thrill of the chase and the satisfaction of bringing evil men to account. The Torah tells us to pursue justice, and I was doing just that. Each time I nailed one, it was a small measure of revenge for what the Nazis did to my family. But lately, I'd been having nightmares. The scenes usually came to me just before dawn when I was halfway between sleep and waking. They were in black and white, like wartime footage. Faces, terrified, puckered with cold. Sometimes I thought I glimpsed my mother. Guttural shouts, the dull thud of gunfire—and I jerked awake in a cold sweat. I tried seeking calm through prayer, saying the familiar words of Modeh Ani, with which all religious Jews begin their day: *"I gratefully thank you, O living and eternal king, for You have returned my soul within me with compassion. Abundant is Your faithfulness."*

The prayer was intended to bind me to God in a way that would make me continuously aware of His presence throughout the day. But with dreadful images still in my head, it was hard to achieve the proper mindset for prayer — what we Orthodox Jews call *kavanah*. I tried to empty my brain of extraneous thoughts and direct it upward and inward. I tried hard, but I didn't always succeed.

I thought of seeking counseling, but I was ashamed of my weakness. I considered talking to my rabbi, but he was a new guy, three years out of rabbinical school, hopelessly naive and idealistic. I had no one else to confide in. My most recent girlfriend had dumped me six months ago.

"That's the trouble with you," Jennifer had told me in one of our final and most hurtful fights. "This Nazi-hunting thing has taken over your life. All your anger is channeled into it. You're relentless. There's no room in your head for anything else except that and religion. When was the last time we did something fun together? You're always working, always scribbling on your legal pads, filing your files, building neat piles of papers. I can't live like this anymore!"

There wasn't much I could say. We'd been dating on and off for almost a year, but it wasn't working. Jennifer Osterman was an editor in a small publishing house that specialized in books about self-esteem — where it comes from, how it grows, how you lose it, how you get it back. Jennifer read them all as if they contained spiritual manna from heaven. On paper, she was perfect for me. My mother, dead these twenty-two years, would have loved her. My father approved. She said she was willing to live a traditional life, keep kosher, observe the Sabbath, give our children a religious education. But something held me back. I knew she wasn't the one. Where was the passion, the look, the touch that would make my pulse race? In Genesis, when Jacob met Rachel, his muscles bulged with the superhuman strength to move a giant boulder from the mouth of a well. And then he kissed her and lifted up his voice and wept for joy. I wanted that same fervor, not a pale imitation from a self-help book.

So Jennifer left and found herself someone else. Mutual friends expected an engagement announcement any day.

She was right about one thing, though. My work obsession was unhealthy. I needed to separate myself from the job, but the beasts who had murdered my grandparents might be living in comfort, right here in the United States. If I couldn't sleep at night, why should they?

Whenever one of those hateful dreams wrenched me awake, as it did two days after my meeting with Sophie Reiner, there was no going back to sleep. I got up, said a prayer, splashed my face with water, and went for a run. My usual five-mile circuit took me through Rock Creek Park, just under forty minutes. After that, there was still time to do the laundry, iron some shirts, vacuum the living room, and read the *Washington Post* over breakfast. I poured out my granola, added skim milk, waited for my first coffee of the day to brew, and sat down. That's when I saw what had happened to Sophie. She was on the front page, below the fold.

As had been the case for most of the past month, the lead story covered the new House speaker, Mitch Conroy. He was promising to shut down two or three government departments. He had his eye on Energy and Education. He could hardly dismantle Justice, so my job was probably safe. The ceasefire around Sarajevo was holding, but the Serbs were still slaughtering Bosnians in other enclaves, while the world looked on and did nothing. There was talk Jimmy Carter might fly to the region on a peace mission. Then, a smaller headline, near the bottom of the page: "Woman Found Dead Near Museum." I scanned the first couple of paragraphs and suddenly felt queasy. The cup in my hand started shaking. I thought I was going to throw up.

The woman was about fifty years old. She carried no identification, and the police were appealing for anyone who might recognize her description. She had been wearing a trench coat and a red pin. She had been sitting in my office, droplets of rain still caught in her hair. Someone had slashed her throat. Her body was found under a tree a couple of blocks behind the Air and Space Museum. There were no witnesses.

9

Washington is used to murders, but they usually take place well away from the tourist areas. Sophie's body had been found almost within sight of the Capitol. The police commissioner promised speedy action. The mayor insisted the city was safe and urged tourists not to change their plans. Mitch Conroy, who had an opinion on everything, had also joined the act. Crime was out of control, he opined. We needed zero tolerance for criminals and swift executions for murderers. Someone needed to clean house, and, like a Texas sheriff, Mitch was the man to do it.

I had not really known this woman — we spoke only for ten minutes — yet I felt strangely bereft. Why had she been killed? I felt disoriented, out of my depth. I write everything down, puzzle it out step-by-step. But I could see no logic here.

And it's different when the victim was sitting in your office two days before, dripping on your carpet. The whole thing seemed so bizarre, so random, and I might be the only person able to identify her. I reached for the phone, but decided to drive to work and call from the office. I needed time to digest all this.

A sheet of paper had been stuffed beneath one of the windshield wipers of my car. I unfolded it, thinking it was a flyer from a local business, and saw written in large red characters "6-6-6." Probably a prank by some neighborhood kids, I figured, screwing it up in a ball and shoving it in my pocket.

It started to rain as I drove, a freezing, wind-driven rain. Crawling along Connecticut Avenue in my battered Civic, I mentally replayed my conversation with Sophie Reiner, as waves of water smacked like drum rolls against the roof and windshield. Had she seemed fearful? Had she known death was stalking her? There was no sign of it that I could recall. She had been nervous, certainly, but fearful? No, she fully expected to meet me the following day.

Washingtonians hate the rain. They somehow feel that in the nation's capital, everyone has the right to life, liberty, the pursuit of happiness, and perpetual smoggy sunshine. People rarely complain about the summer's stifling humidity and polluted air. But if it rains — or, even worse, snows — it's an offense against the natural order. Traffic slows to a stately five miles an hour. Normally, this doesn't bother me — I like to think in the car or listen to the radio — but I was jumpy, and the slow crawl made me even edgier.

Forty-five minutes later, I finally reached the office, shucked off my coat, and sat down behind my desk. I thought about a cup of coffee, decided against it, and adjusted my tie, even though it was already straight. I knew I should call the police, but first I wanted to speak to Eric Rosen, my boss and the head of the OSI. He should know if I was about to get involved in a news story.

It was already almost ten o'clock. Eric was in his office, sitting behind one of the larger desks in Washington, D.C., where outsize desks match outsize egos, reading a piece of paper. "What's going on?" I asked.

"Just another hate letter," he said, waving it at me, "which I'm about to send over to the FBI, where they will no doubt shove it in a folder with all the other dreck I've been sending them and forget about it. We've been getting more than usual recently." I caught a glimpse of a swastika scrawled in red crayon.

"I've received a few, too," I told him. "I've been collecting them in a file under *W* for wackos."

"Send them to me. I'll pass them all on to the FBI. Maybe they'll find a pattern. Anyway, what do you want? Make it quick. I'm leaving for the airport soon."

"Where to this time?"

"Boston. I'm the keynote speaker for the Union of Concerned Scientists. Fascinating group. Should be an interesting discussion."

Eric was a *macher* — a mover and shaker, a man who gets things done. He was in constant demand as a speaker, which suited him just fine. He fed his Napoleonic self-image on a steady diet of public acclaim, while I stayed in the background and kept the office functioning. A hyperactive little man, Eric was certainly a commanding orator. No one was better at whipping up an emotional froth. Afterward, he would stand on the podium, thrusting his barrel chest out, smiling with satisfaction, letting the applause wash over him in warm waves.

"Concerned scientists, eh? How many concerned scientists does it take to change a lightbulb?"

"How many?"

"One. All the rest will be so enthralled by your speech they won't notice the dark," I said.

"I hope that awful joke isn't why you came to disturb me," Eric said, frowning.

"No, I came to ask whether you saw that item in the *Post* today about the woman murdered on the Mall." I sank irrevocably into his overstuffed plush leather couch.

"Yeah, I saw it, but I didn't pay much attention. I was more interested in who the Republicans want to appoint as chairman of the Judiciary Committee. I assume you've been following the speculation. They're talking about Senator — "

"She was here a couple of days ago," I said, puncturing his stream of consciousness.

"Who was here?"

"The dead woman, the one in the article."

"She was *what*?"

"She came to see me in my office. At around four o'clock."

"Here? In this building?"

"I recognized her from the description in the paper. The police said she was wearing a red pin. She was wearing it when she came to see me."

"*Gotenyu*! Have you called the police?" In moments of stress or surprise, Eric always lapsed into Yiddish.

"I wanted to tell you first. And I really need some coffee."

"Help yourself." He indicated the machine in the corner. I pulled myself off the couch and asked if he wanted a cup.

"Mark, what on earth did she want from you?" My name is Marek, but everyone except my father calls me Mark. I poured the coffee and sat back down.

"She said her name was Sophie Reiner, and she had some documents she wanted to show me. She said they concerned Belzec."

"What documents? Where are they?"

"She never handed them over. She said she would bring them the next day — that would have been yesterday. But she never showed up. Now I know why."

"Why did she come to see you? I'm the *balebos*, the one in charge here."

"How the heck do I know? Maybe you were busy. Maybe she was too scared to approach the Great and Mighty Oz himself. Perhaps she was intimidated by the many reports she'd read about your towering intellect."

"Did you ask her why she came to you?"

"She told me she'd read about me in the German newspapers."

"You're not supposed to talk to reporters without my permission. Especially not the foreign press. Remember, I speak for this office."

"Relax, Eric, and let's focus on the dead woman just for a second. Anyway, it's been years since I've been quoted over there — that's what was so strange about her remark."

"What about that *New York Times* profile of you last month, which you persuaded me to authorize against my better judgment? A German paper might have picked it up and translated it."

The *Times* had latched on to me after a big case I'd won against a former Romanian priest. He'd organized a mob to kill a couple of hundred Jews in 1944. The judge had stripped him of his U.S. citizenship and expelled him from the country. Eric had wanted to do the interview himself, but the reporter insisted that I was the focus of the story, since I was the one who had argued the case in court.

"Well, that might explain it," I said thoughtfully.

Eric asked, "Are you sure she said Belzec? Maybe she meant Bergen-Belsen." This was the concentration camp in Germany where 70,000 people died of starvation, exposure, and disease. Anne Frank died there, so it was better known to the public than Belzec, though less significant in the history of the Holocaust. People often confused the two.

"No," I told him. "She said Belzec, although she mispronounced it. She was quite definite about it."

Eric fell silent. I took a sip of his coffee and grimaced. *I should have known better.* It was extremely hard to get a decent cup anywhere in any government building. I brought my own beans to work and ground them fresh each morning. I knew Eric and I were both thinking the same thing. Where were the documents? Did they even exist?

He sighed. "Do you need me to be there when the police come? I can cancel Boston."

I took off my glasses and started polishing them. I was feeling a little better now that I had talked to someone. "No, I can handle it. You go ahead and speak to your concerned scientists. They need you more than I do," I said.

An hour later, I was telling the story to two detectives. Sam Reynolds, a burly black man with gray hair, had the weary look of a man who wanted you to know he had seen and heard just about everything. The other detective, Connie Novak, was half his size and not much more than half his age, with twice as much hair and bright red lipstick. They both sat up straight in their seats when I said I could identify their Jane Doe.

"She was here in your office?" Reynolds asked, chewing gum furiously.

"That's right. Two days ago. She sat on the same chair you're sitting on now. She was wearing the red pin they described in the newspaper. That's how I knew it was her. She said her name was Sophie Reiner." I spelled it out for them. "She was German."

"Shit. That means the State Department, ambassadors, political pressure, all kinds of crap," Reynolds said grimly.

"I spoke to her in German. She had a north German accent, I would say."

Novak immediately got on the phone. "If she was staying in a D.C. hotel, we should be able to track her down pretty quickly," she said.

There was a knock on the door, and my assistant poked her head in. "Got a sec, Mark?" she asked, flashing an infectious grin in my direction.

"Not now, Lynn. Maybe in an hour. I'll give you a call when I'm free." She left, and I turned back to the detectives.

"What did this Reiner woman want with you?" Reynolds asked. I described our conversation as well as I could remember, referring to my notes.

"You're a pretty careful guy, Professor, writing it all down like that," Novak said. I wasn't sure if her voice held a note of approval or censure.

"I try to be."

"Tell me about this Belzec place," Reynolds said. I explained how it was the first real extermination camp, the first place where the Nazis had erected gas chambers, early in 1942. I described how they murdered their victims with carbon monoxide pumped from a large truck engine, how it sometimes took as long as thirty-five minutes to kill them all, and how they dumped the bodies in trenches, first wrenching the gold fillings out of their mouths. In the middle of my recitation Reynolds stopped paying attention. The Holocaust often has that effect on people. So I shut up.

Novak shivered. "My husband is Jewish," she said, somewhat irrelevantly. There was a pause. The detectives spat out their gum, inserted new sticks, and resumed chewing. Novak offered me a stick, which I declined.

"Were these documents worth killing someone for?" Reynolds asked.

I shrugged. "I never saw them. If they named people who are still around . . . but it seems so unlikely. I've never heard of such a thing."

Reynolds frowned. "On the other hand, it may just have been a robbery gone wrong. Although a slashing murder like this is uncommon in a robbery. Usually the perp uses a gun."

"What does that tell you?"

"Not much. As I said, you usually only see stabbings in domestic abuse, but to be honest, Professor, we still have a long way to go in this case. Until ten minutes ago, we didn't even know who she was. Tell me more about these papers. What do you think they could have been?"

"I wish I knew. There aren't many documents about Belzec. Only two people survived, and they both died years ago. That's why any kind of firsthand testimony could be so significant. If it's legitimate, that is. If you do come across any old papers or documents, I'd ask you to be careful with them and call me immediately."

Reynolds nodded. "Okay, Prof, we'll take it from here. Just keep your mouth shut. Don't talk to the media. We may need to come back to you if this Belsen stuff adds up to anything."

"Belzec," I corrected him.

"Whatever," he said.

I had done my civic duty. My part in the whole horrible mess was over. The police would handle it from here.

Wrong again.

3

I must pick my way myself
Through this darkness.

— "Good Night" by Wilhelm Müller, music by Franz Schubert

A week passed before I heard from Lieutenant Reynolds again. As usual, I was busy shuffling papers, attending committees, and reviewing documents. But Sophie Reiner never quite left my thoughts. Impatient to learn something one afternoon, I called the number the lieutenant had given me to ask what was happening. I was put on hold, to seasonal elevator music — "God Rest Ye Merry Gentlemen." Christmas spirit had spread to every corner of the land, turning the entire country into a vast shopping mall. After a few minutes, since I was neither merry nor a gentleman, I grew tired of waiting and hung up. The rest of the day we played phone tag.

Next afternoon, we had our weekly staff meeting. For once, most of the department's nine historians and thirteen lawyers were in town, which meant we could fully review our current caseload. As we sat down, I looked around the conference table. It was interesting to see the difference between the two tribes. The lawyers, both men and women, wore the same uniform as me — dark suits with white shirts or blouses, sober ties and gold cuff links for the men, silk scarves and discreet jewelry for the women. Some of them, not me, had their monograms stamped on their custom-made Egyptian two-ply cotton shirts. Most of us sat up straight, writing copious notes on yellow legal pads. The historians, mostly younger, wore their own uniform: jeans or cords, tweedy jackets, and loud shirts with their top buttons undone. They sprawled in their chairs, occasionally sitting up to scrawl hieroglyphics in spiral notebooks. If they bothered to wear ties, the men always left them hanging several inches below their necks. For that reason alone, I could never have been a historian. That and the fact that there was no future in history.

We had several cases working their way through the system. The biggest involved one Lazarus Bruteitis, who had been chief of the security police in Vilnius Province, Lithuania, during the Nazi occupation. Bruteitis had been living quietly in Rhode Island for the past four decades. We had been investigating him for several years and had compiled a thick dossier of crimes committed under his command. The problem, as always, was proving his personal involvement and knowledge. The typical Nazi document did not generally record the names of the killers. Orders were often disguised in euphemisms. Once, I remember seeing a planning document for "the resettlement" of Jews from a certain village. The proposed location turned out to be two pits. And near the end of the war, when the Nazis and their acolytes realized they were defeated, they built huge bonfires and burned much of the evidence.

"So where do things stand?" Eric asked Janet Smart, our chief historian. "I heard you had a breakthrough. It's about time."

"A mini-breakthrough, maybe. We dug up a new document with Bruteitis's name typed on it ordering fifty-two Jews to be shot at a place called Paneriai," Janet said, shoving a photocopy around the table for us to look at. It was written in German, and sure enough, there was "Bruteitis" typed neatly at the bottom. Unfortunately, it wasn't signed.

"Remind me, what was Paneriai?" Eric said.

"It was a wooded hamlet outside of Vilnius, where thousands of Jews were stripped, lined up in trenches, and shot. Only five thousand of Vilnius's sixty thousand Jews survived the war," Janet said. She looked like a refugee from the 1960s who had spent too much time on the beach without sunscreen. She had to be pushing sixty by now. I had worked with her on a dozen cases, and despite her appearance, she was a formidable partner with a steel trap of a mind, capable of filing away and effortlessly recalling references, citations, facts, and figures in several languages.

"Where did the document come from?" Eric asked.

"Soviet archives in Moscow," Janet said.

"Are we sure it's authentic?"

"It matches other similar documents. I'm confident it's genuine."

"Okay then, let's serve the bastard with papers and issue a press release," Eric said. "How soon can you get it done?"

"Are you sure?" I asked mildly. "I know we've been waiting a long time, and I see his name on the document, but . . ."

"But what?" Eric snapped.

"But there's no signature. Is this enough?"

John Howard, a department lawyer who was handling this case with Smart, looked up from the legal pad on which he had been doodling. "I agree with Mark," he said in a thin, reedy voice. "Personally, I'd feel more comfortable if we had something with his actual signature. We can't go forward on just this. He could always claim that somebody typed this up on his behalf without his knowledge. We've been through this before."

"Shit!" Eric exploded, slamming his pencil down on the conference table. "How long have we been sitting on this fucking case? Five years? Seven? We all know he's guilty, even if we don't have his signature. We may never get his signature. The world isn't perfect. We need to move ahead before the *mamzer* dies on us. How old is he now?"

"Seventy-six," Janet replied.

"The older he gets, the harder it will be to win. No matter how healthy he is, we all know he'll bring a whole team of doctors to court, swearing that his health is too fragile for the poor old man to be deported. They always do," Eric observed bitterly.

We all took Eric's frequent outbursts in stride. We also knew he was anxious to find a high-profile case that we could take to the media to prove to the new Republican majority that we were still alive and kicking. And we all knew we were in a race against time. The crimes we dealt with happened half a century ago in faraway corners of Europe. The criminals were now elderly immigrants — Germans and Austrians, Ukrainians, Estonians, Latvians, Hungarians, Romanians — all with their long-repressed memories and secret guilt. A few more years, and they would elude justice once and for all. Then we'd have to shut up shop, unless Congress passed a new law authorizing us to investigate other human rights abuses, like the slaughter in Bosnia or last year's Rwandan genocide. Eric had been lobbying lawmakers to do just that, but it wasn't clear where things stood after the election.

"Janet? You haven't told us what you think," Eric asked, tapping his pencil against the edge of the table. "If we delay further, is there any chance of getting new information on this guy?"

"Maybe. There is one more avenue we haven't tried yet. We've been pressing the Lithuanian government to give us access to their archives ever since they became independent four years ago. As you might expect, this was hardly their top priority. The Red Army only finally left the country just over a year ago — "

"Enough with the history lesson, get to the point," Eric growled.

Janet shot him a look. "The point, Mr. Rosen, is that a source I know at the State Department tipped me this morning that things might be about to change. He has it on good authority the Lithuanian government is going to agree to our request."

"That's great," I said. "When might this happen?"

"Maybe even this week or next, certainly before Christmas," Janet said.

"How soon could you get there?" Eric asked.

"The minute they give their formal assent, I'll be on the next plane," she said.

"How's your Lithuanian?" asked George Carter, the department's brightest young historian and best linguist. He was wearing a particularly inappropriate tie that afternoon — panda bears cuddling baby panda bears and eating shoots and leaves.

"Nonexistent, but my guess is all the material is in German," Janet said.

"Okay, I guess we'll have to wait to see if the Lithuanians come through," Eric sighed. "But I'm not prepared to let this file sit there much longer. One way or another, we're moving ahead with this case. Is there any other business?"

"I got another one of those hate letters," I said, brandishing a message that had arrived in the afternoon mail.

"What's it say?"

"The usual. 'We know who you are and we're coming after you. We will rescue our country from the grasp of degenerates like you.' And other friendly sentiments appropriate to this joyous Christmas season."

"Has anyone else been getting this kind of dreck?" Eric asked. There were a couple of nods around the table.

"I generally just throw them in the trash," John Howard said. "It's just part of the job."

"You're probably right, but I'd like you all to send all hate mail to me from now on," Eric said. "I want the FBI to know about it."

Leaving the meeting, I took the elevator to the top floor and hurried to a small conference room where a small group of men from different divisions of the Department of Justice met at around five thirty each afternoon to recite the afternoon and evening prayers. I couldn't always make it, but I tried to whenever possible. The group needed a minyan, or quorum of ten, to include certain prayers, including the Kaddish — the prayer for the dead, which those in mourning recite each day for thirty days after the death of a spouse or sibling and eleven months after the death of a parent, to fulfill the fifth commandment to honor one's mother and father.

Nine men stood in the room as I arrived, facing a window to the east in the direction of Jerusalem, already *davening,* swaying and bowing to the prayers. My arrival completed the minyan. I closed my eyes and softly recited the opening words of the Amidah, the eighteen benedictions: *"Praised are You, Lord our God and God of our ancestors, God of Abraham, of Isaac, of Jacob, great, awesome, mighty, exalted God who bestows loving kindness, Creator of all."* The Amidah, which means "standing," is said quietly so that each individual can approach God in his own way. Like Jacob, I often found myself wrestling with Him and with my better self.

In our minyan, everyone prayed more or less together, but each of us was lost in his own world. I recited these blessings several times a day; the Hebrew words slipped off my tongue in a rush, without thought. I sometimes had to force myself to concentrate on their meaning, but even on distracted days the prayer had significance. The fact that Jews have said these same words, unaltered, for millennia makes saying them a powerful act of affirmation. When I reached the line about giving life to the dead, I added a small, silent prayer for the soul of Sophie Reiner.

The service took about twenty minutes. When it was over, we all quickly shook hands and hurried back to work. As I opened the door of my office, the phone was ringing. I lunged across the desk and grabbed it just before voice mail picked up. It was Reynolds. "Professor, how ya doin'?" he asked.

"I'm pretty good. But you know, I'm not really a professor," I said. "How's the case coming?"

"There's something I want you to see that you might be able to help me with. Could you come down to the station?"

As I drove through wet streets, the car radio carried more bad news from the Balkans, where Sarajevo remained besieged, its residents targeted by snipers whenever they ventured out of their homes for food or fuel. Then the subject turned to domestic issues and the Texas twang of Mitch Conroy took over, sounding his usual alarm about the horrors of big government, until I switched him off.

Reynolds and Novak were waiting in an interview room. They offered me a cup of coffee. I took a sip and put it aside. It tasted like boot polish dissolved in hot water.

"Professor, I want you to take a look at this," Reynolds said, handing me a piece of paper. "I recall you saying how you're fluent in German, and all."

I took a look at the half dozen lines, scrawled on a piece of hotel stationery in a large, undisciplined hand, automatically noting a couple of spelling mistakes in the first paragraph. "Sure, I can read it. It seems pretty clear."

"So what does it say?" Reynolds asked.

I scanned it quickly. "Rather melodramatic," I told them. "It appears to be a letter to her mother . . . and it's unfinished, like she was writing it before she left the room and put it aside to finish later. Was there an envelope or an address?"

Novak shook her head. "Nothing. Just that piece of paper." I thought maybe her lipstick was a different shade this time, less scarlet. It didn't quite match her fingernails.

"Let me write it down for you in English," I said. Reynolds shoved a writing pad across the table. For the next five minutes, we all sat in silence while I worked. "Okay, this is it, more or less," I said, setting down the pen.

Mama, Mama, how on earth did I come to be here, alone in this grubby room, in a strange city in a strange country?

You ought to know — it's because of you I'm here, thousands of miles from home. You're the one who sent me here — sent me through your silence. So many things you left unsaid. Why were you not honest? All we had was each other. I did everything for you. And you, you shut me out. You could have trusted me. I would have kept your secrets.

Now, I wrestle with them night and day, trying to find my way through the forest.

Reynolds looked disappointed. "That doesn't help," he muttered.

"Were you expecting something in particular?" I asked.

"I didn't know what to expect. I was hoping maybe for some idea about what she was doing here in D.C."

"I assume you confirmed her identity."

"We did, and she was who you said she was," Novak said. "She was staying in a motel out on New York Avenue. Not very classy. Didn't find much there. No solid leads, no idea why anyone would want her dead."

"Well, maybe like you told me, she was just in the wrong place at the wrong time," I said hopefully.

Reynolds sighed. "Could be. We haven't ruled anything out. And just so we're clear, we're talkin' here off the record. I don't want any of this in the media."

"Don't worry," I assured him piously. "I'm not allowed to talk to the media without the permission of my boss. And he almost never gives it."

"All right."

"What else can you tell me?"

"She was seen leaving the hotel probably around five, six o'clock. The medical examiner puts the time of death at anywhere between seven and eleven. Her body was found early next day."

"What about her hotel room? Did you find anything there, apart from the letter?"

"Some clothes, toiletries, a few books, magazines, some CDs, ashtray full of cigarette butts even though it was a nonsmoking room," Novak said. Her nicotine-stained fingers flashed into my mind, and I imagined her puffing away in the seedy privacy of the last room she would ever see.

"No suspicious prints," said Reynolds. "We're trying to track her movements. We know she arrived in the country October 26. Flew in on Lufthansa to JFK from Frankfurt. That means she was here about a month. We're trying to figure out where she was, who she saw, and what she did. We know she was in Florida and in Boston, but we don't know why. She used a credit card, which makes it easier to follow the trail."

"Do you know anything about her mother?"

"The German police are trying to come up with a more detailed profile. We know she was single, apparently never married. She worked as a medical aide at a retirement home. Seems to have lived a totally ordinary life," Novak said.

A lonely life, I thought. *A bit like mine.*

"Any connection to the Nazis? Like a family member maybe?" I asked.

"Not that we know, but the Krauts are still looking into it."

"Just so you know, they don't appreciate being called Krauts," I said. "They prefer Huns."

"Really?" Novak said. "I never knew that."

"No, not really. It was a joke." I coughed in embarrassment and tried to think of a more serious question to ask them. They both looked at me as if I were crazy.

"Did you find any documents? She said she wanted to show me some documents."

"No documents, Prof. There were some books. I have them in my office, but they're all in German. They don't look like much, just trashy romance novels. You can take a look if you like," Reynolds said. He stood up and led the way through the squad room into a tiny cubicle in the back. A small pile of books lay on the table. I examined them briefly. They appeared to be translations of American romance novels, the type you can buy in any supermarket. The covers showed swarthy men with long swept-back hair and bulging biceps clasping half-undressed women with heaving breasts. The sorry collection of paperbacks fit with the picture Reynolds had painted of a middle-aged spinster leading a dull, lonely life. Not at all the kind of person who would have access to important historical documents.

I flicked idly through one of the books and came across a piece of paper acting as a bookmark. "Did you see this?" I asked Reynolds.

"What?"

"It's a ticket," I said, examining it. "To the Holocaust Museum. Dated November 27 — that's the day before she came to see me."

"Yeah, we saw it. Hell of a way to spend one of your last days on this earth," Novak said.

"She didn't know she was going to die," I said. Glancing at the CDs on the desk, I saw Abba's greatest hits, Nat King Cole, Burt Bacharach favorites, *Be My Love: The Definitive Mario Lanza Collection* — sickly stuff — and one more entitled *Der Winterreise*, a collection of songs written by Franz Schubert. It jogged something in my mind.

"This one may be interesting," I told Reynolds.

"How so?"

"She said something to me that day we met about being a music lover. It struck me at the time as kind of a strange remark, one of several strange remarks she made. To tell you the truth, I was half convinced she was a nutcase."

"What's interesting about it?" he asked. "She said she liked music, and she has a bunch of CDs. Seems perfectly logical to me."

"This last one here doesn't fit the pattern. Everything else she has is easy listening, and all her books are romances. This one is different." I picked up the case to examine it. *Der Winterreise — The Winter Journey* — Roberto Delatrucha, baritone. The face of a man in late middle age stared out from the cover. He was partially obscured by shadows, his steel gray hair swept back, eyes half closed, large, prominent mouth framed by a thick gray beard and mustache.

"Can I take out the liner notes?" I asked. Reynolds nodded. I glanced through the material quickly. "We read it," Reynolds said. "Nothing there." Actually, there was a hint of something there. I kept my mouth shut. It really was a minor point, hardly worth mentioning.

"Can I keep this one?" I asked.

"Nope, it's evidence," Novak said. "You can get one at a record store if you're that interested. Why?"

"I don't know. Probably nothing."

When I got back to my car, I made a quick note in my legal pad before I forgot the details. Jennifer used to make fun of my need to take notes on everything that ever happened to me. She called it excessively anal. She was probably right, but I had been doing it for years, and I wasn't about to stop now. Anyway, she was gone, so what difference did it make?

I was tired and hungry, but the thought of going home to an empty apartment didn't thrill me. So I drove to the mall, found a record store, and headed for the section on Schubert. To my surprise, there were fifteen different versions of *Winterreise*, three of them by Roberto Delatrucha, including the one I had seen on Reynolds's desk. I hadn't listened to classical music for years, not since my mother's death, when the piano she had loved playing so much had fallen silent. Strains of Chopin's mazurkas still occasionally floated uninvited into my head on invisible wisps of air. But this music was unfamiliar to me.

I picked out four discs — *Winterreise*, a couple of other Schubert compositions, and one of Delatrucha singing Schumann, who, beside

Chopin, was my mother's other favorite composer. I remembered practicing some of his easier piano pieces as a kid. Mama would sit down beside me on the piano bench, playing the bass while I played the treble. Then we'd switch. Sometimes we'd swap hands without switching places, leaning across each other so that our arms crossed over the keyboard. Sometimes she'd put her other arm around me as we played, and I snuggled against her, safe and warm and loved.

Our home had been full of music then. Mom always hummed to herself as she went about her daily tasks. When she left us, the music went with her. My father and I lived together in virtual silence for another five years, until I went off to college. When I became religious, it only increased the gulf between us. He rarely mentioned her name. I wanted to, but didn't. I quit piano lessons shortly after the funeral and never sat down at the instrument again. A year later, my father sold it. Sometimes, when I was alone in the house, I'd gaze down at where the piano legs had squashed little round indentations in the carpet. I'd lie down with my eyes closed and gently stroke the patch of rug worn bare by Mom's heel from working the sustaining pedal — almost the only sign that was left of her in the entire house.

I snapped out of my reverie. "Is this stuff popular?" I asked the man behind the counter as he rang up my purchases.

"Not mega popular, like *The Four Seasons* or Beethoven's Fifth," he said. "We sell a few from time to time."

"And this Delatrucha guy, is he well known?"

"I'd say. Next to Fischer-Dieskau, he's the king of lieder."

Fischer who? I had no idea who or what he was talking about. I paid for the discs and left. They seemed innocent enough on the outside. Inside, they were emotional dynamite primed to blow up in my face.

As I wander around Washington, peering into the lobbies of government buildings, I keep asking myself how this nation fell so low.

For there is no doubt, we are steeped in evil. The souls of 50 million unborn babies cry out for justice. Sometimes, I can hear them weeping.

Yesterday, I was at the Vietnam Memorial. I stood in the cold, reading the names — name after name after name — and while I was reading, I thought about Dusty Briggs and Stan Knight getting their heads blown off in that hellhole they call Iraq. One day, they'll be names on a monument too, if anyone cares enough to build one. They'll write on it, "They died for cheap gasoline." What a joke! At least they didn't have to come home and watch what's happening here with the queers, kooks, and kikes running the country. I felt a migraine coming on and rushed back to my room before the torture hit.

The truth is, nothing was ever the same after the war. Everything led up to that one moment in the desert. We're pinned down, taking mortar fire from an Iraqi position about a half mile away, waiting for air support that's not coming. We've already lost Briggs and Knight, and if this goes on for much longer we're all fucked. There's only one person in the entire platoon who can take out a position at that range. One! The lieutenant calls me forward. "This one's for you, Shorty," he says. I put my eye against the scope, watching and waiting, ignoring the shit flying around us, the explosions, the cussing and yelling, the radio crackling. It's just me and the scope. Everything's frozen. Then I see a flash of light in the distance. An Iraqi pops up his head for a micro-second. I press the trigger; his upper body explodes. Everything above his shoulders disappears, like on a video game. Our guys are cheering and whooping. "Way to go, Shorty, did you see that shot, did you fucking see that shot?" they're yelling. Nobody can believe it. I keep on shooting, even after they try to surrender. Until the lieutenant grabs me by the shoulder and tells me, "That's enough, son." As if it's ever enough, once you get started.

As we roll through the desert, we see more Iraqis, crawling along on their hands and knees. And dogs chewing on the corpses. Once you see that, believe me, nothing's ever the same. Nothing.

4

*During the time that I myself was at Belzec, the gas installation was still housed
in a hut which was lined with sheet metal and which held about 100 people.*

— TESTIMONY OF JOSEF OBERHAUSER

I THREW MY JACKET ON THE BED, grabbed a Diet Coke from the
fridge, shoved some leftover ravioli into the microwave, and flicked
the CD player on. I had moved into this apartment after Jennifer and
I broke up. It seemed like a good idea at the time — move to a new
neighborhood, put some space between me and the office, get
involved with a different social set. The apartment was within walking distance of an Orthodox shul, or synagogue, vital for Shabbat, the
Sabbath day, when I couldn't drive. I had two bedrooms, one of
which nobody had ever used. The building itself was immaculate. It
boasted a resplendent lobby with marble floors and wall-length mir-
rors so you couldn't tell whether you were coming or going. But the
place never quite felt like home. My one major purchase had been a
king-size bed, which seemed as big as a swimming pool when I lay
in it alone. I drowned in it every night.

Truth was, I longed for female company. Most of my friends
were deep in married bliss, with two or three kids already in tow. At
the synagogue, nearly every week, some amateur matchmaker tried
to fix me up on a blind date, but none of these led to anything. Word
had gone around that I was too picky and difficult to please.

Lately, I'd been having lustful thoughts about Lynn, my assistant,
who had to be eight or nine years younger than me. She had a law

degree, but she still carried the air of a student about her. Her energy level and enthusiasm were scary. Just the sight of her tearing down the corridor, perpetually in a hurry, sent a low-level electrical jolt through my body. But she was off-limits. Making passes at personal assistants, even those wearing glasses, was strictly verboten.

A Simon and Garfunkel disc was in the CD player. The song was one of Jennifer's favorites — "Bridge over Troubled Water." The words seemed to mock me. As the song ended, I slipped *Winterreise* into the machine, hung up my jacket, took off my shoes, and lay down on the bed. It began with a series of falling chords on the piano. Then Roberto Delatrucha began singing.

It was an extraordinary voice — deep, soft, and velvet, resonating with a haunting tone of longing and regret. I had never heard anything quite like it. It's unreasonable, I know, but after years of poring over SS documents, German for me had become the language of mass murder. Yet from these lips, it sounded lyrical and gentle. The sound of his voice reaching for the high notes was like a caress. A lump formed in my throat, and I blinked away a tear. I'd banished music from my life, and now it had snuck past my defenses.

I extracted the sleeve notes and followed the lyrics of the songs. The word *lieder* simply means "songs" in German, particularly songs set to German poetry. This composition consisted of twenty-four poems sung with piano accompaniment. They told the story of a rejected lover condemned to wander through a bleak winter landscape, looking for, but not finding, redemption. The first song set the tone:

> As a stranger I arrived here.
> A stranger, I go hence.
> The path is dismal, veiled in snow.

No one who is even a little lonely should have to listen to such despair. For months, I had tried to bury myself in work. These songs brought me face to face with my isolation. *Typical morbid Germanic nonsense,* I told myself, yet there was something about these songs that demanded attention. Partly the tunes, deceptively simple yet full of surprising changes of mood and tempo. Partly the intimate dialogue between singer and pianist. But mostly the voice itself, rich and dark and bitter, like strong black coffee.

The leaflet contained some sketchy biographical details. Delatrucha received his musical education in Buenos Aires and at Juilliard in New York. There, he met his accompanist, later to become his wife, Mary Scott. There was a small black-and-white picture of the two of them. Mary was sitting behind the piano, a small woman, her features hard to discern in the fuzzy photograph. Delatrucha posed behind her, one hand over his heart, the other flung artistically in the air.

After his arrival in this country from Argentina, Delatrucha slowly built a reputation as a serious interpreter of German 19th-century art songs. Not for him the easy path to fame and fortune. Not for him the facile rendition of operatic favorites and popular encores. Through four decades, Roberto Delatrucha has remained true to his singular mission, almost single-handedly reviving American interest in this beautiful but neglected repertory.

The songs still played in my head as I lay down to sleep, and they welled up again when I awoke. The first thing I wanted to do, after reciting the morning blessing, was listen to them again, but the music would have to wait. Struggling into my coat, I rushed into the chill, dark air, anxious not to miss the daily minyan, which began at six thirty each morning. Some of the most fervent worshippers met half an hour earlier each day to study a page of the Talmud, but that was too much devotion even for me.

Back home, I played the disc during breakfast while skimming the *Post*. It was an unequal contest; the music won hands down. I had to switch it off to concentrate on the newspaper. Good thing I did, too. After days of no news, a story about Sophie Reiner appeared in the Metro section. Her earthly remains had been returned to Germany for burial. The article said Sophie had no family to mourn her. Her elderly mother had recently died; her father had been killed in the war, before she was born. So Sophie had been writing that letter to a ghost. I felt sad for her. Nobody should have to live and die alone. The police said they were still investigating. "We are pursuing several possible leads," a spokesman said. It didn't sound promising.

I cut out the article to add to the file I had started on the case, then looked at my watch. Time for one more song from another of the Delatrucha discs. This time, the voice of a younger, more assertive Roberto Delatrucha filled the room. This performance had been recorded in the mid-1950s, when he was just starting to build his career. You could hear the youthful vigor and confidence in his delivery. The first song was called "Der Erlkönig," "The Elf King" in English. It began with a rush of powerful piano chords, pounding and throbbing to mimic the sound of a galloping horse. The words by Wolfgang von Goethe told of a father and son riding through a forest in winter, the father nestling the child to keep him warm. The son senses a ghostly figure, the Elf King, lurking in a shadow, beckoning to him. "Father, father, look over there," the young boy cries. But the father sees nothing. The evil spirit begins whispering seductively to the child, "Come with me, come with me." Still, the father remains blind and deaf to the threat. The Elf King creeps closer, ever closer; he reaches out and seizes the child. "Father, he's hurting me," the child cries in anguish. His soul is being wrenched from his body; the father is helpless. The horse gallops on, the father clutching his still-shuddering child to his breast. They reach safety, but it's too late. The child is dead.

The song required Delatrucha to sing in three different voices. The father's voice, deep and gruff; the son's, high-pitched and terrified; and then the voice of the Elf King himself—soft and beguiling, creepy and tempting. It was artistry of the highest order, and deeply disturbing. Every father tries to protect his children, but what happens when he can't? What happens when the evil is so great it overpowers him? It made me think of my own father. I picked up the phone and called him.

"Well?" came the brusque response.

"Dad, it's me, Marek."

"Why are you calling at seven thirty in the morning? What's wrong?"

"Nothing. I just wanted to hear your voice. I guess I was feeling a little lonely. How are you doing?"

"You're lonely? You need to find yourself a wife. What happened to that nice young lady you're seeing? What's her name?"

"Jennifer. And I told you six months ago. We broke up."

"Well, call her up and say you're sorry for whatever it was you did. She was nice, that one."

"It's too late," I said. "We couldn't get along. She was way too nice for me."

"It's not too late. It's never too late. Only after death is it too late. Remember that, Marek. Only after death," he said in his harsh, guttural accent.

"Okay, Dad, I get it."

"So you will call this Jennifer?"

"Forget Jennifer, Dad. She's history. It's over. Done, finished, kaput."

"History, your whole life is history. Why don't you find a proper job, make some money, and live in the real world with the rest of us? You're thirty-six years old."

"Thirty-five."

"Thirty-five, thirty-six, it's time to stop this nonsense and get a real job before it's too late. Who would have thought my son would grow up to be a fanatic?"

My spirits slumped. It was always like this between us. We couldn't have a conversation without exchanging reproaches. The two of us had been abandoned to face the world together, but the tragedy had only driven us apart. He had retreated into a shell, leaving me to cope with my own sadness the best way I could. Judaism offered a channel through which to be angry at God and — eventually — a salve for my wounds.

"Dad, I only called to say hello, not to fight. How are you coping with the winter?" My father had retired five years ago when he hit seventy. Spurning Florida, where most of his friends had fled, Jacob Cain bought a cabin deep in the hills of West Virginia, where

33

he faced the bitter winters alone, chopping his own firewood and stomping defiantly through the snow. He said it reminded him of Poland.

"I'm coping. Winter is winter. It's cold, thank God. Some things you can still trust to stay the same." He spoke precise English with few mistakes, but he had never lost his accent, a mixture of Polish and Hebrew. He had been lucky. The eldest of four children, he had rebelled against his religious upbringing to join a socialist, Zionist organization. In 1937, when he was only eighteen, he said farewell to his family and left Poland for a kibbutz in Palestine. That decision saved his life. Letters arrived regularly from his village until the Nazis occupied Poland in 1939. After that, news occasionally trickled through. He knew his family had been evicted from their home and herded into a ghetto early in 1941. Then, nothing. He volunteered to fight with the British and took part in the invasion of Italy. Not until after the war did he discover the truth. All the Jews from his village had been deported to Belzec in August 1942. None survived.

He paid a brief visit to Poland after the war, looking for traces of his loved ones. Nothing. Poles were living in the family home. They refused even to let him inside. He returned to Palestine with a bitter heart. He fought again in 1948 in the Israeli War of Independence. Later, in the 1950s, tired of fighting, he moved to the United States, where he met my mother, an Auschwitz survivor, and changed his name from Cohen to Cain, a name denoting perpetual exile. He opened a liquor store in D.C. I was their only child.

"Maybe I'll come out there one weekend. We could do some cross-country skiing and sit in front of the glowing embers, drinking hot punch," I suggested.

"You don't like cross-country skiing. You're no good at it."

"I do occasionally. It's not as bad as ballroom dancing or mud wrestling," I joked. "I'd like to see you. I miss you."

"There's no synagogue and no kosher food. You know all this."

"I'll pray on my own and eat vegetarian. God won't even notice I'm gone."

"It's a long drive just for a weekend, especially when the roads are snowed up. They don't plow very often around here."

"That doesn't bother me. I'll find a free weekend and let you know."

"Don't come because you feel sorry for me."

"I don't feel sorry for you. I feel awesome filial respect. Aren't you even a bit lonely, Dad?"

"Why should I be lonely? I'm comfortable with my own company. You're the one who lives in the past, chasing ghosts."

"Not ghosts, Dad. They're real men, your age, who murdered people — who may have murdered your own family, or Mother's. Doesn't that mean anything to you?"

"What I know is this, Marek. My parents, my brother, and my sisters have been dead for more than fifty years, and there's hardly a day I don't think of them. But life goes on. I built my life, got married, raised you. And now you're an attorney. You could be rich and successful. You could live in a big house and fill it with my grandchildren. But instead, you poke about in the past and make yourself miserable."

"But Dad, there is such a thing as justice."

"What justice? If you find some old man who killed Jews fifty years ago, will that bring my sisters back to life?"

"It might prevent the same thing happening again."

"Ah, you are so naive, Marek. It already has happened again. It's happening right now in Bosnia, it happened last year in Africa."

He had me there. The slaughter of 800,000 innocent people in Rwanda, while the world stood by and watched, had plunged me into despair. I agonized over what to do. Several times, I started drafting an angry resignation letter. To its eternal shame, the United States did nothing to stop the killing until it was too late. But my letter remained unfinished. One day, the world would need people like me with experience finding and prosecuting war criminals to settle accounts with the new generation of mass murderers.

But my father was still fulminating.

"Justice. Pshaw, you talk of justice? Justice is showing the Nazis we won because we chose life. But what's the use? We've had this conversation a thousand times."

"Dad, just so you know, I love you! That's an official statement."

35

"Bah! Find a woman to love, Marek. Get out of that rut you're in. Raise a family. Then you'll learn about love."

He was right about that, I knew. But it didn't make me feel any better.

Where do you begin to right the wrongs? Do you start with the doctors and nurses who lend their hands to the slaughter? No, executing one or two would achieve nothing. They will burn in hell, along with the mothers who murder the flesh of their flesh. The judges in black robes who defend the baby-slaughterers—they too shall be called to account. I believe this with perfect faith.

These headaches, where my brain splits in half and it feels like someone is winding barbed wire around my head, I never used to get them before the war. Sometimes I see visions, flashes of brightness, wavy lines dancing in front of my eyes, but I welcome them. The more I suffer, the more I see. I see that the root of the evil lies within our monstrous government. I see that death must be fought with death, that lesser means will not suffice. "And I looked, and behold a pale horse: and his name that sat on him was Death, and Hell followed with him. And power was given unto them over the fourth part of the earth, to kill with sword, and with hunger, and with death, and with the beasts of the earth."

I remember the feel of her hair as I grabbed it, the warm saggy skin on her neck as I stretched it back, her terrified eyes, that stale, damp smell, and then the blood.

Next on my list is the man who calls himself the Nazi hunter. The hunter will become the hunted. I am judge, jury, and executioner. I alone decide when to carry out the sentence.

I need more money. I called to ask when I would get the five grand for the German woman.

"It's already in your account in West Virginia," the voice said. "Don't call this number again. We'll contact you again when we have more work for you soon."

5

I hate a life
That unfolds itself easily

—"The Boatman" by Johann Mayerhoff, music by Franz Schubert

I WENT STRAIGHT UPSTAIRS TO ROSEN'S OFFICE, passing Janet in the corridor. "Do you know anything about Schubert?" I asked her.

"Not a thing, babe. But if you want to know about the Grateful Dead—"

"That's okay, I'll pass. Did we ever hear back from the Lithu-anians about their archives?"

"My State Department guy was right. There was an official announcement yesterday from Vilnius. I circked a memo."

"It's probably in my in-box. When are you leaving?"

"Sunday. I hear the food there is vile."

"As long as the beer is drinkable, you'll be fine."

Eric's door was open, so I walked in. "I'm busy," he growled. "Go away."

"Top o' the morning, Eric. Beautiful day. How are you?"

He muttered something without looking up.

"Nice of you to ask. I'm fine," I said.

"Didn't you hear, Cain? I said I'm busy. Come back next January. Better yet, make it February."

"You're always busy. I'm always busy. The whole world's busy. But not too busy for Schubert," I said, tossing *Winterreise* into his lap.

"What's this?" he asked.

"I thought you needed some culture. Read the liner notes if you can take five minutes from your busy life. See if anything strikes a chord."

I glanced around his office, admiring the collection of signed photographs on his desk, showing Eric with each of the nation's presidents from Ford to Clinton. Eric's most prized photo showed him standing next to Reagan. Ronnie was gazing off into space, his eyes gentle and unfocused. Rosen, a good eight inches shorter, glared at the camera, swollen with pride. Those were good days, under Reagan, when our work had unquestioned support from both parties *and* the White House. How times had changed! Mitch Conroy kept reminding everybody how committed he was to slashing "bloated federal programs." Were we a bloated federal program? How much support for Nazi-hunting would there be from this new regime? Already, Conroy was threatening hearings on all aspects of government spending in the New Year. And Jack Doneghan, his chief speechwriter and right-hand man, was no friend of ours. A former conservative columnist, he had once written an op-ed piece denouncing our existence and methods and siding with some of what he called our "victims."

Eric finished reading the blurb. "Hmm, I see what you mean," he said. "There is something here, maybe. Actually, just one word."

The word was *Argentina*. Around 60,000 Nazis, including Eichmann, Mengele, and many other top leaders, fled from Germany to Argentina in the years after the war, many with the help of Catholic priests and Vatican officials.

"You notice it doesn't say where he was born," I said.

"Shouldn't be too tough to figure out. Is he any good?"

"He's extraordinary," I said. Eric removed the disc from its case and inserted it into the CD player on his shelf. Once more, that rich, vibrant voice filled the room. We listened to the first couple of stanzas, then Eric flipped off the CD player, and we sat in silence for a couple of moments. The chords echoed in my head.

"I see what you mean," Eric said finally. "Extraordinary is the right word. Well, he wouldn't be the first classical musician to have been involved with the Nazis. Lots of them collaborated. Von

Karajan for one, the son of a bitch! He joined the Nazi Party, started all his concerts with the Nazi anthem, and carefully weeded all the Jews out of his orchestra when they told him to."

"Shameful," I said. "But that doesn't make him a war criminal."

"True. He was a coward, a scumbag, and a general *shtinker,* and he was an absolute tyrant as a conductor, but he wasn't a war criminal. Still, even collaborators should have paid a price for what they did."

"No one cared that he had been a Nazi stooge?"

"It set his career back a few years right after the war, but everyone forgot about it soon enough. He became a huge star, a member of the international jet set. He was practically worshipped by classical music buffs all over the world. It almost made me puke every time I saw yet another article about him. Plus he made a ton of money." He paused. "Though I did admire his management philosophy."

"What's that?"

"Karajan was asked how he got the orchestra to obey him. He said, 'I give them all the freedom they need to make them do what I want.' "

"Yes, I can see he's been quite an inspiration to you."

Eric looked at the Delatrucha disc again. "What do you think about the beard this dude is sporting? It hides half his face."

The idea of Delatrucha collaborating suddenly seemed repugnant to me. He had brought me back to classical music, and for that I was grateful.

"It's just a beard. It doesn't really strike me one way or another," I replied. I recognized the signs. Once Eric got curious about someone, he wouldn't stop until he had uncovered the truth. And he loved high-profile cases that got him into the newspapers and on TV. Eric never saw a TV camera he didn't want to stand in front of — a common Washington disease.

"Mark, I think it would be worth taking a quick look into his background," he said. "Just to satisfy my curiosity. But keep it tight. With this new Congress, the last thing we need is accusations that we go after people with no evidence. Another Demjanjuk fuckup would kill us."

Just the name made us both shudder. Demjanjuk may have been our most famous case; it was certainly our biggest embarrassment. A Ukrainian, Demjanjuk had emigrated to the United States in 1952 and settled in Cleveland, where he worked as an auto worker until he retired. Based on what we thought was solid evidence, our department had identified him as Ivan the Terrible, a sadistic guard who operated the gas chambers at Treblinka. He was extradited to stand trial in Israel, convicted, and sentenced to death. Then new evidence turned up from the Soviet Union suggesting that Demjanjuk wasn't Ivan the Terrible after all, although he apparently had undergone Nazi training and had served at other Nazi camps. The Israeli court overturned the conviction, and Demjanjuk returned home. The department was trying to build a new case against him, but the whole episode had given our enemies valuable ammunition to attack our methods and existence.

"Can I have a couple of people to help me do some research?" I asked Eric.

"Yes, two. Who do you have in mind?"

"I was thinking maybe George Carter and Lynn, my assistant."

"The pretty one?"

"I hadn't noticed."

"Right. Sure you hadn't."

"We should brief Janet as well. She is George's boss."

Eric thought for a second. "No, she's leaving for Lithuania. Let's keep this to ourselves for now. Don't mention it at the staff meeting. If and when it turns into an official investigation, we'll bring everyone up to speed."

The three of us met next morning in my office. Carter was a lanky, bony man in his early thirties. With short-cropped hair, he looked more like a U.S. Marine than an academic. But he was a brilliant researcher, fluent in Russian, German, and Polish. He was teaching himself Romanian and was often overheard mouthing strange syllables to himself in the cafeteria. Since his recent marriage to a fellow linguist, he'd also taken to singing tunelessly in a language no one could identify. George was that rarest of creatures — a happy man.

40

"What on earth are those awful tunes?" I asked him once.

"Moldavian love songs," he replied. "I like to sing them to Marie in bed."

"You'll have to teach them to me," I laughed enviously.

I gave him the CD liner notes, passed another photocopy to Lynn, and placed the disc of Delatrucha singing Schumann in the CD player. These songs were different from the Schubert — dreamier, more introspective, but equally enchanting. I had spent the previous evening listening to them, and reading the melancholy, haunting lyrics written by the famous German poet, Heinrich Heine, another tortured soul — a Jew who had converted to Christianity not from religious conviction but to escape discrimination and obtain, as he put it, an entrance ticket to Western civilization.

George carefully read the notes, then looked at me quizzically. "What's this have to do with us?" he asked.

I switched off the CD player. "First, this discussion stays between the three of us. We don't share it with anyone, not even colleagues in the department."

George frowned but said nothing. I continued, "I'm interested in this guy's background. Specifically, I want to know where he comes from and what he was doing during the war."

"And your suspicion is based on what?" George asked, dripping skepticism.

"Let's just say we received a tip, and we'd like to check it out."

"A tip? Since when do we investigate tips? What are we, the police?"

A legitimate question. Most of the information the OSI investigated came from foreign governments or was generated by our own researchers searching wartime archives. Forget the image of Israeli hit squads tracking down evil murderers in obscure hideaways. Most Nazi-hunting took place in libraries and archives. The most recent data came from the former Soviet Union, which had captured millions of Nazi documents but had only allowed us to see them in the past couple of years. We trawled the documents for the names of known perpetrators. Once we had a suspect's name, we could run it through U.S. immigration records and other databases. Ironically, the

CIA was still keeping its own Nazi documents — believed to contain millions of pages — secret.

Few Americans know that tens of thousands of Nazi collaborators came to the United States after the war without anyone asking any questions. At that time, our nation eagerly accepted Europeans as long as they were white, Christian, and anti-Communist. Little effort was made to verify their backgrounds. Over the years, our office checked over 80,000 names of concentration camp personnel, SS members, and the like. All these names were placed on the government's Watch List. If anyone on the list ever tried to enter the country, he was stopped and questioned. And people did regularly show up at U.S. airports, especially New York and Orlando. Former SS men were fond of vacationing at Disney World.

Lufthansa and other airlines faxed us passenger lists while their transatlantic flights were still airborne. Once, a guard from the Birkenau death camp arrived in Orlando for a trip to the Magic Kingdom. We had no power to arrest him for crimes committed on foreign soil. The most we could do was to tell him he wasn't welcome in America and send him back to Germany on the next plane. Later, I debriefed one of the immigration officials who had questioned him. The old Nazi told them, "I can't believe anybody still cares about those events of so long ago."

If a name produced a hit from the Immigration and Naturalization Service, it meant someone with that name had once immigrated to the United States. The next step was to figure out if he was still alive. If we could prove he had lied about his Nazi past, we could deport him. With Delatrucha, we were working backward. We didn't have the name of a war criminal. All we had was that Sophie Reiner had called herself a lover of German songs and had one of the guy's CDs in her room. George and Lynn didn't need to know that.

"I'm not comfortable with this, Mark," George said, frowning. "Have you run it by Janet?"

"Janet's about to leave for Lithuania. Eric approved it."

"But what is it that we suspect this guy of? What are we looking for? Isn't this an invasion of his privacy? We don't go around investigating people based on tips. That's not what we do."

"Look, George, we're interested in knowing if this guy had Nazi connections. If we can't find anything, we'll drop it. We won't be invading his privacy. I want to find out what there is about him on the public record. Lynn, that will be your baby. He's well known in his field, so there has to be a paper trail — magazine articles, interviews, profiles, TV documentaries. Are you okay with that?"

"Totally cool," Lynn said, tossing back her curls, delighted to be included. Even after months in the staid Department of Justice, Lynn still sounded like an eager sophomore sometimes.

"If you're uncomfortable, George, you can bow out. It's purely voluntary. Otherwise, I'd like you to put in a standard request to Immigration to figure out where this guy came from and when he arrived. I'd like to know if and when he changed his name. Somehow I doubt he was born Roberto Delatrucha."

Once the war was over, it didn't take long for the army to decide I was "surplus to their requirements," and before I know it I'm out of the service and back home in Knott County, the armpit of America. Momma was smart; she ran off a long time ago, when I was little. I don't even remember what she looked like. When I was a kid, I used to think it would be cool to track her down. If I found her, I could get away from Dad and his drinking and beatings, and we'd live together and be happy. Now, if I ever did see her, I'd ask her, "Remember me? I'm the son you dropped like a used tampon."

My father hasn't changed much. The old buzzard's still just as mean and ornery as he ever was, only now he doesn't dare raise a hand to me because he knows I'd beat the shit out of him. Most of the time, he's too fucked up to even try. I tell him, "Dad, the meth is dissolving your teeth; pretty soon your whole face is going to collapse." He says, "Who the fuck asked you to open your pussy mouth, you undersized little fuck?" Some things never change.

I needed work. But the only jobs are down the mines, and I'm never going down there. I filled out forms to drive a coal truck; the boss just laughed at me. "Your feet won't even reach the brake pedal, shrimp. Isn't there anything else you can do?" My high school diploma didn't impress him. "Didn't they teach you anything in the army?" Yeah, they taught me one thing real well. They taught me to kill people.

I never planned the pretty lady. It was a crazy impulse. I started trailing her, not for any particular reason, more to test my skills. I need to stay sharp for the mission. So when she went down into the subway, I bought a ticket and went right down after her. And there she is, standing on the edge of the platform, and the thought comes to me to see how close I can get without her knowing. The train's coming, and by now I'm just behind her, and she still hasn't seen me or even felt me. My hand shoots out, giving her a shove, and just like that she's gone. At the exit, nobody says boo. Anyway, it was quick; she hardly suffered. It wasn't a cruel death, like those poor people in Waco, Texas. I was there, I saw the whole thing, the flames, the fire, the stinking federal agents who stood there and let them fry without lifting a finger.

So if you want to talk about murder, talk to me about Waco, talk to me about Randy Weaver at Ruby Ridge and his family, shot down like dogs by the ATF and the FBI. And while we're discussing murder, allow me to point out that infanticide is murder last time I checked. And when the regime in Washington legalized infanticide, they gave up any legitimacy they might have had. And when they started tolerating queers walking around in public flaunting their vile ways, it became the duty of all right-thinking folk to rebel. And when they built a museum with our tax dollars to glorify the historical lie they call the "holocaust," it's time for the entire white nation to reclaim its history. So that's what we need to talk about, not this other shit.

Burl called from West Virginia. He's already bought a couple thousand pounds of fertilizer with the five grand. He found an abandoned barn to store it. The plan is finally coming together. I tell him we need more, but not to buy it all at once and not all in the same place.

I've been tracking the Jewish guy. He has no idea. It's just a question of where and when I carry out the sentence, but his death should also send a message.

Timing is everything.

6

I could see that the lips and tips of their noses were a bluish color. Some of them had their eyes closed; others' eyes rolled.

— Testimony of Karl Schluch

A LARGE POSTER HUNG over the entrance of the health club. "Be all you used to be," it exhorted. "For a no-nonsense workout, join the Sarge's Boot Camp. No music, no dancing, no spandex, no nonsense." There was a picture of a line of balding, middle-aged men standing to attention, sucking in their bellies. Shuddering at the sight, I vowed never to let that happen to me. A little skinny guy was hanging around outside the gym. He looked familiar, but I couldn't place him. When I caught his eye, he looked away.

After five miles on the treadmill and half an hour lifting weights, I came home feeling unusually virtuous, preening in front of the wall-length lobby mirror while I waited for the elevator.

In the apartment, messages were blinking on the answering machine. Jennifer, my ex, saying she'd be over later that night to collect her CDs, and another one from Detective Novak, asking me to call her back. I was put on hold — naturally — to a mushy string orchestra playing "White Christmas," composed by one Israel Isidore Baline, better known to the world as Irving Berlin. Further evidence that musicians do often change their names. Novak finally came on the line and got straight to the point: "What do you know about criminal activities of Nazis in the United States?" she asked in her breathless voice.

"During World War II?"

"No, I mean now, today."

"You mean neo-Nazis? I don't know much. It's not my field. Lately I've been getting even more hate mail from them than usual. I have a friend who's an expert. I can give you his number if you like. Is there a connection?"

Muffled talking in the background, as if she were consulting with someone. Then she was back. "Okay, I'm going to tell you something, but you have to keep it strictly confidential."

"Sure, no problem," I agreed.

"We found something that may show a neo-Nazi connection. On the other hand, it may be nothing. Have your kind of Nazis ever gotten involved with the American type?"

"My kind of Nazis?"

"The ones you investigate."

"My kind of Nazis generally keep a low profile and stay out of trouble. Most of them are solid, upright citizens. The last thing they want is to get involved with a band of crazies. They generally keep their noses clean. What did you find?"

More background muttering before she came back on the line. "It was a piece of paper in her pocket. It had the numbers '6-6-6' written on it."

"Six-six-six?" I repeated, not understanding. "I found a piece of paper like that stuck under my windshield the other day. I thought it was some kind of prank."

"Do you still have it?" she asked.

"I think I threw it away. No, wait, I balled it up and stuffed it in my coat pocket. It's probably still there. Why? Is it important?"

"Send it over here if you still have it. We can analyze the paper and handwriting to see if it's the same. Has anything like this ever happened to you before?"

"No, never. But you still haven't told me what it means. What's going on here? Should I be worried?" I was getting nervous.

"Six-six-six is the 'mark of the beast.' From the Bible, I forget where. It's a symbol used by white supremacists, especially the Aryan Brotherhood."

"Aryan Brotherhood?" I kept repeating everything she said, but I couldn't help myself. The whole conversation seemed unreal. Was I in some kind of physical danger?

"They're a prison gang," she said calmly, unaware of how much she was rattling me. "Very strong in federal prisons and now spreading outside as well. Very violent. Involved in lots of murders, often against their own guys — anyone they suspect of snitching."

"What do you mean, 'snitching'?"

"Cooperating with the police. Informing, squealing, whatever you like to call it."

"You mean the people who killed Sophie may be after me as well? What the hell am I supposed to do about this?"

"Hey, Prof, calm down. It's just a piece of paper. Maybe it's a coincidence."

"I don't believe in coincidences. And I bet you don't either."

"No, you're right, I don't. Send the paper over. That's the first step. We'll take it from there."

"How would anyone link me to the Reiner murder?"

"You're jumping to conclusions. You don't know there's any such link."

"There has to be a link. Maybe they were following her and knew she came to see me. Maybe your office leaked the fact that I was helping you."

"Stop right there, Professor. You're way outta line. It didn't come from this office."

"Okay, okay. It's just that I didn't expect this. She walks in off the street one day, she gets killed the next. She gets the 6-6-6, I get the 6-6-6."

"I still think you're jumping to conclusions."

"So you think I should ignore this?"

Novak paused. "No, I think you should have a word with the head of security at your office about possibly providing some protection. The FBI tracks neo-Nazis. Maybe you should call them. After all, don't y'all work for the same government department over there?"

I didn't know what to say. She hung up.

When Jennifer showed up, I wasn't in the mood for conversation. I made the pretense of offering her coffee, but she was equally anxious to get this over with. It already felt like years since we had been together, and now we were strangers to one another. I handed over the discs, and she went on her way.

That night, I had a new dream. I was in some kind of boot camp doing exercises to the tune of Schubert's "Military March." *"Schnell, macht schnell!"* shouted the drill sergeant. "Faster, go faster!" I tried to jump up and down, but my body was heavy and awkward. Then I realized I was carrying something on my shoulders. I tried to shake it off. "No dancing, no singing!" shouted the drill sergeant, pulling out a pistol and aiming at me. The weight fell off my shoulders and crashed to the ground. It was a head wrapped in a white cloth. "No, no," I yelled, jerking myself awake before I could see whose head it was. Even in my sleep, I knew I didn't want to know. In the half-light, disconcerted, I wondered if I would ever be free of these nightmares. At least now there was a reason to have them.

I tossed and turned the rest of the night. When the alarm went off at six, I pondered whether I ought to be going to minyan. Some Nazi might be waiting for me on the street corner. Hell, this was no way to behave. I pulled myself together and drove the few blocks to shul, looking in the mirror every few seconds. I didn't see anyone following me.

The minyan usually met in a small chapel rather than in the main sanctuary. It drew a smattering of people, many of them mourners saying Kaddish for a loved one. I slipped my *tallis* around my shoulders after kissing the corners of the embroidered neckband and saying the blessing. Then I put on my tefillin, or phylacteries, binding the first one on my left arm, strapping it once above the elbow and seven times between the elbow and wrist. Next I said the blessing, *"Blessed are You, Adonai, God and Ruler of the Universe, Whose commandments make us holy, and Who commands us concerning tefillin. Blessed be that Sovereign Name for ever."* I lowered the second tefilla over my head until it rested just below my hairline and tightened the straps. Last, I took the remainder of the strap still lying loose below my left wrist and wound it around my second and third fingers and

49

around the back of my hand to form the Hebrew letters *shin, dalet,* and *yod,* which form the word *Shaddai* — Almighty. I was ready to pray.

I decided to stay after the service, joining the rabbi and half a dozen others for bagels, coffee, and a quick study session in the library to discuss the weekly Torah portion, which told of Joseph's travails and triumphs in Egypt. The section dealt with dreams, starting with Joseph's visions predicting how his brothers would all bow down to him and culminating in his prediction of the seven years of plenty followed by the seven years of famine in Egypt. I wished Joseph was still around to decode my own dreams.

The 6-6-6 was, as I thought, still in my coat pocket. Back at the office, I made a few copies of the balled-up paper and messengered the original to Detective Novak. I went upstairs to show it to Eric. He was immediately grim. "This is different from regular hate mail. Whichever meshuga put that under your windshield took the trouble to find out where you live and what kind of car you drive."

"I'd already figured that out."

"I'm going to call the FBI again," he said. "Perhaps now they'll take it more seriously. If it's any consolation, if they come after anyone, they'll come after me as head of the office." Eric's monumental ego, again. It was amazing the way he twisted every situation — even a death threat — to emphasize that he was the head honcho. It was beginning to piss me off.

"Actually," I said, "I was thinking that everybody here could be in danger, not just Your Eminence. You ought to put out a bulletin to the entire office, laying out what's going on and warning people to take precautions."

"Good thinking. I'll do that."

"I'm going to call a friend who knows about neo-Nazis."

"Who's that?"

"David Binder. I was at law school with him. He works for the Anti-Defamation League. Part of his job is tracking extremists."

"I think I've met him a couple of times. Let me know what he says."

I ran into John Howard in the corridor, as if he'd been waiting

50

to corner me. "Mark, a word in your ear," he said in a low voice, ushering me toward his office. He shut the door behind us and gestured for me to sit down. I remained standing.

His thinning, fair hair was beating a rapid retreat across his head, leaving an expanse of forehead behind it. A bead of perspiration was sliding down his temple. He seemed nervous, refusing to meet my eyes.

"What's up?" I asked.

"Can I speak to you in confidence?" He glanced around the room. "Do you ever wonder about Eric?"

"Wonder what?"

"Whether he's the best man to lead this department, especially now that the Republicans have taken over Congress." I stared at him in amazement. Eric had enemies outside the department, but it never occurred to me he had them inside as well.

"No, I've never thought that. Eric is pretty nonpartisan. He doesn't care about politics, only about the department. He has good contacts in both parties."

"Come on, Mark. He's getting nuttier and nuttier," Howard said and clasped his hands together. "Just look at the Bruteitis case. Eric's champing at the bit to file charges, whether we have the evidence or not. He would have done it if you and I hadn't stopped him at the last staff meeting."

So now we were allies? "Eric sometimes talks a bit wild, but he's pretty cautious when it comes to making decisions."

"Sooner or later he's going to cut one corner too many and land us all in serious trouble."

"What do you suggest?"

"I have friends on the Hill you should talk to. If Eric has lost your confidence as well . . ."

It was time to cut this short. "No, John, he hasn't. And I don't think we should be having this discussion. The president nominated Eric for his position, and as far as I know the president and the attorney general still have full confidence in him. If you don't, I suggest you resign."

"Oh, come on, Mark, get real. With Conroy running Congress,

Eric's days are numbered. That's a fact. We ought to be looking to the future. If Eric goes, you're next in line, but you need to make your intentions clear. If you're not interested in taking over, plenty of others are."

I stalked out of the office without another word. It took me a couple of minutes to regain my composure. The problem was, there was some truth to what John had said. Eric could be unpredictable; he didn't always go by the book. Look at the way he was handling the Delatrucha inquiry. And I was going along with him. But Eric had been like a father to me, or at least like an uncle. For a second, I thought about calling him to report the conversation, then decided not to. I had agreed to keep it confidential, and I had to honor that commitment. But John Howard would bear careful watching in future.

Getting back to business, I phoned David Binder, the neo-Nazi expert. When I told him about the 6-6-6, David told me to come right over to his office. It was a cold sunny day, and normally I would have enjoyed the walk across town. But I took a taxi. I didn't even try to come up with an excuse; I knew I was nervous. As I stood on the sidewalk waiting, I kept glancing around to see if anyone seemed suspicious, though I wasn't sure what to look for. People walked past me, their shoes and boots clattering on the cold sidewalk like distant thunder, my senses on red alert.

David poured us both some coffee and hauled out the latest pictures of his budding young sports stars competing at pee-wee soccer. It had been several weeks since we'd spoken. We saw each other rarely since he had joined the growing club of proud, sleep-deprived fathers, while I remained in the opposing camp of frustrated singles still looking for love.

"You should come to dinner on Friday. There's someone Judy and I would like you to meet," he said, peering at me through spectacles even thicker than my own.

"Not another introduction, David. I'm hardly in the mood."

"This one's different. She's a couple of years older than you and getting over a rough divorce. But she's charming and intelligent. She works in the library of the Holocaust Museum. You'll have a lot in common."

"Please. I can just see us spending romantic evenings talking about Bergen-Belsen. Moonlight walks through Babi Yar. A romantic honeymoon at Treblinka. No thanks."

"Come on, what do you have to lose? You can't win the lottery if you don't buy a ticket. It's just dinner with friends, not a date. The worst that can happen is you get a good meal out of it. If you like each other, you can meet again. If not, then don't."

"Great, now I'm your charity project."

"A guy like you needs to be married. I don't know why you're not. You're bright, you're kind and decent, and you're not bad looking. I'm no fashion model, but even I managed to find someone."

"Thank you, David. That's a real morale booster."

"Maybe it's that aura of sadness you carry around with you. And anger, too. Your own personal Mark of Cain."

"Ha, ha. Very original. The first time I heard that joke was in the third grade."

"A family would be good for you. It would give you something to think about other than yourself and all your troubles."

"Why do you married people always pity us singles so much? We're the ones having all the fun."

"So you'll come?"

"All right. At least she sounds like a grown-up. Most of the dates they keep pushing on me at the shul are shy, demure little religious girls barely out of high school who know nothing about the world and want to get married as quickly as possible and start having babies. What's her name?"

"Sara Barclay. She's perfect for you. Now, tell me about this note you received."

I showed him a photocopy of the "6-6-6" written on it and explained how another had been found in Sophie Reiner's pocket.

"That's all? No message? No warning?"

"Wouldn't you call this a warning? I just don't know what they're warning me against. Why do they call it the mark of the beast?"

"It's from the Book of Revelations," David said. "It's a symbol used by several extremist groups. Some of their guys have it tattooed on their bodies, along with swastikas and the like. It's like a sign of membership in the club."

He rummaged in his desk and pulled out a battered, well-read Bible. Flicking through the pages, he came to the relevant passage. "Here it is, chapter 13, verse 16. 'Let him who hath understanding count the number of the beast; for it is the number of a man; and his number is six hundred, three score and six.'"

"Strange. What does it mean?"

"For that, you need to talk to a Christian theologian. It's way out of my league."

"And they murder people, these Aryans?"

"There's a lot happening on the extreme right these days, and nobody is paying attention. Not the FBI, not the police, nobody," he told me. "These groups are getting more and more violent and organized. And increasingly, the federal government is their prime target. That means people like you, Mark. I'm surprised your department hasn't been threatened before. You're a natural enemy for them. You're in the government, you go after Nazis, and you're Jewish."

"I have had the weird feeling lately that someone's been watching me."

David looked a little worried. "Can you be more specific, Mark? What does he look like?"

"I'm not sure — a little skinny guy. I think I've seen him maybe a couple of times. It may be my imagination working overtime."

"This isn't good."

"You don't believe they'd actually kill?"

"They do kill; they have killed."

"I knew there were neo-Nazis around, but I thought they were just mouthing off."

"We used to think that, too, but not anymore. There are dozens of these groups — Aryan Nations, Knights of the Ku Klux Klan, Liberty Lobby — the list goes on. Some of them have started doing military-style training and building homemade bombs. They liaise with each other and form cells like a real underground army. Sooner or later, one of them is going to do something big and kill a lot of people."

"Why do they hate the government so much?"

"They see our government as part of a vast international conspiracy to take away American independence and put us all under the United Nations, which according to them is controlled by so-called international Jewry."

"The UN keeps passing anti-Israel resolutions all the time."

"They would say it's all part of an incredibly devious plot to fool people."

"They're nutty."

"But the threat is real. I hope I'm wrong, because we're all so vulnerable. We don't know the meaning of the word *security* in this country. Even one person acting alone could be extremely dangerous and do a lot of damage. Have you heard of the Unabomber?" There was real passion and urgency in his voice.

"No. Who's he?"

"Nobody knows. He sends very dangerous, intricately crafted, booby-trapped parcels through the mail to people, mostly science professors at major universities. At least one person has been killed, and several others seriously injured. The FBI has been after him for years, but they still know hardly anything about him. One person with some technical expertise can defy the most powerful law enforcement agency in the world. And his bombs are quite sophisticated. There are lots of easier ways to build massive bombs, out of common materials that are easily available, like fertilizer, for example."

"Stink bombs?"

"Real bombs, capable of killing hundreds of people."

There was a pause while I let all this sink in.

"What do you know about the Aryan Brotherhood?" I asked.

"Up to now, they've mainly been organized inside the prison system, but they're trying to grow on the outside. They're into drug trafficking, extortion, sex rings — classic organized crime."

"And they've murdered people." I was feeling queasy again.

"Lots of people. They would go after anyone who challenges them or betrays them. They've also been known to do contract work — killing for hire," David said.

"So what am I supposed to do? Rent a bodyguard?"

David chuckled mirthlessly. "Too expensive to keep up for more than a week or two, unless the government's paying. But there are some things you should do."

"Such as?"

"Get a good alarm system on your apartment and your car. Keep your eyes open when you're walking around or driving. Vary your routine. Maybe get a gun."

I still couldn't believe all this was happening.

"You can take a course. Local gun clubs or the NRA give them. Or if you don't want a gun, you could buy pepper spray. Carry a whistle so you can summon help if needed. Always try to let other people know where you are and where you'll be."

I didn't hear any more from the police for the next couple of days, though I called several times. I tried to follow David's advice and had an alarm system put in my car. I bought a whistle and ordered a few canisters of pepper spray from a mail order outfit I found in the yellow pages. They had a bewildering array of items for sale. I opted for a dispenser guaranteed to work at a range of eight feet. I asked the salesman how it worked. He said it would swell an attacker's mucous membranes almost instantly, force his eyes closed, and make breathing difficult. "It will put him flat on his back and out of action within seconds. Guaranteed or your money back," he assured me. The effects would wear off after twenty to thirty minutes.

I found myself calming down as I buried myself in work and no further threats materialized. The week passed in an endless series of meetings, which were comforting for a change for being so boring.

On Thursday, we had our weekly staff meeting, poorly attended this time because staffers were already away on vacation. John Howard had spoken by phone with Janet, who had arrived in Lithuania and accessed the archives.

"Sounds promising," he said. "She said she's already found some documents mentioning Bruteitis that we've never seen before."

"Has she found anything with his signature?" Eric asked.

"Not yet."

I listened carefully, but there was no hint of any hostility between them. Howard ignored me completely, which suited me just fine.

On Thursday evening, we had the annual Christmas party, now officially known for reasons of political correctness as the "seasonal party." I found myself sitting next to Lynn, sharing a bottle of below-average chardonnay in a darkened restaurant. I wasn't quite sure how I got there. Had she maneuvered herself next to me, or had I maneuvered myself next to her?

"Tell me, Mark," she said, somewhere between her second and third glass. "What does a Nazi hunter do for fun?" Her eyes shone in the candlelight. Her dangly earrings swinging, she leaned closer to me. She smelled delicious. My glasses were steaming up. I took them off to clean them, rendering her fuzzy, but still lovely.

"Not much," I said. "I like to work out, I run a lot and bike. I read, eat out, go to the movies once in a while, read Nazi-hunting magazines — that sort of stuff."

"God, how staid," she said. "Like those white shirts you always wear. Every day, white, white, white. You should loosen up a bit. Try wearing blue for a change. It would accentuate those beautiful blue eyes of yours that you hide behind your glasses. Aren't you religious types ever allowed to have fun?"

Beautiful blue eyes? I was blushing like a teenager. Lynn looked at me and giggled. "Oh, God, I must be really tipsy, talking to my boss like this. I'm embarrassing you. And myself. Forget I said that. It's not me talking, it's the wine."

"No, it's okay. I like it," I said. "And for your information, although I don't eat bacon or shellfish, there's nothing at all in Judaism about not having fun. I like all the same stuff as you do — movies, theater, parties, good food . . ." *And sex*, I thought.

There was an awkward silence. "So what kind of music do you like?" she asked.

"Mostly stuff from the sixties and seventies — the Beatles, Dylan, Baez, Joni Mitchell — you may have heard of some of them. I've been listening to a lot of Schubert and Schumann lately, for obvious reasons."

She grimaced. "That's work. I asked about fun. How old did you say you were? Sixty? Seventy?"

57

"Well, what do *you* do for fun?" I asked, a bit stung. "I suppose you like staying out all night drinking and carousing."

"No, that's not me at all. I'm an early-to-bed kind of girl."

"So strolls on moonlit beaches and romantic evenings in front of the fireplace?"

"Now you're talking. I love that kind of thing. Wouldn't you, if it was with the right person?"

It did sound nice. With the right person.

Half an hour later, I was standing on the sidewalk with Lynn, hailing a taxi. The cab pulled up, she stood on tiptoes and kissed me on the lips, and it was over. "Happy holidays," she said, climbing into the cab. And she was gone.

That night I listened to Delatrucha sing a cycle called *Die Schöne Müllerin*, "The Beautiful Miller Girl." It began with the piano mimicking the sound of water gurgling down a stream toward a water mill. The narrator is in love, and for a brief moment it seems the miller's lovely daughter returns his feelings. Delatrucha's voice lifted to an incredible, ecstatic climax. "Let one song alone echo today; the beloved miller girl is mine! Mine!" I found myself rooting for the guy. In my mind, I was the narrator, and Lynn was the beautiful mill girl.

Of course, in the song cycle, things pretty soon go sour for the poor old narrator, as they usually do in German poetry. It's the age-old story: the miller girl catches sight of a dashing hunter, a much more glamorous fellow, and makes eyes at him. Jealousy seizes the narrator. He can't bear it, and by the end of the song cycle he's done away with himself and is resting comfortably in his grave, where all gloomy German poets end up. For a moment, I felt sorry for the poor schmuck. But then I asked myself, Why am I identifying with a loser like him, when the hunter gets the girl? I'm a hunter myself, of sorts. Of course, she was all wrong for me. For one thing, she wasn't even religious. My mind knew that, but my body wasn't listening.

As for Delatrucha, he may or may not have lied about his past, but he was a wonderful singer. In that one delirious stanza, he captured all the dizzy, heady exhilaration of the beginnings of love. I went to bed thinking about the kiss, Schubert playing in my head.

I had a small hangover next morning, but Lynn seemed totally unaffected when we met to discuss Señor Roberto Delatrucha. Just seeing her produced a rush of blood to my head (and elsewhere). Delatrucha's file had just arrived from the INS, George reported. Today he was wearing a tie depicting ducks in flight that clashed violently with his bright red shirt.

"Delatrucha arrived here in 1951 from Argentina," George said, stretching his legs halfway across the office. "In 1952, he married a woman called Mary Scott. That was his basis for applying for U.S. citizenship, which he obtained in 1958."

"Place of birth?" I asked.

"L'viv, the Soviet Union."

"And the date?"

"October 8, 1920." I wrote it down on my legal pad, frowning.

"L'viv wasn't in the Soviet Union then," I said. "Before 1918, it was ruled by Austria. And after the Treaty of Versailles, it was in Poland."

"It did have a large population of *Volksdeutsche*," George observed.

"Of what?" Lynn asked. "English please, you guys."

"*Volksdeutsche*. Ethnic Germans," I said. "When did he pick up the name Delatrucha?"

"He already had it when he arrived here," George said. "But on his U.S. immigration form, he was required to provide his former name. He gave Roberto Schnellinger, definitely a German name. I did a search of CROWCASS files for Schnellinger. And guess what I found?"

"What?" we both asked.

"Nothing," George said flatly. "There are no Schnellingers listed."

CROWCASS is the Central Registry of War Criminals and Security Suspects. It's a list that was drawn up by the U.S. military after Germany surrendered in 1945. A CROWCASS listing was equivalent to an arrest warrant. Anyone on the list who was found was supposed to be arrested and handed over to the Allies for trial.

"What about German sources?" I asked. The best source of

German war records was the Berlin Document Center, operated for many years by the U.S. State Department but recently remanded to the Germans. It was the world's largest trove of captured Nazi personnel files, and included an almost complete collection of SS records.

"I put in requests to see if the document center has any Schnellingers on file," said George. "It will probably take a couple of weeks for them to respond. We won't get anything until well after Christmas. Germans take the holiday season very seriously. Have you ever spent Christmas in Germany, Mark?"

"No," I said. "Nor do I want to. I dread hearing 'Rudolph the Red Nosed Reindeer' in German." I turned to Lynn, who was clutching a folder bulging with press clips and photocopies. She was wearing a pink turtleneck cashmere sweater and a pair of dark honey earrings that complemented her eyes. She put on a pair of granny spectacles, which she probably didn't need, shuffled a couple of papers, and began.

"First the name," she said. "Roberto of the trout."

"What?" we chorused again.

"Delatrucha. It's Spanish for 'of the trout.' "

"As in the *Trout Quintet*," said George. He began warbling tunelessly. From his lips, it sounded like a Moldavian love song.

"Okay, okay, we get the picture," I said. "There's also a song called 'The Trout' on one of the CDs I bought. About a guy who hooks a trout and watches it die."

"Why would he choose such an obviously fake name?" George asked.

"Lots of artists and actors take stage names, so let's not jump to conclusions. It doesn't necessarily mean anything. What else do you have, Lynn?" I asked.

"There's a bunch of material about his accompanist, Mary Scott," Lynn continued. "They divorced in 1985, and he got a new one."

"New accompanist or new wife?" George asked.

"Both," Lynn said. "Her name is Elissa Horne. She's like thirty years younger than him, which is totally gross, if you ask me."

"What else?" George asked.

"Delatrucha came here on a fellowship for young foreign musicians to spend a year at Juilliard. That's where he met Mary. She was a piano student. They teamed up to give a concert. It was a huge success. I called the *New York Times* archives, and they dug up the review for me and faxed it over." She handed each of us a photocopy, dated February 20, 1952.

Roberto Delatrucha, a newcomer to our shores from Argentina, revealed himself last night as a mature and gifted artist of caressing subtlety and poetic expression. Ably accompanied by Mary Scott, Delatrucha masterfully crafted a mood of profound engagement in a performance of Schubert's *Winterreise*. His powerful voice effortlessly led a rapt audience into the very heart of darkness at the center of the cycle.

"It all comes back to *Winterreise*," I muttered.

"It's like his signature piece," said Lynn. "He says it's the work he feels closest to." I found myself suddenly recalling our kiss. God, she was cute in those silly glasses. She flashed me a grin. I wrenched my mind back to the subject at hand.

"What else have you got?" I asked.

"A whole bunch of other reviews, but they're basically more of the same. Everyone agrees he's an awesome singer. He quit singing in public a few years ago, but he still teaches down at the University of Florida. He seems totally into his privacy, with one exception, which is that he's listed as a major Republican Party donor. He gave a lot of money to the GOP in the past election, and even took part in a fundraiser for Mitch Conroy, where he sang 'America the Beautiful.'" She passed around a clipping from the *Orlando Sentinel* describing the event.

"Interesting but probably not relevant to this inquiry," I said. "It's certainly no crime to be a Republican. Some of this office's best friends and supporters are Republicans. So let's drop that one. Tell us more about his new wife."

"He dumped Mary in 1984 and teamed up with this new Elissa chick, who was actually once one of Mary's pupils. She's apparently not nearly as good a pianist as Mary, but she's probably better in the sack."

"How do you know that?" I asked.

"About her bedroom talents?"

"About her talents as a pianist."

"I spoke to a music professor at George Washington University. Bill McDuffy. My friend Amy takes singing lessons from him. He's a big Schubert buff."

"Did you tell him why you were interested in Delatrucha?"

"I said I was a student doing a paper. Anyway, once he got going, there was no stopping him. He said Roberto had this almighty blowup with his wife and daughter a few years ago."

"Daughter?" George asked.

"Roberto and Mary's one kid, Susan, born 1958. She took her mother's maiden name after her parents divorced. Apparently, she was a promising musician as a child, but she never made it. Now she works as a book agent in Boston. A couple of years ago, Mr. Trout won some big award. They got Isaac Stern, the famous violinist, to present it, but then Mary shows up in the audience and goes bananas, cursing at Roberto from the bleachers. They had to drag her out. McDuffy remembers it 'cause he was there."

"Good stuff," I said.

"There's more," said Lynn. "Roberto hasn't performed in Germany or Austria for ages, not since the early seventies, even though he's mega popular there and it's the birthplace of lieder. He hasn't set foot there for twenty years. It's raised some eyebrows, but he's never given an explanation."

"Interesting. Maybe he didn't want to be recognized by anyone who knew him during the war," George said. It was in the 1970s that interest in the Holocaust and war criminals had started to reawaken in Germany. In the 1950s and '60s, former Nazis still made up a large part of the population. Most led untroubled lives in a nation that was still sympathetic to them. "Did you find anything about his early years?"

"Almost nothing. I mean, this guy is truly fanatical about his privacy. If he gives interviews, it's just to speak about music, never about himself."

"That might indicate he has something to hide," I said.

"You're stretching it, Mark. It might just mean he likes his privacy. I like mine, too," George countered.

"You're right. I'm reaching," I conceded.

"But this guy goes further than that," Lynn said. "I couldn't find anything in the clips even about where he was born, not a single word. Nothing about his mother or father. Nothing about where he went to school. Nothing about the war, which he must have lived through, wherever he was. Just a totally blank slate."

"So we're not left with very much," I said, summing up. "Just a bunch of unanswered questions and some vague suspicions."

"The response from the Document Center might clear up some things when it arrives," George said. "But I wouldn't get my hopes up too high. Even if this guy is originally German, there's no guarantee that Schnellinger's his real name. People took on new identities all the time in the confusion at the end of the war."

"I have more sources I can check, if you think it's worth it," Lynn said. "I haven't finished going through all the newspaper databases. And I also want to find out more about his wife and daughter."

"Well, you've piqued my curiosity, even if you didn't find much," I said. "What you didn't find is almost more interesting than what you did. I don't really have a sense about this guy yet one way or the other. It won't do any harm to keep searching. Let's meet again next week to see if there's any point continuing."

"Fair enough," said George, and left the room. Lynn got up to follow. I gestured for her to stay. "Lynn, about last night," I began.

"I was a little drunk. But you're allowed to kiss anyone you want at the Christmas party," she interjected. "It doesn't mean anything. Everyone knows that."

"Oh," I said, failing to disguise my disappointment. "All right. Fair enough. As long as that's understood, then."

"Totally," she said.

Then she leaned forward and kissed me again.

7

A friendly light dances in front of me;
I follow it hither and thither.

— "Pretense" by Wilhelm Müller, music by Franz Schubert

On Friday evening, after Shabbat services, I dutifully appeared at David and Judy's home, bottle of wine in hand. They were getting ready to put their kids to bed, but first the seven-year-old had to play the piano for us. The proud parents beamed as he struggled through the first two pages of "Für Elise." We all applauded enthusiastically. The kids were settled for the night, and the grown-ups sat down for dinner. I was seated opposite Sara Barclay, a petite woman with an attractive oval face, limpid gray eyes, and a quiet air of unflappable calm about her. We assessed each other across the table like fencers looking for an opening. To my surprise, I enjoyed the evening. Sara was both attractive and sharp-witted, and conversation flowed easily. Judy asked us both if we didn't find our jobs too depressing, having to deal with the Holocaust all the time. I ducked the question, mumbling something about justice, but Sara jumped right in.

"It's not at all depressing. It's uplifting. Just today, a middle-aged man came in with his mother, a survivor, to make a video recording of her story. We collect survivors' stories in the museum, as you may know. They brought two of her grandchildren as well—both teenagers. I listened in. It was truly inspiring," she said.

"Tell us," we all urged her.

"The woman was only about thirteen when they transported

her entire family to one of the camps. She was already half-starved and very skinny. There was a slight opening in the cattle car they were traveling on, and her parents saw she could squeeze through the gap. They made her jump off the train. They knew they were going to their deaths, but they were too big to fit through themselves. And they were desperate for her to live. She landed in the snow and hurt her leg; a Polish peasant found her and sheltered her for over two years. Of course, she never saw the rest of her family again."

"That's not depressing?" David asked.

"Well, of course it is tragic. But it's also inspiring. It shows her will to live and her family's will for her to live and the humanity and heroism of the family that sheltered her. As the Torah teaches, she chose life. And there she was today with her son and grandchildren by her side. Her parents' hopes were fulfilled. So, yes, it was sad, but not depressing."

David was right. Under different circumstances, she would have been perfect for me. As we said good night, I brushed her cheeks with my lips, wondering if I should see her again. But it would have been unfair; my mind was too full of Lynn, whose very touch produced an electric spark. How can you explain the power of two brief kisses? I couldn't stop thinking about them.

I walked home after dinner. I never drove on Shabbat, but there seemed little reason to be worried about walking through the city alone. Nothing had happened since the windshield-wiper incident, and I had recovered my nerve.

But as I turned the first corner, I had a strange feeling I was being followed. It was difficult to explain — a creepy sensation on the back of my neck. I kept looking around, but it was hard to see anything in the dark. Stupidly, I had left the whistle in my briefcase. The pepper spray hadn't arrived yet. All my senses stretched extra thin. The least little sound seemed ominous. I started jogging, then broke into a sprint, wearing my overcoat and dress shoes. I doubled back down a couple of streets, then realized how irrational I was being. They'd been to my apartment building. I stopped running and walked the rest of the way, looking over my shoulder the whole way.

At home, I touched the mezuzah with my fingertip, kissed it, and entered the darkened apartment. The only light was in the kitchen. It remained on throughout Shabbat, while all the other lights stayed off. But as I went into the bedroom, I saw the light blinking on my answering machine. Usually I disconnected the phone on Friday afternoon so nothing would intrude on the day of rest; this week I had forgotten to. I threw a pillow over the machine so I wouldn't have to keep looking at the light blinking all day.

At shul next morning, the rabbi spoke about the situation in Bosnia. "Just as they did after the Holocaust, some will ask, 'Where is God?' " he said. "To go around blaming God for man-made tragedies makes no sense. The question is not, 'Where was God during the Holocaust?' The right question is, 'Where was man?' " Agreement rumbled from the congregation.

"Look at it from God's point of view. Faced with our accusations, what would He say? God might say, 'I created this world, but I asked you to care for it and for each other. Go ahead and pray to me, but understand it is you who have the responsibility for your actions. You can look to the heavens and charge me with cruelty but it is you who are killing each other all over the world, not I. So don't ask where I am. The real question is, Where are you?' "

The rabbi continued: "Our task, which God gave us, is to perfect the world. As *The Ethics of the Father* teaches, we do not have to complete the work personally, but the enormity of the task does not excuse us from not trying. God asks, 'When will you take steps to perfect My world?' "

In the afternoon, I had a long nap before returning to shul for afternoon prayers. The sun set by late afternoon, so Shabbat ended early. Once it was over and I had recited the Havdalah blessings welcoming the new week, I removed the pillow from the answering machine and retrieved my messages. There were four; the first three callers had hung up without saying anything. The fourth was from someone called Jerrold Osterman—Jennifer's elder brother—asking me to call and leaving a number. He lived in Silicon Valley, and I had never spoken to him. Strange. I dialed the number. A woman answered and told me to wait a second. There was a rumble of conversation in the background, as if a large number of people were there.

"Thanks for calling, Mark," Jerrold said in a tired voice.

"What's up?"

"Mark, there's no easy way to tell you this. Jennifer was killed last Thursday."

"What?"

"She died last Thursday. My sister is gone." He swallowed a sob.

"Last Thursday? That can't be right. I saw her last Thursday. She came by my apartment to pick up some CDs."

"I'm afraid it is true." He sighed.

"But she was here, standing right here in my living room. She only stayed a couple of minutes, but she seemed perfectly fine."

"She must have been on her way home from your place when it happened."

"I can't believe you're telling me this. What happened?"

"She fell onto the Metro tracks just as a train was approaching."

"She *fell?*"

"She was apparently standing very close to the platform. She must have slipped or lost her balance."

I closed my eyes. This couldn't be happening. Tears welled up in my eyes and overflowed. Suddenly I was sobbing. At the other end of the line, Jerrold was keening along with me. Then I had an even more appalling thought. "Jerrold, she wasn't pushed, was she?"

"That's what we wanted to know, but nobody saw anything."

His answer calmed me down a little. "Oh, my God, Jerrold, I'm so sorry. You must be devastated. Is there anything I can do? Anything at all?"

"Thanks for offering, Mark, but I don't think so."

"When's the funeral? I'd like to come."

"We're burying her tomorrow out here in Palo Alto."

"I'll catch the first plane I can."

"Mark, I don't think that's such a good idea. Her fiancé, Jeff, is here. He's pretty broken up, as you can imagine. I think it would be better if you didn't come. After all, you two weren't really in each other's lives anymore. Perhaps sometime in the future, in a month or two, we'll have a memorial service for all her friends in D.C., and you could come to that."

"Of course. I'm so sorry for your loss. Jennifer was such a beautiful person. I can't believe it. I just can't believe it."

"Neither can we. Be well, Mark. I know at one time you two were close. I hope you'll remember her fondly." He choked up, and I felt myself doing the same.

The rest of the day passed in a fog. The next evening was the first night of Hanukkah. I lit two candles, reciting the blessings alone, thanking God for sustaining us in life and bringing us to this day. The blessing had suddenly acquired a new meaning. Life was so fleeting, so ephemeral. As the psalmist wrote, "As for mortals, their days are like grass. They flourish like a flower of the field, for the wind passes over it, and it is gone."

I tried to recall how Hanukkah was when I was a kid, my father chanting the blessing, my mother coming out from the kitchen spattered with flour from frying the latkes, the potato pancakes. It used to upset me how messy she looked, but I loved the smell of hot oil that suffused the whole house. Suddenly, I missed her desperately. The room I was standing in, my entire home, was spotlessly clean, but it was as empty as my life. The best way to honor Jennifer, I decided, was to grasp hold of life and live it more fully for as long as possible. I resolved to invite Lynn to help me light the candles at least once before the festival ended.

That night, I dreamed I was sitting on a workbench with two piano keyboards on either side of me. I was playing one with each hand, better than I had ever played before. My right hand swept up and down the keys in dazzling glissandi. My left kept a steady um-pa-pa beat, which gradually transformed into the sound of a telephone ringing. Still three-quarters asleep, I snaked my hand out, groping for the receiver. "Who is it?" I muttered, eyes closed.

"Have you seen today's *Post* yet?" It was Rosen.

"What's happened?" I croaked, feeling for my glasses. My hand swept over the bedside table, accidentally knocking them off. "Shit!"

"What's the matter?"

"My glasses fell. Hold on." I scrabbled on my hands and knees until I felt the metal frame, put them on, and the world came back in focus. It suddenly hit me that today they were burying Jennifer, putting her broken body into the cold ground.

"This had better be good. I've had it with bad news. What time is it, anyway?"

"Almost seven. You're not still in bed, surely?"

"On a Sunday morning? Why on earth would I be in bed?"

"I never took you for a late sleeper."

"Only once a year. Today was going to be the day. What did I miss that couldn't wait?"

"Take a look at the Style section and call me back when you've read it."

Before I could go downstairs to get the paper, the phone rang again. It was Lynn. "Have you seen it? — our Trout guy's in the *Post!*" she said breathlessly. My heart jumped at the sound of her voice. "I didn't wake you, did I?" she asked.

"No, Rosen just called and did that. What's it about?"

"He's won a major prize. Something called the McCready Award."

"Is that all?"

"I thought it was pretty interesting. I'm sorry I called so early."

"No, it's okay." Then, before I could think about hesitating, I blurted out, "Lynn, can you come and light Hanukkah candles with me tonight?" I felt as though I were sixteen again, asking my first girlfriend on our first date.

"Not tonight," she said calmly, as if she were expecting this. "I'm doing a shift at a soup kitchen in D.C. My friends and I do it every week. I could come next Saturday, the eighth night. We'll light them all, sing the dumb song about the dreidel, the whole bit."

"Great," I said. "I'll make the latkes."

"Cool."

"It's a date, then. Oh, and did you get Eric's memo about the hate mail we've been getting?"

"I saw it, but I didn't take it too seriously. I know you guys get hate mail all the time. It goes with the territory, doesn't it?"

"This time it might be a bit different. One of these kooks took the trouble to find out where I live and what I drive and left a note under my windshield. And a close friend of mine died last week. She fell under a Metro train."

"Mark, that's awful. I read about that poor woman in the paper. I had no idea she was a friend of yours."

"We had been close once. Anyway, the point is, I want you to take seriously any threats you might get and keep an eye out for anything suspicious. Don't walk around on your own late at night."

"Right, boss."

The line beeped, telling me there was another call waiting. It was George. Apparently everyone in Washington but me had seen the *Post,* which was reporting that Delatrucha was one of six winners of the prestigious McCready Prize, awarded annually for lifetime achievements in the arts. In the middle of the front page were photos of the six honorees: two elder statesmen of the theater, a feminist author, a little-known sculptor, a well-loved poet, and Delatrucha, his beard bushier than ever. I got the coffee going and sat down at the kitchen table to read the article.

> Roberto Delatrucha is honored for his honest, unflinching interpretations of classical songs. Delatrucha, a native of Argentina who came to the United States 42 years ago, said he was overwhelmed. "Never in my wildest dreams could I have imagined such an honor," he said.
>
> The prizes will be awarded at a special ceremony at the Kennedy Center in the presence of the president of the United States on February 20 and broadcast on public television. Admirers of Delatrucha can catch the singer in a rare appearance next week when he gives a master class at the University of Virginia in Charlottesville.

When I called back, Eric was bubbling with excitement. "This is big," he said. He was already envisaging the publicity potential of unmasking a major new catch. He adopted a tone of righteous indignation. "Whatever happens, I'm not going to let the president of the United States award a prize to a Nazi. Not on my watch. We must defend the honor of the presidency," he intoned in his best imitation of Winston Churchill.

"We don't know he's a Nazi," I said. "We hardly know anything about him at all except that he's an exceptional singer."

"Mark, we have seven weeks to find out the truth before the ceremony. We need to get moving right now. What do you know about him so far?"

"Not much. His previous name was Schnellinger, and he came here from Argentina in the early fifties. That's about it. We've put in requests to the Berlin Document Center, but it's going to take time to get answers."

"We don't have time anymore. You'll have to go over there yourself. How quickly can you leave?"

"Whoa, slow down." Was John Howard right? Was Eric coming unglued in his zeal for publicity?

"What do you mean, 'slow down'?" he asked. "We need to go full speed ahead."

"Eric, it's almost Christmas Eve. You'll get nothing done in Germany until after New Year's Day. I'm snowed under with work. The Bruteitis case is still up in the air, and Janet will be back from Lithuania soon. We've got a major appeal coming up, and the new Congress is coming in, plus there's the budget to complete. My entire week is meetings. We're still checking sources on Delatrucha. So far, there's really nothing to go on."

"Okay, I suppose we can wait a few days," he said reluctantly. "But from now on, Mark, this is your top priority, the first thing you do in the morning, last thing before you leave. And I want to be briefed on this every couple of days."

"We should bring Janet in as soon as she gets back."

"I'll consider it."

"Speaking of priorities, what about that meeting with the FBI to talk about my personal security?" I asked him.

"You haven't received any more threats, have you?"

"No, just the one I showed you." I didn't mention Jennifer's death or my suspicion that someone had followed me the other night.

71

"We'll do it after New Year's. Everyone's busy right now," he said.

The next day, Detective Novak left a message on my voice mail, saying tests showed no match between the note found in Sophie Reiner's pocket and the one on my car. Different paper, different pen, different handwriting.

Twice during the week, I was invited by the families of synagogue congregants to light candles. Both times there was a single girl there, dangled before me like bait. But now, with my date with Lynn approaching, I wasn't biting.

Christmas Day passed slowly. I said my prayers at home and went for an early-morning run in Rock Creek Park. It was so bitterly cold that even the most fanatical neo-Nazi wouldn't want to be out. The sky was gray with impending snow, and almost no one was out. I warmed up after the first couple of miles and started to enjoy the solitude. My thoughts kept jumping from Delatrucha to Lynn and back again. I had that song on my brain — "In and out of the grove, let one song echo today; the beloved miller girl is mine. Mine!" If only.

I spent the afternoon at the office, reviewing everything there was on the Delatrucha case. Sophie Reiner kept coming to mind. What had brought her to America? If I closed my eyes, I could almost see her sitting in front of me, brushing her scraggly hair from her forehead. There was something nagging at me, some connection I was missing, but I couldn't put my finger on it.

I passed the evening camped in front of the TV, watching a video and eating chocolate-covered macadamia nuts at 96 fattening calories apiece. Each one was a bitter personal defeat. So far, the macadamias were up five to nothing. The phone rang.

"I was thinking about you," Lynn said. My heart soared.

"I was thinking about you, too. Where are you?"

"Philadelphia, with my parents. So boring."

"I could drive up tomorrow and bring you home," I said, thinking of her joyous grin and bouncing curls.

"I'll be back in D.C. in a couple of days. And we have our date on Saturday." Aha! She called it a date.

"Saturday might as well be next October, the days will pass so slowly."

"I never pegged you as such a romantic. How sweet."

"You caught me at an unguarded moment," I said gruffly. "Usually, I behave like a seventy-year-old, as I believe someone once told me."

"Anyway, I'll see you in the office on Thursday," she continued, ignoring my jibe.

Where I could look but not touch, I thought sourly.

Just before midnight, as I was about to go to bed, the phone rang again. Silence on the line. For a moment I thought nobody was there; then I heard the breathing.

"Who's there? *Who the fuck are you?*" I hissed. Still silence. I slammed down the receiver. These people wanted to intimidate me. The horrible thing was, they were succeeding. I was almost completely defenseless if someone really wanted to do me in. If someone came at me with a knife or a gun, what was I supposed to do? Make like Jiminy Cricket and give a little whistle?

Next morning, I phoned the police and asked them to page Novak.

"Working the day after Christmas, Professor?"

"Putting your tax dollars to work," I said. "I notice you're working, too."

"Not by choice."

"I received an anonymous phone call last night."

"Did he threaten you?"

"Just heavy breathing."

"Not much we can do about that. I'd get your number changed, or delist it."

"Thanks for the advice, but I don't want to kowtow to a bunch of thugs."

"Anything else?"

"Where in Florida did Sophie Reiner go?" I asked.

"Orlando. Why?"

"Did she rent a car?"

"Yes. Why?"

"Delatrucha, the singer whose CD was in her room, teaches music in Gainesville at the University of Florida. She may have gone to visit him. It's an easy drive from Orlando on 75. I've done it myself."

Novak paused. "We don't think this singer guy has anything to do with it. We're pursuing a new lead."

"So what was Sophie doing in Florida? And why did she also go to Boston, where his daughter lives? Another coincidence?"

"We don't think that's why she was killed. Listen, Prof, I can't tell you any more right now. I've already said too much. If any of this shows up in the media . . ."

"Don't worry, it won't. But I don't think you should dismiss the Delatrucha angle so quickly."

"Professor, do I tell you how to do your job?"

"No," I admitted.

"So don't tell me how to do mine. Hopefully we'll have something to announce pretty soon."

Saturday went by even more slowly than usual. At shul, I couldn't concentrate on my prayers. I was waiting for the evening to come. When the buzzer finally sounded and I opened the door, the sight of her in a chunky woolen cardigan caught my breath. The sweater was three sizes too large, but she still looked incredible. I stood there trying to think of something to say before speechlessly ushering her into the apartment.

"This is the first time I've seen you not wearing a suit and a white shirt," she said. I was wearing jeans and a black sweatshirt. "You look human."

I made havdalah and was delighted to see Lynn knew how to sing the blessings. "Learned them at Jewish summer camp," she told me after she plunged the multibraided candle into the wine to extinguish the light of Shabbat and begin the new week.

I switched some lights on, and she wandered around the apartment. "Have you read all these books?" she asked, indicating my shelves. "They all look so dry."

"They're not all as dry as they seem," I said, pulling down a translation of the Song of Songs. I read from the first page:

Kiss me, make me drunk with your kisses.
Your sweet loving
Is better than wine.

"That's hot," she said, looking at me. I wanted to kiss her. Like a coward, I held back.

We cooked the latkes together, grating the potatoes by hand, then deep-frying them until they were brown and crispy.

"What do you like to eat these with?" I asked her.

"Applesauce and yogurt, like everyone else."

"Actually, people eat them lots of different ways, depending on where their families came from."

"Really?"

"Some people like them with salt. That's the Lithuanian way. In my father's family, which came from Galicia in southern Poland, they'd always sprinkle them with sugar. Actually, we Galicianers sprinkle pretty much everything with sugar."

"Latkes with sugar? Yuck!"

"That's what my mother said. Her family were Litvaks."

Before eating the latkes, we lit the candles and sang "Rock of Ages," and the dreidel song in both Hebrew and English, and the one about the great miracle that happened in days of old. Lynn suggested we sing the song about a hero arising in every generation to redeem the people. She had a sweet soprano that soared effortlessly over my tuneless tenor.

It wasn't that difficult to imagine doing this again next year. I felt so much at ease. I didn't have to pretend, I could be myself. I could tell her anything — almost everything — and it would be okay.

"So what kind of a Jew are you?" Lynn asked.

"Modern Orthodox. I live in the modern world and accept everything about it, or almost everything, but I try to live my life according to the commandments."

"What about the role of women?"

"What do you mean?"

"Do you consider women equal to men?"

"Absolutely."

"Would you count a woman to make a minyan?"

The conversation had suddenly taken a very serious turn.

"In my shul, they don't count women in the minyan, and women are not allowed to chant the Torah. I've been going there a long time, and I feel comfortable there. Would I personally count a woman in the minyan? Yes. Would I worship in a place where women were called up to the Torah? Yes. Would I allow a woman to feed me a ham sandwich on Shabbat? No."

She leaned forward and touched my *kippah*. "What about this? I've heard the kind of yarmulke people wear has political significance."

"For some people it does. Like those large crocheted ones with patterns the Israeli settlers wear. But not mine. I wear it out of respect for God and to remind myself we are all living here on earth under His sovereignty. It's not so much a statement to the world as a reminder for me. That's why I prefer to wear a plain black *kippah*."

"You said His sovereignty. Does that mean you believe God is a man?"

"If you read Deuteronomy or Maimonides, you know that God has no form, not of a man or a woman or any living creature. 'Him' is a kind of shorthand, and I'm used to it. But do I see him as a muscular guy stretching out his hand, like the one painted in the Sistine Chapel? No."

"Okay, enough theology. Do you have some music we can listen to?" I turned on the CD player. Delatrucha's voice came on. I read the translation.

> We sat so quiet together,
> In the cool shade of the alders.
> We looked down so quietly together
> Into the babbling stream.
> I did not look at any moon,

Nor any star shine.
I looked at her form
At her eyes alone.

As the song ended, I leaned forward, no hesitation. She tilted her head ever so slightly, inviting me in, and I kissed her. I've read the Song of Songs a thousand times. We read it in shul every year at Passover. Now, finally, I understood it. She was fragrant, she was myrrh and aloes, she tasted of honey and almonds, her lips were yielding and sweet as figs and pomegranates, and each kiss was better than wine.

We talked for hours. She told me about her family; her father was a keen outdoorsman who loved hunting and fishing. Lynn, his eldest, was apparently a grave disappointment because she was not a boy and did not share his enthusiasm for firearms. To be kind, she occasionally allowed him to drag her out to the firing range.

I told her about my dad in the wilds of West Virginia and how I had promised to visit him. Lynn was immediately enthusiastic and said she would like to come too.

"Really?" I said, visualizing us tramping through the snow together and roasting chestnuts over an open fire. "Let's go. When are you free?"

"The weekend after next, maybe. Is there room for both of us?"

"Sure, there's a spare bedroom, and I can sleep on the couch." I brought up office regulations about not dating your boss. Lynn replied tartly that she might be a few years younger than me, but she was not a child, and I should shut up. If we really were going to be dating, we shouldn't be working together. But I pushed that thought to the back of my mind. Right now, I was too happy. If it lasted, I'd figure something out later.

Lynn left shortly after midnight, lingering at the door for half an hour before finally tearing herself away. I made sure she was safely in a taxi before going back upstairs, wondering when I could see her again.

My buddy Clint has come up to help. I hauled his fat ass around the city, showed him the Jewish dude's apartment building, pointed out his car. He wanted to see where I slit the German bitch's throat. So we went over there, but there was nothing to see—they even cleaned up the blood stain.

It's time to let Clint know about the plan. So far, the only person that knows is Burl. I told him, "Clint, we've got to think a lot bigger. We've got to think on an entirely different scale."

"What do you mean, shrimp?" he said. I've told him a thousand fucking times not to call me that, but I let it pass because I need him to listen to what I'm saying.

I tell him, "Millions of patriots in this nation are sick to their stomachs. They're like dried kindling waiting to ignite, waiting for a spark to set them in flames."

He says, "For a small guy, you sure like to use big words." This is the kind of shit I have to put up with all the time. Was it like this for Julius Caesar or Alexander the Great?

I tell him, "Just 'cause you come from West Virginia, doesn't mean you're stupid, so don't make like you are." I look him straight in the eye to show I'm serious. I say, "We can be the spark, Clint. By God, we can be the spark that ignites the conflagration that brings freedom back to this country. You and me and Burl. How do you like that?" I'm not sure he gets it, but he nods anyway.

"Damn right, shrimp, damn right," he says. I grab him by the collar, press my forearm against his fat neck, shove my face about an inch from his, and I tell him, "Don't fucking call me that ever again." I feel a little bad doing it, but a leader needs to be respected. I tell him, "If you call me by that name again, Clint, so help me God, I will cut your fucking balls off and stuff them down your fucking throat. Are we clear?"

His face turns red, and he gurgles a bit, but the look in his eye tells me he comprehends what I'm trying to communicate. I let him go.

Then I explain to him that random acts of defiance aren't going to cut it anymore. They're not the kind of spark that can start a conflagration. Which is why I sat in my car outside the Jewish temple

78

for four hours on Saturday and drove away without pulling the trigger. It took real self-control because I had those people in my sights, each and every one of them, as they streamed in and out. It's a lot harder not to kill someone than to kill them. The Scripture says, "I know the blasphemy of them which say they are Jews, and are not, but are the synagogue of Satan," so it would have been okay to plug one or two of them, which I could have easily done and still gotten away. But I held back.

Lying flat on the back seat, looking through the slit I made in the trunk of my car, I subjected them, one by one, to my personal examination and scrutiny. I held the power of life and death over each one of them. But the Lord gave me the strength to hold back. Now was not the time. So I let them live, even the one who calls himself the Nazi Hunter. I had him in my sights for at least ten seconds. His day will come soon enough, but nothing must compromise the mission.

And I'm wondering whether it was a mistake to kill the jogger.

8

I saw a mountain of clothes of all types behind our locomotive shed.
Petrol was poured over items of clothing that were no longer
wearable and then they were burnt.

— TESTIMONY OF OSKAR DIEGLEMANN

I BOUGHT SOME NEW SHIRTS, one dark blue, one green, and — in a gesture of unbelievable daring — a black one. I couldn't actually imagine wearing it in the office, but perhaps the day would come. As I left the store, a man bumped against me. I swung around instantly ready to defend myself, my breath coming short, my muscles tensed. But it was nothing, just two guys brushing shoulders in a crowd.

The *Post* reported that a runner had been murdered in Rock Creek Park. No witnesses. The body was found lying by the side of the road with a bullet in his head. I had run this same stretch the day before. Maybe it hadn't been too cold. I called to ask why the pepper spray hadn't arrived yet and was told it was in the mail.

George had disappeared on a short ski trip, so it wasn't until after New Year's Day that we convened again to discuss Delatrucha. But at least I knew Lynn was working hard on the assignment. While we were waiting for the Germans to finish Christmas, there wasn't much I could do, so I busied myself with other tasks. So much paper was rolling into my office, it was difficult to keep the files straight. Each day brought another hate letter or two, which I sent — unread — straight upstairs.

The *Post* ran a series of interviews with the six McCready Award winners. Delatrucha's was the last to appear. The writer mainly seemed interested in his pretty young wife. "She has rejuvenated my creative life," Roberto said. "When we make music together, we are one being." There was a picture of the two of them sitting side by side in front of a grand piano. I scoured the article, hoping to find some clue about Delatrucha's early life, his childhood, his parents — anything. There was just one little snippet. "I had music in my life from birth," he said. "My mother named me after Robert Schumann, her favorite composer. I remember her singing me some of his songs when I was quite young. She died when I was twelve." Now we had something in common — my mother had also died when I was twelve.

On January 4, five weeks after her murder, the police held a press briefing to announce a breakthrough in the Sophie Reiner case. Local TV carried the highlights on the five o'clock news. The police commissioner said the suspect was a known violent felon and drug addict who had been caught with Sophie Reiner's wallet in his pocket. Reynolds was standing behind the commissioner, grinning, like a cat who had caught a canary.

Next morning, I called Detective Novak to find out if the police had found any documents.

"Nope, no papers."

"Did you ask the guy? Maybe he had them and threw them away."

"You know, I did ask him. He said he didn't know what I was talking about."

My last chance of finding Sophie's documents had just gone down the toilet. Why the hell hadn't she just brought them with her that first day? "So who is this guy?" I asked.

"A drunk, a junkie, and a scumbag."

"How did you track him down?"

"The moron had her credit card in his pocket, and he couldn't resist using it. Bought a shitload of booze. We had a watch out on the card. We were on the scene within minutes and picked him up on the street. When we searched his room, we found her pocketbook."

"That didn't come out in the press briefing."

"What I just told you is strictly off the record, between us."

"Of course."

"Inside the pocketbook we found a knife wrapped in a silk scarf. Forensics confirmed it was the murder weapon. Reynolds is the department superstar right now."

"So what was the motive?" I asked.

"Theft, pure and simple."

"He confessed?"

"Not yet. He says he found the pocketbook lying around on top of a garbage can."

"Do you believe him?"

"He has no alibi and a record longer than your arm. I'm with Mitch Conroy on this; we need to fry scum like him. Save the taxpayer the cost of locking them up."

"What about gangs and neo-Nazis and the mark of the beast and all that stuff you were asking about?"

"False leads. We get them on every case."

"How do you know he wasn't paid by someone to murder her? That 6-6-6 in Sophie's pocket has to mean something."

"Professor, we examined the neo-Nazi angle, but it didn't add up. There was no evidence. You can't build a whole theory on one piece of paper."

"So that's it? Case closed? Chalk another one up for Washington's finest?"

"That's it. Case closed."

"What about Sophie's mother's secret?"

She hesitated, then said, "Look, Prof, that's the way it usually is in this business. You always have a few unanswered questions. But we got the guy who did the killing, and that's enough. The DA's happy, and if the DA's happy, we're happy. There's no way Reynolds will reopen this case."

"What about the threats against me?"

"Like I told you before, when you have the FBI in the same department, why do you need us?"

I wandered upstairs to consult with Eric, who had seen the same TV reports and the morning papers. "Now that we know Delatrucha had nothing to do with the murder, where does that leave our investigation?" I asked him.

"I'm not sure. What do you think?"

"I'm meeting with Lynn and George this afternoon. We can reassess after that," I replied. "I know you're suspicious, but the evidence seems thin to none right now."

"Maybe, but if there's any lead, any little snippet, no matter how small, I want you to keep digging. Remember, the president's giving a prize to this guy."

"Yeah, I know."

"By the way, have you received any threatening phone calls recently?"

"You, too?"

He hesitated. "Not exactly threatening."

"Just quiet breathing, and then they hang up."

"It makes me nervous." he said.

"How do you think I felt about that note under my windshield? Plus my ex-girlfriend falls on the track in the Metro. Then some guy gets shot dead in Rock Creek Park, where I go running almost every day."

"You're sounding paranoid."

"Just because I'm paranoid doesn't mean someone's not out to get me. Did you call the FBI? I want to hear from an expert."

"I was just about to."

"Do it, Eric. I've been nagging you for days. You won't feel good if something happens to me. The guilt will haunt you. I wouldn't want that."

"Calm down, and remember I'm the boss. That makes me the number-one target."

Right, Eric, you're in charge, always numero uno.

When I got back to my office, David Binder called. "Have you heard of an organization called White Klan Resistance?" he asked. "They're small, but they put out an underground newsletter that gets circulated among many of the extremist groups. It's called the *White Patriot*. I got their latest issue, and guess what."

"What?" I asked, hoping it might open a new trail.

"It identifies Rosen and you by name as senior agents of the International Zionist Conspiracy. It says you're moles working inside the federal government to dismantle the United States, outlaw Christianity, and contaminate the racial purity of the white race."

"Shit."

"They're calling on their supporters to harass you. Now that they know who you are, you can definitely expect more threats."

"Did they print photos of us?"

"No, but the text is pretty vile. They call Rosen a 'dwarf-like degenerate organism subverting the law, who takes his orders from the Secret Council of Zion and perpetuates the myth of the Holocaust.'"

"Not too far off."

"Not a joking matter, Mark."

"Sorry. Gallows humor. What do they call me?"

"You're his 'slavish lackey who lives only to suck up to his foul, mongoloid master.'"

"Now all these crazies are going to be sending mail and calling me?"

"You should definitely delist your home number if you haven't already."

"That's what the police said. I'd been putting it off. It's not right letting those thugs decide how I should behave."

"You should still do it. It's a precaution you should take to protect your privacy. On the bright side, it doesn't look like these folks are connected to the creep who killed your German woman, if what the police said is true. We're forwarding the material to the FBI, as we always do. I'll fax you a copy as well."

I took a deep breath. "David, be honest. How much danger am I in? I've been getting the creepiest feeling that someone's watching me or following me around. My ex-girlfriend died in a freak accident, and a runner got shot in the park where I go running all the time."

"Disturbing, I agree, but it may also be a coincidence."

"I'm totally spooked."

"Was your girlfriend murdered?"

"They say it was an accident."

"And this other guy, the runner. I don't see the connection. If someone wanted to kill you when you were out jogging, why would they kill someone else?"

"Mistaken identity?"

"Seems far-fetched. On the other hand, it doesn't hurt to be careful. Report this to your security people. Don't just ignore it and hope it goes away."

It was hard to focus after that. I ate a sandwich while going through a memo about something, but I couldn't concentrate. I put a Schubert disc into the machine and leaned back in my chair. Ironically, the voice of Roberto Delatrucha was the only thing that seemed to calm me.

George and Lynn trooped into my office a couple of hours later. George looked fit and rested from his vacation and was holding a thick sheaf of papers. Lynn was also carrying some files and flashed a broad smile when she saw the dark blue shirt I was wearing. And just like that, seeing her smile, the sun was shining again.

"Okay, let's get going. George, I assume you received some responses from the Berlin Document Center. What do you have?"

If there was anything on this Schnellinger character, that's where it would come from. I had done my own research in the center and knew it contained an unbelievable amount of information — 75 million documents stored in over 11 million files. The Nazis tried to destroy their records at the end of the war, shipping them to a paper mill to be pulped. U.S. troops showed up to seize the precious files just in time. One wing of the Document Center included the files of thousands of writers, artists, and musicians who had thrown in their lot with the Nazis. Perhaps one of them had Schnellinger's name on it.

"Sorry, Mark, I think we struck out," he said cheerfully. Nothing made George happier than bad news, but he'd had his doubts about the case from the first and would be just as happy to see it die.

"What did you find?"

"They found three guys named Schnellinger in the archive, but none of them looks like our man."

"Tell me about them."

"Okay, we have Otto Schnellinger. Born Hamburg, 1920, served in the Wehrmacht, died at Stalingrad, 1942. Roughly the right age, but definitely not Delatrucha. Strike one."

"Yeah, being dead would seem to rule him out," I said.

"Then there's Herman Schnellinger, served in the Luftwaffe, shot down over Britain in 1940, never heard from again. Strike two. The third one is Heinz Schnellinger. He's the only one who may have survived the war, but he's certainly not the Trout Man either. They faxed over a photo in his file, and it doesn't match. He was bald, and his face was all pockmarked. He was born in 1902, which makes him way too old to be Delatrucha. Strike three."

"What did he do, this third one?"

"He was in the Wehrmacht and then a police reservist."

"Some of those reserve units were sent to Poland and the Soviet Union. They did horrific things, massacring Jews and loading them on transports to the camps. What happened to him?"

"I don't know. He was never listed as dead. I could probably check with U.S. Army records to see if he was ever registered as a POW. But I think it's a waste of time. This isn't our man." He pulled the photo out of his folder to show us. It bore no resemblance to Delatrucha.

"Maybe there is a connection," I said. "Maybe Delatrucha appropriated this guy's identity."

"Anything's possible, but how do you prove it? There's nothing to go on. We both know how easy it was for Nazis to get new identities after the war. Look at Eichmann and Mengele."

In the summer of 1945, U.S. forces found themselves in charge of three million German POWs. There was no way to feed such a vast number, so the U.S. Army released them all, except SS men and suspected war criminals. The trouble was, it was tough to identify who was in the SS and who wasn't. Some, but not all, had their blood types tattooed under their left arms. Mengele, the infamous doctor of Auschwitz, didn't have a tattoo. Did Delatrucha? The way things were going, we'd probably never know.

Another problem was that before September 1945, the U.S. Army never even collected the names of all the POWs it had under its control before releasing them. It was ridiculously easy for Nazis to change identities. Adolf Eichmann was in U.S. custody that summer. First he gave his name as Adolf Karl Barth. Later he said his name was Otto Eckmann. After they released him, he got fake papers and escaped to Argentina. He was finally kidnapped by Mossad agents and brought to Israel in 1961, where he was tried, convicted, and executed for crimes against humanity.

We were stymied. I had to agree with George. There was nothing there. I turned to Lynn, stifling the spark I felt every time our eyes met. "Okay, what do you have?" She'd been fidgeting throughout George's presentation, as though she could hardly wait her turn.

"I've got tons! Let me start with Trout Man's daughter," she said, removing a photocopied newspaper article from her file. She was wearing those cute granny glasses again. The clip included a picture of a tallish, slim woman with short dark hair dressed in a fashionable black cocktail dress, being escorted by a dude with a ponytail wearing a tuxedo. The dude had a possessive arm around her waist. The woman glared straight at the camera. Even in the poor reproduction, she was strikingly attractive and radiated strength of will.

"That was taken at the National Book Awards ceremony in 1989," Lynn said, brushing her hand against mine and sending a low-level surge through me. *The beloved mill girl is mine.* "She's a literary agent. Her specialty is what you might call scandalous memoirs — books by people accusing their famous parents of abusing them when they were kids — that kind of gross stuff."

"Who's the guy with her?" George asked.

"That's probably her most notorious client, Jimmy Williamson. They were romantically linked for a while, but they parted ways several years ago."

"That sleazy guy's an author?"

"He wrote a memoir about growing up in a tough neighborhood in Boston, joining a gang, going to jail. Word on the street is that Susan wrote most of it herself. It was nominated for the prize, but it didn't win. Then, it turned out that she — how do I say this nicely? — gussied up some of the details."

"She made some of it up?" I asked.

"Apparently. It caused a minor scandal a few years ago. That's when her business started tanking. Some of her top clients deserted her. Now she's apparently persona non grata in the book trade."

"What about the mother?"

"Mary Scott. She lives in Alexandria, Virginia," Lynn said. "After she divorced Delatrucha, she used to give occasional piano recitals at local churches and schools, but she hasn't played in public for a few years now."

I looked at the photocopy again. "Well, this is interesting, but I don't see the relevance."

Lynn's face reddened adorably. She pulled out another document and handed us each a copy. This was clearly the climax she had been building to. It was in Spanish. We looked at it blankly, then back at her. "Okay, you have us hooked," said George. "What's it say?"

"Gentlemen, what you're looking at is an interview Mr. Trout Man gave in 1958 to *Diario ABC*, a big-time Spanish newspaper. He was on his first foreign tour after coming to the States."

"How did you find this?" asked George, impressed.

Lynn grinned. "*Diario ABC* reprinted part of the interview in 1988, just before Delatrucha went back to Spain for a series of concerts marking the thirtieth anniversary of the first tour. I found it in the Nexis database."

"That's amazing," I said.

"It was totally luck," Lynn said. "Most news databases only started around ten years ago. There's no way I could have tracked down a 1958 news story if they hadn't reprinted it thirty years later."

"Not just luck. There was also hard work and persistence," I said. Lynn reddened even more. George shot me a glance, and then looked back at Lynn. He couldn't figure out exactly what was going on between us, but it was obvious he'd felt a vibe.

"Enough with the mutual admiration," George said. "Just tell us what it says." Lynn handed us an English translation with one paragraph highlighted in yellow.

"I vividly remember the very first time I performed *Winterreise* in public. It was in Berlin in early 1944.

There were air raids almost every night at the time. I was so scared I could hardly sing. I didn't know if it was fear of the bombs or stage fright. My voice wobbled through the first song. The second went better. Then the sirens sounded and everyone hurried away to the shelters, leaving me and my accompanist on an empty stage staring at the darkened hall."

"Eeenterestink," I said in my best German accent. "Veddy eeenterestink."

Sometimes I wonder, do I really have what it takes? Will the others follow me? So far all we've done is talk. There are hundreds of groups all around this nation full of big talk, but not one of them has ever done anything worth shit.

I keep thinking about the jogger, trying to understand what happened. It's been weighing on me. There're so many thoughts and feelings jumping around inside my brain. Sometimes I feel them pressing up behind my skull until it's fit to explode. I wake up in the middle of the night, shaking with rage at all the cowards and baby murderers running our nation into the ground. Why don't the American people rise up?

One thing's for sure: I would never have shot that jogger if it wasn't for tracking that kike. He can call himself what he likes, but he sure ain't no hunter. I was on his trail for a week, and he never even felt me, except maybe once. Looking through the scope, I had him in my sights the whole time he ran up the hill. One easy shot, and I could have had his head stuffed and mounted on the wall of my cabin. But the phone call said "Not yet." When he ran past and out of sight, the fury was still boiling up inside me. Suddenly, I was dizzy and nauseous. Everything was fuzzy and distorted. I saw flashes of light, like Saul on the road to Damascus. I stuffed a pill in my mouth and swallowed it dry. I closed my eyes because I knew the pain was about to begin. My tongue was already numb; I'd lost feeling in one side of my face. It felt like someone hit me with a two-by-four, like a drill boring through my skull. I lay there for Lord knows how long, praying to Jesus, until the pressure eased. My heart slowed down, and I could open my eyes again. The first thing that came into focus was a man running up the hill, puffing and sweating. The sun was setting, and I was shivering with the cold. The light was shining on him in a weird and unnatural way, like his head was on fire, and it came to me that it was a sign. Someone had to pay for all the suffering. I wasn't even sure I could hold the rifle steady, but once I had him in the crosshairs, everything slowed down to its normal pace again. So I let him have it — one clean shot — and it brought me back to myself. But afterward I wondered if it was the right thing, especially when I saw his wife and young kids on TV bawling their eyes out at the funeral. Then they said he worked for the federal government, and I felt better about it.

I'm running low on pills. What will I do after I run out? How will I manage if the pain strikes during the mission?

9

And if the little flowers knew how deeply wounded my heart is
They would weep with me to heal my pain.

— "And If the Little Flowers Knew" by Heinrich Heine,
music by Robert Schumann

There was silence while George and I reread the interview. "This is incredible," I said at last. "This changes everything."

"His one slip," George commented. "In 1958, he was probably feeling pretty secure. Nobody was looking for Nazis then."

"I'm going to Rosen with this," I said. "George, you'd better come, too. I have a feeling you may be packing your bags for Germany. This is fantastic work, Lynn."

For the first time, we had evidence from Delatrucha's own mouth that he had been in Germany during the war. More than that, we now knew where he was at a specific time and place. He had given a concert, or at least started to give one. If we could find someone else who had been there, we might be able to discover his actual name. I was sure it wasn't Schnellinger, any more than it was Delatrucha. Without his real identity, we had little chance of making progress. But now we had a foothold. I bounded upstairs to Eric's office and barged in without knocking.

"We've had a breakthrough on Delatrucha. Now's the time to send someone to Germany," I said excitedly. "I suggest George. He's been on the case from the start, and he knows what to look for."

"What the hell are you talking about, Cain?" Eric asked.

I explained what Lynn had found and showed him the

interview. He slammed his hand down on the desk. "That's my boy! Now we're in business. When can you leave, George?"

"Within a day or two, I guess. How do you suggest I go about it?" George asked.

"Start with the Nazi press," I said. "You'll probably be able to find newspapers on microfilm at the university library. If Delatrucha gave a concert, it was probably reviewed. Concerts leave traces and memories; they have their own half-life. Someone somewhere remembers, you can bet on it."

"What if the concert was held in a small hall and didn't rate a review?" said George, seeing the glass half empty.

"With a voice like his, Delatrucha was probably already marked as an up-and-coming star. There may have been a lot of interest in his debut."

"I'll try to get a plane over there tomorrow night. That would put me in Berlin Friday morning. But don't expect miracles. This may take some time. I'm not even sure what's open on the weekend."

"We don't have a lot of time," Eric cautioned. "Hire a couple of local students to help you if necessary. Work as fast as you can. You know the deadline. The president is slated to give Delatrucha the prize on February 20."

After George left, I showed Eric the fax David Binder had sent over. "This might explain all the hate mail we've been getting."

"Bastards!" Eric said, standing up and thrusting out his chest. "I'm not a dwarf! I'm just below average height."

"And I'm not your lackey. You've been promising a meeting with the FBI for a couple of weeks now, and it hasn't happened. I want that meeting. No more delays."

"I know, I know. They keep stonewalling me. They say they have bigger fish to fry. For some reason, they don't take these neo-Nazis seriously."

"That's exactly what David Binder says. He thinks the government's being negligent, and they'll only wake up when something really bad happens. I don't want to be the one it happens to. You have pull in this building, Eric. Use it. Get me the meeting. I mean it. I'm sick of always looking over my shoulder. I want that meeting, and I want it now."

Two days later, we had our first full staff meeting of the new year.

"This is the outcome of my visit to Vilnius," Janet said, indicating a thick pile of documents. She passed around copies for everyone to examine. I flipped through the file, which held order after order, all neatly signed by Bruteitis, a dozen in all. One sent a list of people with recognizably Jewish names to prison, another authorized a transport to a labor camp, and a third handed people over to a killing squad.

"Not bad," I told Janet. "All this from the archive in Vilnius?"

She icily stared me down, saying nothing. Eric looked across the table at John Howard, who had a thin smile across his thin face, as if he knew something that none of the rest of us knew.

"Counselor, I assume this meets your standards for opening proceedings against Mr. Bruteitis," Eric said coldly.

"Of course," Howard replied, smiling his humorless smile. "This is exactly what I've been hoping for. I'm very happy. Filing earlier would have been premature, just as I argued. It underlines the importance of insisting on the highest standards in all our cases and never, never cutting corners."

Eric ignored the slight. "Very good. When Mr. Howard is happy, everybody's happy. Janet, I want you to prepare a press release. We'll make a formal announcement tomorrow. The timing couldn't be better." Members of the new Congress were even now arriving in Washington, ready for the formal handover of power to the Republicans.

As the meeting broke up, Janet took Eric's arm. "Eric, we need to talk," she said, pointing to a seat. "Mark, you, too."

I sat down again. Janet stood in front of us, glaring, waiting until everyone else had left. "What the *fuck* is going on? I want an explanation, and it'd better be good."

"What are you talking about?" Eric asked.

"You know bloody well. I'm talking about George Carter

dashing off to Germany without my knowledge or approval." I could see from Eric's face that the accusation had struck home. But he was an expert in taking a punch and staying on his feet. "Let's go back to my office," he said, playing for time. He led the way down the corridor, shut the door behind us, sat behind his desk, and indicated the couch for Janet and me.

"Oh, no, you don't," Janet fumed. "I know what you're trying to do with your massive desk and your ridiculous furniture, so you can look down on me from on high. Not this time. Quit the bullshit, and tell me why George left last night for Germany on a private investigation that I know nothing about." Her voice was taut with fury, her face drawn tight. Her chest was heaving below her blouse. Embarrassed, I looked down, noticing her hands trembling. She grabbed the edge of Eric's desk to steady herself. I had never seen her like this.

I had warned him this might happen. There was no way I was going to bail him out. He coughed a couple of times and reddened. "Well, Janet, my dear, you were away — in Lithuania, of course — when this little thing came up. I decided, since it concerned a public figure, we needed to keep it secret for the time being until we knew what we might be dealing with. Of course, I was just about to brief you today, but someone evidently beat me to it. How did you find out?"

Vintage Rosen, putting his opponent on the defensive.

"George tried to call me from the airport. He left a message on my answering machine," Janet said, slightly mollified. "I called John Howard, but he didn't know what was going on either."

Shit! Now Howard was involved. More ammunition in his campaign to depose Eric. No wonder he had looked so pleased.

"Well, of course we always intended to bring you in as soon as possible, Janet, my love. But speed was of the essence. We had to get George over there immediately. It's no slight to you, and no harm's been done. Mark, why don't you take Janet down to your office and bring her up to speed?" Eric said, waving us both out.

"No," Janet growled. "*You* bring me up to speed. Here and now."

"Mark knows more about this than anyone. He's running the

file. We can talk about this later. If you'll excuse me, I have other pressing matters to attend to. Someone has to run this office." Eric picked up his phone. We were dismissed. The audience was over.

Downstairs in my office, Janet asked, "What the hell is going on? Is he really losing his grip, the way John Howard says?"

"Nonsense," I said. "He's the same old Eric. Howard has delusions of grandeur. He thinks that just because his Republican buddies are suddenly ruling the roost, Eric's days are numbered. He doesn't know who he's dealing with."

"We'll see," said Janet. "Howard is devious and ambitious. You don't want to underestimate him. If Eric carries on like this, he won't have any friends left in the office except you. I am *seriously* pissed, and I don't want anything like this ever happening again."

Eric issued his press release on Bruteitis. The story made page three of the *Post*, which wasn't bad. The stack of files on my desk seemed higher than ever and had never looked more uninviting. Untidiness threatened. By the following afternoon, I was thinking of taking a break when Lynn came bursting through the door.

"Aren't you going to Charlottesville?"

"Why?"

"Delatrucha's music tutorial. It's this afternoon at the University of Virginia. Remember?"

I slapped my forehead.

"Well, let's get going! It starts at four. We can make it if we leave right now and drive like hell."

"You're coming, too?"

"If you want me." She smiled as I glanced at my watch.

It was about 120 miles to Charlottesville, two and a half hours if the traffic wasn't too bad. For an afternoon alone with Lynn, I would have gone, music or no music. "Brilliant," I said. "Let's go."

I felt like a schoolboy playing hooky as we drove through the heavy Washington rain. With Lynn beside me, I was in absurdly high spirits, almost dizzy with euphoria as we crossed the Potomac into Virginia. Lynn had come equipped with a collection of cassettes in her pocketbook. She slipped one into the machine, and a distinctive soprano sang of love coming to the door, looking for a woman. *It's you, you're the woman*, I wanted to cry out. Instead I said, "Joni Mitchell. That song was popular when I was in college. You know it?"

"Are you kidding? It's a classic. Anyway, most of the stuff I like is from the sixties and seventies."

I reached out and stroked her hand for a second. The car felt warm and safe. We continued into the Virginia countryside in the company of Bob Dylan, Carole King, and James Taylor.

The downpour had slackened by the time we reached Charlottesville. We raced across the campus, splashing through puddles. The darkened auditorium was about three-quarters full; the master class was already under way. I paid eight dollars for the two of us, took a program, and found two empty seats toward the back, just behind an elderly woman.

The first surprise was Delatrucha's appearance. I expected a larger man to own such a large voice. He wasn't more than five foot six, a barrel chest thrust out in front of a muscular body. His truncated frame made his head, with its shaggy halo of grayish black hair, seem unnaturally large. He was coaching two singers, a tenor and a baritone, through the opening song of *Winterreise*. Another student was playing the piano.

The baritone sang first. Delatrucha listened in silence, arms crossed on his chest. He didn't move until the last note had died away; then he approached the young man, gesturing as if to embrace the air.

"You need to be more desperate," he said softly. Together with the rest of the audience, I leaned forward to hear. He still had a noticeable accent — German was his native language.

"You must think about love. But this love is not easy. It is not about pleasure and happiness. On the contrary, love always goes together with pain. Even the words rhyme in German. *Mein herz, mein schmerz* — my heart, my pain. This is a love that is desperate, never far from grief, from anguish, from heartache. Like this." He placed his right hand over his heart and sang the first few measures unaccompanied. His face was expressionless, his body motionless, yet full of tension, his chest thrust out, his neck stretched tight. There was a rustle of appreciation around the auditorium. His voice was still rich and true, if a little strained in the higher notes. "You feel it in here," he said, thumping his chest. "You feel it echo inside your body. The emotion comes through the singing, through the color of the voice, never through the loudness of the voice. The tempo must be steady, as steady as your heartbeat. It must sound . . . inevitable. Now please, again."

The audience murmured appreciatively. I was completely entranced. I pushed to the back of my mind the possibility that he might also be a Nazi. The woman in front of us was muttering to herself. She kept folding and unfolding her program, squashing it as hard as she could into smaller and smaller rectangles. The more we sat there, the more absurd it seemed, to think that this brilliant man, so totally absorbed in his art, could have been drawn away from his calling by the evil appeal of Adolf Hitler.

The next two hours passed quickly. Both of us were completely under Delatrucha's spell. Everybody was. He had enmeshed the entire audience in an invisible web. When the students were singing, he was absolutely still. As soon as the music stopped, he was seized with animation. Delatrucha had strong views about how the songs should be sung. He insisted on an absolutely rigid tempo. He also had several suggestions for the pianist. "Make your notes harsher," he said at one point. "This music is not nice, it is not pretty. It is hard and cruel. It is never cozy." He imbued the word *cozy* with such contempt that the whole room flinched.

Occasionally he added little asides about Schubert's life and times. "He lived in a unforgiving world, not soft and sentimental like today. Death was all around him. He knew already in his early twenties that he was dying of syphilis. He knew himself to be unclean, imperfect, a sinner. As we all are. Yet out of this came such beauty."

Delatrucha turned his attention back to the young pianist. "You must let the singer set the tempo, not force him to a certain pace. That's what my first wife always tried to do with me." The audience laughed. The woman sitting in front of us shot to her feet, clutching her pocketbook. A man sitting next to us asked her to sit down, but she ignored him and moved unsteadily to the aisle, heading slowly down the steps toward the stage.

"Bastard! *Bastard!* How dare you make me one of your jokes!" she screamed. Everyone jerked upright; nobody moved. In the dim light, it was like watching a scene from a play.

Delatrucha stood illuminated in a pool of light on the stage, the woman half hidden in the darkness just below him. The student stopped singing; the accompanist played a few more notes and tailed off. Everybody was frozen. Delatrucha took a step forward, squinting down at her from the stage. She pulled something from her pocketbook, and someone screamed. A red stain spread across Delatrucha's white shirt. The audience panicked. People clambered over seats in a rush for the exits; others hit the floor. Lynn was screaming as I shoved her to the ground.

Above the noise, the woman was shouting, "*Pig, you pig!*" Delatrucha just stood there. I pushed my way forward, thinking I could tackle her from behind if only I could get close enough. Most of the audience was rushing in the opposite direction.

"Ladies and gentlemen, don't be alarmed," Delatrucha called out. "This woman cannot hurt me." His face was twisted with pity and contempt. "Mary," he said, "when will you stop this nonsense?"

"Never, as long as you live!" she yelled, pulling the trigger again. A stream of dark liquid shot out, spattering Delatrucha's shirt. I laughed in relief. She was firing red ink from a water pistol.

A couple of young men rushed forward to restrain her and wrest the toy pistol away. "Ladies and gentlemen, please do not be alarmed," Delatrucha bellowed. "This woman is known to me. She is my former wife. She has done this kind of thing before."

A measure of calm returned to the auditorium. The young men still held the woman, who was writhing with fury, struggling to get free. Delatrucha addressed what was left of his audience again. "Please forgive me. Unfortunately, we must end our studies now. If you will allow me, I will return on another occasion." You had to admire his dignity and poise. There was a scattering of applause. Campus security arrived, weapons drawn, and grabbed the woman from the students. Delatrucha leaned down toward them. "Please let her go. She is quite harmless."

"We need to take her in and file a report," one said.

"You will do no such thing. She has committed no crime, and I will not press any charges. She is no threat to anyone except herself. I insist you release her."

They let her go.

He turned to her. "Mary, I pray you find peace. Don't do this again, or I will have to take steps." He gave a sketchy bow in the direction of the audience and strode offstage. She slumped down into a front-row seat and began to sob quietly. I approached her and took the next seat.

"Mary, do you need any help?" I asked softly. She glanced at me through red-rimmed eyes.

"Who are you?"

"I'm a friend. I'm from Washington, like you. Can I help you?"

"I want to get out of here. Please take me out of here," she said. Lynn had recovered enough to join me. Mary stood up, and we ushered her out of the hall. Her thin body trembled through her winter coat as I steered her around puddles. We walked slowly, without speaking. She was oblivious to her surroundings and to us. As we reached the edge of the campus, I noticed a café across the street. "Let me buy you a cup of coffee," I said.

I brought us each a cappuccino.

"You're very kind," she sniffed, wiping her eyes with a tissue. "I must look a sight."

She did. She looked nothing like the photos I had seen of her when she was still married to Delatrucha. Her eyes were swollen and bloodshot, her wrinkled face pitted with smudges of mascara, her hair gray and unkempt. She looked at least ten years older than her ex-husband.

"Mrs. Scott, my name is Mark Cain. This is my friend Lynn Daniels. We admire your work."

"Thank you for saying so."

"It must be hard to be an accompanist, always in the background while the singer gets the limelight," I continued, hoping to draw her out.

"Anybody who knows anything about music knows she's not even half the pianist I was. Not even half." She spat out the word *she*.

"I own several of the recordings you made with Delatrucha. Your contribution shines through," I said. "And critics agree that those performances have never been equaled."

"How dare he make fun of me like that. Don't even mention his name to me. To be dumped like that, cast out like trash after thirty years."

"It must have been so hard," Lynn murmured sympathetically.

"It was the end of my life."

"But you still have your music. That must be a great comfort."

Mary stared at us for a moment, her eyes filling with tears. She thrust her gnarled hands in front of Lynn's face.

"Look at these, look at them," she groaned.

"Arthritis," Lynn whispered.

"Yes, arthritis. What could be worse for a pianist?"

Lynn took one of her hands and gently stroked it. Tears were welling up in her eyes. "Mrs. Scott, I'm so sorry. It must be awful for you," she said.

"You are a nice young lady," she said, as Lynn continued to caress her hand. "Thank you."

"There's no need to thank me. I wish I could do something to help."

"You are helping. Just by being here, by being so kind."

"Why did you come here, Mary?" I asked, bringing the conversation back to business.

Mary began sobbing quietly again. "He didn't have to throw me aside the way he did. A real man would have stood by me. He has no shame, cavorting with a woman younger than his own daughter."

"But why . . ."

"I didn't mean to," she said, reclaiming her hand from Lynn. "I just wanted to hear his voice again. It's still the most beautiful voice I ever heard. It's so unfair. My hands are ruined, but he still has his voice."

"You brought a water pistol filled with red ink," I noted.

"I hadn't decided whether to use it. If he hadn't mocked me, I probably wouldn't have. This wasn't the first time he's told that joke against me, by the way. It's part of his routine. He had no right to ridicule me in front of all those people. I just wanted to scare him a little. I didn't mean any harm, Mr. . . . What did you say your name was?" She looked at my *kippah*, her face suddenly full of suspicion.

"Cain. Mark Cain."

"Are you a reporter?"

"Hardly," I laughed. "We're doing some research into your ex-husband's life."

"Ah, the authorized biography, to polish up his image."

"Something like that." I was lying, but I wanted to keep her talking. "I'm particularly interested in his early years," I said.

"You mean, when we first met? Those were wonderful times. I could tell you a lot about that."

"And even earlier than that, before you met?"

"Before we met, he was in Argentina. I don't know that I can help you much with that. We never spoke of it. We were in Buenos Aires together a couple of times on tour, and I asked if he had any family there, but he said they were all dead. Why don't you ask the almighty maestro himself?"

"I'm interested in your perspective. Perhaps we could meet for lunch back in Washington? I really do need your help with this."

Mary wavered. Part of her wanted to relive those days. Another part was resisting. I could see her mind working, wondering what I was really after. "That part of my life is dead. Why bring it up again?" she said.

"Any account of Roberto Delatrucha's life would be incomplete without your side of the story. It would be like writing about Sullivan without Gilbert, Rodgers without Hammerstein."

"Lennon without McCartney, Simon without Garfunkel," Lynn added, piling it on.

Mary hesitated, but the temptation was too great. It must have been years since anyone paid any attention to her, and attention, after all, is what all performers crave. "Lunch. Chez Louis, next Tuesday, twelve thirty. You pay," she said.

"Wonderful."

She stood to go.

"Are you sure you're up to driving, Mrs. Scott? We could give you a lift home, and one of us could drive your car," Lynn said.

"Thank you, my dear, but I'm perfectly capable," she said, tottering toward the door. "I may be an old woman, but I'm not dead yet."

Lynn said she was hungry and knew a cute little inn we could stop at for a meal. "I'm sure they have something vegetarian," she pleaded.

It couldn't have been more romantic, with Victorian chintz all over the place and an open fire crackling in the hearth. I ended up ordering bread and a large salad.

Still, I could drink the wine. Even before the first sip, I was intoxicated with anticipation and yearning, mixed with a liberal dose of guilt and fear. Why had she brought me here? There could only be one reason. *This is wrong,* my brain was screaming, but my body sent a different message — that nothing, nothing could have been more right. I couldn't stop staring at her in the candlelight, drowning in her lovely eyes. The tension built between us, stoking my desires until I was close to bursting. I had spent my entire life following rules, commandments, admonishments, all those "Thou shalt nots," analyzing everything from every conceivable angle, distrusting my feelings. Now, I abandoned myself to feelings.

We finished a bottle of wine, and I waved to the waiter for a second.

Lynn said, "Haven't we had enough? Perhaps we should switch to coffee. We still have to drive back to Washington tonight." Her words were a bucket of cold water over my head. I was sure we'd be getting a room upstairs.

Mortified, I closed my eyes, both ashamed and relieved. Trying to recover my poise, I said, "You're right. I got carried away."

"No problem. Everything's cool."

"Lynn, this isn't how I usually behave. I don't know what got into me."

She smiled again and kissed me softly on the cheek. "Stop worrying so much. Just go with the flow. You enjoy spending time with me, don't you? You want us to keep on seeing each other?"

"Of course."

"Then let's just do that and see where it leads. Things have a way of working out if the karma is right."

"Okay," I said, feeling like she was the grown-up and I was the kid.

"And for now, Mr. Nazi Hunter, I think you should get back to hunting Nazis."

"Give me coffee, and I'm up for anything."

10

*The diesel started. . . . After 28 minutes, only a few were still alive.
Finally, after 32 minutes, all were dead.*

— Testimony of Kurt Gerstein

T HE WIND HAD STRENGTHENED while we were eating and was
whipping sheets of rain against the windshield as we set out on the
journey back. For a while, we sat in silence, with only the swoosh of
the wipers and the drum of the rain for company. I was concentrat-
ing on the road ahead. I assumed Lynn had gone to sleep when she
suddenly spoke my name.

"Yes?"

"There's something else I have to tell you."

"Yes."

"I love working for you, but you were right about what you
said. We so can't be doing this if you're my boss."

My heart sank.

"On the other hand, I'm totally into the Delatrucha case. I told
them there's no way I could leave while it was still ongoing."

"Them who?"

"I interviewed with a human rights organization to be their
legal counsel, and it looks like they want me."

"You're leaving?"

"I think so."

"We can get you reassigned, promoted even."

"No, I was thinking of leaving anyway. I don't want to spend my whole life chasing after gross, nasty old men. And this is a step up. Actually, I ought to thank you. What's happening with the two of us pushed me into going for this job."

I exhaled. "That's wonderful, Lynn. Congratulations."

"So it's okay? I can stay until Delatrucha is settled?"

"You know we have a February 20 deadline. If it's okay with your human rights people, you could start with them after that."

"That's what I already told them. They're cool with it."

It was after two in the morning by the time I had dropped off Lynn at her apartment and reached my own. I emptied my mailbox on the way upstairs. More letters than usual. There was also a small package, which gave me pause but turned out to contain the pepper spray I had ordered.

I headed straight for bed, but the message machine was blinking furiously, demanding to be heard. Perhaps George had called from Germany. I hit play.

"This is a message for Marek Cain," said a soft male voice with a slight southern accent. "Mr. Cain, listen real carefully because I'm only going to say this once." He paused. "It's time for you to back off. I'm telling you this for your own good, Mr. Cain. I wouldn't want anything to happen to you. Stop what you're doing, and everything will be just fine." He spoke so calmly that it took a second to process what he was saying. A wave of bile coursed up my throat, and I stumbled into the bathroom, coughing and retching. He sounded like the Elf King. The evil was creeping closer. It had slunk under my door into my bedroom. I ran the cold water and took a large gulp, then splashed my face, reminding myself that I was not that boy in the song. I could fight back. But how and against whom?

I unplugged the phone from the wall, threw my jacket and pants on the floor, lay down, and closed my eyes.

The alarm rang at six as usual. I thought about calling the police. A couple of hours wouldn't make much difference. I got up, stretched, said Modeh Ani, went downstairs, looked around in all directions, and set off for a quick run in the park, clutching the pepper spray. The streets were almost completely deserted, still wet from the previous day's downpour, and the air was saturated with moisture.

For the first couple of miles, I moved sluggishly. But my energy returned by the time I was done.

I showered and started the coffee going before tackling the previous day's mail. After the message on the phone machine, I had a good idea what awaited me. Setting aside routine bills and flyers, there were nine letters. I slit open the first envelope and unfolded a single sheet of paper with a crudely drawn swastika and the word *DIE* emblazoned in large black letters. None of the other eight was quite as succinct. A couple were actually rather eloquent in a repulsive way. Together, they informed me that I was a rat, a germ, a traitor, a whore, a bastard, a degenerate, and — most of all — a Jew. The postmarks had come from all over the country: Idaho, Nebraska, Kansas, Texas, West Virginia. Obviously the result of the article in the neo-Nazi newsletter. I washed my hands, as if soap and water could erase the slime. With little appetite for breakfast, I gathered up the letters and headed for the office.

When I reached my desk, there was a note from Eric asking me to call him. He had received his quota of hatred as well. Maybe now he would finally call the FBI. I was about to rush upstairs, but then I decided to make Eric wait another ten minutes. I phoned George in Berlin first. I wasn't going to let those Nazi bastards control my agenda. I was going to do my job, and right now my job was the Delatrucha case. And I wasn't going to give up my morning coffee for any damned neo-Nazi either.

George was in his hotel room. Reaching for my legal pad, I asked him how far he had gotten with his inquiries. "I was just about to call you," he said. "It's not going too badly. I located a library where most of the Nazi newspapers are stored. I already started with the *Völkischer Beobachter*," he said, citing the official mouthpiece of the Nazi Party.

"Makes sense."

"Don't get your hopes up too high. It's going to be slow work, and it's going to take a while. I went through the first half of January 1944 this morning, and all I got was a terrible backache."

"Poor George, excuse me while I get a Kleenex."

"Not funny, Mark. You're the one who ought to be here. This

was your brilliant idea. I had to stop working after a couple of hours when I started seeing double. Plus I'm still getting over the jet lag. And I guess you know by now I told Janet about the trip."

"That's all sorted out. Don't worry about it. Just keep your mouth shut to anyone else in the department or outside. Report only to me, and I'll make sure everyone who needs to know knows what's happening. I'm assuming you haven't found anything of interest so far."

"Not yet. I'm working as fast as I can. I know you and Eric are in a huge rush, but you have to take your time and scan every single page. I'm afraid of missing something. The print is so tiny."

"Ignore what Eric told you about hurrying up. Never mind his deadline; take as much time as you need. Whenever you feel yourself getting tired, take a break. You can't risk missing something. I'd rather you spend an extra few days and do it right. The evidence is there. You just have to find it."

"You'd be amazed at the amount there is about music in these newspapers. I had no idea how devoted those Nazis were to classical music. They sponsored an enormous number of orchestras and concerts. I read an account of a fantastic performance of Beethoven's Ninth by the Berlin Philharmonic in the middle of 1943 that almost made me want to be there."

"Doesn't that end with Schiller's 'Ode to Joy,' about all men uniting as brothers?"

"Ironic, isn't it? By then, the orchestra had already kicked out all the Jews and sent them to Auschwitz."

Eric burst through the door. "You look like shit," he said. "Your home phone isn't working. Why didn't you call me? I need you in my office right now."

"In a minute," I told him, gesturing to the phone. "It's George. I'm wrapping up with him." *I* looked like shit? His hair was shooting ten different directions, and he had dark moons under his eyes. He stood at the door, fuming.

"It'll only be another minute," I told him. "I'll be right up."

He stalked out.

"George, where were we? You were talking about music."

"The Nazis were always printing articles about German composers and how they upheld the Aryan race. I knew Wagner was an anti-Semite, but according to them even the music of Bach and Beethoven glorified Nazi ideals. Music was very important to their ideology."

"Interesting, but keep your eye on the ball. Don't get too caught up in the details."

"I know, I know. Listen, I'm going to take a nap, and then I'll get back to work. Call me early tomorrow, your time. I'll know more by then."

Eric was in a state of agitation rare even for him. "I suppose this is about all the hate mail you've been getting," I said, dumping my latest pile of letters on his desk and flopping down onto his couch.

"Every day there seems to be more. Somebody needs to do something," he said angrily.

"Funny, that's what I've been telling you for weeks."

"The FBI is finally taking it seriously. They're sending a couple of agents over this afternoon. Four thirty, right here in my office," he said.

"About time," I said. "I had nine hate letters in yesterday's mail alone. And one particularly menacing phone call as well."

"Calls? Here?"

"At home." I tossed him the mini-cassette I had brought from my answering machine. "You might want to send that over so the FBI can listen to it before the meeting. It's delightful."

"They're a bunch of sewer rats. I've always known they're out there, crawling around underground, but you don't think about them much because you never see them. And suddenly one day they've come to the surface and they're running around the streets. Well, fuck them! I'm not going to be intimidated!" He swept the pile of letters off his desk. They skidded across the floor, a couple landing near my feet. We sat in silence for a few seconds, staring at them.

"That's not the only reason I asked you up here. Something's come up. We've got to prepare for a meeting on the Hill next Tuesday afternoon. I've been summoned by Mitch Conroy's office. I'll need you to come, too."

"Surely he's got bigger fish to fry."

"We'll be meeting with Jack Doneghan, his chief of staff, who is possibly an even bigger *putz*."

"What do they want?"

"Conroy has asked Doneghan to examine every budget line of every government department to see what he can cut. That's why I need you. I want you to go through the budget with a fine-toothed comb. I need to be able to justify every item."

"Our budget is tiny compared to most government departments. The Pentagon spends more on toilets than we do in an entire year. Why us?" *John Howard*, I thought, but there was no way to prove it.

"It's not a good sign," Eric said. "We're definitely under attack. On all fronts."

I spent the afternoon reviewing the figures. At four thirty, I returned to Eric's office for the meeting with the FBI. An attractive woman of about thirty-five wearing an austere black suit was already there, sunk deep into his plush sofa, while a younger man with a buzz cut leaned against the desk. She struggled to her feet. "Agent Teresa Fabrizio," she said, holding out a perfectly manicured hand for me to shake. Her colleague introduced himself as Agent Steve Bennett.

Fabrizio did all the talking, while Bennett stood there looking rugged and manly. "We've reviewed these letters you've been getting and the phone calls as well. We believe they're the result of the article that was published in the *White Patriot* newsletter."

Thank you, Captain Obvious. "What are you going to do about them?" I managed.

"Sir, we've analyzed them, and on the whole we don't think you're in any real danger. They're unpleasant, and we sympathize, but we think they'll decrease over the next few weeks, and things will return to normal."

"What about the note under my windshield?" I asked. "Someone took the trouble to come to my home to plant it there." I showed her the "6-6-6," which finally caught her attention.

"I wasn't aware of this. You say this was under your windshield. Where were you parked?" she asked.

"At home."

"This is the original?"

"A copy."

"Where is the original?"

"I sent it to the D.C. police."

"Why did you do that?"

"Because they discovered a similar message in the pocket of Sophie Reiner, the German tourist who was murdered in the city last November."

Again she betrayed her surprise. "How do you know about that? That detail was never released to the media."

"I was trying to help them in the case. Sophie came to visit me the day before she was killed. I was the one who ID'd her after she died."

Eric intervened to describe how her death had launched us into an investigation of Delatrucha. "What I just told you can't go any further," he cautioned. "That investigation is still ongoing."

Fabrizio nodded, her face expressionless. "And did the paper or the handwriting match?" she asked.

"Not according to the police. Anyway, they've lost interest in the neo-Nazi angle. Lieutenant Reynolds got his man. As far as he's concerned, case closed."

"We'll see about that. I'll talk to this Lieutenant Reynolds."

"Good," I said.

"Mr. Cain, have you seen anyone suspicious around? Maybe someone following you or watching you?" she asked.

"I had a feeling someone was following me the other night, but I can't be sure."

"Do you feel like you need protection?"

I tried to imagine myself walking around with a protector. Would he move in with me? Would he go out on dates with me and Lynn? I wasn't sure I wanted that. "You're the expert. You tell me," I said.

"Well, sir, my initial reaction based on what you've described is that it would be a stretch. If we assigned personal bodyguards to every federal employee who ever found a strange piece of paper, the government would soon go broke, and Mitch Conroy would have apoplexy. But let me contact the D.C. police about this Reiner woman. Meantime, here's my card. It has my direct line and a number where they can contact me after hours. If anything even slightly suspicious happens — anything at all — don't hesitate to call me."

It was Friday, which meant I had to leave by three thirty to make it home in time for Shabbat, which began at sunset. I wanted to spend the evening with Lynn, but she had her weekly shift at the soup kitchen. She invited me to come, but I explained I couldn't do any work on Shabbat.

There were several more letters in the mail. I pitched them into the garbage without opening them. No point sending them over to the FBI.

The foulness of the messages still lingered in the empty apartment like a bad smell. The holiness of the day was defiled. Shabbat is supposed to be a foretaste of paradise, a span of sacred time, set aside from the rest of the week. We rest because God rested, and by doing so we become, if only for a few hours, closer to Him. I hurried out to Friday-night services. The singing cheered me up. Sara Barclay was sitting across the aisle in the women's section, wearing a stylish red beret over her dark hair. After the service, she greeted me. I felt a little awkward about not calling her, but she put me at ease, and we chatted for a couple of minutes.

"Do you have any plans for the rest of the evening?" she asked.

"No, not really."

"Why don't you come back to my place? I have a chicken roasting." Observant Jews didn't cook on the Sabbath, but it was permitted if the food was already in the oven before sunset.

I hesitated.

"Don't worry, Mark." She smiled. "I won't seduce you."

Sara's apartment was tastefully furnished with sleek Scandinavian furniture, pastel-colored carpets, and delicate impressionistic landscape watercolors on the walls.

"Did you paint those?" I asked.

"I'm afraid so. Make yourself comfortable."

Everything was beautifully understated and coordinated. The

delicious smell of cooking suffused the apartment. She opened a bottle of white wine. The table was set for one, but she quickly added a second place. I said the blessings over the wine and the bread, and we began eating off elegant china. It was all immensely comfortable and civilized. I knew Sara was an intelligent, graceful woman who cared about many of the same things as me. I also sensed that if I tried to kiss her, she wouldn't resist. But there was no snap, crackle, pop the way there was whenever Lynn was near. At the end of the night, I pecked her briefly on each cheek and left.

The next night, just before midnight, the phone rang.

"Is this Marek Cain?" It was the same greasy, insinuating voice from the answering machine, like some character out of Tennessee Williams. I imagined a middle-aged, red-faced, paunchy man wearing a grubby white suit.

"This is Cain. Who are you?"

"An American patriot."

"What did you say, asshole?" Rage gathered in my chest.

"I said, I'm —"

"You're not scaring me. You don't know who you're messing with, scumbag." Shaking with fury, I slammed the phone down, balled my right hand into a fist, and pummeled the pillow, imagining I was slamming it into his doughy gut. It made me feel better, but then the fear returned.

I paced the apartment for a while, my mind churning. I switched on CNN for five minutes, turned it off, made a cup of cocoa, threw a load of laundry in the machine, ironed a shirt, did twenty five pushups and thirty sit ups, and punched the pillow a couple more times before I went to bed.

At 5:30 a loud knocking woke me up. Fumbling for my glasses, I staggered toward the front door, grabbing the pepper spray on the way. "Get the fuck out of here before I call the police," I shouted.

"It's your neighbor from 4A," came a voice. "Your car alarm is going off in the parking lot. Turn it off!"

"Oh," I said, relieved and embarrassed. "Sorry." I hurried to the parking lot and turned off the alarm.

Someone had deliberately gashed the paintwork. I was looking at half a swastika.

Since the incident with the jogger, I've been nervous to go out more than I have to. Every time I give way to my impulses, I risk being identified, so I stay in the room working on my Declaration to the American People. *I made Clint stay here as well after he came back one morning with a big grin on his face and he tells me, "Shrimp, I done something. I think you're gonna like what I done." Straight away, I think he's blown our cover and we're busted but he tells me all he's done is scratch a swastika on the Jew's car. "To put a righteous scare into him," he said.*

"Did anyone see you?" I asked.

"No, it was too early. I ran when the alarm went off."

"From now on, you stay here until it's time to do the job," I tell him. "Also, I want you to leave that Jew alone. Do you understand?" He says he does. I tell him, "This is an army. We can't have you going off and doing stuff by yourself without telling anybody." So Clint sits watching soap operas and game shows on TV.

Occasionally I let him go out to Burger King or Taco Bell to bring back food, but still he complains all the time. "Why do we have to stay in here? It's like being in jail."

"Don't be such a fucking asshole," I tell him. "It's just for a couple of days. And it's nothing like being in jail."

Clint asks, "How did you get in jail anyway?" I tell him it was after Waco. I was so broke up and heartsick about those poor people, I wasn't thinking straight. All I wanted was to get as far away as I could. When I reached the Oklahoma state line, my truck broke down and I was out of money. So I did a dumb thing. I tried to borrow a used car. I'm not going to tell him what happened to me the first night, when they put me in a holding cell with Dwayne Robertson. I'll never tell anyone about that. So I just say, "Aw, it wasn't so bad. I got educated in jail. Most of what I know about the world I learned in there."

"Like what?" he asks.

"Like about the Jews, for one thing. I didn't know nothing about the Jews. There weren't none around where I grew up, and I never met one all the time I was in the army. Now I know why. Jews haven't got no interest in serving the nation. They just suck the blood out of it."

When you're sitting in jail with nothing to do all day, you read pretty much anything that comes your way. Some of the screws were sympathetic, they knew what Dwayne had done. They could see it in my busted nose and black eyes. The doctors tested me; they even gave me some pills for my headaches. A guard gave me a newsletter from one of the Aryan groups down in Texas. For the first time, I understood what's really happening in America, how the Jews took away power from the white race and gave it to the blacks and the mixed races, how they want to make us all mixed. When I asked him if he had any more, he gave me The Turner Diaries. Easily the best book I'd ever read.

"What's it about?" Clint asked me.

"Imagine a country run by Jews and mixed races where they take away your guns. I mean, just think of it, Clint, a country where you can't go out hunting with your daddy, like you and me did when we were coming up." I never did go out hunting with my daddy. Anyone who put a hunting rifle in that old drunkard's hands had to be crazy. "Anyway," I tell Clint, "turns out that taking away our guns is the Jews' biggest mistake. It's what causes the spark that sets fire to the kindling. Remember how I explained about the spark?" He nods. "Well, in the book there's this huge rebellion and a group of the God-fearing white folk decide to blow up the FBI's computers so they can take back the country."

"How they do that?"

I tell him, "They use ammonium nitrate mixed with heating oil—thousands of pounds of it—to make a huge bomb. Just like we're gonna do. We're going to make it real."

His eyes cloud over. "We're gonna do that?"

"We sure are. Burl's already buying it back home. I've been sending him the money. It's gonna be the biggest fucking explosion this goddamn country's ever seen."

11

The rose said, "I'll prick you
So that you'll always think of me."

— "Hedgerose" by Wolfgang von Goethe, music by Franz Schubert

I looked around, but of course there was no one there. No point calling the police now. *The hell with it,* I decided. *I'm going for a run.*

I didn't realize how angry I was until I found myself sprinting up a hill at a tremendous pace, overtaking a lone cyclist. Adrenaline was flooding through my body. I almost wished someone would try to accost me. I'd have beaten the shit out of him.

Back home an hour later, I had my number delisted, then phoned Berlin. George was in his hotel room. He sounded drained.

"What's the time over there?" I asked.

"Four in the afternoon. I feel as if I haven't slept for a week. You know, if we had that new communication system everyone's talking about, we could just send each other electronic messages whenever we wanted."

I could just imagine his bony face knotted in a scowl of earnest self-justification. "E-mail? What good would that do? We'd still need to talk. Anyway, it's in the budget for next year, along with cell phones for everybody, if Congress doesn't cut it all out. How far did you get with the Nazi newspapers?"

"I'm up to February 21, 1944."

"I hope you're not rushing it. I don't want you to miss anything."

"Don't worry, I'm not."

"How far do you think you need to search? Delatrucha said his concert was near the beginning of 1944. I would think that would be in the first three months. Unless he was trying to throw people off the scent."

"He wasn't," George said.

"Did you find something?"

"You have no idea how many pages of garbage I had to go through today. I deserve a hefty raise."

"You aren't getting one, George. Did you find a concert review?"

"No."

"Then what? Godammit."

"A tiny announcement advertising a concert for the following evening, just a little box at the bottom of a page."

"Excellent. What did it say?"

"It was for February 18, 1944 — the debut performance of a young baritone. And guess what else."

"His name was Schnellinger?" I said eagerly.

"No, it wasn't. It was Franz Beck."

"Never heard of him."

"Me neither."

"Did it say what he was singing?"

"Unfortunately not. It just said it would be a recital of lieder."

"No picture, I suppose."

"No, it was really small, like I said."

"But it could be our man."

"Well, it could be, but it's not definitive. There could have been more than one song recital around that time. There was plenty of musical activity going on even in wartime. Concerts, recitals, you name it. I looked through the newspaper for the following three days for a review of the performance, but I couldn't find one."

"It was interrupted by an air raid, so that's not so surprising," I said.

"Right. And when I looked in the newspaper for February 19, there was some mention of a bombing attack the previous night, which fits what he said. But still, I wouldn't go rushing into a court-room on the basis of one little announcement in the Nazi newspaper."

"What did you say his name was — Beck?"

"Franz Beck."

"Interesting. He told the *Post* he was named after his mother's favorite composer, Robert Schumann. Maybe he was mixing a little truth with a little fiction."

"What do you mean?" George asked.

"Maybe he was named after his mother's favorite composer just like he said, but it wasn't Schumann, it was Franz Schubert." George, who believed strictly in verifiable facts, chose to ignore this flash of insight. "Anyway, nice work," I said. "Now we have a possible name for this guy."

"Perhaps."

"Your next move is back to the Document Center to see if they have a file on Franz Beck."

"I'll be there first thing Monday morning. I'll probably have something for you on Tuesday."

"Get a good night's sleep and treat yourself to a fancy meal with an expensive bottle of wine. It's on me. You deserve it," I told him.

"I'll do that after I get home so I can share it with my wife."

"Have two bottles, then, one now and one later."

"No fun drinking wine when you're alone."

"So find a nice plump little fraulein to drink with you."

"Mark!" He was shocked. *Shocked!*

"Just kidding. George, okay, I'll say *auf wiedersehen.*"

"There's one more thing," George said.

"What's that?"

"A very tiny detail." He paused. "The concert was under the patronage of someone pretty famous."

"Who?" Von Karajan? Strauss?"

"Much bigger."

"*Who?*"

"Heinrich Himmler."

"My God!" I breathed. How would a man like Himmler, head of the SS and the Gestapo and second in the Nazi hierarchy only to

Hitler himself, become involved with a young singer? Was he a friend of the family; perhaps they had common acquaintances? Or perhaps they had crossed paths somewhere.

"So how about that raise now, boss?"

"I'll run it by Mitch Conroy and get back to you," I told him. "Keep this strictly confidential. I'll brief Janet, but I don't want it going further. If you get any calls from anyone else . . ."

"You mean John Howard," George said.

"He called you?"

"He seems pretty interested in what I'm doing."

"What did you tell him?"

"Nothing, but he knows we're investigating Delatrucha."

"Yeah, I figured."

"Eric brought this on himself by acting like a secret agent."

"Whose side are you on, George?"

"Nobody's. I'm just a tiny pawn in your chess game. I want to be friends with everyone and get the job done." Then he hung up.

The rest of the weekend passed uneventfully. Sunday was Tu B'Shvat, the New Year for Trees. In Israel, the almond trees would start blossoming. In D.C., we were still deep in the grip of winter.

On Monday morning, I briefed Janet and Eric on George's discovery.

"Is there anything we can do to speed things up?" Eric asked.

"I wish we had a picture of him without that great bushy beard," I said. "If he was in Nazi Germany in 1944, he was definitely clean-shaven."

"There's software now that can generate computer images of what a person might have looked like when he was younger or what he might look like when he's older," Eric said. "Send me a picture. I'll contact the FBI, see what can be done."

"Now that the investigation is making progress," Janet said, "I'd like you to put it on the agenda for the weekly staff meeting."

"Still too sensitive," Eric replied firmly.

Janet frowned, but said nothing more.

★ ★ ★

I spent a lot of time thinking about Delatrucha. Only now was his true character coming into focus. He was a formidable adversary. Most ex-Nazis just try to disappear. Delatrucha had been in the public eye for forty years, flaunting his presence. He must have been driven by a gargantuan ego; he was utterly determined but also enormously shrewd. He could be charming and courageous, but he was also ruthless and cruel. I would need to be equally relentless and resourceful to nail him.

I was hoping my lunch with Mary Scott would add more details to the portrait. Chez Louis turned out to be impeccably snooty and unbelievably expensive. Delatrucha's ex-wife had lavish tastes. I blanched at the prices on the menu. Luckily I'd be eating salad. Everything else was *treif*—nonkosher. I spent ten minutes staring at a $10 glass of fizzy water, watching people come and go, wondering if Mary was standing me up. A striking woman in a luxurious fur coat sailed into the restaurant on the arm of a man sporting a dirty blond ponytail. She imperiously handed him her coat. Under it, she was wearing a shimmering black dress. Everything about her smelled of glamour and money. I realized I was staring and returned to studying the menu, wondering which of the wonderful-sounding concoctions would be most fun to eat, if only I could.

The restaurant was swarming with lobbyists and activists, presumably on fat expense accounts. Republicans were still celebrating the election that had brought them back to power after decades in the minority. One corner of the joint, reserved for cigar smokers, was full. A happy hubbub rose from the diners. I caught a glimpse of the woman gliding through the restaurant as if she owned the place. Then she was at my table. She glared at me for a moment, then sat down without saying a word. She had short black hair and wore long, silvery earrings that accentuated her high cheekbones and matched the silver necklace around her neck and the bracelets hanging loosely around her thin wrists. Then I realized I knew who she was.

"You must be Susan Scott," I said, offering my hand. She ignored it. I tried again. "I'm Mark Cain."

"I know who you are and what you do," she said. Her voice was thin and hard. She was wearing a kind of pale silvery lipstick that complemented her gray eyes, which glinted metallically. "I looked you up because I was suspicious about this strange man who suddenly appeared, wanting to talk to my mother. I want you to leave my mother alone. She's not going to talk to you. She's in a fragile mental state, and I don't want you driving her over the edge. Leave her alone."

A waiter came up; she waved him away with an imperious flick of her fingers. "Well, don't you have anything to say for yourself?" she said.

I took off my glasses and started polishing them with the tablecloth to buy time. "I had no idea about your mother's mental state. I certainly wouldn't want to cause her any harm," I said.

"As long as that's understood." She stood to go.

"Perhaps you'd be willing to speak to me for a few minutes." I gestured her to sit down again.

"Why should I? You investigate war criminals, like that Demjanjuk. My father may not be perfect, but he's no Nazi. I have no interest in talking to you. In fact, if you know what's good for you, you'll stop what you're doing before I hire a lawyer and file a restraining order. I will not be known to the world as the daughter of a Nazi."

I didn't know how to respond. "I have nothing against your family, nothing against your father either. He's a wonderful singer. But let me ask you something: What do you really know about him?"

"What the hell do you mean by that?"

"I mean, do you know where he was born, where he grew up? Do you know his real name?"

She sank back into her chair. "His original name was Schnellinger. That's no secret," she said.

"Are you sure that's the name he was born with? How do you know?"

She inhaled audibly. "So you really are investigating him," she muttered under her breath. "Damn that crazy German woman!"

"Ms. Scott, I can't discuss internal department matters," I said, playing for pomposity. "But I can assure you all our investigations are

121

carried out fairly, impartially, and within the law. Our interest lies simply in finding the truth."

"Is that so? Then why did you try to trick my mother into talking to you, posing as some kind of a writer?" she said with some of her former feistiness. "I wonder what your boss would say if he knew. Or perhaps that's how you people operate. You can sneak around my father all you like, but you won't find anything. He and I may have our issues, but he's not a Nazi."

She stood up again, but I wasn't ready to let her go yet. "You said something about a German woman. I assume you mean Sophie Reiner."

Her face went pale. "How do you know about her?"

"I know she was in Boston before she was murdered. She contacted you, didn't she? What did she tell you?"

She sat down again, swallowed hard, and started fiddling with one of her rings. She wouldn't meet my eyes. Her skin seemed too tightly stretched over her face. I had seen that look often enough in court during cross-examination. It was the look of a witness who was rattled. I stayed on the offensive.

"Ms. Scott, you probably don't know that Sophie came to see me the day before she was killed. She had documents she wanted to give me. I think she showed them to you."

Susan grabbed the glass of water on the table and took a sip. I locked eyes with her. "I think you should talk to me. This is a murder case. I can help you. Or you could talk to the police instead." The police had made it clear they had their man, but Susan didn't know that.

"I won't be a part of it," she gasped, rising to her feet. "If one word of this gets out, you're toast. I warn you."

She swiveled and strode toward the exit, shoving a waiter out of her path. The ponytail was waiting. He helped her put her coat on, and they hustled out of the restaurant.

It had started to snow as I left to see Jack Doneghan. I grabbed a taxi for the short drive to the Capitol, my mind still churning. A picture was forming in my head, but it didn't entirely make sense. If Sophie had really gone to Florida to confront Delatrucha, he may have had a motive to kill her. But how would a classical musician with no criminal background arrange a murder?

As I paid the taxi driver outside the U.S. Capitol, I couldn't help looking around for suspicious characters. It was becoming a habit, even though I knew it was ridiculous. If I wasn't safe here, under democracy's dome, I wasn't safe anywhere.

Eric was waiting outside the minority leader's office. Conroy would soon be moving into the grander quarters of House speaker after Congress reconvened. His office buzzed with activity. Aides, frustrated by decades in the minority, salivated at the prospect of real power, none more than Jack Doneghan, who was said to be the muscle behind Conroy's throne. After a 20-minute wait, Doneghan's secretary ushered us into his presence. He waved us into two chairs facing his desk, glaring at us from beneath bushy eyebrows. His domed head sank into a doughy neck, pushing the skin into deep folds.

"Let's make this quick," he said in a broad Texas accent. "We've been going through your record, the speaker and me, and we're not sure what the American taxpayer is gettin' for his money. All y'all seem to do is chase after a bunch of old men."

Eric bristled. "With respect, Mr. Doneghan, what the American taxpayer is getting is an office created by Congress and staffed by dedicated individuals who uphold U.S. laws, American values, and the Constitution."

"That so? Tell it to that poor sonofabitch Demjanjuk." Doneghan sneered. "How much longer do y'all expect to find more Nazis to hunt? Seems to me most of 'em should have died by now," he continued.

"There are plenty of Nazis still out there, and we aim to find them. When that's done, we plan to go after other war criminals as well — Bosnians, Rwandans, anywhere there's genocide. We're already working on a bill."

"I don't think so. You missed your chance. That kind of legislation might have passed in the old Congress, but things are going to be quite a bit different around here from now on. There's a new team in charge. You boys have conducted your last witch hunt if I have anything to do with it. Next time you persecute some poor old man for no reason, we'll be coming down on you like a ton of bricks. And don't think I won't know. From now on, no sparrow in Washington is going to fart without me hearing about it."

"If you look at our record, you'll see we very seldom make mistakes," Eric said dryly. "We have the best conviction record of any division within the Department of Justice."

"And we'll be cutting your budget, of course," Doneghan went on, as if Eric hadn't spoken.

"If you can get the votes," Eric interrupted sharply, his face reddening. He puffed out his chest. "We still have friends in this building, Republicans as well as Democrats. You might be surprised."

"We'll be cutting government departments all across the board," Doneghan said, his voice rising. "Nobody's exempt. You boys think you're above everyone else? The era of big government is over for everyone, mister, and that includes you."

It was like watching a prizefight, two heavyweights beating each other senseless. But I was also proud of Eric. He wasn't backing down an inch.

"We're not 'big government,' as you put it. Our department is small, our budget is tiny, and we can account for every cent. If you come after us, you'll be making a big mistake."

"Don't you tell me how to do my job," Doneghan responded, slapping his meaty hand down on his desk. A secretary poked her head in. Doneghan shooed her away angrily; he was sweating profusely.

"I don't care how you do your job. You can cut all the government you want, as far as I'm concerned," Eric's voice was cold as ice. "Cut Health! Cut Welfare! But I'm going to protect my office and its mission, because it's important and because it upholds the values of the United States."

"Spare me the speech, boy. Just get me the information I asked for," Doneghan said. "Then we'll see what we want to cut."

"You'll have it within a week," Eric snapped. "And now, if you'll excuse us, I'm sure you're a busy man." He swept from the room. I hurried after him as he plowed through the tourists in the Rotunda and out of the building. We shared a taxi back to the office.

"That went well," I deadpanned. "Why didn't you tell him what you really think?"

"He threw down the gauntlet. I had to pick it up. He's just another Washington *schmekel* blowing off steam," Eric replied. "He'll back off. It's not worth the political price to go after a tiny department like ours."

"I hope you haven't made an enemy for life." I said. "We have enough already."

"Relax. Doneghan doesn't represent anyone but himself."

"But he has the ear of Mitch Conroy."

"Conroy's a realist. He has a slight majority, but that doesn't give him absolute power. We'll be okay. We just have to be even more careful with our investigations, especially if someone high-profile is involved, like this Delatrucha guy."

"I am being careful." I didn't mention my lunch with Susan Scott and the possibility we might soon be hearing from her lawyer. "But you have to be careful too, Eric. You have enemies inside the building as well as outside."

"Nonsense."

"You do, Eric."

"Who?"

"John Howard, for one."

"He loves the department."

"He may love the department, but he doesn't love you. He knows about our secret Delatrucha operation. George Carter told him. He'll use it against you if he gets the chance."

Eric slumped down, floored by the revelation. I paid and we got out, shivering in the wind. I was about to go inside, but Eric just stood there, stray snowflakes flurrying around his head. "John's plotting against me?"

"He wants your job."

"I can't believe it."

"Believe it. It's human nature, and it's been going on forever. Just read the Book of Kings about the struggle for power after the death of King David."

"What the hell are you talking about, Mark?"

"Never mind."

"That little pissant wants my job?" He really couldn't comprehend it.

"He's a big Republican, and he thinks this may be his opportunity."

"Well, fuck him! He can kiss my *toches*. And fuck Doneghan as well. They can both kiss my ass." He turned on his heel and strode into the building.

Lynn and I had agreed to cook dinner together at my apartment that night. I picked her up at Metro Center. She greeted me with a peck on the cheek that turned into a series of pecks — not all of them on the cheek. Snowflakes on her hair melted into little droplets that shone like diamonds. God, she was beautiful. . . .

"Now that we have a lead on Delatrucha's real identity, we can look for his Nazi Party file. That may tell us a lot," I said, snapping back to business.

As we got out of the car, I looked carefully in both directions. As usual, nothing suspicious. The mailbox was stuffed with a fresh crop of hate mail. "Have you been receiving any threatening mail or phone calls lately?" I asked.

"No," she said.

"That's a relief. I've been getting more than usual. Some neo-Nazi group mentioned Eric and me by name in their newsletter, and that unleashed a flood. I even had to unplug my phone for a day. The FBI and the police think it's nothing to worry about. And I have my trusty pepper spray," I told her.

"I wouldn't put my trust in pepper spray. I'd want something stronger."

We went up to the apartment, and suddenly we were all over each other. My nerve endings stood at attention. Her cold hands were under my shirt, raising goose bumps on my skin; I kissed her neck, her earlobes. My hand found her breasts, not listening to that "still, small voice" asking if this was the right thing to do.

And then the phone rang. "Ignore it," I panted between kisses.

"It may be important," she gasped.

"Probably just another neo-Nazi."

"Answer it." She slithered out of my grasp, picked up the receiver, and handed it to me.

"Mr. Cain?" A female voice, shrill, agitated, vaguely familiar.

"Who is this?" I asked.

"It's Susan Scott."

"How did you get my number?"

"You're in the book." *Not for much longer,* I thought.

"What's wrong?" I gestured to Lynn to pick up the extension to listen in.

"I don't know what's going on. I'm afraid," Susan said.

"What happened?"

"I think someone was following me today. I keep catching glimpses of some man." Her voice sounded rattled, almost hysterical.

"Are you sure?" I asked.

"No, I'm not." I knew the feeling. It wasn't pleasant.

"Ms. Scott, please calm down. You need to calm down."

"Okay, I'll try," she whispered.

"What does he look like, this person you're seeing?"

"A man dressed in a black coat, not too tall, not too short. Whenever I look around, he disappears. I'm not even sure my mind isn't playing games with me."

"Ms. Scott — Susan — how many people know you're here in town?" I asked her.

"I don't know. It's not a secret. I was doing business, meeting clients."

"Where are you now?"

"The Four Seasons in Georgetown."

"Are you alone?"

"I am right now."

"Call the police. I'll give you the name and number of a detective." I dug through my notes for Novak's number. "Call her, explain who you are and what you saw."

"Can you come here? There are things I need to tell you. I can't keep it all bottled up any longer."

"What things?"

"About Sophie Reiner. You were right. She came to see me. I feel so terrible. Poor woman."

"What did she say? Did she show you the documents?"

"She said lots of things, but I didn't believe her. What if she's dead because of me? I wouldn't listen to her. I sent her away." She sniffled quietly over the phone.

"Don't blame yourself."

"If you knew what she told me, you wouldn't say that."

"What did she tell you?"

"I can't, I just can't. Not tonight, over the phone." She let out a sob.

I didn't want to push her too hard. "I'll tell you what; it's late, and we're both tired. Let's meet tomorrow morning, eight o'clock, in your lobby," I said. "We can have breakfast."

"Mr. Cain, do you know why this is happening?"

"I don't. But I think it all revolves around Sophie. She stirred something up and paid for it with her life."

"Mr. Cain, Mark — can I call you Mark?"

"Sure."

"Mark, you have to help me. I don't feel safe on my own. Couldn't you come here and spend the night with me?" Lynn shook her head vigorously. She needn't have bothered, I had no intention of going.

"Don't open the door to anyone, and you'll be perfectly safe."

"Okay."

"I'll see you tomorrow morning."

She hung up.

Lynn came back and put her arms around me. "Do you have any other secret admirers I should know about?"

"She's scared," I said.

"Right."

"Lynn, are you jealous?"

"Of her? No way. I just don't trust her. Remember, I did research on her. She's a practiced liar. Remember that book about her boyfriend."

"I've dealt with a lot of lies in my time. I think I can tell the difference."

"Can you?"

I leaned forward to kiss her again, to pick up where we left off, but the mood was broken. We disengaged sheepishly. She stroked my cheek and smiled. "Don't worry, Mark. It's okay."

"It's not okay. We need time together without other stuff getting in the way. I don't want to be sharing you with the Delatrucha case."

"What about that weekend you promised me in West Virginia?"

I had forgotten about that. "How about this weekend? It's beautiful out there right now with the snow. We could leave on Friday, get there before Shabbat. I need to check up on the old man anyway. I haven't seen him for months."

"That'd be great," she said. "Let's do it."

"I'll call my dad and tell him to expect us."

Lynn called a taxi. "Go to bed," she said as she left. "And don't let that woman sweet-talk you too much tomorrow."

12

I heard of one incident in which a Jew threw a six-year-old child at an SS man as a distraction while other Jews stormed the guards, strangling one ethnic German and one SS man before they were subdued. This happened on the way to the gas chamber.

— Testimony of Tadeusz Misiewicz

"Shit!" I swore under my breath, jumping out of bed and groping for some clothes. It was already seven thirty in the morning. I must have forgotten to set the alarm on this of all days. This never happened to me. I quickly said Modeh Ani, skipped shaving, struggled into my suit, and rushed out the door. Washington traffic was hopelessly snarled, and it was almost 8:20 by the time I reached the Four Seasons. Susan wasn't in the lobby. I waited for a few minutes, then called her room. No answer.

"She checked out," the desk clerk told me. "Are you Mr. Cain? She left you this." He handed me an envelope. Ripping it open, I found a single sheet written in German, and a short note in English:

Mr. Cain —

Please forgive me. I was up all night thinking about this. I can't stay here any longer. I want no part of this. I'm going home. Sophie gave me this. I hope it means something to you. I have nothing else to say. Please leave me and my mother alone. She doesn't know anything.

Sincerely,
Susan Scott

The sheet of paper was written in German in a small, crabbed hand. It was a photocopy. The date caught my breath—July 1, 1942—then the first few words, "I think of her day and night." There were a few more lines of text. I sat down in an armchair and quickly scanned them, reaching for my legal pad to write down the translation.

July 1, 1942.

I think of her night and day. I know it's wrong. I know in some sense she is not fully human, but who of us in this place is? And yet her form is human and lovely, and I am but a man. I will be strong. This is a test of my will, and I shall not fail it.

I read it twice, making sure I had it correct. It sounded like part of a journal. If so, the date meant this entry had been written during the height of the Holocaust. Was this one of the documents Sophie Reiner wanted to give me? And who was this mysterious woman? Was she connected to Sophie? Did Sophie Reiner have in her possession an entire journal written at Belzec? The historical importance of such a document was unthinkable. This fragment raised more questions than it answered.

At the office, a message from George asked me to call immediately. He was in his hotel room, bubbling with uncharacteristic enthusiasm.

"I found it!" he said.

"Found what?"

"Franz Beck's file."

"So he was a Nazi."

"Not just any old Nazi. He was an SS officer."

"Tell me exactly what you found," I said. "No, wait, I'm going to conference Janet in on this." I dialed her in. "Tell us what you found."

"According to the file, Beck was born in 1918 in Hesse. He signed up with the Nazi Party in 1937 and joined the SS in 1939."

"That makes him what, seventy-six?"

"About the same age as Delatrucha," George said.

"What else? Does it say anything about what he did?" Janet asked.

"Sent to Poland in 1941. After that, the information becomes sketchy. But get this—he won the Iron Cross First Class in 1943."

"What for?"

"For duties performed in Operation Reinhard," George said flatly.

My heart was racing. The telephone felt hot in my hands.

"What did he do in Reinhard? Does it say?" I asked in a hushed voice.

"It doesn't."

"Not surprising," Janet interposed. "Reinhard was conducted in total secrecy. It was kept within a very tight group."

"Still, it could mean we're dealing with something really big," I said.

"If we can prove Beck is Delatrucha, it's huge. Just about everyone connected to Reinhard was up to his neck in mass murder," Janet replied.

Reinhard was the Nazi code name for the operation launched at the beginning of 1942 to murder all the Jews of Poland within a year. A small group of SS was selected to carry it out, helped by Ukrainian volunteers. The Nazis built extermination camps at Belzec, Sobibor, and Treblinka where, in the space of eighteen months, they murdered almost two million Polish Jews, a crime unparalleled in human history. By the end of 1942, the Nazis were able to declare vast tracts of Poland *Judenrein*—free of Jews. Very few of those who served in Reinhard were ever brought to justice. Some died later in the war. Most just melted away. A handful were tried in Germany in the 1960s and received light sentences. I even remembered reading some of the sickening trial transcripts several years before. If Delatrucha really was Franz Beck, he had enjoyed a unique career. Could the same man have been operating death camps in Poland in 1942 and singing Schubert in a Berlin recital hall in 1944?

"It would be remarkable," George said. "But remember, we still don't have *proof* it's the same guy. There could have been more than one Franz Beck. It's a common enough name."

"Maybe, but the string of coincidences is getting longer and longer. If he was in Reinhard, it would explain the connection with Himmler," I said.

Himmler was in charge of the Final Solution and therefore Operation Reinhard. His orders had created Belzec and Treblinka. Silence hovered while we all tried to absorb the possibilities.

"George, how much do we know about SS rosters at the extermination camps? Could we possibly place this Beck character at a specific place at a specific time?" Janet asked.

"I'm not sure. I don't think there are rosters. The best way would be to find witnesses. A few Jewish survivors from Treblinka and Sobibor may still be alive; none from Belzec as far as I know. And there must be some Germans and Ukrainians still around who were there, if they'd be willing to talk."

"George, I'd like you to stay over there a few more days. Draw up a list of possible witnesses — live ones — anyone who might be able to identify him from the camps. If necessary, I'll come over to help interview them," I told him. "Is that okay with you, Janet?"

"It's okay with me if it's okay with George."

"George?"

"No problem, Mark. I started out thinking this was a wild goose chase, but now, with Himmler mixed in, I'm hooked. I want to nail this bastard as much as you do. Let me confer with some German colleagues, and I'll get back to you."

Next I briefed Eric on George's discoveries in Germany and my conversations with Susan Scott. I showed him the German extract she had left me.

Eric whistled softly as he scanned it. "Pretty interesting," he said. "It definitely whets the appetite. The big question is, where's the rest?"

"Sophie Reiner probably hid it somewhere. Susan Scott may know, but she's scared to death and isn't talking. I was supposed to meet her for breakfast this morning, but she bolted back home to Boston."

"Does anyone else know about this?"

"Just you."

133

"Let's keep it that way. With the department leaking like a sieve, we need to keep this information out of the wrong hands."

"So what next?"

"You have to go up there and talk to her. She's hiding something. I can feel it. That extract you showed me, it proves there really are documents, and I want them."

"If I chase after her, she may freak out even more. She's completely unnerved; she begged me to stay away. Maybe I should let her calm down for a few days first."

"I'll leave that for you to decide. What about George? What's his next step?"

"I asked him to locate any surviving witnesses from Operation Reinhard. And before I forget, I'm going to see my dad this weekend in West Virginia. I haven't seen him for months. Lynn is coming, too. We'll probably leave Friday morning and come back Sunday night."

Eric smiled. "No hanky-panky in the office. I should transfer her so she isn't working for you anymore."

"No need. She found another job with some human rights outfit, but she's agreed to see the Delatrucha case through to the end first."

"Okay. And Mark . . ."

"Yes?"

"I'm glad to see you happy."

"I'm not used to it. It feels dangerous, like walking on a high wire."

"Just remember this case is your top priority. Keep the romance to after hours."

I spent the afternoon doing research at the Holocaust Museum. It had opened the previous year and had already become one of the top attractions in Washington, always with a long line of visitors waiting to get in. As I waited in the austere brick-lined lobby to pass through the metal detector, I saw the words of President Clinton displayed on a wall: "The Museum will touch the life of everyone who enters and leave everyone forever changed."

I spent a couple of hours reviewing testimony from some of the war crimes trials from the 1960s involving people who had served in Reinhard. None of it contained any reference to anyone who might fit Delatrucha's description. One thing that did emerge from the testimony was the heavy psychological toll that mass murder took on the murderers themselves. Many spent months in a drunken haze — the only way they'd been able to keep on doing their jobs.

The afternoon minyan afforded a short but welcome break from Nazis. From there, it was back to my office, where I found a long fax from George lying on my desk. Before I could read it, the phone rang again.

"I heard you had a good meeting with Doneghan," said Howard, his reedy voice even more oily than usual.

"It went well. Doneghan and Eric got along like a house on fire."

"Jack thought it went well, too. Another performance like that, and Eric will be out of here faster than a greased pig."

"Howard, do you have any actual business to discuss, or did you just call to share nonkosher idioms?"

"I like you, and I respect your work. You're not a blowhard like Rosen. I consider you a valued colleague. I want you to know there'll be a place for you here after the revolution." He cackled.

I hung up. The man was becoming more and more brazen, and he always seemed to be a couple of steps ahead of us. Shaking my head, I returned my attention to the fax.

```
FROM: George Carter
TO: Mark Cain
RE: Franz Beck


    Here are some thoughts following our
phone call:
    I think my next move should be to
research what we know about Himmler's vis-
its to Poland in 1942. If Beck knew Himmler,
they may have met in Poland. As you sug-
gested, I've hired a couple of local grad
students to help me with that. There are a
```

number of published sources we can look at, including the diary of Hans Frank, the Nazi governor of Poland, who kept a detailed record of all his meetings. That shouldn't take too long. I should have some details for you on that within a day or two.

On the question of witnesses, I con-sulted some German colleagues. They believe there is probably still a relatively large number of Germans alive who took part in Operation Reinhard—guards, railway work-ers, police, builders, suppliers, etc. However, the list of people who actually served in the camps is much shorter, and it's not certain any will agree to be interviewed. The Germans are trying to track down names and addresses. There are also probably witnesses still living in Ukraine, and possibly survivors in Israel.

At your end, you should brief the State Department. We're going to need official cooperation from the Ukrainian government to locate witnesses and interview them.

Lastly, it would help a lot to narrow the search to one specific camp to focus the inquiry.

There was a voice in my head — a tired, wheezy German voice. Sophie Reiner had started this investigation, and she was still guid-ing it. I sent George a one-line fax:

Concentrate on Belzec.

We've been given a new assignment. "Once we've done this next job, we should have enough money," I told Clint.

He asked, "Enough money for what?"

I said, "Enough money to buy all the rest of the stuff we're going to need for the big operation. Remember what I said about the spark and the kindling?"

I think he does, but you can't always tell with Clint.

I'd love to aim for the White House or the Capitol, but they're too well guarded. The Supreme Court would be good, but it's set too far back from the street and up a bunch of steps. The State Department's a possibility. The guards there were slow to move vehicles along, especially from the side entrances. Would blowing up the State Department provide the spark? Does it send the right message?

Clint asks, "How many people have you killed, anyway?"

I tell him, "I don't rightly know. I killed an awful lot over in Iraq."

"Not counting Iraq," he says. "How many since you've been back?"

I try to remember them all. "Half a dozen. Maybe more."

"Who was the first?" Clint wants to know.

"That's easy. I was still in jail. When I got out of seg and back into general population, I hooked up with my white brothers for protection. When they asked what I did, I told them, 'I kill people. I'm real good at it.' They said, 'We've got a cocksucker in here who needs killing.' I said, 'What's he done?' They said, 'He's a snitch.' They gave me a shiv and made sure he was alone when he went to the shower. He was eight inches taller than me, but he didn't give me any trouble. The screws tried to investigate, but of course no one saw anything, so I was in the clear."

"Who was the last you killed?" he asks.

I tell him about the jogger. Clint's awful quiet. So I ask him, "What's the matter?"

"I never killed no one," he says. "Could you take me out with you, show me how?" I told him not to be stupid, he'll find out soon enough. "Couldn't we just kill another jogger?" he asks. "Or that Jew guy?"

"Maybe," I tell him. "If you're good, I'll let you kill a jogger."

The Jew is mine.

13

I smile at you, O skeleton;
Lead me lightly away to lands of dreams.

— "The Young Man and Death" by Joseph von Spaun,
music by Franz Schubert

By the time I was done drafting a request for Eric to submit to the State Department so we could brief our embassies in Berlin and Kiev and formally request the help of the German and Ukrainian governments, it was already eight thirty, and I was dog tired. Lynn poked her head into the office. "Ready to quit for the day?"

"Sure, let's go eat. Just let me straighten everything out here." I started sorting the papers on my desk.

"You really do need things to be organized, don't you?" she said, mussing my hair.

"What's wrong with that?" I said, removing her hand.

"Nothing. I'm just trying to bring a bit of chaos into your orderly life."

"Where do you want to eat?"

"How many kosher restaurants are there in D.C.?"

"Not many, but there are a few veggie places that are okay."

We ended up at the Green Pepper in Bethesda. Over eggplant lasagna and a cabernet, I brought Lynn up-to-date on the investigation. She agreed with Eric that we should press Susan Scott for more answers and volunteered to fly up to Boston with me to interrogate her.

"Maybe she'd be more inclined to talk to another woman."

I said I'd think about it.

Then the subject turned to West Virginia. I said we probably wouldn't be doing any downhill skiing, but we might try cross-country and even tobogganing if the weather was okay.

We split a serving of tiramisu for dessert and decided to get coffee back at my apartment. She noticed the scratch on the hood as we got into the car. "I'm going to get it filled as soon as I can," I said.

We drove back; I grabbed my briefcase from the backseat, and we walked toward the building, snuggling and exchanging little kisses. I pushed open the swinging glass doors — the lobby was dark. The lights must have been broken. Then a shadow formed in front of us. Metal shimmered, slashing toward my throat. Time froze; everything moved in slow motion. I jerked my briefcase upward and felt the knife scrape across the leather. I heard myself yelling and shoved Lynn backward. I remembered the pepper spray in my coat pocket and tried to pull it out.

The assailant was dressed in black, a big, fat son of a bitch, but that made him move slower. Pockmarked face, teeth bared in a snarl — as he reached back to stab again, I ducked and swayed to one side, and my glasses clattered to the ground. "Get out, get out!" I shouted to Lynn.

I yanked the pepper spray from my pocket and aimed in the general direction of the man's face, while thrusting my other hand straight out in front of me. The effect was immediate. He doubled up, clutching his eyes, screaming wildly. I aimed a kick at his fuzzy image, catching him on the knee. He fell in a heap, engulfed in a spasm of coughing. Never in my life had I hit another person, but I stomped as hard as I could on his wrist and felt the bones crunch. It felt good. He shrieked in agony and let go of the knife.

There was another faceless ghoul half hidden in the shadows — a slim, insubstantial figure — and then Lynn's voice came, shouting, "Back off, asshole!" She had stepped just inside the entrance, half squatting, a gun held firmly in both hands.

The small man was holding something in his hand, I couldn't see what. There was nothing I could do, he was out of pepper spray range. "Back off or I'll fire!" Lynn screamed again. Something exploded a few inches behind my head. The wall mirror across the lobby shattered. Deafened and disoriented, I scanned for the exit.

"Let's get out of here!" I shouted, shoving the door open and holding it for her. The assassin had retreated to the back of the lobby for cover. Burglar alarms were howling all over the building as residents hit panic buttons. I pulled her out, and we stumbled into the dark. Flinging the car door open, I threw myself behind the wheel and shoved the gearshift into drive. Lynn tumbled into the passenger seat as I hit the gas pedal. We shot out of the parking lot, tires squealing.

"Calm down, don't go so fast," Lynn panted. Without my glasses, it was like driving through a fog. I got a grip, slowed down, looking for somewhere to stop, and finally pulled into a strip mall.

"What's the matter, why are you stopping?" Lynn asked.

"Glasses," I muttered. I pulled my spare pair from the glove compartment. She sprang into focus, cheeks flushed, eyes flashing. We held each other for a long time. I could feel her trembling. She started to cry quietly, the tears tracking down her cheeks.

"I can't believe I did that," she said. "Tell me I didn't hit him."

"I don't think you did. I couldn't see that well."

"I was aiming high, trying to miss. I just wanted to scare him. He was coming for you. He wouldn't stop."

"I'll never forget it." I stroked her cheek, brushing away the tears. "It's okay, it's okay, Lynn."

"I warned him. You heard me. But he kept coming."

I asked, "How come you have a gun?"

"My dad made me get it when I moved to D.C. Murder capital of the nation and all. I agreed to buy it just to shut him up. I never thought I would use it," she said, half laughing, half sobbing. "I kept it locked in a desk at home until a couple of weeks ago, when you warned me you were getting these threats and I should be careful."

"Do you have a permit for that thing?"

"You don't need one in Pennsylvania. That was the first time I fired it. I hope I never have to again."

"Where's the gun now?"

"In my pocket."

"The safety's on?"

She took it out. The black, blunt-nosed weapon in her hand made me nervous, but she seemed to know what she was doing. "Yes. What do we do now?" she said.

"Get to a phone and call that FBI agent I met the other day, Agent Fabrizio," I said. As we edged back into traffic, two cruisers hurtled by in the other direction toward the apartment building, sirens wailing. "The office is the safest place I know."

I parked in the underground garage below the building. In my office, we removed our coats and fell into each other's arms. We were both shivering. I heard her murmur in my ear, "Thank God you're safe. Thank God you're safe." At the butt end of the worst day of her life, she still smelled delicious: a heady mixture of sweet perfume and fresh shampoo.

I fished Fabrizio's card out of my pocket and called the number she had given me. A few seconds later, I was patched through to her. "I've been attacked," I stated bluntly. "Just now, in the lobby of my apartment building. I was with my girlfriend. Two men came at us. One had a knife, the other may have had a gun."

"Are you hurt?"

"We're okay. I pepper-sprayed one of them and left him coughing his guts out on the ground. Hopefully the police got there in time and arrested him. My girlfriend fired a shot to scare the other one off."

"Did she hit anyone?"

"I don't think so."

"Where are you now?"

"In my office at Justice."

"I'm coming right over. Don't move."

She arrived twenty-five minutes later, accompanied by a grim-faced, gum-chewing Lieutenant Reynolds. Fabrizio took one look at the two of us and pulled out a hip flask from her pocketbook. "Here, this'll settle your nerves," she said.

We each took shots of the burning liquid.

"This is a quite a mess you folks got yourselves involved in," Reynolds said, chomping angrily on his gum. "What the hell did y'all think you were doing?"

"We were attacked. I'm lucky to be alive. Didn't you arrest the guy I pepper-sprayed?" I asked.

"There was no one to arrest when the squad cars arrived. If you'd been there, we'd probably have arrested you."

"It's not too late," I said, holding my wrists out. I was getting more and more infuriated with the police, and judging by Reynolds's expression, he wasn't too thrilled with me either.

"Let's not get so dramatic," Fabrizio said soothingly. "Nobody's getting arrested. That's not why we're here. Just tell us what happened. Don't leave anything out."

"We were walking into the apartment building when a guy dressed all in black came at me with a knife." I showed them my briefcase, the leather scarred by the assailant's weapon.

"Did you get a look at his face?"

"Not enough to identify him. I think he was white. A big guy, maybe six-one or six-two, and heavy, built like a football tackle. Pocked face. The other one was small and skinny — he was lurking at the back of the lobby. Lynn fired a warning shot at him. Did you see his face, Lynn?"

"No."

"Where's the gun?" Reynolds asked. Lynn took it out; he examined it, sniffing the barrel. "How many shots did you say you fired?"

"Just one."

"I'm assuming you registered your weapon with the police here in D.C.?"

"I didn't know you had to."

"You most definitely do. Carrying a concealed weapon in the District of Columbia is illegal. All firearms must be stored safely at home or at a place of business. We have enough problems already with people shooting joggers in parks for no reason. I'm going to have to take this. We may file charges later."

Lynn looked crushed.

"Lieutenant —" I began. He turned on me immediately.

"Are you still chasing conspiracy theories about that German lady's death? Because we got the murderer, and the case is closed. Or it was until the FBI started sniffing about — with all due respect, Agent Fabrizio." He spat his gum into the trash bin next to my foot. The FBI was meddling in his case, threatening to spoil his triumph. That's why he was giving Lynn such a hard time.

Fabrizio stood there with arms folded, a faint smile on her face. I turned back to Reynolds. "First of all, back off my girlfriend. She just saved my life. Second, I'm not chasing any theories, Lieutenant. That's not my job. I'm investigating whether the singer Roberto Delatrucha was a Nazi. Whether that turns out to have something to do with Sophie Reiner's murder, I have no idea. That's your job, not mine."

Reynolds was still fuming but said nothing more.

Fabrizio had a few more questions, but neither of us was able to add much. She looked grim. "I must admit, I didn't take your story all that seriously. This puts a different light on things. I'm thinking maybe we should give you some protection as you move around the city. You're obviously safe in your office, but I hate to think of you wandering unprotected around town."

"We're going to Boston tomorrow to interview a witness, and after that we're going to West Virginia for a long weekend," I told her.

"Does anyone else know of these plans?" Fabrizio asked.

"No. I only decided to go to Boston just now. You're the only people who know."

"Call me when you get back, and we'll see where we are with your security. Maybe you should go to a hotel tonight. You don't want to go back to your apartment. It's bound to be crawling with local media. They'll devour you."

"We'll stay right here," I said.

Fabrizio and Reynolds left, and Lynn and I went upstairs to Eric's office. She lay down on his couch. I took off my jacket, stretched out beside her, and wrapped my arms around her. It was a narrow space, too tight to be comfortable. Our bodies pressed together; she snuggled close, trying to find a good fit. I kissed her again, tasting her, my hands exploring her body, intensely aware of my arousal. She had to be aware of it, too; it was pretty damned obvious. Each time I touched her, my mind went off duty and told my body, *Okay, you're in charge here now. Call me when you need me again.*

"This is our first night together," I whispered.

"Not exactly how I imagined it," she replied, half giggling, half crying.

"Me neither. But it's still a night I'll never forget."

Our limbs were as entwined as our lives had become. She brushed my cheek with her lips. "Good night," she whispered.

Lynn fell asleep almost immediately. For a long time, I couldn't relax. I kept seeing that flash of metal as the knife thrust toward me. It still seemed so unreal.

I woke up about 4:30, stiff, dry-mouthed, and shivering. It was pitch-black in the office, and cold. Lynn was still asleep. I disentangled myself from her, covered her with my jacket, and limped down the corridor to the bathroom. After splashing some water on my face, I padded down to my own office. I had a lot to thank God for. I took the small prayer book out of my scarred briefcase and turned to the psalm of the day.

> God of retribution, Lord God of retribution, appear.
> Judge of the earth, give the arrogant their deserts.
> How long, Lord, how long shall the wicked exult? . . .
> Were it not for God's help, I would be in my grave.
> When my foot slips, the Lord's love supports me.
> When I am filled with cares, His comfort soothes my soul.

Silence washed over me. Where was God? In my heart of hearts, I didn't believe that God intervened in the lives of men and women. He had created the world and given humans the gift of free will — the ability to choose between the good and evil in each of us. God wants us to choose good and gave us the means to do so, but all too often evil prevails, and when it does, God doesn't intercede to stop it. If I learned anything from the Holocaust, it was that.

There was a long fax from George:

FROM: George Carter
TO: Mark Cain
RE: Himmler

Here's what I dug up about Himmler's
visits to Poland from a review of the published literature. He made two known visits to Operation Reinhard death camps. The
first was in mid-July 1942; the second in
the first quarter of 1943. There may have
been others we don't know about. The first
trip preceded the liquidation of the Warsaw
ghetto. He was almost certainly at Belzec,
and we know he also traveled to Nazi headquarters in Lublin, where he held an important meeting to review the operation. After
that, Himmler issued an order dated July
19, 1942, confirming the timetable under
which all the surviving Jews of Poland were
to be sent to death camps by the end of the
year.

The second visit was late February or
early March 1943. By that time, Operation
Reinhold was virtually completed. Around
1.7 million Polish Jews had been killed.
Himmler visited Sobibor and Treblinka;
there are several accounts of the visits.
At Sobibor, the commandant arranged a special gassing of over 1,000 young people in
his honor. After the gassing, the Nazi VIPs
all went to the camp canteen for a special
meal. Himmler also inspected the gas chambers and crematoria at Treblinka.

The main purpose of this visit seems to
have been to decide what to do with the
three death camps because they would soon
no longer be needed. Himmler ordered them

to be dismantled. He instructed that all
the victims' remains should be burned,
their bones ground up, and all traces of
the crime erased. The mood was apparently
jubilant. Himmler recommended promotions
for 28 SS officers who had distinguished
themselves during the operation. I checked
the list, but the name Franz Beck isn't on
it. Himmler also seems to have hosted a
celebration in Lublin at which there was
music and entertainment. That's all I've
been able to find. It's possible Himmler may
have met Beck on one of those visits, but
I can't prove it.

Bottom line: I still can't place Beck at
any of the camps, and we still don't know
what he did during the war. My German contacts are still searching for witnesses.

I switched off the desk lamp and sat there thinking. I began a
long memorandum, setting out all that had happened since Sophie
Reiner had first poked her head into my office. I wanted to leave a
complete record in case anything happened to me. I addressed one
copy to Rosen and left another in my filing cabinet.

After about an hour, my fax machine started buzzing again and
slowly spat out an image of a young man. Eric's FBI friend had come
through. It was Delatrucha, without a beard, as he might have been
as a young man. I made a few photocopies and stuffed them in my
wounded briefcase.

The sickly gray light of day began seeping into the office. Lynn
came in, yawning and stretching. She sat on my lap, put her arms
around my neck, and wished me a good morning.

"How did you sleep?" I asked, as she laid her head on my
shoulder.

"Not bad, considering. God, I must look awful."

She did, but I didn't care. There was something precious about
her disheveled hair and puffy eyes. She smiled. Despite everything,

she was happy to be here, happy to be alive, happy to be with me. My glasses were steaming up again. "Take me with you to Boston," she said.

"Absolutely. Especially after what happened last night. But don't you think we should call ahead and let her know we're coming?"

"I think we should surprise her."

"What if she's not there?"

"We have to take that chance. If we call to say we're coming, she might disappear on us again."

"Okay. We'll go this afternoon. That'll give us both time to go home and freshen up."

"Before we ambush her."

"Right."

14

At night, when they locked us into the barracks, we heard from the pallets whispers of the Kaddish. We prayed in memory of the dead.

—— Testimony of Rudolf Reder

Susan's office turned out to be in Medford, a suburb north of Boston, on the third floor of a shabby building on Main Street. A sign announced that this was "The Scott Literary Agency." Underneath it, a piece of paper taped on the door promised that someone would be "Back Soon." The door itself was unlocked. We walked into an empty waiting room that contained a couple of ancient leather armchairs and a sofa. Old issues of *Editor and Publisher* and the *New York Review of Books* lay strewn on the coffee table. An adjoining workspace was empty, the desk bare except for a computer monitor covered in plastic. Lynn said Susan's business had gone downhill in recent years. Judging by the clothes and jewelry she wore and the hotels she stayed in, she hadn't let it affect her lifestyle too much.

Two walls of the waiting room were decorated with framed covers of books by some of Susan's more notable clients. My eyes landed on one that had achieved notoriety a few years back, *Surviving Daddy: A Poet's Experience with Sexual Abuse.*

"This is the book that got her in trouble," Lynn pointed at another cover showing a menacing individual, his head covered in a dark blue bandanna, his outrageously muscular forearms festooned with tattoos.

"Who is this guy?" I asked.

"Her former lover, Jimmy Williamson." There was some kind of bird, perhaps a crow, tattooed on one arm, and a spider's web on the other. The image glared at us with undisguised hostility. Williamson's memoir was entitled *Gangster: From the Hood to the Joint and Back Again*.

"I wonder what Susan saw in him," I said. "He doesn't seem the type for sunset walks along the beach and evenings in front of a log fire. I think he may have been the guy with her at the restaurant last week."

"I thought I'd read somewhere that they weren't an item any more," she said.

Shadows obscured a third wall. As I walked toward it, three small framed photographs of Roberto Delatrucha came into view. In one, he was bowing to the audience at a concert hall; the second showed him singing, his arm stretched out in that characteristic pose I had come to know so well. And there was another of a more youthful Delatrucha with his arms around a young girl, both of them smiling broadly.

"Take a look at this," I said. "It's Delatrucha and Susan when she was a girl. Makes you wonder whether she really hates him or worships him, like an adoring daughter."

"Could be both," Lynn said. "Fathers and daughters are complicated stuff. Very Freudian. Look at me and my dad with his guns, wishing I was the son he never had."

"Fathers and sons can be problematic, too," I said.

The door opened behind us, and Susan walked in, looking brisk and businesslike in a navy suit and crisp white blouse with an elegant string of pearls around her neck that matched her silver fingernails and dangly earrings. She was clutching a leather briefcase in one hand and a cup of coffee in the other. For a moment, she appeared not to recognize me. Then a sharp intake of breath, and a splash of coffee down the outside of the cup. "Mr. Cain. What are you doing here?" she asked harshly. "I told you to leave me alone."

"I respect your wish for privacy, I honestly —"

"Then why are you here?" she snapped. This was the Susan who had accosted me in the restaurant, not the tearful creature I had spoken to on the phone.

"Last night we were attacked in the entranceway to my apartment," I said.

"How terrible. By whom?" The right words, but she didn't sound concerned.

"Perhaps the same men who were following you. We weren't hurt, though we might have been."

"I don't see what this has to do with me."

"What about the man who was following you?"

"Maybe business problems. It was probably my mind playing tricks on me."

"I don't think you were imagining it," I said. "And running away to Boston won't make you safe."

"But why would anyone threaten me? I haven't hurt anyone. It's absurd."

"I believe it has something to do with Sophie Reiner," I said. "We haven't hurt anyone either, but that didn't stop two men with knives from coming after us. This is what one of them did to my briefcase." I held it up. "That could have been my throat. Now, I must ask you to cooperate. We are government agents on Department of Justice business. Whatever passed between you and Sophie, even if it's distasteful or personally embarrassing, could be vitally important. If you require protection, I can arrange it."

"I don't want your protection," she said dismissively.

"That's your choice, of course. I will keep whatever information you give us strictly confidential."

"I don't believe you. I asked you to stay away, and here you are. Why should I trust you? Give me one good reason."

"You don't have a choice. The FBI is involved. If you don't speak to us, we'll get a subpoena, and you'll have to speak to them."

"What information do you think I might have?"

"I don't know. Perhaps it involves your father. Whatever it is, someone may be willing to kill you to stop it."

Susan lifted both her palms. "I don't want this. I told you I can't be a part of it. I have a right to privacy, a right to remain silent. You may be used to this kind of thing, but it's not part of my life, or my world." Under the veneer of anger, she was fighting to hold herself together.

Lynn intervened, "Maybe we could sit down and discuss this more calmly? Perhaps over a cup of coffee. There's a café across the street. We're all too stressed out to think straight right now." Susan looked at her, exhaled, then nodded her agreement.

Lynn and I ordered black coffee; Susan asked for a cappuccino. We sat for a couple of moments. Susan's hands were in constant motion, tapping the table, fiddling with cutlery, picking up and putting down the salt and pepper shakers. Just watching her made me nervous.

I wanted Lynn to take the lead in the questioning. She had established a tenuous rapport with Susan. I nodded discreetly for her to go ahead.

"The point is this," Lynn resumed. "You're no safer in Boston than in D.C. We found you in the phone book, and anyone else could easily do the same. You can't run away from this. You're totally part of it now, whether you like it or not. We can help you try to deal with the danger, but you need to help us as well." Susan sighed deeply, shrugging her shoulders in defeat.

"Okay, Mr. Cain, you win. What do you want to know?"

"Sophie Reiner. How did she contact you?"

Susan glanced around the room, picked up her coffee cup, replaced it without taking a sip, and ran her fingers through her short hair. "In November, just before Thanksgiving, I was in my apartment when I got a phone call out of the blue," she began. "I could tell from her accent she was German. She sounded excited — she said she had to see me."

"Did she say why?" Lynn prompted.

"She said it was personal, that it concerned my father. I told her I hadn't spoken to him for years. She said it was important and she wouldn't take much of my time, but it concerned me as well." Susan fell silent again, played with a stray lock of hair, looked around the room. "She told me she had something to show me," she said.

"What was it?"

"That's what I asked. She said her mother had known my father as a young man in Germany—they were quote unquote *dear friends*—and she had some pictures she wanted me to see. I was intrigued. You were right, what you said the other day. My dad never spoke about when he was young. Not to me, not even to my mother. And we knew never to ask. It was as if his life only really began when he arrived in the United States. Anything that happened before was a closed book, off-limits. Occasionally, reporters or music critics asked about it, but he always avoided the questions. So I was curious. I said I would meet her the next day in my office."

"Then what happened?" Lynn asked.

"She showed up and started babbling about her mother, how she had recently died, how sad it was and how she had been close to my father many years ago when they were both young. It was hard to understand her. She kept breaking into German. So I asked her to show me what she had come to show me. And then . . . And then she did."

"What was it?"

"She brings this huge packet of papers out of her bag and starts spreading them across the desk. They were all photocopies, nothing original. I asked, 'What's all this?' She said they were his letters to her mother and a journal from the war. All in German, of course. I asked, 'Where are the originals?' She said they were safely hidden someplace. I was suspicious. I mean, they could have all been forgeries. How was I to know? She picked up one of the letters and started reading from it. I told her I didn't speak German, so she tried translating it, but her English wasn't good enough. She didn't know half the words and said them in German. I was getting impatient. She was getting more and more emotional; she had tears dripping down her face, and she was waving her arms around like a demented woman."

"Were the letters dated?" I asked.

"The one she read from was from 1941, June or July, I think."

"Did you see who signed the letter? Was there a name on it?"

"I didn't even think to look. Neither one of us was thinking rationally by that time."

"I understand. So what happened next?"

"I was just about to show her the door when she pulled out a photograph — a small print not much bigger than a passport photo. And that's when I realized that she did have a connection to my dad. He was sitting with his arm around a young girl in her early teens. Sophie pointed at the girl and said it was her, aged thirteen. It must have been taken around 1957 or 1958."

I fell back on my courtroom training. Rule number one: never betray surprise, no matter what the witness says on the stand. I took a sip of coffee — by now getting cold. My thoughts were racing. I focused on my next question and on keeping my voice neutral.

"Okay, she had a picture of herself as a girl with your dad. Then what happened?"

"I asked where she had gotten all this stuff and what she wanted from me. She embarked on this long, drawn-out story of her life." Susan looked at her empty coffee cup.

"Do you want another cappuccino?" Lynn jumped in.

"No, thanks. Let's go back to the office. We can continue there."

I wasn't sure we should break the flow of the conversation, but Susan had already stood up and was leading the way. We filed back across the street and up the three flights of stairs. Susan sat down behind her desk. She clearly liked to be in control. She quietly slid a manila folder sideways under some papers, then looked back at us, expectantly.

"You were saying how Sophie told you her life story. What do you remember about it?" I asked.

"She said she was born in 1945. Her mother was called Hildegard Reiner. She brought Sophie up alone. They lived from hand to mouth in West Berlin. Hildegard told Sophie her father died in the war. When Sophie was a girl, a man used to show up from time to time for quick visits — maybe once a year. I figured it out. He visited whenever he was in Germany on tour. It must have been tough; my mother was his accompanist, so she was usually with him. He must have snuck away for an hour or two at a time."

After a knock on the door, the man with the ponytail stuck his head in.

"Not now, Jimmy," said Susan. Then turning to us, "Excuse me a minute." She grabbed him by the arm and hustled him back outside. I could hear heated conversation, but I couldn't make out the words. Lynn crept to the door to see if she could hear, but I wanted to see what was in that manila folder. I picked it up and peered inside: a single newspaper clipping. Reading upside down, I deciphered the headline, "Canadian Ranchers Fear Mad-Cow Disease." Why would Susan want to conceal that? Puzzled, I replaced the folder.

Lynn dashed back to her chair just before Susan returned to the office and sat back down behind her desk. "Sorry about that. Where were we?" she asked.

"You were saying how your father must have snuck away to visit Sophie's mother during concert tours."

"That's right. Hildegard told Sophie the man was one of her father's old army buddies. She called him Uncle Robert. He used to bring her presents — dolls, toys, later nylons, and once he brought a gold bracelet. He gave her a big red pin that she was wearing that day."

Rule number one: Remain calm. "She was wearing it when she came to see me as well," I said carefully. "She was wearing it when she died."

"Oh, God," Susan held her head in her hands.

"What else did she tell you about your father's visits?"

"She said he would kiss and hug her — she liked him because he always came with a gift, and he would also leave money for her mother. She didn't know he lived in America or anything else about him. Then the visits stopped, and she rather forgot about him."

"And then?"

"Then, about a year ago, her mother got very sick. She told me the name of the disease in German. Some kind of cancer maybe. Sophie nursed her until she died. A few weeks later, Sophie was going through all her mother's things and she found a suitcase hidden away at the back of a closet — it was stuffed full of photos, letters, postcards, even a journal dating back to 1940. Also a couple of my father's old records."

"Go on," I said, struggling to keep my poker face in place.

154

"When she saw the photos, she recognized the man she vaguely recalled from her childhood — Uncle Robert. Then she looked at one of the record sleeves and recognized my father. She started reading the letters and realized . . . and realized . . ." Susan broke off, reaching for a tissue.

The letter Sophie had left in the hotel now made sense, the letter she had been writing to her dead mother but had never finished. *"You could have trusted me. I would have kept all your secrets. Now, I wrestle with them night and day, trying to find my way through the forest . . ."*

"She realized Robert wasn't her uncle," Lynn said gently.

"That's right."

"I can't imagine," Lynn continued. "You must have been totally freaked out."

"You could say that."

"And did you believe her?" I asked.

"Of course not. I still don't quite believe it. It's like one of those movies about someone leading a double life."

"So what did you tell her?"

"I was angry. I thought she was trying to get money out of me. I was ready to give her some just to make her go away. I took out my checkbook and asked her how much she wanted. She said she wasn't interested in my dirty money. She wanted us to be real sisters. I mean, can you imagine? Sisters?"

It was hard to imagine the dowdy, bedraggled Sophie as sister of this sophisticated creature. Susan gathered herself, speaking in a low monotone. "That's when I told her to leave. I shouted at her to get the hell out."

"And did she?" I asked.

"Not at first. She said I was making a mistake. All she wanted was to be a sister to me and a daughter to my father. She knew it was a shock, but she'd give us time to get used to the idea. Imagine it — she wanted us to be one big happy family. I didn't know whether to laugh or cry. We haven't been a happy family for years. The last thing my father would have wanted was a new daughter, especially not a Raggedy Ann like her. He gets all the fathering he needs with Elissa. The child bride, I call her. I told Sophie she was crazy, but she wouldn't listen. She said she was going to Florida to see him — she already had her ticket — and if he wouldn't listen to her, she would make him sorry."

"How?"

"She said she'd go to you and tell you all his secrets."

So much for rule number one. I was stunned, and my face showed it. "Me? She mentioned me?"

"Marek Cain, the Nazi hunter, she called you. I'd never heard of you. She said you'd be very interested to hear what she had to say. She said there were some things about my father — awful things — that would be of great interest to the U.S. government. At that point, I completely lost it. I started yelling and throwing her papers on the floor. We were both crying. . . ."

"And then?"

"She picked up all the papers, stuffed them in her bag, and slammed the door behind her. After she'd gone, I noticed she'd missed a couple of pages that had fallen behind the desk."

"Did she leave the photograph she showed you?"

"No, she took it."

"When she said she knew some awful things, do you have any idea what she might have been talking about?"

"I've been trying not to think about it."

"And then what?"

"Like I said, then she left."

"And that was it?"

"That was it. Until . . ." She dabbed at her eyes again.

"Until?"

"Until I did something I probably shouldn't have done. I called up my dad. I hadn't spoken to him for a long time . . . and I guess I was waiting for an excuse. I wanted to hear his voice. I missed him. So I called. Elissa answered. She didn't want to let me speak to him. I said it was a matter of life and death. I told him the whole thing. I said Sophie might be on her way to see him in the next few days. He listened very calmly, asked a few questions, and then very politely thanked me. Like I was a complete stranger. He didn't even ask how I was. And now she's dead, and it's all my fault," she wailed.

But I wasn't finished with her yet. I still had a few more questions. "Did you ask your father what the awful things might have been?"

She dabbed her eyes with a tissue. "No, of course not."

"Do you know if Sophie actually did see your father?"

"No. He didn't call back, and I never heard from her again. The next thing I knew, she was dead." She stifled another sob. "Excuse me for going all soft on you. I haven't told anyone about this, and it's been eating away at me."

"But Susan, surely you're not suggesting that your father had something to do with Sophie's death?" Lynn asked.

"I don't know."

"It's not so easy to have someone killed. You can't just look up 'hit men' under the letter *H* in the yellow pages," I observed.

"My father, he knows lots of people. He's a member of a gun club. He loves guns, never goes anywhere without one."

"My dad's the same way. That doesn't make him a murderer," Lynn countered, shaking her head. "You don't think he asked one of his gun club buddies to commit a murder? That's totally wacky. Gun club members are the most law-abiding people in America."

"No, of course not." Susan reddened. "But, like I said, my father knows all kinds of people. A few years ago, he hired an ex-con to do his gardening. He said it was a good deed because everyone deserves a second chance. They became quite friendly. Maybe they're still in touch. Maybe that guy has friends from prison, criminal types, he could have asked to do him a favor."

"What's this gardener's name?" I asked.

"I don't know. I forget."

Lynn butted in. "I thought you said you hadn't spoken to your dad for years. How would you know about his gardener?"

"That was when we were still speaking from time to time."

"So that gardener was years ago."

"But that doesn't explain why someone would be following you. Your father wouldn't harm you," I said.

"I don't know what to think. He may not want me in his life, but I don't think he wishes me harm. I think what he's really after is

Sophie's papers. Maybe he thinks I know where they are, and he's hoping I'll lead him to them. Do you know where they are?"

"I never saw them. Sophie told me she'd hidden them somewhere safe. I don't even know if they still exist. As far as we know, you're the only person to have seen these documents. Do you remember anything else about them at all?"

"Not really. Some of them were letters, but it was all in German. I couldn't tell you anything about what was in them, apart from the pages she left behind."

"Pages? You only gave me one page."

"There were two. Here, take it. I never want to see it again." She rummaged in her desk and came up with a piece of paper. It was badly crumpled, as if someone had balled it up to throw away and then smoothed it out again. It was in the same crabbed hand as the previous document.

"Did Sophie describe the contents of these documents?"

"All she said was they were shocking." Susan looked sad and worn out.

"I assume you had these translated. Did they mean anything to you?"

She shook her head.

"What kind of man is your father? I asked. "You said you hadn't spoken to him for several years. Was he a loving father?"

She looked at me blankly. "Yes, when I was a little girl, he was a wonderful father. That's why he can't be a Nazi. It's not possible." Her voice held layers of pain and anger.

It was all too possible. Many Nazis I had encountered were great family men. "And later?" I asked.

"When I was a teenager and in college, he was still wonderful. Of course, we had our ups and downs. For several years, he struggled on and off with depression, which made things difficult for everyone. There was a time when he was drinking too much. Sometimes he had bad dreams. But he got through it, and we were all pretty happy together. Until Elissa came along, and he didn't want my mother or me around any more."

"You're an only child."

"Yes. So was Sophie. I never had a sister. And now I never will."

"So you believe her? You think she really was your half sister?"

"How can I know for sure? But there was a connection between her and my father, that I do know."

"Susan, I'm going to give you the name and phone number of an FBI agent. She's investigating the attack on us yesterday. Please call her and tell her about the man who was following you."

She hesitated. "I'll think about it."

"Call her. She might be able to tell you some simple things you can do to protect yourself."

"Okay."

"And if you remember something else, or you just want to talk, here's my direct office number."

"What are you going to do?"

"I'm not sure. We need to get back to Washington."

"I have to ask you." Susan paused, her face stricken. "Who do you think my father really is? What do you think he did?"

My turn to hesitate, but we owed her an explanation after all she had told us.

"We're not certain yet, but we believe he may have served in something called Operation Reinhard."

"A military operation?"

"No, it was concerned with killing Jews. Maybe two million."

"Oh, my God. No!"

"As I said, nothing is confirmed. The evidence may disprove it. We're still at a fairly early stage of the investigation. And contrary to what you may have heard, we're very cautious. We won't take any steps against him, or say anything public, until we are 100 percent sure. But you must promise not to tell anyone about this conversation, especially not your father. It may put you in more danger."

She nodded. "Just tell me one more thing: What was his name, his real name?"

"Franz Beck," I said. "Does it ring any bells?"

"I never heard it before."

There was a long silence. I half wanted to offer some comfort, but it didn't feel right.

"Oh, one more thing," Lynn said, as we were halfway out the door. "When you phoned your dad and told him Sophie might be on her way to Florida, did you mention Mark by name to him?"

"Yes, I did." Susan averted our gaze. "I guess that was a mistake. How bad is it?"

I shook my head. "Probably not so terrible. The FBI has been briefed. If I need protection, they'll be there to provide it."

I doubt I convinced her. I hadn't even convinced myself.

When you're at war, you're bound to have setbacks. I tell this to Clint, but he's not a happy camper. He sits there, with a towel over his head, pressing a bag of ice against his wrist, shivering and moaning. I tell him not to be such a crybaby, but he carries on whimpering. His eyes are red and swollen almost shut. He looks like shit. "We can draw strength from this," I tell him. "We were tested and we survived. I got you out, didn't I?" It was a miracle I was able to drag the fat lug out of there before the cops arrived.

"You never said nothin' about them being armed," Clint says. "They could've killed me."

He has a point. I blame myself. I should have done the job myself instead of leaving it to him. But he begged me. Thinking about all of this, I feel a headache coming on, and I pop a pill to stop it before it starts. I tell Clint, "I'm gonna kill that bastard and his bitch, too, for what they did to you. I promise you, Clint, I will take care of him if it's the last thing I do."

It's time to go home and make final preparations.

15

Why this solitary tear?
It clouds my vision.

— "WHY THIS SOLITARY TEAR?" BY HEINRICH HEINE,
MUSIC BY ROBERT SCHUMANN

"WHAT DID YOU THINK?" I asked Lynn in the taxi back to the airport.

"I think she was telling the truth. I'm not sure it was the whole truth, but I ended up feeling sorry for her. Imagine someone announcing she's your long lost half sister and your dad's some kind of Nazi. Her reaction seemed credible."

"I agree, although I wish she'd kept my name out of it," I said.

"Some little things struck me wrong, though. That stuff about the gun club, that was ridiculous."

"What she said also casts Sophie in a different light. She wasn't a do-gooder devoted to truth and justice. She wanted to be Delatrucha's daughter despite his crime. She only started crusading for truth and justice when he turned her down."

I called Agent Fabrizio from a pay phone at the airport. "You just caught me," she said breathlessly. "That perp who was charged with the Reiner murder — I'm on my way to see if I can get more out of him. I'll call you when I'm done."

"I have something for you, too," I said, relaying what Susan had said about her father's ex-con gardener. "He may link Delatrucha and the murder," I said.

"We'll try to check that out. Gotta go."

Once the plane had taken off, I took the photocopy Susan had given me out of my scarred briefcase and smoothed it out. I started translating out loud, with Lynn writing down the English. The style was a little dated. I stumbled over a few words, but mostly it was easy enough to understand. We both leaned over to read the completed text.

The piano is a fine German instrument, a Bechstein. I was able to stretch my fingers and even my voice. After weeks without practice, I was very rusty. To think that music was once my entire life. Those days seem long ago. Still, sometimes I hear the notes of a song echoing in my head. The other day, I seemed to hear the sounds of Schubert's "Trout" — that much-loved song so dear to us both. I tried to banish the notes from my mind. They have no place here. And yet, though I perform my duties with enthusiasm, I must confess that I sometimes miss singing. My comrades were surprised and delighted at my abilities. They want to organize a concert at which I would sing for the entire unit. I told them music was in the past for me. There is no time for singing now. That time will come again after victory. Life meanwhile continues on its rigorous path. I strive each day to harden my soul. The future is not built by weaklings. Unpleasant jobs need to be done, and we are doing them. In the meantime

"That's it?" Lynn asked.

"That's all we have. It looks as if it continued on another page, but there's a lot we can learn from this."

"It's clearly a letter," Lynn said.

"Yes, he talks about the beloved song 'so dear to us both.'"

"And we assume this was written by 'Uncle Robert' to Sophie's mother?"

"Presumably."

"It's interesting that the beloved song turns out to be 'The Trout.'"

"Trout — Delatrucha."

"It was definitely written during the war," she continued. "By someone serving in the army. He speaks of his comrades in the unit doing unpleasant jobs."

"Not necessarily the army. Could be the SS or even the police. They were experts when it came to unpleasant jobs. It's frustrating. If we knew where this person was writing from, we might be able to figure out what the unpleasant jobs were. The more I see of these documents, the more I want to see the rest. I wish there were some way of knowing where she hid them."

"For all you know, she could have rented a locker at Union Station and stuffed the papers in there."

"If she did, they could sit there for the next fifty years without anyone finding them," I mused.

When we arrived in Washington, Lynn headed for her apartment. I wasn't sure I wanted to return to my own place, but no group of thugs was going to drive me from my bed. We agreed to meet in the office the next day to drive down to West Virginia for the weekend. I felt physically and emotionally drained, but it was nothing that a few days of fresh air, snow, and scenery couldn't cure.

The lights were shining brightly in the lobby. The landlord had quickly repaired the damage. You would never have known it had been the scene of an assassination attempt twenty-four hours before.

My apartment was dusty; I couldn't be bothered to clean it. The fridge was almost empty, but a couple of cans of soup huddled in the cupboard, and some old bread looked suitable for toasting. As I sat down to eat, the phone rang. Eric wanted an update.

"Sophie Reiner may have been Delatrucha's daughter."

"Wow! That is big news."

"The problem is, we can't prove it. That's the way it is with this case. We keep turning up interesting possibilities, but we can't prove any of them."

"Perhaps it will all fall into place when you arrive in Europe."

"I'm going to Europe?"

"I heard from the State Department today. The Germans have

tracked down some witnesses, and they've scheduled interviews for next week. You should be the one to talk to them. George is a historian, not a lawyer."

"When do I have to be there?" I asked.

"The travel office booked you a flight for next Tuesday night. Drop by the office tomorrow morning to pick up the ticket. After that, you'll probably have to go to Ukraine. Our embassy in Kiev wired back that the Ukrainians have identified a couple of witnesses there as well."

"Tuesday night? That means I can still have my weekend in West Virginia."

"Never let it be said that the Office of Special Investigations stands in the way of true love. But once you get over there, don't waste any more time. Just get the job done and come back home. Remember, the clock's ticking."

Again, I slept badly that night. I lay in bed thinking about Lynn, about what it would be like to embrace her and undress her and make love to her. It had been years since I had known such an intense physical longing. I literally ached for her. I told myself it wouldn't be a sin, even if we weren't married. The Torah doesn't forbid premarital sex, even though the rabbis frown on it. I had checked out the question many years before when I was in my early twenties and in the throes of a previous love affair. We were so dissimilar, though. Would Lynn be able to adopt my lifestyle? Would I be willing or able to compromise?

Toward morning, I dreamed my mother was warning me about something. "They're burning, they're burning!" she cried.

"What's burning?" I asked her.

"The potato pancakes." When I went into the kitchen, it turned into a vast field full of people. I was the only one wearing clothes. I started running, looking for a way out, but arms grabbed me, and I couldn't move.

Lynn and I had agreed to meet at noon to begin our trip. That way, I could catch up on paperwork before we left. I was nearly finished when the phone rang again. "Jack Doneghan called," a grim-sounding Rosen said. "He wants to speak to you. He said he'd call back within a quarter of an hour, and he wants you on the line."

"Tell him all the budget information he asked for is being typed up and checked. He'll have it Monday afternoon."

"He doesn't want to talk to you about the budget. He wants to talk about Roberto Delatrucha, and he sounded mighty pissed," Eric said.

"*Shit.* I'll be right up."

Eric was pacing around his office, bristling like an angry little terrier. "Mark, how the hell did Doneghan find out about Delatrucha? This is just what I wanted to avoid. I told you no leaks. How the hell did this get out?"

"Two words, Eric: John. Howard."

"Howard? I don't believe it." His voice shook. "I built this department. Christ, I *am* this department. What would he be without me? Just another little *pisher* wandering around D.C. looking for some big shot to pay him some attention," he said. There were times when Eric made it really difficult, even for people who loved him, to tolerate his egomania. But this was no time for recriminations. I had nailed my colors to his mast. I had to stick by him.

"Eric, I told you he knew we were investigating Delatrucha. He'll use any weapon he can against you. That Delatrucha has political connections makes it worse. He hosted a GOP fund-raiser for Conroy last summer."

"Oh, great. Now we're deep in the political stew. Watch what you tell Doneghan. Don't get him even more riled than he already is."

"That's rich, coming from you, after that dustup you had with him last week," I said. "Before I speak to him, tell me there's no way you'd give in to political pressure to stop the investigation."

"Of course not," Eric said. "*Khas v'shalom*, over my dead body. Even if it costs me my job. Which it won't!" The phone rang. Eric pressed the speakerphone.

"Good morning, Mr. Doneghan," I said. "This is Mark Cain."

"Cain, are you *totally* fuckin' crazy? Why else would you be investigating one of our nation's finest citizens and greatest musicians?" he snarled.

I envisioned him sitting in his office like Jabba the Hut. "I can't discuss ongoing investigations with you," I answered piously.

"Don't give me that bullshit. You know what I'm talking about. Delatrucha's a personal friend of speaker Conroy. Hosted a fundraiser for him, sang the most incredible 'America the Beautiful' any of us will ever hear. The speaker values his friendship and support very highly."

"He is a good singer," I understated. "Nobody's questioning that."

"Don't get cute with me, y'hear? You gotta have a very good reason to go after a man like that. The speaker can't believe what he's hearing; neither can I."

"Again, I can't comment, but I can assure you we're not 'going after' anyone," I told him.

"Not good enough, son. Are you trying to embarrass Speaker Conroy? Is that your game?"

"Nothing we're doing will embarrass the speaker. As far as I know, he is not connected to this."

"So you're not investigating Delatrucha."

"That's not what I said."

"Son, you need to remember you work for the U.S. taxpayer. You can't refuse to answer my questions."

"First, I am not your son. Second, I would like to help, Mr. Doneghan, but I will not discuss ongoing cases, and it's not your job to ask me. I report to Mr. Rosen; he reports to the attorney general, and *he* reports to the president, who presumably reports to God Almighty. If you have a problem, take it up with one of them."

"Son, you just destroyed your career. If you don't answer, we'll call a hearing and haul you up to the Hill with a subpoena if necessary. I'm telling you to call off this witch hunt. You're entering a world of hurt if you don't. Don't you know Delatrucha's up for a big prize in a couple weeks? The speaker plans to be there, and he's hosting a party in honor of Mr. Delatrucha afterward."

"Let the chips fall where they may," Eric said. "You might want to keep an open mind about this. If the speaker accepted money, even unknowingly, from someone who turned out to be a former Nazi—

and I'm speaking purely hypothetically here — I would think he'd like to know about it so that he could return the money before it becomes public knowledge. Good-bye, Mr. Doneghan."

Eric sat down next to me. "What next?" I asked. "Do you think he'll go to the attorney general?"

"He's a fool if he does. Don't worry about the politics. That's my job. You just focus on finding the truth."

"You have to do something about Howard. We can't have a snitch in the department undermining you all the time."

"Yeah, I know, but I can't fire the schmuck without cause."

"Leaking stuff can be a two-way street."

"What? Don't be so fuckin' mysterious."

"What if Howard were to hear some information about you . . ."

"What kind of information?"

"Something that made you look particularly unethical, something that would force your immediate resignation if it became public."

"Like what?"

"Like cooking up evidence, for example."

"I'd never do that."

"Of course you wouldn't, but what if Howard thought you had? What's the first thing he'd do?"

"Leak it to the press? Call up his buddy Doneghan, maybe?"

"Probably both. And if the information was juicy enough, Doneghan would go to his buddy Mitch Conroy. But what if the information turned out to be false?"

A slow smile spread over Eric's face. "You are evil, Cain. Pure evil. I never knew you had it in you. But it's risky, it would have to be done carefully."

"Yes, it would."

"Let me think about it. For now, take that pretty young thing and get the hell out of town. You'll be with your dad until Sunday?"

"Monday."

"If I need you, I'll call you."

There was one more thing I wanted to check before we left — that newspaper clip on Susan's desk. I went to my own filing cabinet

167

and pulled out a folder of newspaper articles, rustling through the papers until I found what I was looking for. The *New York Times*— on one side an article about mad cow disease, on the other a profile of none other than the famous Nazi hunter Marek Cain.

The sky was cloudy as Lynn and I left D.C., but by the time we crossed the West Virginia state line the sun was shining; it flashed and glinted through the snow-draped pine forest on either side of the road. It was a glorious day for a winter journey—our own *Winterreise*. The road twisted and turned deep into the hills. It had been plowed some hours before, but driving conditions were treacherous. Clumps of snow, melting in the sun, kept falling from the trees, sometimes thudding against the car roof. Lynn slept much of the way, the brilliant light sparkling in her hair.

Leaving the sky bruised a deep purple, the sun was already beginning to drop toward the horizon as we reached the dirt road leading to my father's house. Dad lived at the top of a steep hill, commanding a tremendous view of wooded terrain. The nearest village was two miles away in the valley below. The road hadn't been plowed, and the car would never make it. I parked outside the 7-Eleven in the village. Lynn woke up, stretched, and gave me a warm, sleepy kiss.

"We have to walk the rest of the way," I said.

"How do you know he's home?" Lynn yawned.

"He refuses to leave. He likes being cut off by snow. It reminds him of his childhood in Poland. I should warn you, he can be a bit abrupt. Don't worry if he snaps at you. It's nothing personal. He does it to everyone, especially me."

"How does he survive all alone?"

"He has weeks of supplies. You'll see when we get there."

"What about heat?"

"He has a big barn full of firewood next to the house."

It took us half an hour to trek through the snow, carrying our bags. To lighten my load, I left my briefcase in the trunk. The air was cold and bracing. Smoke was rising from the chimney as we approached the cabin. He didn't seem particularly happy to see me, but he brightened up considerably when he saw I had brought a pretty young woman along.

"Come in, come in, my dear," he said, grabbing her by the arm and ushering her into the kitchen. "What did you say your name was?"

"I'm Lynn Daniels," she said, holding out her hand for him to shake. And before I knew it, the handshake had turned into a hug. He'd only known her for twenty seconds, and they were already hugging. He hadn't embraced me like that in twenty-five years.

"Thank you for inviting me, Mr. Cain." She gave him her broadest smile.

"Pshaw, never mind about the Mr. Cain nonsense. Call me Jacob." He was already smitten. But who wouldn't be? "A cup of tea, or coffee, or perhaps some hot chocolate?"

Lynn also seemed quite taken with him and his old-world charm. I had to admit, the old man seemed pretty fit for his seventy-five years. His shock of white hair became him, setting off his vivid blue eyes above a bony nose that was getting more craggy with age, like the beak of a bird of prey. Suddenly, I was really glad to be there, glad to see him, despite the cold welcome. West Virginia would be perfect. We would sleep late, enjoy the scenery, and recharge. Just for a couple of days, I wanted to forget Delatrucha and stop the endless tape of Schubert songs that had taken up permanent residence in my brain.

"Hot chocolate sounds good," Lynn said.

"Black coffee for me, no sugar," I said.

"Marek, your office has been calling," he said.

"Marek?" Lynn asked.

"It's my real name. It's Polish. Nobody but my dad ever uses it." I said. "This person who called, did he give a name?" I asked.

"I think he said Eric."

"I'll call him back. There's just enough time before Shabbat begins. But after that, no more calls." I picked up the phone to return the call. "Mark here, what's up?"

"I had a call from that FBI woman, Fabrizio. She wanted to speak to you. I gave her your number down there. She'll probably be calling some time this evening."

"I don't want to speak to her until after Shabbat."

"Then have Lynn tell her that when she phones. Also, there was a call from Susan Scott. You may also hear from her."

"Eric, please don't give my number down here to anyone else."

"Give your dad my best." He hung up.

We dumped our stuff in the spare bedroom, and Lynn got to work with my dad, cooking up a vegetarian stew. He and Lynn were getting along like a house on fire.

To my surprise, before dinner, Dad hauled out a pair of silver candlesticks I had not seen since my mother died. "My dear, would you light the candles and say the blessing for the Sabbath?" he asked Lynn.

"Of course," she replied.

He said the blessing over the wine himself in an old-fashioned Eastern European–accented Hebrew that you rarely heard anymore. Modern Hebrew, with its throaty guttural stresses, sounds completely different. My father's blessing was like a message from a lost civilization.

After dinner, we played Monopoly. My dad was a demon player, buying up property like Donald Trump, building houses and hotels with abandon. I kept going to jail and not passing Go. As I sat around that table, I realized it felt like a family — a feeling I hadn't known for years.

Fabrizio called around nine. I took it, despite the Sabbath. After all, you're allowed to break Shabbat in matters of life or death. Lynn came into the bedroom to listen.

"Cain, why didn't you tell me this Delatrucha is so connected?" she asked. "There I am, investigating his gardener, and all of a sudden I've wandered into a political minefield."

"What happened?"

"An agent in the Orlando field office called him up to ask about the gardener. Delatrucha denied ever employing any ex-cons. An hour later, my boss is on the phone to me, asking what the hell I thought I was doing messing with one of Mitch Conroy's best friends without clearing it with the director."

"The director?"

"The head of the FBI — that's how high this goes. You can't go rummaging around in the life of a man like that without cast-iron evidence. Forget about investigating the gardener, buddy. It ain't happening."

"So that's it?"

"What do you expect?"

"My boss told Mitch Conroy's office to go to hell when they tried to lean on us."

"You both may find you have no jobs by the time this is over. I plan to keep mine."

"I've got bigger worries. Don't forget, a guy with a knife came at me two nights ago. What about Sophie's murderer?"

"Quite a personality. He still denies the murder. Says he found the pocketbook with the knife inside it lying on top of a trashcan."

"Do you believe him?"

"We need to do some more checking. Reynolds is fit to explode because his case is unraveling, but I think there are lots of holes in it. There's nothing in his record to suggest he's capable of murder, and he had no motive. He claims he'd never even heard about the murder until he was charged with it."

"So the murderer may still be out there."

"Right."

"And by now the trail is cold as ice."

"Right."

"Nice."

"By the way, tell your girlfriend not to worry about charges being brought against her because of the gun. I managed to talk him out of that."

"Thanks. I'll tell her."

"Any signs of anything unusual or suspicious out there?"

"No, nothing at all."

"Well, then, enjoy yourselves, and don't fall off the mountain."

16

Since the stink in the summer was no longer bearable,
the method of burning bodies on pyres was adopted.

— Testimony of Samuel Kunz

By six thirty the next morning, I had had enough of the lumpy couch in the living room. My father was already in the kitchen, eating his daily oatmeal. I poured myself a cup of coffee and sat beside him.

"You're up early," he observed.

"I've got a tough case. It's worrying me."

"What case?"

"I don't want to talk about it."

"Then forget about it for a couple of days. You can't always be living your work. This girl, this Lynn, do you love her?"

"I don't know, Dad. We haven't known each other that long."

"I knew I loved your mother the moment I saw her." He swept the back of a bony hand across his eyes. If I hadn't known him better, I would have sworn he was brushing away a tear.

"Maybe it doesn't work like that for me," I said. *Or maybe I didn't dare admit it.*

"Let me tell you something, Marek. I've only known her a day, but already I can tell she's special."

"Maybe *you* should marry her. She was smitten with you, too."

"Pshaw, don't make such stupid jokes. Listen to me, I know what I'm talking about."

"Dad, you've been hoping for grandchildren for years. Every girl I've ever introduced you to is the one."

"Not like this one. This one is different. She's pretty, she's smart, she knows how to cook. . . . What are you waiting for?"

"Let us do this our own way, at our own pace."

"Fine, do it your way. Just do it!"

We hadn't exchanged this many words in years.

The weekend unfolded slowly. I went into the spare bedroom and recited those parts of the morning service I was permitted to say without a minyan. As I approached the end, Lynn slipped into the room and listened quietly.

"It's nice the way you have such strong faith," she said as I took off and folded my prayer shawl.

"Actually, you know very little about my faith," I said, stung. "It may be more complicated than you think."

She shrugged. "I guess I'm an agnostic. I don't know whether there is a God. I do like some of the traditions, like lighting candles on Friday and celebrating the holidays, but I can't see the point of all the laws. How does keeping kosher help you become a better person?"

"It teaches you self-discipline, for one thing. It's God telling us not everything was put on this earth for the benefit of humans. We're allowed to enjoy food, but not without limitations, not without restraint. It's a good way to live."

"Doesn't that apply to every religion?"

"I guess, but we're Jews, so we do Jewish stuff, or at least we should. We've been doing this for thousands of years. It's what's helped us survive as a people. The prayers I say in the morning are the same prayers Jews have said for centuries. Touchy-feely Judaism doesn't have that power. If everyone thought the way you do, we would have disappeared as a people long ago."

She shook her head. Great, now I was driving away the one person I was beginning to care about most.

"Does it bother you, my being religious?" I asked her.

She hesitated. "Maybe a bit. I don't know what to make of it. I've never really known anyone who was Orthodox, much less kissed one.

Most of the time, you seem just like everybody else, but then you go off into this place where I can't follow you. I envy you a little. It seems like an easier way to live, having all the answers. On the other hand, being agnostic leaves your mind more open to examine ideas, I think. Life is uncertain, and I kind of like that uncertainty."

"I don't have any more answers than you. I struggle with this stuff every day. My religion actually has very little to do with faith and much more to do with how to live a good life, a life of value."

"You have doubts, too?"

"I don't doubt the existence of God. If I did, I'd be even more lost than I am now. But I still have to wrestle with the same dilemmas as everyone else in the world. Being religious doesn't automatically make you a good person or a happy person or even a wise person. It doesn't solve your problems or make the choices you face easier. It just gives you a rough roadmap of how to live."

"Does my lack of religion bother you?"

"You're sweet and kind and compassionate. I see how you are with other people, like Mary Scott, or my dad. They respond to you in a way they'd never respond to me."

She blushed a little. "Flattering, but you didn't answer the question. Does the fact that I don't believe in your God bother you?"

"I'd like to think you were someone who could share the things that are most important to me, or at least understand them. But what you believe or don't believe doesn't bother me at all. You don't have to believe in a laundry list of things to be Jewish. You don't even have to believe in God. But you do have to want to stay Jewish. If you couldn't make that commitment, then I would have a problem."

She looked at me for a minute, then nodded.

My dad only had one pair of cross-country skis. Lynn said she didn't mind just hanging around the cabin reading. I skimmed the weekly Torah portion, the first in the Book of Exodus. The section I was reading reached a climax when Moses asked God to tell him His name. God replies, "I am who am." Some people translate this as, "I shall be as I shall be." Either way, scholars have been puzzling over the meaning ever since. I couldn't help thinking about Roberto Delatrucha and all his names, wondering who he really was.

Then Lynn discovered our old family photo albums. I hadn't looked at them since my mother died, which is when we stopped taking photos. We spent the afternoon going through them. Lynn wanted to know who every single person was and what had happened to them. There were a couple of pictures of my grandparents, who had died at Belzec. Lynn said I looked like my grandfather.

"He was a wonderful man, my father," Dad said. "He was one of those men who could fix things. He'd go around with a pocket full of screws and nails, ready to fix anything that was broken."

There is a concept central to Judaism called *tikkun olam* — the idea that we humans are put on earth to repair the world. But my grandfather's hammering and screwing had been of no avail against the Nazis.

My father became uncharacteristically talkative. Lynn even managed to coax him into speaking about his childhood, growing up in Poland in the 1920s and '30s. He spoke about the excitement of going to the weekly market in the main square and watching the Jews and Gentiles haggling over their wares; of wandering through the Jewish quarter, where beggars pleaded for alms, and Hasidim with beards and sidelocks congregated in black coats; and of swimming in the frigid waters of the river running through the town and climbing the mountains surrounding it.

"You ought to write all that down. Or do a video for the Holocaust Museum in Washington," Lynn said.

"Nah, that's for victims and survivors. I got out before the madness started," he said.

"Some of these pictures from before the war are really wonderful, Dad," I chimed in. "I'm sure a museum would be interested."

"I want you to have these albums, Marek. If you wish to give them to some museum, feel free." He picked one up and shoved it into my arms.

"But they're yours, Dad."

"Then I'd like you to take care of them for me. I never look at them anyway. We'll put them in your car tomorrow so you don't forget to take them."

Lynn was looking at a picture of my parents taken some time in the late 1950s, shortly after I was born. "She's so pretty. What happened to her?" she asked. "You never mention her."

All life left the room. The temperature seemed to drop twenty degrees. My father held himself stiff and edged imperceptibly away from me on the sofa and closed the album. I looked at Lynn and took her hand. A glacial paralysis had enveloped me. I had to break out of it, and there was only one way to do that.

"I'll tell you," I said, holding on to her hand.

"No, Marek, don't!" my father shouted.

"You would have found out sooner or later. Now is as good a time as any," I said, disregarding him.

"Don't do this to yourself," he said.

"I was in the seventh grade, and I'd been sent to the principal's office for messing around in class that day. I missed the school bus; I had to call my mom. She said she'd come get me, that she'd be there in a quarter of an hour. It was a rainy, windy day, like when we drove home from Charlottesville last week." A lump formed in my throat, but I held my voice steady.

"I waited and waited, but she never showed up. I thought maybe she was punishing me. An hour later, or maybe more — I can't really remember — a policeman came and took me home. They told me she skidded on the road, and the car hit a tree. She was already dead by the time they got her to the hospital. That phone conversation was the last time I heard her voice." A huge, wrenching sob was stuck somewhere in my throat, but it wouldn't come out. I took off my glasses and started polishing them, blinking unshed tears from my eyes. Lynn's hand was stroking the back of mine.

My father sat motionless at the other end of the sofa. He was enraged, but he would never let his true feelings out. Since the day my mother died, there were two things my father and I had never done: we had never washed our dirty linen in public, and we had never expressed our true feelings. Now I had broken the first taboo.

He cleared his throat. "I suppose that you feel a sense of relief, of — what's the word they always use? A sense of *closure*." He said the word scornfully.

176

"I wanted Lynn to know what happened."

"Why did she need to know? After all these years, why can't you forgive yourself and forget about it?"

"Dad, I have nothing to forgive myself for. And I will never, ever forget about it, any more than you will. My whole life, everything I do, is based on memory. For a long time, I did blame myself. I told myself, *If only I'd been a good boy, if only I hadn't misbehaved.* But I didn't kill her. It was an accident. It wasn't my fault. I stopped blaming myself years ago. What I'm wondering, Dad, is whether you're ever going to stop blaming me. That's the real question."

A long, charged silence. Nobody moved. My father breathed. He stood up and left the room, closing the door behind him. Lynn said nothing. Now she knew everything about me. I had given her the dark key to my soul. We remained on the couch for a while, but there was a distance between us. I could feel her pitying me. Could a woman as lovely as the beautiful mill girl ever love someone as messed up as me?

Next morning, my father had reverted to his role of avuncular host. He was almost too jolly, cooking us a mountain of French toast for breakfast, singing the praises of the local maple syrup in terms usually reserved for a rare vintage wine. Clearly the previous day's conversation had never happened. I decided to play along. We were both masters at this game.

We drove down to the village in his four-wheel drive to buy supplies. First, though, we had to pick up the newspaper and wait while he went through all the coupons. On the way back, we stopped at the bottom of the hill, where my car was parked. At his insistence, we transferred the precious photo albums to the trunk. He acted relieved to be rid of them. Once they were stowed alongside my briefcase, he abruptly stepped forward and gave me an awkward hug. Surprised, I returned the embrace. Lynn silently squeezed my hand when I got back in the truck.

It snowed lightly again that afternoon, adding a fresh inch or two. For a while, Lynn and I watched the flakes falling. She read her book, and I fell asleep on the couch. When I woke up, the skies had cleared, and the sun was beginning to set. I decided to call Susan Scott. When I picked up the phone, there was no dial tone.

"Dad, there's something wrong with your phone. Could the snow have brought the line down?" I asked.

"It's never happened before," he replied.

The hair bristled at the back of my neck. My heart started thumping.

"You think someone's out there?" Lynn asked.

"I don't know. Maybe. I wish the police hadn't taken your gun. All I have is my pepper spray."

"Peppers? What are you talking about? What's going on?" Dad said, bewildered.

"We may be in danger."

"Danger? What danger?"

"Nazis. They attacked us outside my apartment a few days ago, and they may be here now."

"Nazis?" He laughed. "Now I know you're crazy."

"No, Dad, we're serious."

"There haven't been any Nazis since 1945. And besides, this is America."

"Not real Nazis, neo-Nazis."

"Ah, neo-Nazis. Of course. How stupid of me. That explains everything."

Lynn took him gently by the arm. "Mr. Cain, Jacob, I know this sounds unlikely but there totally are neo-Nazis in America, and they did try to attack your son. I was there. He's not joking."

"Who attacked you? What happened? What's going on?"

"I'm sorry, Dad, I didn't want to worry you. Lock the door, and I'll tell you everything."

"What nonsense! I don't believe what you are saying. Such things do not happen. Maybe in Europe. Not in America," he said doubtfully. He could see we were serious. Lynn went to the door and slid the bolt into place.

"That ought to hold," she said. "Are there any other doors?"

"No," I said and glanced out the window for movement or

bright colors that didn't belong. Nothing. If anyone was out there, he wouldn't want to hang around for long in the cold. The last hues of sunset were slowly draining from the sky; the snow still reflected a rosy tinge, but that, too, was fading. The trees in front of the house were already half swallowed by the encroaching blackness. *Maybe we could try to reach the truck and make a run for it.* In their place, the first thing I would have done was immobilize the vehicle. Too risky.

"They'll wait until it's completely dark," I muttered.

"Are the windows secure?" Lynn asked.

"All are barred except the workroom at the back," Dad said. "But the hill behind the house is steep. A person wouldn't be able to get in that way, unless he was a ghost." He still hadn't accepted that this was no joke.

"Let's see," I said.

He led us through the house. One window at the back of the workroom commanded a spectacular view down the side of a slope that fell precariously to a field of virgin white. A harvest moon — so huge and round it seemed unreal — cast a dim glow, floating low in the sky like a massive orange balloon. The window was just big enough for a man to climb through, but it would be difficult because of the way the ground fell away. If anyone tried to enter, we'd have time to take care of him.

What next? I didn't have a clue. There was a hunting rifle leaning against the wall, next to a pair of cross-country skis and a plastic sled. "Does that thing work?" I asked.

"It can take down a moose," he replied.

"Is it loaded?"

"No."

"Then load it. If I'm wrong, there's no harm done, and you can have a good laugh at your crazy son." I had no proof at all, just an incredibly strong feeling, but I was learning to trust my feelings.

"Do you have any other weapons?"

"I have a pistol from my liquor store days, a Colt Commander." He went to a cupboard and took it out.

"Will it fire?"

"I keep my things in good shape."

"They'll probably try to weasel their way in through the front door," I said. "They have no reason to think we'd be suspicious."

"Then maybe we should surprise them," Lynn suggested.

If anyone came, we needed to hit hard. I studied the layout. The front door opened into a hallway leading to the kitchen, with rooms on either side. At the back of the kitchen, five steps led down to the workroom.

"Help me lay this on its side," I told my dad, indicating the kitchen table, a massive antique that had been in the family ever since I could recall. We tipped it over and dragged it in front of the kitchen door. "Do you know how to use this thing?" I asked Lynn, handing her the Colt.

"You unlock the safety and pull the trigger, right?" She was amazing—calm, brave, beautiful. I loved her. And I was the one who had brought her here, leading her into danger. I'd give my life to keep her safe.

I made them crouch behind the table with their weapons while I took up a position by the front door. "This is what we'll do." I said. "When I open the door, you both shoot. Aim high, above their heads. If you hit them by accident, so be it. As soon as you've fired, I'll slam the door shut."

"Then what?" Lynn said.

"Then hopefully they'll realize we mean business, and they'll go away."

"*Hopefully?*" she said. She didn't sound all that hopeful.

"What do you mean 'shoot'?" my dad said. "You can't just shoot at someone. It could be anyone there."

"Dad, when was the last time anyone visited you on a night like this?"

"People never visit me at night. They don't come much during the daytime, either."

"So if someone does knock on the door, they're not likely to be asking for a jug of milk or a donation to the Salvation Army," I said.

We lapsed into tense silence as he digested this. A faucet was dripping in an upstairs bedroom, and the kitchen clock was ticking like a bomb. He and Lynn occasionally shifted positions, their impa-

180

tience mounting. After twenty minutes crouching behind the table, he'd had enough. "This is ridiculous," he snorted, struggling to his feet. "There's nobody there."

"Dad, get back behind the — "

A sharp knock on the door. Lynn yanked him back behind the table.

"Who's there?" I shouted.

"Police. We found a strange car down your driveway."

"What's your name?"

A pause. "Sergeant Jenkins," the voice called. My dad shook his head gravely.

"Which station house?" I yelled back.

Another pause. "County police," the voice replied.

"Go away."

"Open up," the voice shouted again.

"Get lost," I volleyed.

The door shuddered. *They're trying to break in.* It was only a matter of time. We couldn't just wait there. Biting down my fear, I gestured to Lynn and my dad to get ready. She nodded, leveling her weapon. My dad looked stunned. Not surprising, considering the way his entire world had been turned upside down in the space of half an hour. I just hoped he would keep his head down behind the table.

I waited another second, drew the bolt on the door, and swung it open as fast as I could, crushing myself between the door and the wall.

"*Now!*" I screamed. Lynn fired. The blast was numbing. The man in the doorway dropped to the ground, a big heavy guy, like the one who attacked us in D.C.

"Christ, they're armed! Get back, get back!" someone shouted. A couple of bullets hit the kitchen table, ripping scars in the wood. Glass shattered, and I switched the light off, plunging the house into darkness.

"Shut the door!" Lynn shouted.

The man lying in the doorway was blocking it. I slammed the door into his fat body, and he screamed in pain. He scrambled to his knees, and I kicked him in the guts as hard as I could. He flopped down, still in the way. One of his buddies pushed the door from the other side, trying to shoulder his way into the house.

"You're dead, you fucking pigs!" someone yelled. Then another burst of gunfire.

"Open it!" my father commanded. His rifle was sticking over the tabletop. Swinging the door back, I cleared a line of fire. His rifle boomed in the narrow corridor. There was a shriek of terror as I slammed and bolted the door. I dived behind the table. My ears were ringing. I was shaking uncontrollably. So was Lynn.

"Dad, are you all right?"

"So far," he said. He seemed unnaturally serene; maybe he was in shock. I was ready to throw up.

"What next?" he asked, revealing the strength that had carried him and his generation through so many horrors.

"*Hopefully* they'll go away now," Lynn mocked as a burst of gunfire smashed through the window. We hunkered down behind the table.

"You're all dead meat, you fuckers!" one shouted.

"Yeah, we're gonna slice you up and chop you into little pieces," yelled another voice, betraying a strong hillbilly accent.

"What do we do?" my father asked.

"Wait them out," I said with more confidence than I felt. "They can't break through that door. They know we'll shoot them if they try. Did either of you see how many there were?"

"Three, maybe four. Did I hit one of them?" Lynn asked.

"I don't think so," I said uncertainly.

A raw wind blew through shattered windows, billowing the curtains like sails. Thank God for window bars. We could hear them scurrying around the house, checking it from all sides.

Lynn stood. "I have to pee," she announced.

"Can't it wait?"

"No, goddammit, it can't!"

"All right. But crawl. And be careful where you put your hands. You don't want to cut yourself."

She crawled off, sweeping her path clear of broken glass.

"How you doing?" I asked my dad.

"I'm not as young as I used to be." He shrugged.

"Nor as old as you're gonna be."

Lynn returned. "That was fast," I said. "What's wrong?"

"Something's burning," she said. We all sniffed the air.

"She's right," Dad said.

Then it hit me. "They've set fire to the woodshed, maybe even the wood stacked outside the cabin." *Maybe even the cabin itself.*

What now? We had a little time, but not much. The fire would soon catch hold; the snow might slow it down a bit, but not for long.

"The back window's our only shot," I decided.

"They may be waiting for us," Lynn warned.

"There's nowhere to wait. You saw how the ground falls away from the back of the house. We have no other choice. We have to get out of here. Dad, I saw a pair of cross-country skis in the workroom. Can you ski down that slope?"

"Ten years ago I could have. Now I'm not sure."

"What if your life depended on it?"

He smiled. "Well, if you put it like that . . . What about you two?"

The smoke was thickening, and there was something else — the deep-throated roar of a fire about to run wild.

"There was also a plastic sled in the workroom."

"I use it for dragging firewood into the house."

"We don't have much time," I said. "Dad, get your ski boots on quickly."

We crawled back to the workroom. Opening the window quietly, I peered out. No sign of the enemy. The moon was higher now and smaller, a silver coin haloed in a starry sky. There was no choice. If we stayed, we'd burn to death.

"Lynn, you first," I said. She perched awkwardly on a picnic basket, swung a leg over the window ledge, and lowered herself to the ground. She couldn't quite reach and landed clumsily, scrabbling for a foothold, sliding a little way down the slope before stopping herself. I handed her the backpacks, the skis and poles, and the sled.

"Go on, Dad," I said. He clambered up and squeezed through

the narrow space. A fall now would be fatal. Lynn caught him as he flopped to the ground. I handed her the rifle. There was a large crash somewhere; the roof of the woodshed had partially collapsed.

I climbed through the window. "The fire's spreading," she hissed. "*Hurry!*"

17

I don't know what happened to me, nor who gave me the idea;
I had to go down there . . .

— "WHITHER" BY WILHELM MÜLLER, MUSIC BY FRANZ SCHUBERT

OUR BODIES WERE SILHOUETTED black against the snow. Had anyone been looking, we would have been sitting ducks. The first hundred feet were too steep to ski. My dad set off on foot, skis tucked
awkwardly under one arm. I breathed short, shallow breaths and
concentrated on putting one foot in front of the other while keeping my balance with the rifle under one arm and the ski poles under
the other. Lynn carried the plastic sled, no more than a child's toy.
Would it hold us both? Every few seconds, I looked back for signs of
pursuit.

Flames had engulfed the woodshed completely and were
spreading to the house. Snow sizzled on the roof as the fire growled
and hissed, like a savage, caged animal that suddenly finds itself
unchained. Sparks sprayed high in the air, as if from a fiery fountain.
My dad heard the noise, too. "Don't look back," I told him. "Keep on
moving." Salty tears were forming in his eyes.

Traversing the slope, up to our shins in snow, pants sodden, feet
frozen, grabbing at shrubs for balance, we moved as unsteadily as
toddlers.

"Another little bit, and we'll be safe," Dad panted. I looked back
again and instantly lost my footing. Lynn shrieked as I rolled down
the slope, dropping the ski poles, reaching out to grab anything to
halt my fall, finally crashing shoulder-first into a boulder twenty feet

away. The pain was intense. I ground my teeth together so as not to make a sound.

The others scrambled down to join me, Lynn retrieving the ski poles on the way. Where was the rifle? A couple of yards away, my dad picked it up and brought it to me.

"Are you okay?" Lynn whispered. One of my arms was numb, but that was the least of our troubles. A distant shout, barely audible, rose above the conflagration. Lynn's cry had alerted them; perhaps they had seen us moving below. They were coming after us.

"Never mind me. Dad, get those skis on," I ordered. The flames leapt twenty feet in the air, casting a glow on the two dark figures who had appeared at the top of the slope. One lifted his weapon to fire. I motioned Lynn to drop down. A shot sounded, then another. I aimed at the distant figures and let off a couple of rounds. There was little chance of hitting anyone, but maybe it would give them pause. The recoil slammed the rifle butt into my bruised shoulder. It felt like lightning shooting through my body.

"Faster, Dad!"

"I'm trying," he said, bending down to strap on his skis. We were on a kind of ledge — a natural hollow in the hillside that gave us some protection. We also had a clear view down the mountain, which continued to fall steeply away.

"Where should we go?" I asked.

"See those lights in the valley?"

He was pointing to a distant glow impossibly far away, beyond a dense wood, hundreds of feet below us. "Can you make it?" I said, as a shot echoed from above.

Dad nodded. "I hope so. The fresh snow will slow me a bit; that will help."

"How do we get through the woods?"

"Follow the slope down as far as it goes. There's a trail at the bottom."

"Once we get on that slope, I don't think we'll be doing much steering," Lynn observed. "You'd better say a prayer. If there was ever a time for your God to help us, it's now."

There was no time for praying, and God helps those who help

themselves. A shout echoed over our heads, followed by a burst of gunfire as the pursuers came nearer, two figures slipping and sliding down the hill.

"*Go!*" I yelled. Dad launched himself into the darkness and was gone with a *whoosh.* Lynn plopped down on the sled. I sat behind her, my legs on either side of her body, pressing myself against her back, my arms around her waist. A tight fit, but it was our only chance. I wedged the rifle in between us.

"Ready?" I shouted. Another burst of gunfire kicked up snow around us. I didn't wait for her reply. I shoved off . . . and we sank. We each shoveled furiously with both arms to pick up speed. Then we cleared the ledge and hit the steep grade. Instantly we were plunging down the hill like Olympic lugers. I tried to follow my father, but we couldn't steer the sled. It was hard enough just staying on it as it bucked and bumped its way down the mountain, sending jolts into my tailbone.

The moon was a glint of light in the corner of my eye. My legs were kicking up a shower of powder into Lynn's face. I lifted them clear of the snow, and suddenly, the speed was exhilarating. My fear evaporated. Like a little kid, I whooped aloud. With every second, we were putting more distance between ourselves and the thugs. We sliced through the night as clean as a scalpel. I caught a peripheral glimpse of Dad, bent over his skis. He shouted something, but the night swallowed it. The woods were hurtling at us, faster than I anticipated. There was no way to stop. As we reached the first trees, I tipped the sled sideways and we both cascaded out. A moment of panic washed over me as I released Lynn and rolled blindly, head over heels, mouth full of snow, face in the cold until . . . *CRACK!*

I stopped with a deadening thud.

My head was splitting, my mouth warm and wet. I spat, staining the snow red with blood. I must have bitten my tongue. Everything was fuzzy; I'd lost my glasses in the crash. Shit! That was all I needed.

"Lynn?"

"Over here," a faint reply. She was lying a few feet away.

"You all right?" I asked. She rolled over, groaning, and tried to sit up.

"I . . . I think so. Are you?"

"Lost my glasses. Help me find them. I don't have another pair, and I'm blind without them."

"You're kidding, right?" she said. "How am I supposed to find them in the dark, with a band of killers after us? I'll be your eyes until you can get a new pair."

"Just look for a minute, will you? I need them. They've got to be somewhere around here. I had them until we overturned."

We started scrabbling around in the snow. Lynn was getting edgy. "Mark, I'm scared," she said.

"Keep looking. I promise we're safe."

"How would you know? You can't see anything! Wait a minute, what's this?"

"What's what?"

"You're lucky. They're not smashed."

What a relief. The world was in focus again. Now I could see there was a dark trickle of blood running down her face.

"You're hurt," I said, wiping away the blood and finding a shallow graze around her hairline.

"It's just a scratch," she said, then laughed.

"What's so funny?"

"Oh, nothing. That was some ride. We're still alive."

I kissed her. "I know. I can't believe we did that. Where's my dad?"

"Don't know. Come on, get up. We have to find him."

The burning house was a distant glow. There was no sign of our pursuers.

"Listen," Lynn said. "There, did you hear? Over there." She was pointing at him, eighty yards below us, at the bottom of the hill.

"We're here!" I yelled.

"He can't get to us," Lynn said. "We have to go down to him. Do we need the sled anymore?"

"Leave it. Have you got the rifle?"

She nodded. As we approached, Dad was gazing blankly at the glow in the distance. His shoulders were heaving. I had never seen my father cry. I didn't know what to do. I put my arm around him. "You have insurance, don't you, Dad?"

He turned on me. "You don't understand a *damned* thing, do you? Do you have any idea what this feels like?"

I thought I did. His memories, his possessions, his treasures, the very fabric of his life — all of it was going up in smoke. Twice now, I had been the catalyst by which his life had been destroyed. How would we ever overcome this new blow? It didn't seem possible.

"I'm sorry. Poor choice of words," I stammered. He seethed, too angry and too upset to listen to my apology.

"You are a hunter of the Nazis, but what do you really understand? Do you know what it is to lose a home? This is the story of my life played over again. Sixty years ago, I ran away just before the Nazis destroyed my home, destroyed my whole world. Now the same thing again in America! *America*! The only difference is, this time I get to watch it happen. Do I have insurance? Yes, I have insurance. Thank you so much for your concern."

I was crushed.

Lynn put her arms around my father, who was shaking, with anger, fear, cold — who knew what? She kissed his cheek. "Jacob, he didn't mean it like that," she said. "Mark — Marek cares about you. Very deeply. He loves you so much."

He sighed heavily. "And you are a very good, very kind young woman."

"And luckily we put your photo albums in our car. They're the most precious thing of all — except your life. You still have that. And you have a brave son who loves you. You have a lot," she said, hugging him, trying to inject some optimism into the situation.

"Yes, I'd forgotten about the albums," he said.

"And Mark — Marek was very resourceful. He saved our lives, Jacob."

"I know that, too. I do give him credit. But right now, it doesn't help. It doesn't help at all."

We stood for a moment, watching the distant glow. Still no sign of pursuit.

My father turned to me. "Marek, I was harsh. Forgive me."

"Dad . . ."

"A house you can always build again. Come, we must go now." He turned to the woods.

He said it would take less than an hour to reach the highway, but it seemed a hell of a lot longer. We were soaked and aching from every limb. My shoulder pounded; a numb pain stabbed behind my eyes. Dad showed no sign of fatigue, guiding us around tree stumps, through undergrowth, over fallen branches. I had been magically transported back to childhood: a skinny, unathletic kid forced to go on one of my father's endless weekend hikes.

Eventually we reached the edge of the wood and stepped onto the road.

"Stop," I called. "They may be waiting for us." I peered up and down the deserted highway, but nobody seemed to be around. We had made a large circle and came out only a couple hundred yards from the 7-Eleven where I had parked my car.

"Which way, Dad?" I asked as he climbed into the passenger seat. He pointed backward.

About a half mile down the road, we passed a battered old Ford pickup, parked under a tree. "Wait a minute," he said. "Pull over."

"Dad?"

"I know most of the vehicles in town, but not that one."

The flatbed was loaded with large plastic sacks, fifty or sixty of them. The labels meant nothing to me. Lynn spotted a sticker on the rear bumper: two clenched fists on a red sun rising over a line of hills. Lynn wrote down the license plate and made a quick sketch of the bumper sticker.

"Do you still have any bullets in your gun?" I asked her.

"Sure, I only shot two or three rounds up there."

"Could you spare a couple more to shoot out this guy's tires?"

"It would be my pleasure." She beamed.

She extracted the weapon and carefully discharged a bullet into each tire. The gunshots were deafening in the silent night. Hissing loudly, the tires crumbled.

"Let's get the hell out of here," I said.

"What now?" Lynn asked after we had been driving for a while.

"We disappear. Properly this time," I said.

"But where?"

"Germany. I was scheduled to leave Tuesday night, but I'm going to change it to tomorrow."

"I'm coming with you," said Lynn.

"I also," my father added.

"What about your house?" I said. "There's sure to be police and insurance reports to fill out—all kinds of forms and formalities."

"Those can wait. I'm coming, no matter what." My father's voice was unyielding. Useless to try to dissuade him. And he was right. He deserved to come. They both did.

"Do you have your passport?" I asked Lynn.

"In Washington."

"What about you, Dad?"

"In a safe deposit box in the bank in Elkins."

"Okay, let's drive to Elkins then."

We spent the night in a cheap motel. Lynn insisted on sharing a room with me, saying she was too terrified to be alone. As soon as we closed the door, she disappeared into the bathroom, and I heard the water running. My brain felt like it was wrapped in steel wool. Still, the thought of her undressing and stepping into the bath made me quiver. I took off my glasses and flopped down on the bed. What was stopping me? Religion? No. Sheer cowardice. I could deal with gunmen on a hillside, but not with rejection.

I realized I had lost my *kippah* somewhere on the hillside. The room started spinning, and I closed my eyes. The next thing I knew, a hand was stroking my cheek. She was rosy and fragrant, wrapped in a towel.

"Your turn," she whispered.

"Huh?"

"The bath. Get those wet clothes off and warm up in the tub."

"Help me."

191

She pulled my shoes and socks off and warmed my freezing feet. I sighed, feeling another fierce jolt of desire. How easy it would be to pull away that towel, how easy for her to let it slip.

"Go on, Mark, get in the bath, warm up," she chivvied me. A strange feeling suddenly engulfed me, and I knew that I loved her. *Now's the time, tell her!* But I couldn't. "Hell of a romantic weekend," I said. "Where do we go from here?"

"Germany," she said and started laughing, but her laughter turned into a sob. I kissed her long and deep, feeling her heart beat fast against my chest beneath the towel. It gave me just enough courage for just long enough to spit out the words.

"I love you," I whispered, then again louder. "I love you, I absolutely love you."

She stiffened in my arms. "You are such a dork! Couldn't you have picked a more romantic moment to tell me?"

What? Didn't she realize what I had just said, what it had cost me to say those words? But she was smiling. Her eyes were larger and more lustrous than ever. She would find her own way to tell me when she was ready. "I just wanted to seize the moment," I said. "It's the new me."

"You don't have to reinvent yourself for me. I liked the old you well enough."

"It's the true me, the real me," I said. "You might as well get used to it."

We kissed again. But she wasn't going to return my declaration of love. My ardor cooled. "I think I'll take that bath," I announced.

"I'm going to check on your father. I don't like the idea of him being alone after the night he's had. I want to make sure he's okay." He was such a loner, it hadn't even crossed my mind. When I emerged, warm and clean, she was in bed, asleep, muttering to herself as she thrashed around in the bed.

At 5:30, I woke and thanked God for returning my soul to me. That short and simple prayer had never seemed so appropriate. I closed my eyes and added an even more heartfelt blessing on behalf of Lynn and my dad. Then I said the Shehechayanu blessing, which praises God for keeping us alive, sustaining us, and bringing us to this

192

day. Then I called Agent Fabrizio. No reply. I didn't leave a number for her to call me back. After what had happened, I didn't trust anyone, not even the FBI. Wherever I went, someone seemed to know ahead of time.

I kept calling every ten minutes.

"We were attacked again last night," I told her when I was eventually patched through. "They shot at us, then burned down my dad's cabin. I think one of them was the same guy who attacked us outside my apartment. We're lucky to be alive."

"Christ," she said. "Are you all okay? Where are you?"

"We're fine, but I'm not going to tell you where we are. We had to climb out a window and slide down a mountain."

"Tell me exactly what happened. From the beginning."

"Listen, I don't want to talk about it now. I'll meet you this afternoon, Dulles Airport, Departures Lounge, United Airlines check-in desk, five P.M. Come alone, no colleagues, especially not Reynolds. We can talk then. If you want more details before we meet, you can get them from the local cops. They're probably on the scene by now. When you call them, tell them my dad is okay. He's with me."

"How many were there?"

"Four, five maybe." I read her the license plate of the suspicious truck. "That's it for now. I'll tell you the rest at the airport." When Lynn woke up, she smiled and kissed me as if nothing had changed between us. I asked her if she still wanted to come to Germany with me. "Totally," she said, surprised I had even asked. "We're in this together until the end." *The end of what?* I wondered. *The end of the Delatrucha case? The end of our romance? The end of the world?*

We collected my father's passport as soon as the bank opened. He asked for a notary public and wrote out an affidavit stating he was alive and well and would be back to take care of his affairs within a week or two. He mailed one copy to the local police, and another to a neighbor in the village. We dashed to the nearest Wal-Mart to buy some clothes before heading back to D.C.

We picked up our own passports and packed, and I called the airline to book tickets for Lynn and my dad.

193

"There's one more stop I'd like to make before we go to the airport," I said. "My friend David Binder from the Anti-Defamation League is an authority on neo-Nazis. He may be able to identify that bumper sticker."

David welcomed us into his office and supplied us all with hot coffee and doughnuts. He greeted my father with enthusiasm. When we'd been at law school together, he'd occasionally stayed at our place on vacations. I introduced him to Lynn; he winked approvingly at me when she wasn't looking. I told him the story of our ordeal. It was the first time my father had heard it all from the beginning. His face betrayed amazement as each detail emerged, but he said nothing. David took notes, blinking solemnly through thick glasses like a great owl.

"So you want to know who you're dealing with?" he said when I finished.

"That would be good." I said. "Lynn, show him the sketch you made of the bumper sticker."

"I don't recognize this off the top of my head, but let me make a photocopy, and I'll do some research. It may be in our database or somebody else's."

"Lynn, make two copies. We'll give one to the FBI," I suggested.

"Whoever attacked you is not very good at this," David said. "They may be thugs, but they're amateurs."

"So we're being persecuted by incompetents?"

"Think about it," he continued. "Do you suppose for a moment you would be alive today if you were dealing with terrorists of even average technical ability? If they were any good, they would have killed you *before* you thought you were being followed. They had surprise on their side, and still they bungled it."

"They murdered Sophie Reiner."

"Assuming it's the same group. And even there, instead of killing her quietly and disposing of the body, they managed to carry out the murder in a way that attracted maximum publicity. Was that their aim? Not if they were working for this Delatrucha character. If she had disappeared without a trace, nobody would have missed her for weeks."

"Is that supposed to make me feel better?"

"Do you?"

"No."

At the airport, Agent Fabrizio was waiting by the check-in desk. She hustled us into a meeting room.

"You must be Mr. Cain, Senior," she said, addressing my father. "The police down in West Virginia say your cabin was pretty badly devastated. The fire department tried to salvage whatever they could. The police want to speak to you, of course."

"They'll have to wait," he said, yawning. "I'm going to Germany with my son. I'm boarding in an hour, and I'm going to sleep all the way to Frankfurt. Tell them you saw me, and I'm safe."

"What else did they find there?" I asked.

"Empty shell casings, and of course the remains of the fire. I gotta hand it to you, Cain. You may seem like this mild, scholarly type, but mayhem goes wherever you go."

"What about the tag number I gave you from their truck?" I asked, ignoring the backhanded compliment.

"We've identified the owner. His name is Burl Collins, thirty-two, lives near Elkins. We're gathering more information about him, but so far we haven't found either him or his truck."

"We shot out the tires to keep them from chasing us. They probably had to call a local garage to tow it."

"That's a good lead. We'll check it out. Did you notice anything else?"

Lynn gave her a copy of the sketch of the bumper sticker.

"This is excellent. It gives us something to go on. Very smart of you, copying it like that," she said.

"Thank my boyfriend," Lynn said. "He writes down everything. Seems the habit is catching."

"One more thing," I interjected. "The flatbed was piled high with sacks of something."

"Something?"

"They were labeled ammonia and nitrous, I think."

Fabrizio grabbed my arm. "Ammonium nitrate. Are you sure?"

195

"I think so. There were fifty or sixty sacks of it. Why?"

"Jesus Christ," she mumbled.

 "Why? What is it?"

"Ammonium nitrate is a common fertilizer — "

"So what? Maybe he's a farmer," I interrupted.

"— that can also easily be turned into an incredibly dangerous explosive. Add diesel fuel and a blasting cap, and you've got yourself an *enormous* bomb."

"Oh, my God," Lynn whispered. "If not for the snow in the driveway, they could have driven that truck up the hill, parked it outside the house — and we'd all be dead."

"Or they may be planning to blow up something else, something much bigger," Fabrizio said grimly. "We've been monitoring a lot of wild talk recently among these extremists about attacking the federal government. We know some of them have been experimenting with explosives out in the woods. Maybe it's moving beyond talk. We need to find these guys quickly before they can do real damage."

"Our plane is boarding in an hour," I said. "We're off to do some fishing. Maybe we'll hook a big one."

"Catch one for me, and let me know when you get back," Fabrizio said, without a trace of irony.

Now is not the time to get angry. What happened, happened. It was a fucking fiasco, there's no other way to put it — but it wasn't a disaster. The mission continues. I am more determined than ever to go forward.

Seeing the tires of Burl's truck shot out was a test of my leadership. We had to get the fertilizer and the truck out of there to a safe hiding place before the police arrived.

We had a hell of a night of it. Burl brought out his tractor, and we loaded all the fertilizer on the flatbed. We managed to stow the sacks in a barn a few miles away. Then we hitched the tractor to Clint's truck, towed it out of there, and dumped it in the woods.

196

Thank God for Burl. There's a man you can trust in a crisis. Clint spent the whole night moaning because someone fired a gun at him. He said he wanted out. I grabbed him by the collar and reminded him he took an oath of blood and he'd better stand by it. I also reminded him what happens to snitches. He stopped his moaning and bitching real quick.

Next morning, early, I drove to Charleston to rent a U-Haul. The police or the FBI might search the area and find the fertilizer. We all need to disappear for a while, especially Burl. In a couple of weeks, the heat will die down, and we can resume again.

I called a prison buddy and asked where we could hole up for a while. It took us the best part of six hours due south to get there. It's a good place. As long as I'm in the mountains, I feel safe. After the mission, I aim to head back to Knott County, where I know every cave, every abandoned mine shaft, every holler, every riverbed and stream. I can hide out for months, years if necessary. But it's not going to be that long. Once we've carried out the mission, the decent, patriotic, God-fearing majority of America will rise up. The days of this evil government are numbered. Someone must reclaim this nation before all our sacred freedoms are lost. I am about to strike a mighty blow for the Lord. The Scripture tells us, "And their dead bodies shall lie in the street of the great city, which spiritually is called Sodom."

I haven't forgotten about Cain, but I'm declaring operational silence until we embark on the mission. Nobody will hear another word until we strike. The time has come to speak with deeds, not words.

18

Because of the stench, the people in the surrounding areas left their homes.

— TESTIMONY OF TADEUSZ ZALECKI

THIS WAS POSSIBLY THE FIRST TIME I had ever enjoyed a grueling transatlantic flight. The plane felt safe and wonderfully normal. I ate the kosher meal, put away half a bottle of mediocre wine, snuggled with Lynn, and even watched the movie — an epic thriller in which the hero overcomes all the odds and saves the world, leaving a trail of bodies in his wake. The only thing I couldn't do was sleep. Lynn took out her contact lenses, curled up in her seat like a little kitten, and slept through the whole journey. Jacob also kept his word, closing his eyes just after takeoff, not opening them again until just before landing.

Eight hours after leaving Washington, we emerged from passport control in Frankfurt. I never thought I'd see the day when the sight of German signs all around me and the sound of the German language over the public address system would be so comforting.

George was waiting in the concourse. "You need to call Eric. He's frantic. He phoned me three times yesterday. What have you done?"

"It's a long story. I'll call him later. It's only four in the morning in Washington now. Let's get out of here." George led the way to a rented Mercedes and was soon navigating through the airport traffic.

"Nice wheels, George. Where are we going?" I said.

"First Würzburg. Then Munich. We've traced three potential witnesses who may be able to help us."

"Great."

"Maybe. It's not so simple. Only one of the three actually served at Belzec. It's not even certain he'll agree to be interviewed. There's a guy from the German Ministry of Justice with him right now, trying to persuade him to talk to you. He's been told he personally has nothing to fear. He's the one in Würzburg."

"I've never been there."

"You're in for a treat. Beautiful historic city. Baroque palace. Medieval streets. Totally rebuilt, of course, because it was so heavily damaged in the war."

"Sounds nice. Not that we'll be doing much sightseeing. I feel as if I haven't slept for a week. You said there were two other witnesses?"

"They both live in Munich. They may or may not be of use. Probably long shots."

"What about witnesses in Ukraine?"

"I gave the authorities a list of people who testified at war crimes trials about Belzec. Most of them are dead by now, but they found a couple who are still alive. Our embassy in Kiev is talking to the Ukrainian government about it. It's a sensitive political issue."

"Why so?" Jacob asked from the back seat.

"They're fiercely protective of their independence and very defensive about the past, especially their role in the Holocaust."

"They ought to be," I said.

"On the other hand, they want good relations with the United States. That might help persuade them to help us," George said as we hit the autobahn. He accelerated to 160 kilometers an hour, which I realized was 100 mph. I found myself shaking.

"What's the matter?" George asked. I considered how much to tell him.

"A lot has happened, including two attempts to murder us."

"You're kidding!"

"No, George, I'm not kidding, and please slow down. I'd just as soon get there in one piece."

"Relax, Mark. This is Germany. Lots of people spend their whole lives dreaming about doing what we're doing right now — driving the autobahn at one hundred mph. It's fun, isn't it, Lynn?"

"It's pretty cool," she said from the back seat.

Fast as we were moving, other cars kept passing us and disappearing into the distance. "My only dream is to find a hotel bed," I pleaded. "Please slow down, my nerves are totally shot."

George eased down to a more comfortable speed. As we drove, I told him about our adventures. The more he heard, the slower he drove, and the grimmer his expression became. A couple of hours later, we pulled into Würzburg, ready to confront our first witness from Belzec.

The first witness was Hans-Peter Spengler, one of the few Germans still alive who was known to have served as a guard at Belzec. Now eighty, he had spent a couple of years in jail back in the 1960s for his part in killing half a million people. Next on the list was Manfred Rudigger, a onetime aide of Himmler, who had accompanied his boss on many of his travels. George thought he might have been with Himmler on his trips to the camps. But Rudigger was nearly ninety. The last of the three was Wolfgang Schütz, a retired piano teacher, who was listed as Franz Beck's accompanist in his debut recital in Berlin — the one interrupted by the air raid.

"How did you track him down?" I asked in admiration.

"Elementary, my dear Mark. I called the incredibly efficient German telephone operator."

Würzburg was indeed a medieval gem, with a massive, square castle on a hill overlooking the city and a wonderful medieval bridge lined with statues of bishops, spanning a fast-flowing river. We were met at our hotel by Gunther Scharpf, a sober-faced man representing the German Ministry of Justice who was trying to persuade our first witness to cooperate. He looked at me, unshaven and unkempt, with an almost imperceptible shudder.

"Good news, Mr. Cain," he said in an impeccable British accent as we shook hands. "I think I have convinced Herr Spengler to meet with you tomorrow in the forenoon. That will give you some time to, ah, to freshen up, as it were," he said.

"The forenoon," I said. "How civilized."

We took separate rooms and said good night. As I headed for the elevator, George pulled me aside. "There's one more thing I need to ask you," he said.

I waited.

"Not here," he muttered, ushering me in the direction of the bar. "Privately."

"Can't it wait?"

"John Howard called again this morning, before you arrived. He's raving about how Eric's gone too far this time on the Bruteitis case. He claims to have heard that some of those documents Janet brought back from Lithuania with his signature on them were doctored." Eric had decided to try my scheme, and Howard was biting.

"Who told him that?" I asked.

"He wouldn't say. He just said it was a reliable source."

"And you believed him?"

"I don't know what to believe, frankly."

"George, you've worked with Janet for quite a while now. Do you seriously believe she'd forge a signature on a historical document or allow someone else to do so?"

He hesitated. "No, I guess not. But what should I tell John? He was almost gleeful. Plus, he keeps nagging me to tell him what I'm doing here."

"Don't tell him anything. If he chooses to believe absurd accusations, he deserves whatever he gets."

I was so tired I thought I'd sleep for thirty hours, but at three in the morning, I was sitting up in bed wide-eyed, flicking through TV channels showing pop videos, news, sports, and soft porn.

A knock on the door. Lynn was wearing a hotel bathrobe way too big for her. "Can I come in?" she asked shyly, looking down at the carpet.

"Sure," I said, leading her into the room while hastily zapping off the TV. "I'm wide awake, too. It's the jet lag."

"That's not what's keeping me awake. It felt weird knowing you were in the next room, sleeping alone . . ."

"As you see, I'm not sleeping."

"What I'm saying is, it felt wrong that we were apart when we could be together. If we could be together, that is."

"Lynn —"

"No, let me finish. I need to know. Am I just a ham sandwich to you?"

"Come again?"

"Premarital sex is a no-no for you guys. It's a sin, just like eating a ham sandwich, only worse, probably." She was tripping over her words, looking everywhere but at me. "I would never offer you a ham sandwich. I wouldn't do it. I wouldn't want you to eat it, even if it looked good and you were really, really hungry. And I know how you look at me. I've known for a long time . . . and I'm pretty much the same way with you, which is kind of driving me crazy — only I don't want you to eat the ham sandwich because you'd never forgive me afterward, and I couldn't bear it. Oh, God, did that come out as weird as I think it did? I always babble way too much when I'm really, really nervous."

Was she saying what I thought she was saying? I cleared my throat. "Actually, it's not like eating a ham sandwich," I said.

"What isn't?"

"Sex. The Torah doesn't ban premarital sex. Not specifically. It's not a sin." A pause. "Not as such."

"It's not?" she whispered, finally making eye contact.

"Absolutely not." Another pause. Suddenly, I was the nervous one. "Actually, it's an interesting issue. The Mishna says that if an act of intercourse is intended as a mode of betrothal, it's considered to be lawful." Was I babbling?

"That's in the Mishna?"

"It is."

"What exactly is the Mishna?"

"Part of the Talmud."

"Oh . . ."

"And Nachmanides was also willing to overlook such behavior."

"He was?"

"Yes."

"That's good. I never heard of him before, but he sounds important."

"He was. He was a famous medieval scholar. Rabbi Moshe ben Nachman."

"So Rabbi Moshe said it would be okay for us to sleep together?"

"Yes." He'd been dead for over seven hundred years, so I figured he wouldn't mind that much.

She giggled. "So it's kosher, more like brisket than ham."

"But only if we love each other," I said, anxious to ditch the meat metaphors. "I'm not into cheap sex. It has to mean something."

"I should have told you when you told me," she said. A smile crept onto my face. "I've been thinking about it and kicking myself. I feel so bad. But you'll forgive me because you love me and I'm telling you now, which is better late than never."

"Tell me what?" I said.

"I love you."

I reached for her, and she slid into my arms. My hand slipped through the opening of her bathrobe. Her skin felt impossibly soft. She shivered with pleasure. Her arms crept under my T-shirt, doing wonderful things. My heart was pounding like a jack hammer. "So you really do love me?" I whispered.

"Isn't it obvious?'

"Not to me."

"I felt like I was broadcasting it to the whole world."

"I want to hear you say it again."

She gulped, then looked straight at me with those wide eyes. "I love you. Totally." She shrugged her shoulders, and the bathrobe fell away. I gently pushed her back on the bed, and she pulled me on top of her.

"You're sure this is in the Mishna?" she panted.

"Promise," I said.

We didn't sleep much for the rest of the night, but I had never felt more alive, more complete, more ecstatic, like the narrator in the miller-girl song. At five in the morning, Lynn showered, and reality hit. There was a big day ahead. I needed to focus. I said my prayers quickly, covering my head with a washcloth to replace my lost *kippah.* My tefillin and prayer shawl had been in the cabin and were now presumably ashes. But that morning I prayed with more feeling than ever before, and all my prayers were hymns of praise.

It was already 11:00 P.M. in Washington, and time to call Eric before it got even later.

"What the *hell* have you been doing?" he thundered.

"What do you mean?" I asked. "You knew I was coming here."

"I've had police from West Virginia on the line all day, and the FBI as well."

"We spoke to the FBI before we left."

"What the hell went on there? It sounds like the Gunfight at the OK Corral."

"Something like that. But we're all safe. Lynn's here, too."

"This has gotten way out of hand. God, you're usually such a careful, legalistic son of a bitch. Now look at you. Do you know what you're doing?"

"I might ask the same. Do you know what you're doing?"

"What?"

"That bullshit you planted with John Howard about the Bruteitis signatures being doctored."

He chuckled. "You heard about that."

"Howard called George. I assume you roped Janet into your little plot."

"So he swallowed the bait, the little *pisher*?"

"Seems so."

"Good. Now that I have him hooked, I'll reel him in. But listen to me — I want you to be really careful over there. I mean it. You're on foreign territory now. The last thing we need is a diplomatic incident. By the way, our embassy in Kiev confirms they have a couple of Ukrainians for you to interview next week."

"I'll fly there as soon as we're done here."

"Don't waste any time. It's running short."

When we appeared in the lobby, our friend from the ministry looked glum. "I'm afraid there's a slight hitch," he said. "I just received a phone call from Herr Spengler. It appears he has changed his mind."

"Can't you get him to change it back?" I asked.

"He is a man of fairly strong impulses. However, I shall try."

We toured the Baroque palace while waiting to hear Spengler's decision. I gazed without interest at rococo ceilings and frescoes of plump cherubs tickling the breasts of plump women. My mind wandered. When we returned to the hotel, the answer was still no.

"I'm afraid he is adamant," said Scharpf. "All my efforts to move him failed."

"What's his problem?" George asked.

"He says, and this I believe is entirely understandable, that he doesn't want to reawaken painful memories."

"Poor fellow," I said sarcastically.

"Can't someone make him?" Lynn asked.

"I'm afraid not. We in Germany have learned the importance of respecting the law. He has no legal obligations whatsoever. He has paid his debt to society," said Scharpf. A man who served at Belzec, I reflected, could never pay his debt to society, to history, or most of all to the victims, but I didn't bother saying so. Still, it was a bitter blow. Spengler was the one German witness who had actually served at Belzec. If anybody could have told us whether Delatrucha was there, it was he.

"Maybe if I talked to him personally." I said.

Scharpf shook his head. "He doesn't want to see you. He made me promise to keep you away from him."

"And you promised."

"Of course."

"Now what?" said George.

"The other two, I guess," I shrugged. "But not today. We all need to catch up on our sleep."

Lynn and I didn't get much sleep.

Manfred Ruddiger, the second witness, lived in a nursing home just outside Munich.

"He's very old and quite frail," Scharpf warned us. "You must be patient and gentle with him." Scharpf seemed incredibly sensitive to the feelings of these mass murderers.

Ruddiger had been one of Himmler's secretaries from 1942 to 1944. He was in the second wave of senior Nazi officials tried by the Nuremberg tribunal and received ten years in prison for his role. After serving six, he was released and "denazified." He had enjoyed a reasonably successful career as a middle manager in a German corporation before retiring in the early 1970s.

The nursing home was in a pleasant little town on top of a hill. We drove through an attractive central square surrounded by historic buildings and a beautiful Bavarian-style church. "What's the name of this neighborhood?" Lynn asked.

"Dachau," Scharpf replied.

"Like the concentration camp?"

"The camp is a couple of kilometers from here, just outside the town. Perhaps you would like to visit after our interview, if there's time," Scharpf said.

"No, thanks," said Lynn. "It must be weird living in a place called Dachau. Imagine writing that as your return address."

Scharpf bristled. "What do you mean by that?"

"Why would anyone want to live in such a place? It's infamous."

"This place was called Dachau for hundreds of years before Hitler ever built a concentration camp here. It has its own rich history. For years, it was a celebrated artists' colony. People are proud of the history of their town. What would you have them do?" For the first time in our brief acquaintance, Scharpf displayed real passion.

"Change the name," George said. "They'd still have the history. They'd still have the art. Nobody wants to take that away from them. Leaving the name makes it sound as if they're proud of the camp."

"And changing it would be taken by people like you as a sign that they wanted to cover up the past. Besides, do twelve years of infamy wipe out centuries of cultural achievement?" Both men were heating up.

"In this case, yes," said George.

"Well, sir, you could just as well say the same about the whole of German history. You could argue that Hitler canceled out Beethoven and Bach and Goethe. You may view it that way, but our people have other ideas. I wasn't born when these things happened. Must I be considered guilty, too?"

"It's not the same," said George. "Listening to Bach doesn't remind me of Hitler. Living in a place called Dachau would. I can't see how people stand it. Commuting to work every day from Dachau station. Or taking the bus home to Dachau. But I guess it's none of my business."

"Correct," said Scharpf.

Was it significant that Himmler's assistant had chosen to retire here, of all places?

We met Ruddiger in a formal guest room at the nursing home. He looked like a gnome in a wheelchair, in a starched white shirt and polka-dotted bow tie. It was hard to reconcile this shrunken, toothless figure with the commission of the greatest crime in history. His hands trembled, liver spots mottled his skin, but his watery eyes still looked sharp and focused, and his expression was alert. Unlike most of the old men I had dealt with, Ruddiger was a big fish. He had been close to the dark heart of things. He would have known exactly what was going on.

His nurse said he received few guests. "His children don't come very much, his grandchildren never. They're ashamed of him. He doesn't hear too well, but he still has all his mental faculties. He's amazingly sharp for a man of his age, and he's been looking forward to this. It's a break from his routine. He insisted on wearing his best clothes. He even wanted to put in his false teeth, but they don't fit any more."

Scharpf introduced all the people in the room. "Herr Ruddiger, we want to film you on videotape," I told him. "Do you have any objection?"

His eyes sparkled, and he tried to sit up straight. "Will I be on TV?" he asked, tittering with pleasure. His voice was hoarse, and he slurred his words, making them difficult to understand.

"No, everything will be kept private."

"What?"

"I said it would be kept private," I yelled.

His face fell. "Pity. I like TV. I've been on TV, you know, and in the movies. People find me interesting. Well, never mind, ask your questions."

"Herr Ruddiger, tell us a little about yourself, your life today," I asked.

"What's that?"

"Your life here in this home, tell us about it."

He looked at the camera and smiled a ghastly, toothless smile. "You call this a life? I watch TV. I eat. I try to sleep. I go to the toilet when I can get this bitch of a nurse to take me. They don't let me drink or smoke anymore, why, I'll never know. What are they keeping me alive for? Is it so important I live to be a hundred? Is that to be my punishment? Let me give you some advice, young man. Don't bother growing old. Do yourself a favor. Die while you can still control your bladder." He gave a nasty, mirthless laugh, an old man's cackle.

"Do you believe in a life after death?"

"What?"

"Life after death. Do you think there is another world we all go to?"

"How would I know? When I get there, I'll tell you. Get to the point, young man. I may look like shit, but I'm not a complete block-head."

"Very well. Herr Ruddiger, let's go back, if we may, to the year 1943. Perhaps you could tell us what you were doing at that time."

"Let's see, '43, '43 . . . In '43, I was still with Himmler, that son of a bitch. He led me a merry dance, I can tell you. I remember one time when — "

"And in the course of your duties, would you travel to Poland with Himmler?" I cut him off.

"What?"

"Did you go with him to Poland?"

"He was in Poland a few times, I can't remember how many. I would usually go with him. What a shitty country. I hated going there."

"Thank you, Herr Ruddiger. And do you remember visiting Lublin?"

"Who?"

"Lublin."

"Lublin, Lublin . . . I don't know. I was all over Poland — Warsaw, Kraków, Lemberg — all sorts of places, each one shittier than the last."

"Herr Ruddiger," Scharpf interjected, "please remember you are on the record."

"On that what?"

"On the record. Please use temperate language."

Ruddiger snorted in disgust. I shot Scharpf a withering look that signaled him to keep out of it. This was my show.

"All right, Herr Ruddiger," I resumed. "We want to ask you about one particular visit, probably in early 1943. Himmler went to Poland. He visited some of the camps and also attended some kind of party or celebration in Lublin. Medals were awarded to people who worked in those camps. Do you remember such an occasion?"

"There were many parties, young man. We were always having parties. It was one long celebration. That was before everything went to shit. Those were real affairs, and believe me, Himmler had his own special ways of celebrating. I remember one time — "

"Herr Ruddiger," Scharpf warned.

"All right, all right," Ruddiger muttered.

"At this particular party, there was singing," I said.

"There was always singing, especially after a few steins of beer. We were always singing in those days." His voice broke into a quavering, tuneless rendition of "Deutschland, Deutschland über Alles."

"Herr Ruddiger, really," Scharpf interrupted in a tone of outrage. Ruddiger stopped singing.

"We're interested in whether you remember one particular singer. He was an SS officer, and he often sang classical German music — Schubert, Schumann." I showed him the computer-generated photo of Delatrucha as a young man. "Do you remember such a man?"

Ruddiger fumbled for a pair of glasses with lenses thick as sandwiches. He stared at the photo for a long moment. His hands were shaking; he dropped the photo and closed his eyes. The nurse hurried to his side, but he waved her away.

"I'm all right, I'm all right," he insisted, his voice shaking.

"Herr Ruddiger, can you continue?" Scharpf asked. The old man didn't respond. We waited. Finally, eyes still closed, he whispered, "You have it all wrong. There wasn't any Schubert at the parties I attended. The atmosphere was not suitable for Schubert."

"So you don't remember this man," I said.

"I didn't say that."

"So you do remember him."

"I didn't say that either."

He knew something he wasn't saying.

"What is it that you do remember?"

Long pause, wheezy breathing. "I remember the singing, but it wasn't at any parties. It was somewhere else."

"Where did you hear it?"

I leaned forward to hear him whisper —

"In hell."

19

The beast I'm hunting is death.

— "THE FAVORITE COLOR" BY WILHELM MÜLLER,
MUSIC BY FRANZ SCHUBERT

RUDDIGER FELL SILENT AGAIN. I stared into his rheumy eyes. He tried to avoid my gaze, but I held up the photo in front of him. "This is the man you heard, wasn't it?"

Head bent, he nodded, and quietly, he began to cry.

"Are you sure you can continue?" Scharpf asked again.

"Of course he can," I snapped. "No more interruptions."

Ruddiger looked back at me, his Adam's apple bobbing in the wattle of loose flesh at his neck. "There are so many things I've forgotten," he sniffed. "I'm an old man, a very old man. Old men are supposed to forget."

"Not everything. Not this," I said.

"But not this," he agreed. "Not the singing. I want to, but I can't. Weeks, months, years even will go by, and I won't think about it, and then one night I'll close my eyes, and I'll be there again."

"Where?"

"I don't know. I don't remember the name of the place. I only know what I saw and what I heard. I didn't do anything, I swear. I wasn't a participant. I was just an observer."

Across the room, my father was translating quietly for Lynn.

"Very well, you were an observer. What did you observe?"

"I remember this man. And all that was happening around him."

"You said it was 'hell.' Are you referring to one of the camps in Poland where Jews were being killed?"

There was a long silence. Ruddiger slumped back in his wheelchair. I waited. The only sound in the room was his labored breathing. He lifted his head again and whispered, "Yes, it was at one of the camps."

"Tell us what you remember."

"Above all, I remember the smell. What a smell, what a terrible, awful stench! Indescribable. The stench of death, thousands of rotting human bodies — maybe tens of thousands — and shit and filth and vomit and piss."

He swallowed hard. We all waited, even Scharpf, whose lips had pressed into two white, bloodless lines of disapproval.

"It was the smell of hell. If there is a hell, that's what it will be like. Perhaps that's where I will go — perhaps that's what awaits me. Even now, I sometimes smell it in my nose. I who can no longer smell my own dinner — I remember the smell of that place, and I want to vomit; it was an odor so foul all you wanted to do was escape from it. That's what I remember."

"But you remember more than just the smell, don't you, Herr Ruddiger?"

"Yes, there was more."

"The singer, what did he do?"

"It was a visit to observe the way the operation was proceeding."

"The operation?"

"The operation to cleanse the land of Jews. We were touring the camp, in the middle of that foul stench, and out of the blue we hear singing. But not just any singing. It was beautiful. Ach, if you could have heard it. What a voice, what a wonderful voice." He paused, wheezing. No one spoke. Ruddiger looked at Lynn for a second, grinning a humorless smile, and continued.

"We heard him before we saw him. We stopped to listen. Himmler was charmed — and it took a lot to charm that revolting old boor. 'Who's that?' he asks. We move towards the voice, it's coming from around a corner — and then we see him, under the ramp at the entrance to the *Schlauch,* the tube that leads to . . . to the . . . to

212

the gas." I could feel my heart thumping. I couldn't breathe for fear of breaking the spell.

"He stands tall and proud in his uniform; he's the very picture of young Aryan manhood, except that he had dark hair, as I recall. His uniform is impeccable. The prisoners — the Jews — they're listening to him as well." Ruddiger blew his nose.

"They've just climbed out of the train. Imagine: those people who are about to die, men, women, children, with their suitcases, all listening. You have the year wrong, by the way. This would have been 1942. It was summer. Swarms of flies buzzing everywhere. I remember the flies. Beelzebub, the devil, is the Lord of the Flies."

Lynn was pale, and she half suppressed a shudder. Ruddiger's eyes had shut tight. He was there again, not doing anything, not participating, just observing. He licked his dry, cracked old lips.

"Please continue."

"The Jews were hungry, thirsty. They'd been in those cattle cars for hours, maybe days. Many had died in there. The rest were smeared with their own excrement. They cradled their children; they were frightened, so very frightened. Most of them knew they were going to die. And then they heard the singing. He had a little orchestra behind him, maybe three or four musicians, prisoners I think. One of them was a pretty young girl, a violinist I believe. The people hear the music, and they relax and smile at one another because suddenly there is hope. Schubert! Schubert means this is a place of culture, despite the guards and snarling dogs. It means life. It means nothing terrible is going to happen. So when the guards tell them to undress for the showers and delousing, they obey. One or two even approached the singer to congratulate him, and he smiled back — a sweet, trusting smile — and he told them to hurry and get cleaned up."

"So he was not just an observer, this man. He was a participant."

"Yes. In fact, the camp commandant told Himmler afterward how much easier the singer and his music had made getting the people through the tube and into the chamber."

Now the crucial question. "What was his name?"

"I don't know. I never asked."

Damn! "After you saw him sing, then what happened?"

"Himmler spoke to him. I didn't follow. I think I found a quiet corner to throw up in. Later, we watched those same people from the train . . . inside the . . . inside the chamber. They held a little demonstration for us. Himmler wanted to see a gassing. I would have paid all the money I had not to see it, but I could not say anything. There was a small window. We saw them all . . . saw them all die. Oh, my God, my God."

Lynn was weeping openly. My father had never looked so grim. The video recorder whirred on, capturing the moment. We had just created an important, historical document. I collected myself; we needed to finish the interview.

"What happened to him?" I asked.

"Who?'

"The singer."

"I don't know. Himmler may have brought him back to Germany, but I never saw him again. Nurse, give me a handkerchief, for God's sake."

"And you're sure you don't remember the name of the camp?'

Ruddiger seemed to have shrunk inside his clothes. He blew his nose, shaking his head.

"Was it Treblinka?"

"I don't know. I don't think so."

"Belzec?"

"Maybe. I'm not sure. I don't remember anymore. I'm sorry. Now I must rest." He gestured to the nurse to take him away.

As she grabbed the handles of his wheelchair, Lynn called out, "What was he singing? Ask him what he was singing."

I translated.

"Schubert. I've already told you. Nurse . . . "

"Ask him which song," Lynn said.

"How do I know which song? Nurse, please . . ."

"Was it 'The Trout'?"

"What's that? What did she say?"

"Was it 'Die Forelle'?" I asked and sang the first few bars in my squawky tenor. Ruddiger's snivels turned to wrenching sobs.

"Stop it, stop it, for heaven's sake. How much must I endure? I'm an old man," he cried. "Nurse, take me away." I tried to feel compassion for him, but I couldn't. My grandparents had walked down that ramp, down that tube. The nurse wheeled him away. I hope he would remember that stench every day that remained to him. We don't believe in a hell where the wicked suffer eternal punishment, but if there were such a place, he would find a place of honor within in.

As an observer, of course, strictly as an observer.

That evening, the four of us went for a walk around Munich. I wanted to be a tourist, just for a night. The old man's slurry voice echoed in my head, and I could tell the others were deeply affected, too. My father wanted to eat sausages and sauerkraut with fried potatoes. "It's the best in the world. You can't come to Munich and not taste the sausages," he said.

I had a salad.

Back in the hotel, Lynn and I made love with a kind of desperation, as if we could blot out with our bodies the horrible things we had heard. This case was like sailing through fog toward a huge iceberg. The nearer we came, the more awful it became, looming out of the mist, massive and ugly. And I had a horrible feeling that most of the truth was still submerged.

And Delatrucha—he was now the Elf King, with his beguiling voice, luring children and adults alike to their deaths.

That evening, I called Fabrizio from the hotel, hoping to hear that the police had arrested the thugs who tried to kill us. "We got more information about the truck owner," she said. "But he and his friends have disappeared, gone underground. There's no sign of either them or the fertilizer." She sounded tense and worried.

"That's not good news. Where could they be hiding?"

"Who knows? They probably have friends all over the region. We don't even have any of their identities except this Burl character."

"Does he have a criminal record?"

"He's done some time, but nothing major—just penny-ante stuff like auto theft and drug possession. You can say that about half the people down here. That's not what worries me."

"What does?"

"The ammonium nitrate. For years, these guys have been talking about attacking the federal government. Someone might be nutty enough to do it now. The thought of a bunch of loonies driving around with a truck stuffed with explosives, it's — scary."

Our third witness, Wolfgang Schütz, lived with his wife in a small apartment in the center of Munich, not far from the famous beer hall where Hitler launched his first, unsuccessful attempt to seize power in 1923. Schütz had spent his life as a music teacher in a local high school and had retired several years ago. Alone of our witnesses, he had no trace of Nazi involvement. George had discovered that Schütz had fought in the Wehrmacht at the very end of the war, but he was never a party member.

He turned out to be a genial, white-haired man with impeccable old-world manners. He and his wife received us in a room lined with books and dominated by a massive grand piano. In the hallway hung a row of glass cases containing stuffed fish — trout, for the most part. We couldn't escape them.

My father, recognizing a fellow enthusiast, took to Herr Schütz right away, and they were soon comparing notes on fly fishing. Meanwhile, his wife fussed over us, serving coffee and strudel and an indecently rich Black Forest cake. There are some things that Germany has given the world for which the rest of us ought to be properly grateful. Black Forest cake is one of them. I said so, and was rewarded with another slice and a broad smile from Frau Schütz. Time to get down to business.

"As Herr Scharpf has probably explained, we're investigating the circumstances surrounding a song recital you played in early 1944," I began. Schütz leaned back in an armchair, stuffing foul-smelling tobacco into an old clay pipe.

"I was surprised when you contacted me," he said, puffing and sucking furiously, trying to get the pipe to draw. "It was so long ago. I hadn't thought of it for years. I don't understand your interest."

"I'd be happy to explain," I said. "But first, if you please, Herr

216

Schütz, could you kindly describe the circumstances that led up to that recital."

Schütz sucked on the pipe, and a cloud of noxious blue fumes billowed around his ears. "It was quite a grand affair for those miserable times," he began. "It was, of course, a tremendous opportunity for me. All sorts of Nazi bigwigs were there. The concert was under the patronage of no less a personage than Heinrich Himmler. It was organized in order to introduce to the nation a major new talent, a singer by the name of Franz Beck."

Schütz spoke mellifluous English, marred only by the occasional grammatical slip.

"I was only seventeen, you understand, and only by chance did I receive an invitation to perform. The truth is, many others could certainly have played better than I. But the choice was — how should I say — limited. All our young men had been conscripted; the war was not going so well anymore, and they were taking boys younger and younger. They took me, too, not so long after. There was an audition, I recall. A few girls tried out; I was the only boy. I was nervous and not so confident in my abilities, but the soloist liked me, and so I got the job."

"Tell me about the soloist."

"Franz Beck. He was considerably older than I — twenty-three, maybe twenty-four — and had served on the eastern front."

"Did he tell you that?"

"Yes. He had received some formal musical education before the war, I suppose, but even I could see that his technique needed work. He had a raw, rather untrained talent. But he had a wonderful voice, no question about that. Looking back, I suppose it was not a particularly expressive voice, but, no question, it was a tremendously powerful instrument."

"How well did you come to know this Beck?"

"Hardly at all. First, there was this disparity in our ages. We rehearsed together every day for about two weeks — maybe a little more. We would meet in the rehearsal studio and work and then part. I would not say that we formed a friendship. His behavior toward me was correct, never more than that. He was very demanding. There was no question the recital was all about him, and I was there to serve him."

"Did he speak about his war experiences?"

"Never. I once asked, and he told me he didn't want to talk about it."

"Did he wear a uniform?"

"No, except for the night of the recital, when he suddenly appeared in an SS uniform with a chest full of medals. That surprised me very much, as you can imagine."

"Were you aware if he was married or had a girlfriend or family?"

"No."

"Did he speak about his relationship with Himmler?"

"No, but it was understood that he had a powerful patron who was behind the recital. The show sold out, you know, unusual for a student performance."

"Tell us, please, what happened that night."

"Not much to tell. I was very nervous. I believe he was, too. We were performing *Winterreise*. I remember my hands were shaking. His voice was, as well, unsteady. I was surprised, since at rehearsal it was always so strong and true.

"We made it through the first song in a nervous fashion and the second in somewhat better style. It was then that the siren sounded. Almost immediately, we heard bombs falling. They sounded rather close, but people were quite used to raids and evacuated the hall in an orderly manner. I lost sight of Herr Beck in the dark."

"You have a remarkable memory, Herr Schütz."

He smiled wryly. "I should. That was an important night in my life. As I made my way into the street, I slipped and gashed my hand on some broken glass — quite badly. It took several hours before I could get medical treatment because the hospitals were full. Eventually, I had many stitches. There was a shortage of drugs and medicines. They could give me no anesthetic. Today, that wound would be nothing, but then, it was worse than I thought, and it became infected. Because of my injury, I could not be in the concert, and another took my place."

"So the concert did eventually take place?"

"I believe so. Maybe two or three months later. I could not bear to attend. And shortly after, I was conscripted. I never saw Beck again, and my hand was also never again the same. It did heal, but I did not completely regain my flexibility of movement. My hand was good for everything except the career of a professional musician." He sighed. "Perhaps I would not have been good enough. I'll never know. Those two songs from *Winterreise* were my only performance on the concert stage." He shrugged. "Ah well, so it goes. This was many years ago, and there is no reason to be sorry now. I made myself a good life as a teacher. I have the love of a beautiful woman." He beamed at his plump wife, who beamed back. "Perhaps it was never meant to be. I have no cause to complain."

"Do you know what became of Beck after his performance?"

"No. I often wondered."

"Would you recognize a picture of him?"

"Perhaps." I pulled out the portrait of Delatrucha as a beardless young man.

He studied it carefully. "No, this is not him. It is close, but not the same."

"You say it's close?"

"The eyes — they are precisely the same. Hard, determined. But the lips and mouth — they are not quite the same."

I showed him a photo of Delatrucha, beard and all. "Do you know this man?"

"Naturally. It is Roberto Delatrucha, the famous singer of lieder." He paused as the realization sunk in. "Do you mean . . . ?"

"That voice you heard each day for two weeks — is it possible that Franz Beck and Roberto Delatrucha are one and the same?"

"Never could I have imagined it, never! I know the work of Delatrucha. I even possess one or two of his records."

"So it's not possible?"

"No, I didn't say that. I believe it is possible. Of course,

Delatrucha is a mature musician, a great singer, a singer of subtlety and of wonderful technique. Beck's voice lacked that technique, that subtlety. He was young, without advanced musical education. But, yes — it is possible. The power, the strength of Beck's voice that I remember — you hear that same power in Delatrucha."

"But you couldn't swear it was the same voice."

"No, I couldn't swear it, even if I suspected it."

We said our good-byes. Disappointment again. We had added valuable background information, but we still hadn't proved anything. And now, our work in Germany was done. Time to send George home, while Lynn and I flew to Kiev. It might be our last chance to find the missing link.

"It's still the same problem — proving the connection between Beck and Delatrucha," I told George as he packed his bags. "I'm sure in my heart they're the same man, but how do I prove it?"

"What more do you need? Delatrucha said he sang *Winterreise* at a recital interrupted by bombs, and now we know Franz Beck also sang *Winterreise* at a recital interrupted by bombs. I'm not a lawyer, but isn't that good enough?"

"We need someone to identify Delatrucha as Beck, or vice versa."

"Ruddiger recognized him."

"True, but he's ninety. I need a more reliable witness, and preferably more than one. Listen, George, when you get back, don't talk to anyone about this except Eric and Janet, and especially not John Howard. He'll be pestering you for information."

"Don't worry. I'll keep my mouth shut."

My father, who had been very subdued since the meeting with Ruddiger, thought about returning home with George, but decided to accompany us to Ukraine. "I also have some personal business to conduct," he said enigmatically. I asked what it was, but he just shook his head and said, "You'll see."

Only twelve days left before Delatrucha received the McCready Award from the president.

20

During the disposal of the bodies, I also established that the whole procedure was not entirely satisfactory from the point of view of hygiene.

— TESTIMONY OF PROFESSOR WILHELM PFANNENSTIEL

DAVID RUSSELL, the chief political officer at the U.S. embassy, met us at the snowbound Kiev airport and briefed us on the way to our hotel.

"You've blundered into a sensitive diplomatic situation. The ambassador wasn't happy you were coming. This is a difficult situation for the Ukrainians, and we don't want to upset them if we can avoid it," he said, his brow wrinkled with concern.

"What's so sensitive?" I asked.

"We're involved in extremely complex negotiations right now. Ukraine has a large number of nuclear weapons on its soil from when the Soviet Union fell apart, and we would like them to give them up or send them back to Russia. We don't want them falling into the wrong hands."

"What's that got to do with us?"

"There's a strong nationalist lobby here with an anti-Semitic element, and we don't want to give them any extra ammunition against the government. They have elections coming up in a couple of months, and we don't want the ultranationalists gaining ground. The Ukrainian government would like to help you because they want good relations with the United States. On the other hand, they can't afford anything that would look like an admission of guilt for the Holocaust, which they view as a purely German crime. Which of course it was."

"I can cite thousands of sources that show it wasn't."

Russell was a thin, balding, almost chinless man in his late thirties. He looked at me with distaste. "Let's leave the history to the historians. I was talking from a political and diplomatic viewpoint. You need to understand: this is not a battle we want to be fighting in Ukraine — now, or ever. It's dangerous, and it's against U.S. interests. For the same reason, it's also very important that none of your activity goes public. Be grateful they're cooperating at all."

"I'm not interested in accusing them of anything. I'm pursuing one case about one man. Who have they found for me?"

"They've located two individuals who served at Belsen."

"I hope you mean Belzec."

Another look of disdain. "Right, Belzec. Their names are . . . Their names are Bogdan Kuznetzev and Ivan Voronsov. Neither one is eager to speak to you, but they both agreed under pressure and only after receiving assurances they would not be asked about their own activities in this place. Consequently, they're likely to be reluctant witnesses. The ground rules for the interview are that a Ukrainian official will be present at all times. The Ukrainians will also provide a translator and a note taker and will in due course furnish an official record. The interview will focus solely on this Beck fellow, and there will be no fishing expeditions for extra information. The embassy has agreed to all this on your behalf. The ambassador has instructed me to obtain your specific consent before proceeding. Do you agree?"

"I guess."

"Guessing doesn't cut it. I need to hear from you specifically and unambiguously that you agree to the conditions I've laid out."

"I agree. When can I meet them?"

"They both live in L'viv. We can drive there tomorrow. You can meet them early next week."

L'viv, formerly known as Lwów, was a beautiful Baroque city being strangled to death by the modern world. Cars and trucks clogged its narrow medieval streets, belching clouds of foul-smelling exhaust into a putrid sky. As we arrived, I caught glimpses through the car window of lovely old buildings crowned with terra-cotta roofs, of statues and fountains and elegant church spires. But an all-encompassing smog hung low over the city. Ukraine had yet to discover the benefits of lead-free gasoline, and you could smell the difference. The air itself felt sooty.

We had to wait a day to meet our witnesses. I spent the morning in the hotel, watching Mitch Conroy being sworn in as the new speaker of the House of Representatives on CNN. The unmistakable Jack Doneghan stood in the background, grinning ominously.

In the afternoon, Lynn, my father, and I took a walk. The city was enjoying an unseasonable mild spell, and the snow in the streets had melted into brown slush. We found the Goldene Royz synagogue, ruined by the Nazis in 1941. It was built by a Jewish merchant in the sixteenth century, and only a few traces of its once-glorious Gothic interior remained. Down the street, to my surprise, was a small office with Hebrew writing on the door declaring that it was headquarters of the Chabad Lubavitch movement. Inside, a young man with sidelocks was sitting behind a desk.

"Do you have a daily minyan here?" I asked, after introducing myself. He said they did, and I was welcome to take part. There were still a few Jews in the city, he said, and the community was showing some signs of revival. Next door, there was even a Jewish nursery school, which had recently opened. I made a small contribution and bought a new *kippah, tallis,* and tefillin.

Next day, we were driven to an imposing government building near the central square, where we were introduced to an official of the Ukrainian Foreign Ministry, another from the Justice Ministry, and an interpreter. My father, who understood some Russian, took his own notes and made sure my questions were accurately translated.

We were ushered into a room to find two old men sitting behind a table. They each wore identical flat cloth hats and shabby gray suits, brought out of mothballs for the occasion. The suits were a couple of sizes too large for each man. They had probably once fit, but the men had shrunk over the years. They were smoking cheap Russian cigarettes. They stood up as we entered and offered mottled, nicotine-stained hands for us to shake. The stains on Sophie Reiner's fingers flashed into my mind as I grasped an outstretched hand that trembled in my grasp.

In George's absence, Lynn was to operate the video camera. As she opened the case, the first problem arose. "No video, absolutely not," said the man from the Justice Ministry.

"For the record," I said.

"No. We will provide an official transcript of the meeting, which both sides will sign. That will constitute the record. The faces of our citizens are not to be filmed."

"Very well, no video." I sighed.

They were both in their seventies and showed the effects of hard, unhealthy lives. They looked remarkably similar, almost like brothers. Their noses were spattered by networks of tiny red veins. Their eyes were dull and watery, their mouths full of gold teeth that glinted when they spoke. Both were racked by incessant bouts of phlegmy coughing.

The one who had shaken my hand stubbed his cigarette into an ashtray already overflowing with butts. The other gave me a nervous leer. He had spotted my yarmulke and flashed his colleague a knowing look.

"Perhaps the gentlemen could describe how they came to be at Belzec," I began.

"Out of order," snapped the man from the Justice Ministry. "Not relevant to the subject of the inquiry."

"I'm trying to establish some context."

"What you call *context* is irrelevant. Kindly ask your next question," said the official, his bushy eyebrows twitching.

"Could the gentlemen tell me where they lived at Belzec?"

"Not relevant!" His eyebrows were almost up to his hairline.

I bristled. Russell grabbed my arm to stop me from saying something we would all regret. "Perhaps you could give us five minutes while I consult with my colleague," he said.

We stepped into a corridor lined with buckets to catch the water leaking through the roof.

"Cain, you promised to stick to the agreement," he said, glaring at me.

"This is absurd. I wanted to know if they shared living quarters with the SS. The question is legitimate."

"Stick to what you really need, okay? Otherwise everyone is going to get angry, and you'll end up with nothing. You don't need to know who lived with whom or what they had for dinner."

We returned to the room.

"Very well. I apologize for the irrelevance of my earlier questions." I said. "Could either of the gentlemen please tell me if they recall an orchestra or musical band at Belzec?" The translator translated. After a brief pause, the two old men looked at the official for permission to answer, then mumbled between themselves when he nodded his approval. Eventually, one offered a response, speaking haltingly. When he was finished, the other added a few words. The translator took copious notes, then relayed the answer.

"There was a small band. You could not really call it an orchestra. The number of players varied as people came and went," the interpreter said.

"What people?"

"Musicians. New musicians arrived in the camp and were added from time to time. Usually there were four or five players."

"Who was in charge of it?"

"An SS man ran it."

"When did it perform?" One of the men was seized by a burst of coughing. He spat into a filthy handkerchief before responding. "It played sometimes in the evening for the entertainment of the Germans, who occasionally had parties, and also when the transports arrived. It helped calm the visitors as they were getting off the trains."

"Did he just say 'visitors'?" Lynn interrupted.

The translator referred to his notes. "Yes, that's the word he used."

"I take it by visitors, he means specifically Jewish visitors, who arrived at the camp to be murdered," I said, taking up the point.

Both men nodded, expressionless.

"What kind of music did they play?" I asked.

The men consulted. One shrugged his shoulders and answered, "It was mainly German music — marches, waltzes, polkas, that kind of thing."

"Do they recall anything about the SS man in charge?"

Another consultation. "He was young, not very tall; we don't remember his name. He was just another SS man."

"What did he do? Did he conduct, did he play?"

"He conducted. Sometimes he joined in the music. He had a nice singing voice, very deep, almost like a Russian voice. He was popular with the Jews when they arrived. Also, he often sang in the evening at the parties the Germans had."

"Can the gentlemen remember any of the people in the orchestra?"

A longer, much more animated conversation.

"One was a pretty young girl — nice body, good pair of breasts, cute face — if you like that type."

"What type?"

"Dark, Jewish looks."

"I see. What did she play?"

"The violin. There was talk the SS man was sweet on her."

"What do they mean, sweet on her?"

"He had a soft spot for her, protected her, got her food. We assume he was fucking her."

Interesting. I remembered the first journal extract Susan Scott had given me. What did it say? "*I know in some sense she is not fully human, but who of us is in this place? And yet her form is human and lovely.*" Was this the mysterious creature from the diary?

"Was that allowed between the SS and a Jewish woman?" I continued.

"It happened. They had their urges." "*I am but a man. I will be strong. This is a test of my will, and I shall not fail it.*" Perhaps he had failed.

226

As the interview progressed, the two Ukrainians relaxed, even enjoyed the proceedings, lighting one cigarette after another, inhaling deeply, coughing with abandon. They made me want to puke. I handed over the photo-simulation of the young Roberto Delatrucha.

"Is this the man they remember?" They both studied it carefully, consulted with each other, then shrugged.

"We're not sure. It was a long time ago. It looks familiar, but we can't say for sure," the interpreter said. I was fast losing patience with the whole business. It was hardly surprising their memories were fuzzy. The Ukrainians and many of the Germans at the extermination camp had spent much of their time in a drunken stupor, their way of blocking out the horror. We wouldn't get the evidence we needed here. These two old men certainly remembered Franz Beck, but they didn't even know his name. My last chance of nailing Delatrucha was vanishing into the smoggy air of L'viv.

"Please thank the gentlemen for their help," I told the interpreter.

"Is that it?" asked the man for the Justice Ministry.

"That's it."

"Wait. One more question," Lynn interrupted. "Ask them what happened to the musicians, especially the young girl, the violinist."

The interpreter translated the question, which the Ukrainians found amusing. One of them looked at Lynn and began to chuckle — a donkeylike bray that set my teeth on edge.

"What's so funny?" Lynn said, distressed.

The old man began to speak. The interpreter scribbled notes. "Everybody had the same fate there, whether they could play the violin or not. It wasn't a holiday camp, after all."

"She was gassed?"

"Everyone who was not gassed was shot." The old man cackled. Lynn gasped, which only made him cackle some more. My father looked ready to punch the man. We left.

We reconvened in a café, and I pulled out the journal extract Susan Scott had given me. Now that we knew of the Jewish violin girl, the brief sentences held an unbearable emotional weight.

July 1, 1942.

I think of her night and day. I know it's wrong. I know in some sense she is not fully human, but who of us in this place is? And yet her form is human and lovely, and I am but a man. I will be strong. This is a test of my will, and I shall not fail it.

My heart broke. The poor girl. What must her life have been like, her only hope of survival resting on this Nazi who was determined to suppress every human emotion?

"We're only a couple of hours away," my father said. "It's just across the border. I looked at a map. I want to go there."

"Go where?"

"Belzec. I want to see the place where my parents died, the place where all these terrible things happened. I never said Kaddish for my parents. I told you I had personal business."

"This is your personal business? Saying Kaddish?"

"This is why I came with you to Ukraine."

Strange. After weeks of immersing myself in Belzec, I had somehow forgotten it was a real place that we could actually visit. Now that I had the chance, I wasn't sure if I wanted to go. What would I see? — and what I would feel?

21

When tears flow here, you will realize
If there was no other sign,
That I was here.

— "That She Was Here" by Friedrich Rückert,
music by Franz Schubert

Next morning, I wandered the streets looking for a place to buy some flowers — obviously the wrong time of the year. A few sorry blooms were laid out on the tables of the restaurant at the hotel, already several days old. It took a while to explain the situation, but I finessed the manager into letting me have the lot for twenty bucks, which he pocketed, looking very pleased with himself.

Belzec was less than fifty miles from L'viv — a couple of hours on the poor roads — but I hadn't counted on a two-hour delay crossing the Ukrainian-Polish border. We arrived in Belzec in the early afternoon on another mild, overcast day. It was a shabby little place, maybe a couple of thousand residents, nestled in thick pine forests. Most of the snow had melted, leaving dirty puddles flanking the pot-holed street that ran through the center of the village. Our rented Fiat appeared to be the only car in town. The streets were deserted. We circled the village center for a few minutes, looking for the way to the camp, a mile or two out of town.

"Strange," Lynn noted. "You'd think there would be a signpost. People must come here to pay their respects." But there was none.

"Quick, ask her," I said, spotting a teenage girl crossing the road.

My father rolled down the car window. "Where's the memorial?"

he asked in Polish. She shook her head and muttered a few words. "She doesn't know," he said.

"This is the right place, isn't it?" Lynn asked. She had a point, but how many places called Belzec could there be? How could you live in a place where half a million people were slaughtered within living memory and not know anything about it?

A young man was coming out of a shabby grocery shop smoking a cigarette. He, too, shook his head. Then Lynn caught sight of an old man walking down the street.

"Ask him. He'll know. He looks old enough to have been here then."

"Excuse me, sir. Can you direct us to the memorial?" my father asked.

The old-timer shook his head. "What memorial?"

"Well, the museum then."

"What museum? There's no museum here."

"The place where they burned the Jews," my father snapped. The man scowled, baring a toothless mouth, and retorted in Polish.

"What's he saying?" I asked. My dad's face was white and drawn with anger.

"He says we shouldn't bother going there because there's nothing to see except a memorial for the Jews, as if their lives were worth more than all the Poles who died in the war. Welcome to Poland, land of my youth."

My father addressed the man again, who shrugged his shoulders and pointed vaguely ahead. "He says it's two kilometers this way, near where you cross the railway tracks," my father said.

We had passed it without noticing on our way into the village. The only sign acknowledging the site was half hidden behind some trees and coated with rust. Next to it was another, larger sign advertising agricultural vehicles. We turned onto a muddy track crossing a railroad line — the same line that brought the victims to their deaths all those years ago. The path ended beside a house, from which we could hear pop music blaring. It felt like the most desolate place on earth. Drizzle dripped from the leaky gray sky. There was a palpable sense of evil about this place, deserted and forgotten as it was. We sat in the car for a couple of minutes, not speaking.

My father clearly felt the same reluctance as I did. Neither of us had spoken more than a couple of words the entire way from L'viv. I was almost afraid to set foot inside. He opened the car door.

"We came halfway around the world," he said. "Let's see what there is to see." I took the flowers and followed him through the wrought-iron gate that led into Belzec.

At the entrance stood a large map of the layout of the camp as it had been. It was written only in Polish.

"Where do you suppose he stood with his band, singing?' Lynn asked.

My father studied the map. "Right here," he said. "Just about where we're standing now." Ahead of us would have been the *Schlauch*, the tube that led to the gas chambers. We walked between clumps of bedraggled trees — silver birches, pale and anemic, trunks like malnourished limbs. A faint wind blew, rustling an image of a Christian saint hanging from the branches of one of the birches. The Nazis had planted these trees after they burned the bodies and tore down the camp, as a way of covering up the crime. Just beyond the wire fence enclosing the site, a sawmill was working. Only the high-pitched whine of machinery punctured the silence.

A hundred yards beyond the gate stood the memorial, if you could even call it that. Five crumbling steps led up to a metal sculpture of two emaciated figures, one holding up the other by the shoulders. An image of people struggling to survive oppression, no doubt, but these two figures seemed horribly inappropriate, like space aliens from comic books. They looked like somebody's idea of a bad joke, a caricature of the real humans who had died here. Behind them stood a wall of discolored marble, marred by cracks and fissures, in which was carved a Polish inscription.

"In memory of the victims of Hitler's terror murdered from 1942 to 1943," my father translated.

"It doesn't say anything about the victims being Jewish." I noted. He shook his head.

In fact, there were no Jewish symbols here at all. We were standing in a place forgotten by the world. Who remembered the victims now? It was as if they had never been. Yet each had been a human being, an entire universe unto himself. Now they were just a number conveniently rounded to the nearest hundred thousand — 500,000 victims of "terror" who weren't even classified as Jews. I laid the flowers on the ground below the sculpture and noticed traces of *yizkor* memorial candles. So some people did come here seeking comfort. It was hard to imagine them finding any.

"Marek, do you have your prayer book?" my father asked softly.

"Yes, of course."

"Please, help me say Kaddish. I've forgotten the words."

I bent my head. Softly, together with him, I recited the words, which affirm the greatness of God. Lynn joined in as well. Strange, the power of these words for a person who did not believe in God at all.

When we looked up, a little dog was sniffing around at the flowers. Tail wagging, it lifted its hind leg and pissed on the steps of the memorial. "No," my father said in a choked voice, convulsed by great, shuddering sobs. "O God, O God," he wailed. "My mother, my poor mother. What she must have suffered."

In my whole life, I had never seen my father cry. I had now witnessed it twice in as many weeks. "It's okay, Dad," I said, hugging him, feeling stiff and embarrassed.

"Oh, Marek, Marek," he sobbed, "I wish my parents could have seen you. They would have been so proud of you. And your mother, too. She would have been so proud of the man you have become."

As I choked up, Lynn put an arm around us both. We three stood there for a moment in an awkward triangle. My father broke the union abruptly, turned away, and walked into the woods beyond the statue. Lynn followed him. I gazed at the trees, and a quotation from the Shabbat service came into my head as I stood there: *"It is a tree of life for those who grasp it, and its ways are ways of pleasantness."* But there was no life here.

I had never had a sense of my grandparents as real people. The gap in my father's life and in mine left by their murder had never been completely filled. A great, encompassing anger began to fill me. Was this crumbling edifice, bereft of any dignity, the best that Poland, that humanity, could do to honor the memory of the dead? The marble wall had been scrubbed in several places. There were faint traces of swastikas, scrawled on the memorial and then removed.

The site wasn't very large — about the size of a couple of football fields. Behind the memorial, the terrain dipped into a kind of trench, probably the remains of one of the antitank ditches in which the Nazis had dumped the bodies of the victims. A dirt track led around the perimeter, parallel to a wire fence gaping with many holes. Adjacent to the path stood a row of concrete blocks, which, like everything else in this place, were decaying. Pieces of rubble lay scattered along the side of the path. Weeds poked through the slushy snow. Two women with shopping bags were taking a shortcut through the camp.

"This is disgusting," I said.

"Yes," said my father. "I knew my parents died here, but I imagined they could rest in peace with some kind of honor. There is no honor here. But still, I'm glad we came. It was time to close the circle."

"It's not closed," I said. "In the next few days, one of the murderers who stood at this very spot is going to receive a prize for lifetime achievement from the president of the United States."

"That's your problem, not mine. For me, the circle is closed. This is where my mother and father died. I'll never know how they felt in those last terrible moments, or what they suffered. I almost hope they heard that bastard singing his damned Schubert; it might have made it easier. But now, I'm standing here where they stood, breathing the air they breathed. They are dead, but I survived, and their spirit lives on in me and in you and in the next generation, which, God willing, you will bring into the world."

Lynn bent down and picked something up.

"Oh, my God," she said.

It was a human jawbone.

We dug a shallow hole in the ground with our bare hands and silently buried it.

22

The Jew was tied to a post and two Ukrainians rubbed his naked body
with harsh floor brushes until the bones showed.

— TESTIMONY OF MIECYSLAW NIEDUZAK

.

Iᴛ ᴡᴀs ɴᴏᴡ Fᴇʙʀᴜᴀʀʏ 15, five days before Beck received his award
from the president. We'd missed the Super Bowl. Valentine's Day had
come and gone. It was as if we had been in a strange time warp, but
now time had caught up with us.

I still lacked that vital piece of evidence, the final link in the
chain, to prove beyond doubt that Delatrucha was Franz Beck. And
I couldn't figure out where I might find it.

On our last night in Europe, CNN reported that the UN was
charging twenty-one Bosnian Serbs with genocide and crimes
against humanity. I was devoting my life to a genocide that happened
half a century ago, while another one was going on right now a few
hundred miles away.

I called Fabrizio in Washington. "We're coming back tomorrow.
I want to know if it's safe."

"I don't know."

"What do you mean, you don't know?"

"Field sources have been picking up more and more chatter that
some kind of extremist attack might be coming. The problem is, we
don't know where or when. We think maybe a federal building in
D.C., but that's no more than a guess. The director has set up a task
force; the entire government's on alert."

"Holy shit!"

"You may have set the attack in motion with your little gun fight in West Virginia."

"Me?"

"You identified their vehicle and thereby forced them underground. Now they're hiding somewhere with a truckload of explosives. They can't stay hidden forever. They know we're going to track them down. If they intend to attack the government, they'll do it soon."

"Am I in danger? Or Lynn?"

"Our analysts think they'll go after something of major symbolic value. Nobody will notice a pinprick. They want to shock the country and shake public confidence in the government. You should still be careful, though. You may want to check into a hotel for a couple of nights when you get back."

I couldn't sleep after that. My mind swung back and forth between extremists and Delatrucha. The thought of him eluding justice was driving me crazy. I sat on the bed leafing through my notes yet again, the words all jumbling together. I could hardly read them anymore. Since that first day I had met Sophie Reiner, I had covered page after page of my legal pad with ideas, impressions, records of conversations and events, but what did it all add up to? I'd have to report to Eric, and I wasn't looking forward to it.

Lynn kept badgering me to come to bed. "I don't see the problem," she said. "We know Delatrucha gave a recital in Berlin in 1944, and we know Beck gave a recital in Berlin in 1944. What more do you need?"

"It's not enough. It's the same problem we faced with the Bruteitis case. You know for sure the guy is guilty, but — without that signature on the bottom of the page or some other smoking gun — you can't go after him."

"What about the *Diario ABC* interview? That's Delatrucha in his own words."

"That interview is very old. He could claim he was mistranslated or misquoted. Who could prove otherwise after all these years? And I'm sure if we ever went to court, he'd be able to produce three or four witnesses from Argentina who would swear they remember him eating steak and dancing the tango in Buenos Aires in 1944."

"I just don't think there's any point going over your notes again and again right now. You're making yourself sick. What do you expect to find? You've read them a thousand times. Don't be so anal. Just come to bed, will you?"

Anal? "If you can't help, at least spare me the psychobabble." I snapped back.

"Give it a rest. Why don't you just come to bed?"

"Sex isn't the answer to everything, you know." Even as I said the words, I wanted to swallow them.

"You seemed to like it well enough before," she said icily.

"I did. I do. I'm sorry. I don't want to fight. I'm just so tired and angry about the case. Please forget I just said that."

I tried to hug her, but she edged away, curling up and covering herself with the blanket. "You were just as eager as I was, and it's not like I seduced you."

"You didn't. Of course you didn't."

She spoke coldly from beneath the blanket, her voice trembling. "Perhaps it's better this way. I keep wondering if there's any future for us. You have your work and your religion, and I don't know if there's room for me as well."

"Lynn, stop throwing religion in my face. That doesn't have any-thing to do with this. If I were a professional athlete, or a violinist who was always practicing, you wouldn't say that. But because I pray to God a few minutes each day, it's suddenly a big issue and you don't know where you fit in? At least be honest. What's really on your mind?"

She shrugged off the blanket and sat up to face me. "I keep thinking that if we got serious, I would have to give up a lot. I don't know if I'm willing to do that for you."

"What? That's bullshit! First of all, we already are serious — or at least I am. I don't have time for messing around. I would never have slept with you if I hadn't been serious. I thought you understood that. Second, what would you have to give up to be with me that's so important?"

"I'd have to give up the freedom to eat whatever I like, to name just one thing," she said. "I'd have to keep a kosher home if we were together."

"Is that such a big deal? You don't have total freedom now. Nobody does. You might want to eat three pints of ice cream every day, but you restrain yourself because you don't want to get fat. You might want four glasses of wine, but you don't because you don't want to get drunk. We all limit ourselves in our choices all the time. Millions of people spend their lives dieting and denying themselves things they want. Keeping kosher is just one more limitation. It's a lot easier than being vegetarian. And I bet if I were a vegetarian, we wouldn't be having this discussion. What is it about my being Orthodox that you find so scary?"

"When I give up ice cream or beer, that's totally my choice. I get to decide of my own free will. If I were to keep kosher, it would only be because a God whom I don't believe in told me to."

"So don't do it for God. Do it for me. People who love each other make compromises all the time. I would make plenty of sacrifices for you."

"Not about religion."

"Yes, even about religion." I tried to collect my thoughts, reaching out to take her hands in mine. "You once asked me if you were like a ham sandwich to me, but it's really the other way around."

"Go on."

"The way you're talking, I feel less important than a ham sandwich to you."

"Why would you say that?"

"Because you'd rather preserve your right to eat a ham sandwich than stay with me. I don't see it as a big sacrifice. You could still eat whatever you wanted outside the home. I wouldn't interfere or force my beliefs on you. You could eat your ham and pork and bacon and shrimp and scallops and oysters and lobster and whatever other *hazerei* you want. Just not at home, if we ever decide to make one together. That's what it comes down to. That's the so-called big sacrifice. If that's too much to ask, then maybe we should break up."

"What about Shabbat?"

"What about it?"

"No music, no driving, no TV."

"I guess you have to decide whether you value TV on Saturday more than our relationship. If you really had to go to the mall, I wouldn't stop you. I just wouldn't come. There are six other days of the week for TV and the mall, but if it's too much, we should just part as friends. I don't want to, but . . ." There was nothing else I could say.

She was silent. Then, "I don't want to either."

"Really?"

"Really."

"Thank God. I couldn't bear it. We can figure all this out. We just have to be honest and patient with each other."

I kissed her and felt her trembling. She flicked off the light, and eventually we managed to sleep for a couple of hours.

"There is one sure way to nail Delatrucha," she said the next morning as we packed.

"What's that?"

"Find Sophie Reiner's documents."

"Don't think I haven't thought of that. I just don't know where to look."

"You're the logical one. Put yourself in her place. She was in Washington, D.C., a strange city, where she knew no one. We know she came to see you. Where else did she go? Who else did she see?"

I played "What if . . .?" throughout the eight-hour flight back to the States.

It had taken the best part of four days to get back to Washington. At Dulles Airport, we said good-bye to my dad, who was heading back to West Virginia to start the cleanup. Dad seemed old and tired, lacking his usual vigor. On the flight, he had spoken vaguely about coming back to D.C. to live near me. I think he wanted to see how serious I was about Lynn before committing himself. I couldn't tell him. We were still a work in progress.

With Fabrizio's warning still ringing in my ears, Lynn and I rented a car and drove to a hotel in Baltimore. She collapsed on the

238

double bed. "I feel like I'm still moving," she said, eyes shut. In less than a minute, she was asleep. I was exhausted but still too apprehensive to follow her example. I wanted my life back, my safe routine of prayers and Sabbath rest that created an oasis of sacred time away from the world.

The weather forecast called for a major snowstorm heading our way. Accumulations of a foot or more expected in Washington. Great. Something else to worry about. An inch of snow can upend normal life in the nation's capital. A foot would cause total paralysis.

I decided to call Rosen. The second he heard my voice, he exploded. "I have been trying to reach you for three days! Nobody knew where the hell you were," he shouted. "I told you before not to disappear on me, especially at a crucial time like this!"

"Thanks for the warm welcome, Eric."

"Right, welcome home, blah, blah, blah. Where the hell are you?"

"Baltimore."

"What are you doing there?"

"Avoiding neo-Nazis with truck bombs."

"What kind of crap is that? Did you lose your mind over there? I want you in my office at eight o'clock sharp. Bring that assistant of yours, too, if she still works for us. Delatrucha's ceremony is on Monday. We're out of time. I have to decide whether to alert the White House. I assume you found what we needed."

"We have strong circumstantial evidence. Delatrucha was up to his neck in mass murder at Belzec. He organized a little orchestra and sang Schubert to the victims as they arrived to be gassed."

I didn't fool him for a second. "*Circumstantial* evidence? That's what we had before you left. You're telling me you still can't prove it a hundred percent?"

"Ninety-eight percent."

"Not good enough."

"I know. But I'm still digging. Eventually, I'll get the —"

"Stop right there. I don't want to hear the word 'eventually.' There is no 'eventually.' It's now or never."

"The world doesn't end on Monday. The investigation can continue."

"No, it can't. Once he has the award, I'm closing the file. I have no choice."

"What?" I was shocked.

"I won't embarrass the president. How would it look a few weeks after he was photographed shaking hands with this guy if we suddenly announced that the man in the picture is a Nazi war criminal? Try 'massive public scandal,' and I'd be right in the middle of it. Conroy and Doneghan would have all the ammunition they need."

"You'd let him get away with mass murder to avoid embarrassment?"

"Don't play innocent with me. You know how Washington works. I want to nail this guy just as much as you do, but I have to protect this office and our mission. Once this guy shakes the president's doughy hand, the case is in cold storage until further notice."

"You promised you would never bow down to political pressure. 'Over my dead body,' you said."

"This is different. There's no outside pressure. This is my decision for the good of the entire office. I've still got John Howard to worry about as well. I'm on a tightrope here, with no safety net. The slightest little slip, and I'm chopped liver."

"Why not tell the White House to keep the president away from the ceremony, even if we don't have a hundred percent proof?"

"Don't be so naive. That auditorium is going to be stuffed with movers and shakers who have paid big money to shake the president's hand. It'll be knee-deep in political donors. He's going to be there unless he has a damned good reason not to be."

"So we have four days, one of which is Shabbat."

"If I'm going to alert the White House to change the president's schedule, I need to do it before the weekend. You have until tomorrow morning to come up with a new idea, or I'm pulling the plug." He hung up.

This wasn't just a setback. This was total defeat. I called David Binder, thinking he might point me in a new direction. But he wasn't there. Now what? There was zero chance of falling asleep. I made a pot of coffee, watched the basketball highlights for a few minutes, got bored, and switched to the news. Sarajevo had just passed its thousandth day under siege. *Me, too,* I thought.

I undressed and lay down beside Lynn and closed my eyes. Her sweet body shaped itself into mine. My thoughts raced, bouncing off each other like billiard balls. And then — like lightning — an idea made me sit bolt upright. I scrambled for my glasses, grabbed my briefcase, and padded into the bathroom, stark naked. I sat on the toilet lid, whipping through my notes.

And there it was.

I spent the rest of the night watching reruns of old sitcoms and updates about the looming weather crisis. A massive storm system had formed to the south and was moving slowly up the coast, with Washington directly in its sights. Estimated total snowfall was clocking in at twenty inches.

At 5:30, I prayed the morning service. At 6:00 I called Eric. "I've had an idea," I said giddily.

"Tell me about it when you get here," he said. "I'd get going as soon as you can, if I were you. Everybody will be leaving early today if they bother coming at all. They've been raiding the supermarkets to stock up on supplies. Like locusts in a cornfield."

"Okay, we're on our way."

"And Mark, take a look at the *Post* when you get a chance. I'm going to be up to my ears today."

Lynn grabbed a copy in the hotel lobby. The sky was steely gray and the parkway eerily empty of traffic. As I drove, Lynn leafed through the newspaper.

"Oh, God," she said, finding a headline buried on an inside page. "Read it to me."

" 'U.S. Nazi-Hunting Unit Accused of Forging Papers.' "

"He leaked the story to the press," I said. "What a moron."

"What?"

"Read me the article, then I'll explain."

The article reported that the Office of Special Investigations had allegedly fabricated documents in the Bruteitis case. "Do they quote anyone by name?" I asked.

"No. Just an anonymous source close to the investigation."

"Is there a reaction from Eric?

"It says nobody in the department was available to respond."

"Ha!"

"You're taking this calmly. Isn't this terrible for you and Eric?"

"It would be if it were true. But it's not. Eric got someone to feed the story to John Howard hoping to trap him. Ever the idiot, Howard fell for it."

"It's a setup? Why?"

"Howard's been plotting to get rid of Eric. He wants the job for himself."

"So how does this help Eric?"

"First, they'll determine that the documents are genuine and the story is wrong. That shouldn't take long. After that, the attorney general will proclaim his full confidence in Eric. An inquiry into the leak will lead straight to Howard. If he's lucky, Eric will give him a chance to resign quietly before they nail his sorry ass."

"What a place! Boy, am I glad I'm leaving," Lynn said. "This place has become a nest of vipers. You knew about this, didn't you? Why didn't you tell me?"

"I didn't know the details, and we've been so busy surviving attacks and — "

" — studying the Mishna . . ."

"Exactly."

Back at the department, Eric had convened a full staff meeting in the main conference room. We slipped in the back. The attorney general was addressing the crowded room, flanked by Eric on one side and Janet on the other. Many of the people assembled there hailed from other divisions of the Department of Justice, drawn by the whiff of scandal.

"I have been assured that the story in today's *Post* is completely untrue," the attorney general was saying. He was a largish, pompous man in his sixties, a little on the fat side, with a booming voice.

"Eric Rosen has headed this office for many years. He personifies integrity, and his word is good enough for me." He mopped his red face with a monogrammed handkerchief, glaring at the assembled officials, as if challenging them to defy him. No one did.

"I have total confidence in Eric Rosen, as does the president. Your chief historian, Janet Smart, has told me she personally collected these documents from the official Lithuanian archives. The originals remain in Lithuania, and I have received word this morning from the Lithuanian government that they have not been tampered with in any way. All of these documents are clearly signed. We will be communicating these facts to the press shortly."

There was a collective sigh of relief. Eric sat there impassive, half smiling, self-important, serene and confident, totally in his element. Janet fiddled with her beads, nervously sweeping her unkempt hair away from her eyes. She obviously felt less comfortable at the center of the storm.

The attorney general leaned forward. "To put any lingering questions to rest, I will establish a panel of independent experts to verify the authenticity of these documents beyond any shadow of doubt," he said. "At the same time, we will open an inquiry into this malicious and unfortunate leak. When we find the person responsible, he or she will answer to me. Mr. Rosen, do you have anything to add?" Eric shook his head. "Then this meeting is adjourned."

As people filed out of the room, John Howard came toward me, his thin face pale as paper. "Howdy, Johnnie," I said, slapping him on the back. "How's it going?"

He gave me a haunted look. "Can't talk. Gotta get back to my office," he said. "Important phone calls."

"Yeah, I know. You need to update Doneghan—and your Rolodex."

"I don't know what you're talking about," he puffed.

I grabbed his arm, determined to make him squirm. "You don't look so hot. Maybe you're coming down with something. You've got to watch out for draughts this time of the year in leaky offices." He shoved past me and stumbled down the corridor. "Going to take a leak, are you, John?" I called.

Lynn grabbed my arm. "That's enough," she ordered.

We reconvened in Eric's office. He seemed mightily pleased

with himself. He wasn't flaunting it, but I could read his mind. He was preening. He gestured for us to sit down on the leather sofa.

"First of all, welcome home."

"Thank you," I said. "I'm glad to see the attorney general has such faith in you."

"Why wouldn't he? Anyway, I'm glad to see everyone back in one piece. Mark, you said you had an idea on the Delatrucha case. It had better be good, because we all want to get out of here before the snow starts. The floor is yours."

I cleared my throat and felt a pang of nerves. "This hasn't been an ordinary investigation. We've collected a ton of information, but the key all along has been Sophie Reiner's documents."

"Tell us something we don't know," Eric growled.

"I have an idea where we can find them." I took out my legal pad. "These are the notes I took when Sophie Reiner came to see me. She made a comment I didn't understand at the time, but I wrote it down anyway. She said, 'I want the world to know my testimony.' "

"She had a Messiah complex?" Janet offered.

"That's what I thought. I figured she might have a few screws loose."

I flipped forward a few pages. "After she was killed, the police showed me what they found in her hotel room. That's how I got on Delatrucha's trail in the first place. But look at this." I pointed to one particular item in my notes.

"A ticket to the Holocaust Museum? So?" Eric asked.

"At the time, I didn't pay much attention. It wasn't until last night that it occurred to me there might be a connection."

"How?" George asked.

"If you survived the Holocaust, where would you go if you wanted to put your experiences and memories on record?"

"The Holocaust Museum," Lynn said. "I even told your father he should go there to do just that."

"They have an archive where they collect the stories of survivors. People give accounts on videotape or in writing. The librarian, Sara Barclay, and I were at a dinner party a few weeks ago, and she described an old woman coming with her family to give her testimony. My guess is that's where Sophie went with her documents. After all, they are a kind of testimony. I think they're somewhere in the museum. All we have to do is find them."

Eric was unconvinced. "Nice speech, but, if you're right, why hasn't someone found them already?"

"If no one knew they were there, why would they look?"

"You have no real reason to believe it's there, other than that you want it to be there," Eric said.

"There is a connection. We should start searching right now. There's still time. It's not just a guess."

Silence around the table. Then George said, "Only one way to find out. What are we waiting for?"

I looked at Eric. He nodded his assent.

The first flakes were falling as we walked the short distance down the Mall to the museum. Only a few brave tourists were in the entrance-way. I gazed again at the words engraved into the stone wall: "*The Museum will touch the life of everyone who enters and leave everyone forever changed.*" I said a silent prayer that it would.

Sara met us at the library, looking as unruffled and elegant as ever. I explained the situation and what we were looking for. "Yes, many survivors come here to record their testimonies," she said. She showed us how the computer system worked. Survivors were asked to fill out forms, if possible attaching photographs that could be scanned into the system.

"Do people ever deposit documents here?" George asked.

"Sometimes, but few survivors actually have documents in their possession," Sara said. "What did you say this woman's name was?"

"Sophie Reiner."

She punched "Reiner" into the computer. Three names appeared on the screen—Oskar Reiner, Gina Reiner, and Itzik Reiner. Their photos confirmed that none of these was the person we were looking for.

"There's no record that she left a testimony here. What is it exactly you're looking for?"

"We think she had documents about a war criminal—letters, photographs, maybe a journal," Lynn said.

"When did you say this woman came in?" Sara asked.

"November 27," I said.

Sara checked the log for that day but came up empty. "But that doesn't mean she wasn't here. We're always understaffed, and we're sometimes sloppy about keeping proper logs."

"It wouldn't necessarily be under her own name," I said. "Her testimony was about someone else. Try looking under 'Delatrucha.' "

"Like the singer?" Sara asked. "Are you sure?" I nodded, not bothering to offer an explanation, so she checked the directory again. Nothing.

"What about 'Beck'?" Lynn offered. There were two Becks in the archive, but neither was Franz. We called up their files; both were genuine survivors. I was choking with disappointment. I had been so sure, but my hunch was barreling down yet another dead end.

"Try Belzec," George said.

Nothing.

"Well," shrugged George. "I guess that's it. We should get out of here before the snow starts in earnest. They say we're getting a foot and a half."

"Wait," I said. "It's here! I know it's here. Think harder! What name could she have used?"

We all looked blank.

"Maybe Roberto or Robert, his first name?" Lynn ventured. Worth a try.

Nothing.

"Schnellinger," Lynn suggested.

Nothing.

I still wasn't ready to admit defeat. "It's got to be something really obvious. She wouldn't have put it in a place where nobody could find it," I said.

"Why not? She was just looking for somewhere safe. This isn't some kind of treasure hunt," Lynn said.

"We need to put ourselves in her shoes," I said. "What has this case revolved around?"

"Deceit," Lynn said.

"Death," said George.

"Lying, betrayal, murder, cruelty — you name it," Lynn added.

"All true," I said. "But you could say that about any war crimes case. What makes this one different?"

"Music," said Lynn.

The word reverberated in my brain. "That's right. 'A lover of German song,' she called herself," I said excitedly.

"I don't see it." George said.

And then — in a snap — I did. "That's it, Lynn. You're right. That's the answer, right in front of us!"

"What do you mean?" she asked.

"We almost had it a minute ago, but we stumbled past it. Remember, you suggested looking under Robert. Why did he call himself Robert? According to his own words, he was named after Robert Schumann, his mother's favorite composer. But we know that Robert wasn't his real name. His real name was Franz, and he was named after . . ."

"Look under Schubert," Lynn shouted.

Sara shot me a skeptical look, then punched the name. The hard drive whirred, and slowly a document filled the screen. Lynn threw her arms around me. Even George was smiling and shook my hand. I sighed in relief.

"What does it say?" Lynn asked.

"It's in German," I said. "Here, scroll down." I began to translate:

I am the daughter of Franz Beck, a German who served at the camp of Belzec in Poland and has successfully hidden himself away for 40 years. I believe he was involved in war crimes at the Belzec camp. I have discovered these facts by chance, and also I believe that for all his deeds he feels no remorse. He has played with people's lives and takes no responsibility. He rejects his own flesh and blood. He lives like a king while the one who loved him, sacrificed for him, and kept faith with him struggled all her life and died alone. I have evidence which I have deposited in an appropriate place in this museum. If something happens to me, they may be released to Herr Marek Cain, the Nazi hunter.

Underneath was her signature — *Sophie Reiner.*

Declaration to the American People:

My fellow Americans, by the time you read this declaration, the first blow in an epic battle for freedom and godliness will already have been struck. This is a new dawn of freedom, in which patriotic citizens will finally overthrow the evil that has gripped our beloved nation and return to the ways of God. I call on all right-thinking Americans to rise up against a federal government that slaughters unborn babies, promotes vile sexual practices, and gives away our precious freedoms to the United Nations and World Jewry.

The government will no doubt label me as a terrorist. Do not listen, fellow patriots. It is they who are the terrorists. Abortion is murder. And when the regime in Washington made this vile and barbaric practice the law of the land, it gave up the right to be called a government. A government that allows children to be vacuumed from the wombs of their mothers is evil according to the laws of God and Nature. A government that sends its young men to war for Jewish-Zionist interests under the control of the United Nations has given up all claims of legitimacy. A government that allows sodomites to promote their perverted lifestyle, which God has called abhorrent in His eyes, cannot be allowed to stand.

In taking arms against such monstrosities, I invoke historical precedent. In 1776, our founding fathers decided that the British crown had trampled their rights and therefore forfeited its legitimacy. Were the sins of the British any greater, any more abhorrent, than the deliberate murder of 50 million children? This is the true Holocaust, not that invention of the Jews to which this so-called government raises monuments and museums all over our sacred land.

Some may question the use of force and the shedding of blood, even in a just and righteous cause. I regret the loss of life — even of agents of an evil government — but all must recognize that by lending their hands to this regime, they have made themselves targets. Their deaths are as nothing in the face of the mass slaughter they defend.

I ask all American parents: Would you defend your own children if they were under attack? Of course, every right-thinking parent would. But America's unborn children, all our children, are under attack this very day, this very hour. I ask you all, Would you defend the freedom of the United States against international threats to its sovereignty? We are so threatened by a United Nations controlled by Jews that promotes the awful, ungodly concept of international government. Lastly, I ask, would you defend the sanctity of the two-parent family, one man joined to one woman under God? Our families, the sacred bonds of marriage itself, are under siege by sodomites and the homosexual agenda.

I say to all right-thinking Americans that, together, we can take back our country and restore the nation our founders envisioned, a Christian nation under God, with freedom and justice for all.

Our enemies are powerful and backed by powerful forces that hide in the shadows and work their will in dark and devious ways. But World Jewry cannot stand against the righteous wrath of an America determined to win back its freedom.

Fellow Americans, I have struck the first blow. I call on you to join me. Victory is inevitable. Long live liberty. Long live the United States of America.

23

I've found what I was seeking
However it may be.

—"Thanksgiving to the Brook" by Wilhelm Müller,
music by Franz Schubert

Our jubilation only lasted a minute. We still didn't know where the documents were — only that they were somewhere in the museum.

"Maybe in the library," George said.

We rushed across the corridor, only to be confronted by a vast array of neatly shelved books — thousands and thousands.

"This could take weeks," I groaned.

"It's one of the largest Holocaust archives in the world," Sara said proudly.

"We don't have time to search the entire library. We need to narrow it down," George said.

"Start with books about Belzec and Operation Reinhard," I suggested. We spent half an hour going through them, but found nothing.

"Too obvious," Lynn said. "Put yourself in her shoes."

"Where would you look, then?" George asked.

"She's been totally consistent all along, and it always comes back to music. Maybe there's a section in here on Schubert or something."

"We actually have a special archive devoted to music," Sara said. "Printed material, published and unpublished; also handwritten manuscripts and sound recordings — but I don't think there's any Schubert," she said.

"Let's look," I said.

She led us to into another room overflowing with books and manuscripts.

"How is this collection organized?" I asked.

"As you can see, it's not entirely cataloged yet. New material arrives all the time, so it's a little higgledy-piggledy."

"O God, just what we need," George moaned. "She could have just dumped it in a pile of stuff."

"There are five different sections," Sara continued. "One deals with songs sung in the ghettos and camps and by partisans; another with music suppressed by the Nazis; there's also a section on music composed by exiled or persecuted musicians; we have a collection of anti-Nazi songs, and then works written by and performed by Holocaust survivors."

"How does Delatrucha fit in with that?" I wondered aloud.

"The nearest is music sung in the camps," Lynn said.

"But we have no idea if Sophie knew how the place is organized. She may have dumped her papers anywhere," said George.

"True, but we have to start somewhere," I countered. "Let's start with the music sung in the camps."

"Over here," Sara beckoned, already moving down an aisle.

Much of this material was in loose-leaf folders stacked on shelves and in filing cabinets in no particular order. We had to pull out each folder individually to see what was inside. I tried to put myself in Sophie's position. She wanted her material to be hidden so she could retrieve it if necessary, but she also wanted it to be found by others if necessary.

I glanced in wonder at scraps of paper covered with musical notation — songs written by concentration camp prisoners. If there had been time, it would have been fascinating to go through these files. Even in the depths of hell, these captives had held on to their humanity. They had hoarded every precious piece of paper they could find and used them to write down melodies. Each of these fragments, now preserved in plastic envelopes, represented a profound act of resistance. Delatrucha had perverted music, but these prisoners had redeemed it.

251

A copy of "Eli, Eli," the famous song by Hannah Senesz, passed through my hands. Senesz parachuted into German-occupied territory during the war on a mission for the British. She was captured, tortured, and executed.

> Oh Lord, Oh Lord,
> I pray these things never end.
> The sands and the sea,
> The rush of the waters,
> The crash of the heavens
> The prayers of man.

I went on to the next folder, and the next.

Another folder revealed an entire opera written by a camp inmate. The next contained songs written by partisans in the forest, with words in Hebrew or Yiddish.

"Anything?" I asked the others. They each shook their heads, no.

"This is a waste of time," George complained from across the room.

I was beginning to agree with him when I saw an outsize envelope at the back of a filing cabinet, much larger than all the other folders. I pulled it out. It was labeled, "Franz Beck, Baritone."

My body tingled with electricity. I had goose bumps. This envelope had cost Sophie Reiner her life. I was trembling so hard I had to sit down. Lynn glanced over. "Mark, what's the matter? You look pale."

"I found it," I murmured.

"What?"

"*I found it.*"

She rushed over, pulling me to my feet. "George, Sara, come here. Mark found it!" she shouted.

They flocked around as I carefully pried it open. The envelope was stuffed tight with papers. First out was a photograph of a young Nazi in full SS regalia, his arms outstretched, his mouth open in song. The resemblance was unquestionable. This was Roberto Delatrucha.

"Bravo," said Lynn, hugging me excitedly. "This is *it*!"

Even dour George was smiling broadly. "Will you look at that? Unbelievable, totally unbelievable. Even John Howard would be satisfied. These pictures are conclusive," he said.

"And maybe we'll finally discover what he did," I said. "Hopefully all his dirty secrets are in this envelope."

Sara found us an empty room to work in. Outside the snow was really coming down. The ground was already covered. The city was about to be wrapped in a thick white shroud. We had to work fast. I asked Sara if the museum had a camera we could borrow. She said she'd find one. We had to document thoroughly every move we made.

Lynn returned from calling Eric. "The museum is emptying out," she announced. "Everyone's trying to beat the snow. They're closing early. We have another hour before they throw us out."

"Start taking pictures," I said. Lynn snapped a few close-ups of the envelope. George and I carefully removed the rest of the contents, spreading the papers out on a large conference table. My hands were shaking as George pulled them out one by one and Lynn photographed them.

"If you don't need me anymore, I think I'll go home," Sara said.

I looked up. "I can't thank you enough."

"All part of the service," she told me, smiling faintly. "And Mark? . . ."

"Yes?"

"Be happy," she said as she left.

There were some press clippings that appeared to be German newspaper reviews of Beck's concert performances in the 1950s. Next was a packet of letters still in their original envelopes, addressed to Fraulein Hildegard Reiner. It was in the same handwriting as the two extracts Susan had given me. Each letter was neatly dated. There were perhaps thirty or forty. There were also half a dozen photographs. Two showed Beck in uniform. The others were snapshots, taken years apart. In the first, he was cradling a baby. In the last, the baby was already a teenager — the youthful Sophie. This had to be the picture Sophie had shown Susan Scott. Lastly came two school exercise books, their pages yellowing with age. I opened one. It looked as if it had been written with a fountain pen; the original black ink had faded. The handwriting was the same — difficult to decipher but not impossible.

January 1, 1940. The start of a new year, a new decade and for our Reich a new . . .

what's this word? . . .

a new era of renown. How wonderful to stand at the very frontier of the Reich. To be alive and young at this time, I consider myself the most fortunate of men. History is being made. I pledge to do my part and to live every moment to the absolute fullest. My goal for this year must be to put aside selfish ambition. In the coming months and weeks, our nation and our race will be tested. I dedicate myself to the glory of the Fatherland.

"A loyal, upstanding Nazi," George commented.
"This is his diary." I couldn't believe I finally had it in my hands. I flipped to the last entry in the other book.

October 31, 1943. Today I left Poland and will finally return to my Fatherland. A day of joy in my life. I have seen so many terrible things, but now a new chapter begins. From this day, I swear to devote myself only to music, only to art. The past is dead. I will wipe out the ugliness and replace it with beauty.

Two exercise books. Within their pages, I hoped we would find the truth about Beck's actions during the years in Operation Reinhard and the destruction of Polish Jewry.
"What now? It's going to take hours to translate all these," George said. "I'm worried about the snow."
"I want every single page photocopied. We can't risk working with the originals. They may be fragile after all these years. Be very careful as you photocopy them. We can work all night in my office if necessary. We'll divide the translation, you and me. By tomorrow,

we should be able to give Eric a full report he can use to decide what to do."

"It's going to be Shabbat in about four hours," Lynn observed.

Shit. I had forgotten. That meant no working, no cooking, no writing, no switching lights on or off. What was I going to do? Was it permissible to work on Shabbat to help nail Delatrucha?

"You'll have to do it without me," I said.

George gawped at me uncomprehendingly. "The biggest case of your life, and you're going to sit there and do nothing all day? Couldn't you make an exception just this one time?" Lynn was obviously thinking the same thing.

"The only acceptable reason to break Shabbat is to save a life, and we're not saving lives here. This isn't a small thing to me. The rabbis teach us that the Temple was destroyed because the people broke Shabbat."

"That's nonsense," George said. "It was destroyed because the Babylonians and Romans had bigger armies than the Jews."

"I'm not going to argue ancient history with you. I'll work up to the start of Shabbat and all Saturday night, but I won't work tonight or tomorrow during the day."

George shook his head. "Well, we're not going to work in the office. If we stay there, we'll be trapped. No food and nowhere to sleep. We must have had three inches already. The whole city is hunkering down. Look outside." He was right — the street was deserted except for a thin stream of traffic heading south toward Virginia. A lone truck trundled past the museum entrance. It pulled over for a moment, but a guard came out and waved it on.

"You could come to my apartment, but you can't cook, and I don't want you switching lights on and off all day," I said.

"Come to my place," Lynn countered. "My roommate is out of town, so I have an extra bedroom. Mark can do his Shabbat thing in my room while the rest of us work. We can stock up on food, but we need to decide now. I'll see if I can buy some food and then meet you back at my place in a couple of hours. Mark knows where it is."

"The supermarket shelves are probably already bare," said George, ever the optimist. "We'll starve to death."

I thought about whether I should even spend the day with them while they were working, but I decided not to be unreasonable. If they respected me and my ways, I should be able to do the same for them.

By the time we had finished photocopying all the material, the museum was virtually empty, and the remaining staff was anxious to push us out so they could close for the storm. George called his wife, and said he'd be working at Lynn's apartment late into the night. "I'll probably be stranded there the whole weekend," he said gloomily. "With Mark Cain, no less."

"Tell her to come over, too," I said. "The more the merrier. We'll have a slumber party." He brightened up a bit after she said she would come.

A U-Haul truck pulled up near the entrance as we left the museum. Just like the one I had seen from the window less than an hour before. "Wait a sec," I told George.

"What now?" he asked.

Ignoring him, I jogged back toward the truck, my feet slipping in the snow. The security guard, to whom we had just said good-bye, dashed out of the museum, waving his arms. "I told you already, you can't stop here! What's wrong with you guys?" he yelled at the driver.

The man sitting in the driver's seat, illuminated in the half-light, looked vaguely familiar. Our eyes met for a brief second, but I couldn't place him. Something wasn't right here. I could feel it, but I couldn't put my finger on it. Then they took off. It was too dark to read the plate, and the van pulled out into the swirling snow.

I swept the snow off the windows of my car — one of the few left in the office parking lot — and we started driving toward Lynn's apartment, taking it very slowly. The street lights shed a pale, sickly yellow glow over the sidewalks. Washington was turning into a ghost town.

"What was that about back there with the truck?" George asked.

"I thought I recognized one of the guys."

"Who was he?"

"Not sure." But I couldn't get him out of my head, and the first thing I did once we got in the door was call Agent Fabrizio.

"It's Mark Cain. Where are you?" I asked her after I was patched through.

"Terrorism task force headquarters. Please don't tell me someone attacked you again."

"Nothing like that. I saw a U-Haul try to park twice outside the Holocaust Museum in the space of a few minutes. A security guard moved them on both times," I said. "There were two guys in the cab. One of them looked like one of the thugs that attacked us."

"Are you sure?"

"No, I'm not sure. I only saw him briefly. That's why I'm calling you."

"When did this happen?"

"Not more than an hour ago. The streets were almost deserted. That's what made it so noticeable."

"Did you get the license?"

"They took off too fast."

"Shit."

"I know."

"What kind of truck was it?"

"I already told you: It was a U-Haul."

"Was it one of their super movers, a really big one, a twenty-six-footer? Or was it a van? Or something in between?"

"It was small, but not that small — maybe twelve or fourteen feet long."

"What was painted on it? They all have different slogans and pictures painted on the side."

I tried to conjure up an image from my memory. A vague picture began to form. "I think it was a picture of some kind of creature. A long neck and a big head full of teeth."

"Like a tiger?"

"No, more like a dinosaur. A T. rex or something like that."

"A dinosaur? That means the truck could have come from somewhere out West, like Montana or Utah — a state with lots of

257

fossils. That may help us find out where it was rented. Thank you, Mark. This could be a big help."

"Why would they try to blow up the Holocaust Museum?"

"Sounds to me like they were scouting, looking for a soft target. They may try to attack during the snowstorm when everybody's guard is down. At least now we know what we're looking for, and we can beef up security around key buildings. Gotta go." She hung up.

I put on a pot of coffee while George wandered the apartment. There was still a couple of hours left before I had to light the Shabbat candles. We began with the letters and decided to go on to the journal later, leaving the best for last.

The doorbell rang. It was George's wife, followed closely by Lynn, carrying three bags of groceries. George greeted his beloved in a strange language — Estonian perhaps. She smiled shyly at me as Lynn steered her toward the kitchen.

"This is going to be fun," Lynn said. "We're going to make chicken in wine sauce with roasted potatoes and vegetables. It's the last chicken in Washington, and these are the last potatoes. After this, we'll have to cast lots to see which one of us gets to eat."

Another religious dilemma — to eat or not to eat? I decided to eat everything but the chicken. This was going to be tough enough without acting like a religious prima donna.

"You should see the snow out there. It's piling up like crazy," Lynn said, squeezing my hand. "We're trapped, like in *Little House on the Prairie*."

"Trapped all weekend with Roberto the Nazi," George smirked. "Let's get started."

For an hour, we worked doggedly as delicious smells filled the apartment. George broke the silence. "Listen to this. August 3, 1941, from Kraków." Lynn and Marie came in to listen, too.

"Go on," I said.

Dear Hildegard,
You are always in my thoughts. I hope this letter finds you well.
I have hopes of receiving a furlough some time this autumn.

What bliss it would be to see the leaves turn gold in our beauti-
ful city with you beside me.

"I've been reading that kind of stuff, too. He had his sentimental side, our Franz," I said.

"It's so totally creepy," Lynn said, "knowing what we know
about him."

"The interesting bit is just coming," George said. He read on.

The weather here continues fine, and life definitely has its
rewards. We found a piano in the house we are occupying,
owned by citizens who have relocated to another part of
town —

"Jews," I interrupted.
"Presumably," George said.

The piano is a fine German instrument, a Bechstein . . .

"Oh, my God, that's the letter Susan Scott gave us!" Lynn interrupted. "Now we have the date. What's the rest say?"
George continued:

I was able to stretch my fingers and even my voice. After weeks
without practice, I was very rusty. To think that music was
once my entire life. Those days seem long ago. Still, sometimes I
hear the notes of a song echoing in my head. The other day, I
seemed to hear the sounds of Schubert's "Trout" — that much-
loved song so dear to us both. I tried to banish the notes from my
mind. They have no place here. And yet, though I perform my
duties with enthusiasm, I must confess that I sometimes miss
singing. My comrades were surprised and delighted at my abili-
ties. They want to organize a concert at which I would sing for
the entire unit. I told them music was in the past for me.

*There is no time for singing now. That time will come again
after victory. Life meanwhile continues on its rigorous path. I
strive each day to harden my soul. The future is not built by
weaklings. Unpleasant jobs need to be done, and we are doing
them. In the meantime . . .*

"That's where Susan Scott's extract ended," I said.

"That's the end of the page," George said. "The most incrimi-
nating stuff is coming up."

*In the meantime, we are clearing and cleansing the city of
those who no longer belong. Occasionally, there are forays to surrounding villages, which is not pleasant work. Unavoidable, I
suppose, but it's not easy on the men. Only the strongest can do
this work. I believe I myself am strong but I sometimes wish I
were stronger yet. I tell myself it's like taking medicine. It tastes
bad, but it's necessary, and it makes us all more healthy. I
think of you often and send you many kisses.*

"Pity he's not more explicit," I said.

"Yes, it's full of euphemisms. This was before they had opened
the extermination camps, remember," George said. "They had police
and SS units going into villages and shooting thousands of Jews.
Eventually, they decided they could never get the job done like that.
Too many people to kill, and it was too inefficient and messy."

"And too stressful for the killers," I said. "He seems to hint at that
in the letter. The most interesting one I've found so far is from 1942.
The tone is similar, with all kinds of little hints but nothing specific."

"Let's hear."

May 15, 1942.

*Dear Hildegard,
I have come to a place, the name of which I am not at liberty to
tell you.*

"Belzec," George guessed.

"Could be. Unfortunately, he doesn't say."

Here is war at its hardest and most merciless. About my work I cannot speak. Enough to say that it is not for everybody. Only for the strongest.

"More euphemisms," George commented. "It wasn't war at all, it was slaughtering defenseless people."

Sometimes, I have problems putting behind me the cares of the day when I finally lie down to sleep. Then I think of you and our precious moments together. Our long walks, our talks, the wonderful vistas of our homeland, which seem so far away to me now. How wonderful were those lovely days last October when we were together. I pray for their return after we have achieved our victory. How I admire my comrades. What a fine body of men. We are changing history, totally and irrevocably. One day perhaps, history will tell our story and appreciate our sacrifice. Sometimes I yearn for music again. Surely there will be a place of honor for German culture in this new world we are building.

With all my love,
Your Franz

"Maybe we should skip the letters and go straight to the journal," George said. "Go for the real dirt."

"No, we need to go over everything in order. Let's finish the letters first and then do the journal. I'm going to stop working and ask Lynn to light the candles in another hour."

The phone rang. Eric wanted to know what we had discovered.

"We're going through all the material. There's a lot. It's going to take a while," I said.

"The weather's given us a bit more breathing room. Nothing's going to happen tomorrow. What exactly have you found?"

261

"The photos prove that Delatrucha served in the SS. That makes him deportable from the United States, since he lied on his citizenship application. But I think there's a lot more. We haven't even started on the journal yet."

"I'm going to call the White House chief of staff and the attorney general to give them a heads-up. The city will be at a standstill, but we should probably try to brief them sometime on Sunday. Is George with you?"

"And his wife and Lynn as well. We have quite a party going here. We're just about to eat coq au vin. You wanna come?"

"I'll pass. Nobody's going anywhere tonight unless they're crazy. We've had a foot already, and they say there's another foot to come. I'll call tomorrow night to see how you're getting on. In the meantime, Mark, mazel tov. I'm going to enjoy the look on Jack Doneghan's face when I tell him his precious financial backer is a Nazi."

Lynn stood over the candles to make the blessing. "This feels a bit weird, us all being brought here together because of that rat Delatrucha, but it's a special day after all, and we're blessed to be spending it with friends." She lit the candles, closed her eyes, and passed her hands three times over the flames, the way my mother used to when I was little. Then she recited the blessing, ushering in the holy day. I chanted the blessings over the wine and the bread. We took our time, finishing the first bottle and polishing off a second. Lynn suggested we get a breath of fresh air. We wrapped ourselves in coats, hats, and gloves and trudged out into the parking lot, sinking up to our knees in the soft, virgin snow. With difficulty, I had waddled a few steps ahead when something wet and cold hit me on the neck. Retaliation was swift and certain. It was all-out war, first Lynn and I against George and Marie, then George and I against Lynn and Marie, and, finally, due to unbelievable treachery, everyone against me. I retreated to the safety of the lobby.

Lynn and Marie made snow angels in the parking lot, sinking deep into the powder, emerging white like true angels. We were wet and exhausted by the time we got back to the apartment, but it had been a necessary cleansing. Too much Franz Beck was like wallowing in toxic filth.

"If there's no hurry anymore, I'll leave the translation until tomorrow. I'll work all day, and you can join me in the evening to finish it up," George suggested.

"Suits me," I said, eager to be alone with Lynn. "It's been secret for fifty years. Another day won't make any difference."

24

The whole surface of the camp was covered with human bones,
hair and ashes from cremated corpses.

— TESTIMONY OF EDWARD LUCZYNSKI

IT WAS STILL SNOWING OUTSIDE next morning. I decided to go to shul, which was only a few blocks from Lynn's apartment. To my surprise, she came, too. It took us a while to get there, sinking into the snow almost up to our knees. Another twenty hardy folk had braved the elements, so there was no problem making the minyan. The weekly Torah extract, from Exodus, included a passage on keeping the Shabbat: *"God told Moses to speak to the Israelites and say to them, 'You must keep my Sabbaths, for it is a sign between Me and you for all generations to know that I, God, am making you holy.' "*

After the service, several congregants surrounded Lynn, showering her with polite questions. "Finally, our Mark has brought a lovely young woman to services. Every married lady in the congregation has been trying to fix him up for years, but he rejected all their offerings. They'd just about given up hope," one old man told her. On the way home, she told me she'd enjoyed the service. "I didn't pray the way you do. I just read the words in English."

"That's okay," I said. "There isn't a right and wrong way to do it."

Most of the afternoon I napped and read. George got on with the translating quietly in the spare bedroom. When the light faded and Shabbat departed, I said the Havdalah blessings to welcome the new week, and we all resumed work. Lynn typed up our translations. Our mood grew grimmer as, little by little, the pile of paper grew thicker. I guzzled cup after cup of black coffee until we ran out. Around 10:30 P.M., we finished. Snowplows had circled the neighborhood several times, clearing the roads, and George and Marie were able to leave.

Lynn and I went for a short walk after they left — another attempt to clear the poison from our minds. We were the only people on the street, crunching along the sidewalk, breathing the cold, dark air, and holding hands. This time, though, there were no snowballs, no games. We now knew the whole story. The truth had not set us free, any more than it had Sophie Reiner.

I phoned Eric when we returned from our walk. "It's worse than we could have imagined," I said.

"For us or for him?"

"For humanity. And for him. We're not just talking deportation. We're talking extradition and possibly a major war crimes trial."

"Fax me all the details first thing tomorrow morning."

"There's a lot."

"Boil it down to a fifteen- or twenty-minute presentation. We have a meeting at the White House tomorrow, eleven o'clock sharp. I'll want to review all the material before then, but you'll be the one giving the presentation."

Sunday morning, Lynn and I both woke up well before sunrise. She was haunted by the same horrible thoughts as me. We made love with fierce abandon.

The day dawned cold and sunny. We all met in Eric's office at 9:30 to go over the presentation. Then we made the short walk down Pennsylvania Avenue. Surrounded by snow, the White House looked even more resplendent than usual. We waited at the gate while the Secret Service checked our credentials, then we went through the metal detector, up the curving driveway, past the marine standing stiffly at attention, and into the West Wing. Lynn squeezed my hand. Despite growing up in D.C., I had never been inside the White House — not even to take the tour. We were ushered into a surprisingly shabby conference room. Half a dozen officials sat around the table. Some I knew; others I recognized from TV.

We were introduced to Barry Shields, White House chief of staff; Megan Christie, the president's spokeswoman; and Paul Willett, his chief of communications. I nodded greetings to the deputy attorney general and the Justice Department spokesman.

"Well, Mr. Cain," said Shields, "you dragged us all through the snow on our day of rest. The floor is yours."

"Thank you very much. Tomorrow evening, as you know, the president is scheduled to hand out the McCready Awards for lifetime achievement in the arts. We believe that one of the award winners, Roberto Delatrucha, is an ex-Nazi who should not be in this country and who should never have been granted U.S. citizenship. We also believe he is a major war criminal, who committed vile crimes against humanity." I held up the photo of the young Franz Beck in his full Nazi regalia. That grabbed their attention.

"We believe and we can prove that Mr. Delatrucha's real name is Franz Beck. Beck was an SS officer who served at the Belzec extermination camp in 1942 and participated in the murder of approximately half a million Jews. We have obtained his wartime letters to his girlfriend in Germany as well as a personal journal written in his own hand."

"Can you tell us where you got these documents?" Spokeswoman Christie asked.

"They were stored for many years in Germany by Franz Beck's wartime lover, a woman named Hildegard. When she died last year, her daughter discovered the documents and passed them to us."

"Could these be a hoax, like those Hitler diaries some years back?" Shields asked.

"No, sir, we have verified key parts of the story with actual living witnesses in Germany and Ukraine." We had decided not to get into the Sophie Reiner story. It would only muddy the waters, and we still had no proof that Delatrucha was involved in her murder.

"Please continue," said the chief of staff.

"We have translated these documents. There are many pages. With your permission, we would like to read you a few that illustrate one particular story from Beck's time at Belzec. A full report of the investigation and transcripts of all the documents will of course be available to you later."

I sketched some background on Belzec, explaining how Jews were unloaded from the trains onto a ramp and hustled from there straight into the gas chambers. I showed them the exercise books and some of the letters. Then George read the first extract from the journal, June 23, 1942:

Wonderful day! On the ramp, I saw a young girl get off the train carrying a violin case. She was dark like most of them, maybe 16 years old. She told me her name is Rachel Levitas. She is not unattractive, though dirty, as they all are after the journey. I ordered her to play something. She said her instrument was out of tune. I told her it didn't matter. She played a few measures of a Bach partita. Magical! People stopped to listen; even the Jews smiled. They were on their way to the gas, although they didn't know that, of course. She has real talent; pity she's Jewish. I had a wonderful idea, a true inspiration. There must be many other musicians who arrive here on the transports. What if I collected some? I could form a little orchestra, which would raise the morale of all concerned. I separated her from the rest of her family who went to the "showers" for "delousing." She kept asking for her parents and her little brother, asking when she could see them. I tried to calm her; told her "later." Finally I left her in the barracks with the capos. They'll soon set her straight.

"Capos were Jews who were forced to work for the Nazis," George explained, "doing jobs like pulling corpses out of the gas chambers. If they refused, they were killed."

She ought to be grateful I saved her life. If not for me, she'd be up in smoke by now, like the rest of her family. Commandant

Wirth was very excited about my idea and granted me full authority to implement it.

    The officials were silent. Christie looked shocked, the others more stoic.

I resumed: "Next we want to read you an excerpt from a letter dated August 28, 1942, from Beck to Hildegard."

Lynn picked up the paper and read aloud.

Dear Hildegard,

Excuse me for not writing for so long. You can't imagine the pressure we are under. But wonderful news. We had a very distinguished visitor here today. I can't tell you his name . . .

"We believe this man was Heinrich Himmler," I explained, "Hitler's top deputy, as you know, and the man in charge of the Final Solution. We have collected videotaped testimony in Germany from someone who accompanied Himmler on this visit and remembers the orchestra and a man with a beautiful voice singing as the Jews went to their deaths, just as Beck described."

Lynn resumed.

I think I have told you about my orchestra. Well, perhaps "orchestra" is too grandiose a word for it; it's more a quintet right now — violin, mandolin, accordion, trumpet, and clarinet. A strange combination. The standards are not so high because conditions here are far from ideal. Still, we try our best. My violinist has real talent. We play almost every day. I obtained some sheet music from Warsaw which I have arranged for the instruments we have. Sometimes I sing. The visitor, an important person in the Party, overheard me singing. He said Germany needs talent such as mine. I should be trained, he said, so that I could bring credit to the Reich. When my job

here is done, he said he would arrange for me to be recalled to
resume my musical studies. Imagine, in a few months I may be
back in Berlin! Perhaps this is my reward for all the years of
hard service.

> *With all my fondest embraces,*
> *Your Franz*

"This is particularly significant because it explains how Himmler came to sponsor Beck's debut recital in Berlin in 1944," I said. "We have a newspaper announcement of that event, also an interview that Señor Delatrucha gave to a Spanish newspaper in 1958 describing the concert. We also located the man who was Delatrucha's accompanist that night, and he confirmed crucial details."

George resumed. "The next few entries describe Beck's relationship with the young Jewish violinist, Rachel. First, a journal entry from July 1, 1942:

I think of her night and day. I know it's wrong. I know in some
sense she is not fully human, but who of us in this place is? And
yet her form is human and lovely, and I am but a man. I will
be strong. This is a test of my will, and I shall not fail it.

This of course was the first extract Susan Scott had given me. Now that we knew the context, it made sense.

"One week later, on July 8," George continued, "Beck confided in his diary that he almost kissed Rachel but managed to restrain himself. Two days after that, he wrote about her again:

The witch has captivated me. I must break free of her spell.
Again I almost kissed her. A force I cannot comprehend pulled
me toward her. I am deeply ashamed. I want to protect her,
even though I know it is impossible. I cannot allow myself to
take such risks. Even writing such words could be dangerous.

Hildegard seems but a pale shadow in my memory compared to the creature who presently occupies my thoughts like a black succubus. I must control myself.

"In the following entries, Beck wrestles with his conscience as he becomes more and more obsessed with Rachel," George said.

August 14, 1942. Commandant Wirth approached me with these words — "Listen Franz, fuck the bitch if you must, but stop making eyes at her like a lovesick youth. It sets a bad example. She's a Jewess, for Christ's sake." He's right, of course, but I am helpless. I can neither fuck her nor stop making eyes at her. This must end. She is becoming dangerous to me.

George paused. Everybody was listening raptly. "We have one final document for you, dated September 28, 1942," I told them. Ashen-faced, Lynn lifted the paper.

Today was the hardest of my life, and yet, reflecting on it, I'm sure the shattering experience I have undergone will purify my soul. We were on the ramp, and a transport was pulling in. I had called on the band to play "The Trout," which has become a favorite of the camp personnel, who have heard it so often. Rachel complained once again that she would not play. I grabbed her and cajoled her, after which she said she agreed. The transport came to a halt, and the band struck up. I had just finished the first stanza when she threw down her instrument and started yelling to the disembarking Jews that they were in danger, that they were all about to die, and that they should resist or run away. I have never been so embarrassed or so angry. The ungrateful bitch was alive only because of me. I drew my weapon, approached her, and pulled the trigger. Her blood and brains spattered everywhere. I stomped on the violin until it was completely destroyed. I kicked her body and yelled for an orderly to take it away. The Jews, of course, exploded into panic and had to be forcibly restrained with bullets and dogs. I was afraid I would be blamed, but the commandant congratulated me on my prompt action and said he admired my resolve. So it seems my career will not suffer. My colleagues patted me on the back and later bought me drinks. But now, in the privacy of my room, half drunk, I feel deeply conflicted. I am free of her, yes, but I still see her before me, pleading with those dark Jewish eyes. That she is no longer on this earth has thrown me into utter confusion. For a few moments, I succumbed to darkness. I took out my weapon and pointed it at my own head. My hands shook, and I could not fire. Why could she not accept things as they were? I would have kept her alive as long as I could. I will be happy to leave this accursed place, but how will I free myself of the memories? Will I see her face before me for the rest of my life?

Tears were streaming down Megan Christie's face. The others looked down at the table, unable to move, unwilling to speak. I found myself again in Belzec. Did the ghostly strains of Rachel's violin still haunt those bare woods? No, her only existence was in these long-concealed pages written by her murderer, and in the darkest recesses of Roberto Delatrucha's memory. But that would change. I could not restore Rachel to life, any more than I could bring back my own mother. Things that are done can never be undone. I could not help my grandparents, nor the hundreds of thousands of others who died at Belzec. Only God could bring the dead back to life. But I would make sure the world heard about Rachel Levitas.

"What do you propose we do?" the chief of staff asked finally.

"I've been trying to contact the McCready prize committee," Eric said, "but Chairwoman Sanford can't see me until tomorrow morning. We'll ask her to withdraw the award from Delatrucha. In case the committee hesitates, I suggest that the president find something else to do tomorrow evening. Whatever happens, he should not be anywhere near the Kennedy Center."

"Consider it done," Shields said. "What's your next step?"

"We'll be drawing up deportation papers for Delatrucha. We also plan to alert the German government, which may wish to extradite him to face murder charges, or perhaps the Israelis if the Germans don't want him. Naturally, we'll be consulting the State Department on that. When the time comes, we'll also be scheduling a press conference to expose this man to the world."

As we rose to leave, Megan pressed my hands. "Thank you for doing this. I can't help wondering what I would have done in Rachel's situation. Would I have had that kind of courage?"

"Thank God we'll never have to find out," I said. "As for Delatrucha, it's time for him to face the music."

25

On Sunday night, the temperature dropped another fifteen degrees, and the city froze. Rachel Levitas flitted in and out of my thoughts all night. There was so much I wanted to know about her. Where was she from, who were her parents, where had she learned to play the violin, what did she look like? She was calling to me from beyond the grave, begging me to make her more than just a name in Franz Beck's diary.

I quit the fruitless struggle to fall back to sleep and slid out of bed just after five. Lynn's clothes were strewn around as usual. I picked them up and folded them neatly. In the bathroom, the harsh light accentuated the black circles under my eyes and the deepening creases around my mouth.

Sunrise was still a couple of hours away, but I decided to take a walk in the park. The cold was sharp as pine needles, and the icy sidewalks made walking treacherous, especially while battling a brutal wind. Perhaps some of Rachel's family had survived — not her parents or her brother, of course, but maybe another sibling or a cousin. It was even possible she was listed among the names of the dead registered at Yad Vashem, in Jerusalem, where there were almost three million victims' names on file, submitted by family members and survivors. It was worth checking.

I dropped into the minyan on the way back and was home by seven. Lynn was in the shower when I returned. I peeked in behind the curtain. As my glasses steamed up, her body glowed like a Renoir nude, rosy and wholesome. "I'll make coffee," I called out, my spirits suddenly high.

Lynn emerged wearing a bathrobe, face flushed, curly hair akimbo. "You weren't out running, were you?"

"It's too slippery to run. I went for a walk. I couldn't sleep."

"You're crazy. You should have woken me up. I would have calmed you down." She started pouring granola into bowls. We each grabbed a different section of the newspaper and ate in silence, like an old married couple.

"Here's another writeup about the McCready shindig tonight," Lynn said. "You should see the list of celebrities who are coming. Barbra Streisand, Robin Williams, Yo Yo Ma, Nancy Reagan . . ."

"Wow!"

"Sean Connery is the MC."

"James Bond, my boyhood hero."

"Art Garfunkel is singing a song."

"You're kidding. Now, I wish I were going."

"You are. I bought tickets for us."

"You did? When?"

"A few weeks ago. I thought they might come in handy. I also got tickets for the gala at the Willard Hotel after the ceremony."

"The one hosted by Mitch Conroy?"

She nodded.

"That must have cost you a bundle."

"I'm expensing it," she grinned.

"And did you already know who you'd be taking?"

"Actually I added a third ticket on Friday."

"Oh? Who for?"

"Jacob."

"Who?"

"Your dad. I called him up, and he told me he wanted to come. He should arrive in town later this afternoon."

"I haven't spoken to him since we got back from Europe."

"Don't worry. He knows the pressure you've been under."

"And he's obviously crazy about you," I added.

After I showered, I was about to put on my usual white shirt when I saw the black one I had bought a few weeks ago sitting unopened in its packet. There would never be a better day to wear it. I chose a blood red tie to go with it.

"You look spiffy and just a little bit menacing," Lynn said. "Like you aren't going to take any shit from anyone."

"I'm not."

We drove to work down streets canyoned with huge heaps of plowed snow and ice. Schools were closed, and traffic was sparse. Washington was enjoying an unexpected winter vacation. The department was three-quarters empty. The federal government had given all but essential employees the day off.

In my office, I called Sara Barclay, hoping to find her behind her desk. She picked up. "Sara, I wanted to ask, are you in touch with anyone at Yad Vashem in Jerusalem?"

"Sure, we share information, and I meet their librarians and archivists all the time at conferences."

"I need a favor. I have the name of a young girl. I'd like to know if she's listed in their registry of Holocaust victims."

"What's the name?

"Rachel Levitas. She would have been born around 1925 or 1926, and she probably came from a town somewhere in southern Poland, one of the communities transported to Belzec in late June of 1942."

"She may not be listed at all, if none of her family survived."

"If she isn't, she isn't. But if she is, I need the information fast, today if possible."

"That is fast. I'll see what I can do."

Eric had arranged to meet the head of the McCready Award committee at the Willard Hotel, where all the award winners and committee members were staying. The sun was shining brilliantly, although it offered little warmth. Eric was wearing an extravagant fur hat he had bought on a trip to Moscow that covered his ears and half his face. "You look like an old Soviet commissar," I told him. I think he took it as a compliment.

In the hotel ballroom, preparations were well under way for the evening gala. Workers were hoisting balloons, arranging flowers, and testing the sound system. The organizing committee had commandeered a meeting room on the mezzanine floor and turned it into a makeshift command center. Young people with serious faces rushed around, clutching clipboards. Phones were ringing left and right. Christine Sanford, the chairwoman, was standing in a corner, holding a phone in one hand and a hot drink in the other.

"What the fuck is she doing in *Milwaukee?*" she yelled into the phone. "I don't care. Get her a *limo* to Chicago if you have to. Just get her on a plane. And get me the White House chief of staff. If the president's bailing on me, the least they can do is send me a replacement."

She slammed down the phone. "Welcome to my world," she greeted Eric brusquely. She was a petite woman, dressed in black except for a scarf around her neck that almost matched my tie. She gave us both a harried look. "You must be Rosen. And you are . . . ?"

"Marek Cain, deputy director."

"You've got two minutes. Pull up a chair if you can find one, and tell me what's so important." The phone rang again. She shouted to a young aide, "Robin, hold my calls for a couple of minutes. If it's the White House, I'll take it."

"Pretty hectic around here," Eric noted.

"That's the understatement of the year. It's chaos. It'll be a miracle if we have an event at all. What I wouldn't give for a cigarette."

Sanford had been a moderately successful movie actress, who had left the screen for politics twenty years ago and become a well-known voice for liberal causes. She was often on TV sounding off about abortion rights, human rights, privacy rights, civil rights, gay rights, and animal rights. In person, she somehow seemed both smaller and larger than life, speaking in a low smokers' growl, jabbing her index finger in our direction for emphasis.

"Just our luck that the biggest snowstorm in years hits the weekend before the ceremony. Half our guests are stranded in different

276

airports trying to get here. Whoopi is stuck in *Wisconsin*, for Christ's sake. Why she would be there in the first place is beyond me. Nancy canceled. Plus, just to make things fucking perfect, some White House lackey called yesterday to say the president can't make it now. Or the vice president. Or the first lady. I asked if the assistant janitor could come. They said they'd get back to me. I told them half of the guests only show up for a chance to get their picture taken with the president. What am I supposed to tell them? It's a disaster. Thank God for Mitch Conroy, and I say that as a devout Democrat. His office said he'd be there for sure. If necessary, he can do the honors. What can I do for you guys?"

"Did Roberto Delatrucha make it to D.C.?" Eric asked.

"Delatrucha? He's right here in the hotel. God bless him, he's the one person I don't have to worry about."

"You do now," Eric said. "I'll be brief. We have reason to believe that Roberto Delatrucha is a Nazi war criminal."

"What?" she choked on her drink. "Run that past me again."

"We believe his real name is Franz Beck. He was a Nazi and a member of the SS. He served at an extermination camp. He sang to the victims on their way to the gas chambers," he said.

"Is this some kind of sick joke?"

"No joke. And there's no doubt. We have cast-iron evidence."

Sanford was aghast. She looked wildly around the room, then grabbed Eric by the arm and pulled him toward the door. I trailed along behind. "Come with me, and keep your voice down, for Christ's sake," she hissed. "Let's go somewhere we can talk."

She stalked down the corridor like an assassin, opening doors and slamming them shut until she found a deserted conference room. As soon as the door was closed, Sanford turned on Eric. "Why the fuck did you wait until *today* to tell me?" she asked. "What do you expect me to do now?"

"We didn't have the evidence until this past weekend. We would have told you earlier if we could have."

"Wonderful. Just wonderful. Tell me what you've got."

As Eric laid out the case and showed her the photograph of Beck in his SS uniform, her eyes narrowed, and her lips thinned.

"What a disaster. No wonder the president is running away like a nun from a nudie show. I suppose I have you to thank for that."

"You should withdraw the prize from Delatrucha today and exclude him from this evening's celebrations," Eric said.

There was a long silence.

"Well, this is quite a crock of shit you've landed me in," Sanford said at last.

"I would have thought it was a simple decision," Eric replied.

"No decision is simple around here. First of all, half the committee hasn't even arrived yet. I can't make this kind of call on my own. Some of them won't get here until just before the event. We worked for nine months before deciding to give him the prize. Now I'm supposed to take it away based on a two-minute briefing from you? The programs are printed. The guests are invited. This is a big deal."

"I realize that," Eric said coldly.

"And you don't just make accusations against someone without giving him a chance to defend himself. It's un-American."

"You've seen the picture," I said. "This man is evil."

"Evil is relative. We've all committed acts you could call evil at one time or another. Let him who is free of sin cast the first stone and all that," she said.

"We're not talking about minor transgressions. This man served at an extermination camp and helped murder half a million people," I replied. She was beginning to get on my nerves.

"That's what you say. But evidence can be wrong, pictures can be doctored. It happens all the time. I'm not saying these are. I'm just saying we can't condemn him without hearing his side of it. We're not running a fucking kangaroo court. The Constitution says he's innocent until proven guilty."

"I don't see what the Constitution has to do with him receiving an award. He'll have ample opportunity to defend himself once we initiate legal proceedings against him," Eric said. "He'll have every single constitutional right there is and then some. I wanted to save the president and your organization the embarrassment of being tainted by association with such a man."

"I wish you hadn't told me. We could have pleaded ignorance."

She thought for a moment. "I'll try to convene the whole committee later to brief them on your allegations. But I'm pretty sure they'll say the show must go on. The prize is awarded for a lifetime of achievement in the arts. It has nothing to do with what may have happened before. I assume you aren't questioning his artistic merit."

"He's a wonderful singer," I said. "But he's a wonderful singer who's a war criminal. He got his start in a death camp."

"He still deserves a fair hearing. We can always revoke the prize retroactively."

"Your decision," Eric replied coldly. "But when the shit starts flying and it lands on you and your committee, don't say we didn't warn you."

"This isn't a good sign," Eric said as we walked back to the office. "We don't want people rallying around him because he's such a wonderful singer. I wish we could have stopped him getting the prize. It may strengthen his position once the fight begins."

"When people see the pictures and hear about what he did to Rachel Levitas, no prize will save him. In fact, it makes it a juicier story for TV. By the way, what about Mitch Conroy? Shouldn't we warn him to stay away?"

"We should," Eric said, his eyes narrowing the way they did when he had an idea. "Absolutely."

"What do you want to do?"

"Call Doneghan and send copies of the documents by messenger."

"Done."

"You know, it's amazing how often you hear about important documents being delivered late or not being opened on time, especially on a day like today, when half the city probably isn't working because of the snow."

"That would be regrettable," I said, catching on.

"And phone calls don't always get through. You do your best, leave a voice mail or a message with an intern, but somehow they just don't get through in time."

"Such things have been known to happen," I said.

"It would be a pity if that happened," Eric murmured.

Back at the office, I was surveying the lamentable disorganization that had overtaken my desk when Lynn stuck her head in. "How'd it go?" she asked.

"Not well. I don't think we persuaded her."

"No way. Get out!"

"Their problem, not ours. Meanwhile, we have a lot of work to do here if we're going to have a press conference later this week. Can you prepare an AV display and a background paper for the media? Eric's still considering how to break the story. He may give it as an exclusive to someone like Barbara Walters or *60 Minutes* to drum up more publicity."

"On it," Lynn said.

"And I want George to contact that guy in the German Justice Ministry who traveled with us, what was his name?"

"Gunther Scharpf?"

"Yes. We need him to get permission from that abominable old Nazi Ruddiger to take the video we shot of him public."

Upstairs, lawyers were drafting a court order to revoke Delatrucha's U.S. citizenship. Janet was writing a brief explaining the historical role of Belzec. We were also arranging separate briefings for the German and Israeli ambassadors. The whole office was now working on the Delatrucha case. John Howard had called in sick.

At around 3:00 P.M., just as I was going for my fourth cup of coffee, the phone rang. It was Sara Barclay. "They found your girl in the Yad Vashem registry," she announced. "Rachel Levitas, born 1926, from a small town called Jaslo. Southern Poland. I looked up the Nazi deportation schedules to Belzec, and the dates fit."

"Who filed the papers listing her as a victim?"

"Her brother. He filed in 1964 for his parents as well. Also, another brother, aged four, and several aunts, uncles, and cousins. About fifteen people in all."

"What's his name, this brother who survived?"

"Yitzhak Levitas. At the time he filed with Yad Vashem, he gave an address in Ramat Gan, Israel. But that was thirty years ago. I have no idea if he's still there or even if he's still alive. I asked the guys at Yad Vashem if they could trace him, but it may take some time."

"That's great, Sara. Thanks so much. I'd like to talk to him soon and tell him how heroic his sister was."

"What did she do?"

"She tried to warn Jews they were going to their deaths at Belzec. Delatrucha shot her point-blank in the head. When things are a bit quieter, I'll tell you the whole thing. You won't believe it."

"There's one more thing," she said. "There was a picture of Rachel on file. They faxed it over from Jerusalem. I've already sent it to you by messenger. She was such a beautiful young girl."

"I owe you big-time."

That reminded me that I had to "send" some material to Jack Doneghan. I photocopied a picture of Delatrucha wearing his Nazi uniform and stuffed it in an envelope with a brief note explaining our findings. "If we send this over to Capitol Hill right now, when will it arrive?" I asked the receptionist.

"It will be in their mailroom within an hour or two, but it might take longer before it reaches the desk of the person you're sending it to, especially today with so many people off."

"Do they stamp the date and time when it arrives?"

"I believe so; we do here."

"Perfect," I said. "By the way, I'm expecting a packet myself any minute. Please call me when it arrives."

"It just did," she said, handing me an envelope.

Back in my office, I called Doneghan and was put through to his assistant's voice mail. I left my name and number and asked him to call back. With any luck, he'd get the message tomorrow, when it would be too late.

Lynn popped in as I put down the phone. "What's that?" she asked.

"Rachel," I said, ripping the envelope open. Her features were fuzzy from the fax transmission, but you could see her dark, vibrant eyes framed by prominent eyebrows, delicate cheekbones, and soft dark lips in a half-smile. She was about thirteen or fourteen years old in the picture and gazed out with a mixture of innocence and determination. I gazed back and felt my eyes fill with tears. She was born the same year as my mother.

"Poor child," Lynn said, leaning over my shoulder. "I almost feel like she's talking to me."

"What's she saying?"

"'It's time to nail the bastard.'"

26

Some time later, I heard that during the transport of the Jewish work brigade from Belzec to Sobibor, some mutiny and shooting took place.

— TESTIMONY OF WERNER DUBOIS

T HEN MY FATHER WALKED IN. I hugged him gingerly; he felt skinnier and frailer than I remembered. He hadn't shaved that day, and I had a flashback to that childhood feeling of rubbing my face against his whiskers. "Dad, I think this is the first time you've ever been in my office," I said. "Now you can observe me in my natural habitat."

"It was quite difficult to get in. There's a lot of security inside and outside the building," he said. *That must be Fabrizio's doing*, I thought.

"Hi there, Jacob," Lynn said.

His eyes lit up when he saw her. "Lynn, how wonderful you look, as always."

"It's almost time to leave for the Kennedy Center, and we still have tons to do," I said, breaking up the love fest.

"Can I go dressed like this?" he asked, indicating his checked flannel shirt and blue jeans.

"Why not? Who's going to object? Delatrucha?"

I explained my plan to them.

"Are you sure?" Lynn asked. "If you're caught, you could get into big trouble."

"I know."

"Don't you want to run it past Eric?"

"Eric won't agree. He has to go by the book."

"Don't you?"

"Officially, yes. But this isn't official. This is personal."

"I don't want you losing your job over this."

"I've spent my whole life following procedures. No more."

I made six copies of the picture of Rachel Levitas and stuck them together with tape to form a large rectangle, which I rolled into a cylinder.

On the way to the Kennedy Center, I asked the cab driver to stop at the Willard Hotel, where I bought a bunch of red roses at the florist shop in the lobby.

"I have an important package for Mr. Delatrucha," I told the concierge on duty. "Could you please have it delivered it to his room? If he's not in, have the bellboy slide it under his door. I'd like him to see it as soon as he gets back." He nodded when I slid a twenty into his hand.

At the Kennedy Center, the nation's cultural elite was climbing out of limos and preening into the foyer. Inside, bejeweled women in low-cut gowns and men in tuxedos strutted around, cocktails in hand. And these were just the hangers-on. The truly rich and famous, including all the movie stars, were nowhere to be seen. They were presumably enjoying their champagne and canapés in private rooms upstairs rather than mixing with the hoi polloi in the lobby.

Our seats were in the middle of the orchestra section, about twelve rows back from the stage. My dad was several rows behind. As we sat down, there was a loud cheer as Mitch Conroy, with Jack Doneghan at his side, entered and took his seat. The speaker waved enthusiastically, drinking in the applause. Doneghan clearly had not received my phone message or the letter I had sent him warning him not to show up. *What a pity!*

Sean Connery, wearing a tux with a tartan bow tie and matching cummerbund, took the stage and picked up the microphone, and the evening began. In his soft, Scottish burr, he apologized on behalf of the president who could not be present due to other pressing engagements. Fortunately, Speaker Conroy had gallantly filled the breach.

"God, I love that accent of his," Lynn murmured. "So sexy. Why don't you have a British accent, Marek?"

"Dreadfully sorry, old thing."

Then Connery introduced the six prizewinners who filed one by one onto the stage, acknowledging the warm ovation, and sat down in a semicircle. As his name was called, Delatrucha strolled out, beaming, relishing the moment. He bowed several times, clutching his hands over his heart and blowing kisses to the audience. I wondered if his ex-wife was somewhere in the crowd. If she was, she was probably seething.

To my surprise, the laureates were not required to do anything except listen while others praised them. The evening consisted of a procession of distinguished presenters reading biographies of each winner interspersed by musical interludes. They did show a video clip of Delatrucha singing Mahler, with a full orchestra behind him. His voice soared effortlessly over the massed strings and brass, awesomely powerful and authoritative.

I felt a bit sorry for Art Garfunkel, having to follow that. I had expected "Bridge over Troubled Water," but instead he sang "Sound of Silence" which was possibly more appropriate. Delatrucha listened intently and clapped politely. Whoopi Goldberg miraculously arrived from snowbound Wisconsin and regaled the audience with a racy monologue. A semi-famous pianist played a Bach prelude and fugue and afterward made a big point of hugging Delatrucha.

Finally, Mitch Conroy took the stage to bestow the gold medals on the lucky winners. One by one they came forward, basking in appreciation. Delatrucha was the last to approach. Conroy was waiting, medal in hand. A barrage of flash lights went off as the two embraced. Delatrucha bent his head, and Conroy hung the medallion around his neck. Then he joined the other winners, who had stepped forward to wave to the audience once again.

"Now," I said to Lynn, thrusting the flowers into her hand. She walked forward until she was standing directly beneath Delatrucha, who was near the front of the stage. I hung back a few steps behind her. Other audience members were also handing out bouquets or tossing them onto the stage. "Mr. Delatrucha," she called. She caught his eye, and he smiled at the pretty young woman offering him roses and went down on one knee to accept them.

"These are from Rachel Levitas," Lynn hissed. "She wants you to know that nothing has been forgotten or forgiven." Delatrucha looked puzzled.

"Who?" I heard him say. He looked down at the flowers and noticed something unusual. The flowers were wrapped in paper containing six images of a young girl. He stiffened, and the roses fell to the ground. Reacting swiftly, he picked them up, his eyes glued to the multiple portraits of the young Jewish girl with her wistful smile, come to call him to account from beyond the grave.

Applause swelled again from the audience, and all his years of training reasserted themselves. Like an automaton, he bowed, baring his teeth in a ghastly simulacrum of a smile. We retreated a few steps, melting into the crowd where he could no longer see us. Family members of the prizewinners were taking the stage to congratulate their loved ones and share the moment. Elissa Horne, Delatrucha's wife and accompanist, approached to offer a hug and whisper something in his ear. She took the roses from him and glanced at the paper. He snatched it from her, screwed it into a large ball, and shoved it in his pocket, where it made a noticeable bulge. She asked him something, but he turned on his heel without responding.

"That had an effect," I said.

"Yeah, he definitely recognized her. It took him a few seconds, but I saw it in his eyes," Lynn said.

Conroy was escorting the other prizewinners from the stage. The ceremony was over, and everyone was anxious to get back to the hotel for the party, where there would be lots of free booze and food.

"Now what?" Lynn asked.

"He'll probably want to freshen up a bit in his hotel room before the party."

"And that's when he's going to find that package you had delivered."

"Yeah, the one-two punch. After the initial surprise, I wanted him to be in no doubt we had all the goods on him. He can sit and read his own diary for a while. He hasn't seen it for fifty years. That should really give him something to think about."

Jacob asked, "Do you think he'll have the chutzpah to show up at the party?"

I thought about it for a second. "He'll be there. You can bet on it."

A taxi arrived, and we got in.

"My guess is, he'll resist every step of the way," I continued. "Most of these Nazis do. He may be in shock right now, but part of him is already planning his strategy."

"What strategy?" Lynn asked. "He's totally screwed."

"First, he'll deny everything. He'll claim mistaken identity. He'll hire the best lawyers money can buy, and they'll keep filing legal motions to drag the proceedings out for years. He'll call on his political friends and his musical friends for support. He'll cry persecution and claim that he's the real victim. He'll launch personal attacks on me and Eric. Meanwhile, he'll keep appearing in public wherever they'll have him and behave as if he has nothing to be ashamed of. And if that doesn't work, he'll say he's a sick old man and we should all just leave him be. Tonight is just the beginning."

At the hotel, we joined the throng crowding into the ballroom. It was a bit like an election-night victory celebration. People were electrified, downing alcohol as fast as they could. A loud hubbub rose in the room, practically drowning out the jazz ensemble on stage playing big band music. We joined a long line snaking back from the door for our chance to shake hands with Mitch Conroy, who was greeting the guests one by one as they entered. Suddenly a beefy paw grabbed my sleeve.

"What the fuck are you doing here?" Doneghan growled.

"Nice to see you, Jack. I want you to meet my father, Jacob Cain, and my fiancée, Lynn Daniels."

That slowed him down. "Sir, ma'am," he nodded politely at them. Drawing me aside, he asked again, "What's going on?"

"Nothing," I protested. "I just came to hear if Delatrucha would sing 'America the Beautiful,' seeing how it nearly brought you to tears."

"I don't believe you."

"You should. By the way, Jack, I called you today, but you weren't in your office. I left a message. I also sent you some documents."

"What documents?"

"You'll see. And now, if you'll excuse me. . . ." I extricated myself from his grasp and rejoined the others.

"So I'm your fiancée, am I?" Lynn asked.

"Poetic license." I blushed. "Just to get him off my back. When I propose, I promise you'll be the first to know. And if I'm accepted, you'll be the second," I added, turning to my father.

"Maybe I'll be the one to propose," Lynn said.

A sudden roar rose as Delatrucha entered the room, still wearing the medal around his chest, followed by the other award winners. Elissa trailed a few steps behind him. Conroy escorted him to the bandstand and took the microphone. Delatrucha looked pale, and Conroy practically had to drag him along.

"Ladies and gentlemen, what a night!" Conroy shouted as the room quieted down. "The president sure doesn't know what he's missing." There were a few laughs and desultory boos from the audience. Conroy grinned and gestured for silence. "No need for that, ladies and gentlemen, no need for that. We're dealing with art here tonight, not politics. Anyway, I'm sure y'all will agree that the president's loss is our gain." There was a large laugh from the audience. "I mean, his artistic loss is our artistic gain." Another laugh.

Conroy smiled again. "We're all honored to be here, and I have a special treat for you. My good buddy here, Roberto, has agreed to sing for us. I had to strong-arm him into it. He didn't want to, but he just agreed." A cheer went up.

"Now, some of you may not know that Roberto and I are old friends," Conroy continued. "I've been honored to be a guest in his wonderful home down in Florida. You see, we share a love of freedom and a love of America as well as a love of music. Roberto here grew up in Argentina, but he chose to become an American, and he's made a huge contribution to our nation. I'm personally honored to have the support and friendship of such a great Hispanic American. So, ladies and gentlemen, let's welcome Roberto, and let's not forget his wonderful wife, Elissa, a great American in her own right."

The applause swelled again, but Delatrucha didn't acknowledge it. He stepped onto the bandstand, waving away the microphone. Lynn's hand was clutching mine. What was he going to do? Elissa walked over to a piano set up on the stage and sat down. The room went quiet. Delatrucha closed his eyes for a moment, clutching his hands in front of him as if in silent prayer. Then he spoke in a low voice that penetrated to the far corners of the ballroom.

"Ladies and gentlemen, I am not one for speeches. I have always been a private man. I have always let music speak for me. There is nothing I can express, no emotion I can encompass, that has not been better expressed already by, say, Robert Schumann or Franz Schubert. All of humanity — the good and the bad, the noble and the base — lies in their songs." A few hands started clapping; Delatrucha shook his head to hush them. The crowd had gone from raucous to somber in seconds. Delatrucha glanced up at the mirrored ceiling, as though he were seeking inspiration.

"Schubert and Schumann and Brahms and the great Richard Strauss — whom I was once honored to meet as a young man — these are the men who have spoken for me these many years, as long as God has given me the strength. The music is pure, even when we are not. Perhaps I did not do all that could have been done, but those who were not there have no right to criticize. They do not know what it was like. They do not know how they would have acted. I have struggled with this all my life, and, believe me, many times I longed to end my struggles. And still, even today, I do believe that through music I brought good to the world. I hope that is remembered to my credit."

"What the hell's he talking about?" someone asked.

"And so tonight, ladies and gentlemen," Delatrucha continued, "I wish to sing you a little song. Speaker Conroy asked for 'America the Beautiful,' but I have chosen instead a song by my namesake, a song that has followed me throughout my life.

"I have sung this song in circumstances none of you can imagine, and yet, only now, only tonight, do I suddenly see that strangely, it encompasses my whole life. Tonight Roberto Delatrucha dangles at the end of the hook. I did not choose my fate. It chose me. When all is said and done, I am just an ordinary man with an extraordinary voice." He paused and then repeated, "Just an ordinary man."

A hum formed in the room as people turned to their neighbors, asking what it all meant. Delatrucha whispered a few words in Elissa's ear and kissed her lightly on the back of the neck. Then he took up position in front of her, one hand on the side of the piano.

" 'Die Forelle,' " he announced.

" 'The Trout,' " Lynn whispered.

"Of course," I said.

Elissa bent her head and began to play the introduction, transforming the piano into a gently flowing brook, the water rippling softly over a stony riverbed. A man stands on a riverbank watching a beautiful fish gliding through clear waters, darting about as swift as an arrow. A fisherman on the other bank casts his line, but the fish evades it. You can hear the fish splashing in the sparkling stream in the rippling piano chords. The narrator watches the contest between fish and fisherman, hoping the trout will win. "So long as the water stays clear, the fisherman will never catch the trout," he thinks to himself. But the fisherman is crafty and stirs up the water with mud from the streambed. A second later, the beautiful creature hangs on the hook, bloodied and dying. The piano murmurs out its final breaths and grows quiet.

It is a short song, barely two minutes, a work of miniature perfection, but it deceives. The melody is cheerful, conveying unclouded delight, but the words speak of trickery, treachery, and death. "My blood was boiling as I beheld the victim of deceit," the narrator says in the final line of the song. But of course, he can do nothing but watch.

His eyes half closed, Delatrucha seemed fully immersed in the words and melody. The song ended, there was a moment of silence, and the hall erupted in applause. It washed over him, his arms outstretched as if in benediction. He bowed deeply and acknowledged his wife, who stood by the piano and curtsied gracefully. Then he pulled a gun from his inside breast pocket, put it to the side of his head, and pulled the trigger.

27

The bad old songs, the bad and evil dreams,
Let us now bury them, bring a large coffin.

— "THE BAD OLD SONGS" BY HEINRICH HEINE,
MUSIC BY ROBERT SCHUMANN

PANDEMONIUM OVERTOOK THE ROOM; frightened and screaming, the audience stampeded for the exits, shoving each other aside in the rush to get out. Some took cover behind chairs or under tables. I charged forward to the stage, but Lynn pulled me to the side of the room, where it was safe. "Mark, you can't help him. He's dead," she shouted. "His skull exploded." She was so calm. She might not fold her clothes at night, and she would never fold in a crisis, either.

To his credit, Conroy stood his ground, bending down to Delatrucha, who was lying facedown in a spreading pool of blood. Doneghan, his face a pudgy mask of revulsion, pulled his boss away, pointing at the cameras. A gaggle of photographers approached, snapping furiously. The speaker's face was splashed with blood, and his white shirt was stained red. A group of security agents, weapons drawn, rushed forward, surrounded him, and pushed him to the ground, shielding him with their bodies.

"Where's my father?" I bellowed.

"I don't know," Lynn shouted back. "He was standing just behind me." I looked wildly around the room but couldn't find him.

Christine Sanford had stepped forward and picked up the microphone. "Please calm down, ladies and gentlemen. Please exit the room in an orderly manner. We are not under attack. I repeat, we are not under attack," she pleaded. As people realized no further shots had been fired, her words started to calm the ballroom.

I felt an arm on my sleeve and turned around. It was Dad, apparently none the worse for wear. I hugged him fiercely, feeling his whiskers against my cheek. "Are you okay? Are you okay?"

"I'm fine," he reassured me, patting me on the back.

Elissa had collapsed in front of the piano. Sanford, still holding the mike, called out, "Is there a doctor here? We need a doctor." I wasn't sure what to do next. The scene kept replaying in my head.

Turning to Lynn, I muttered in a daze, "I killed him. Now I'm a murderer, too."

"Nonsense," she snapped. "He killed himself."

"I pushed him to it. I did everything but pull the trigger."

"You made him face the past. Suicide was his own choice."

My eyes filled with tears. I took off my glasses, trying to blink them away. She grabbed me by both arms. "Listen, Mark, this is no time to go wobbly. Put your glasses back on, and look at me!" I tried to focus on what she was saying. "You need to call Eric. Right now. The department has to respond to this." She started pulling me from the room.

"Tonight? It's nearly ten o'clock." Sirens were already blaring outside. Scores of police and emergency personnel had converged on the hotel and were streaming into the lobby, clearing a pathway through the crush of terrified people.

"This can't wait until tomorrow," Lynn said. "You need to get the facts out quickly. The story's going to probably run on CNN in less than ten minutes."

She was right. I scanned for a pay phone, fumbling for a quarter. No more than five minutes could have passed since the shooting. It seemed like an eternity. Conroy, surrounded by bodyguards, was being hustled out of the building. He had wiped most of the blood off his face, but spatter remained on his neck and collar. Doneghan stumbled by as I dialed Eric's number.

"Delatrucha shot himself," I said without preamble.

"Where? When?"

"In the hotel ballroom, a few minutes ago."

"Fuck. Is he dead?"

"He blew his head off. TV cameras caught the whole thing. Lynn thinks we need to issue a statement about our investigation."

"Christ, I don't believe this. Tell me exactly what happened."

"He made a long, rambling speech about how he's just an ordinary man; next he sang 'The Trout' and took a bow. Then, all of a sudden, he pulls out a gun, and *bang*! It happened in a flash. One minute he's standing there, the next . . ."

"Okay, don't panic, keep calm. How did he know we were on to him?"

"It's a long story. I'll tell you later."

"Mark, what the hell have you been up to? Never mind. Was anyone else injured?"

"I don't think so. Conroy got splattered with gore. There was a rush for the exits, but no one was hurt."

"Okay, good. Listen, Lynn's right. We need to put out a statement. Here's what we'll do. I'll call the communications director right now. We'll write up something brief and get it on the wires. Where are you now?"

"Still at the hotel, at a pay phone in the lobby."

"Head back to the office. We'll meet there in half an hour. I'm going to call the attorney general. The White House needs to know, too. Don't talk to anyone before you talk to me. We'll go through the sequence of events."

I hung up the phone and found myself face to face with John Howard, his face whiter than usual. "What the hell are you doing here?" he gasped. "Did you see what went on in there?"

"Yes." I turned to go, but he clutched my sleeve.

"Cain, you didn't have anything to do with it, did you?" I didn't answer. "You did, didn't you? I knew it." I ripped myself clear of him, shoved him out of the way, and found Lynn and my dad.

We started walking down Pennsylvania Avenue. The night was colder than ever, a bone-piercing cold. "Dad, you must be exhausted. Let Lynn take you back to the apartment in my car. It looks like I'm going to be in meetings for a while, maybe all night."

"Yes, I think maybe I have had enough excitement for one night," he said.

I gave Lynn my car keys. "Come back to the office as soon as you've got him settled," I told her. "I'm going to need you."

"I'll be there in an hour."

"Sorry about all this, Dad," I said.

"Ach, don't worry so much. I'm tougher than I look. You're the one always preaching about justice. Now you got it."

But I hadn't.

The department was buzzing with activity when I arrived. Eric hustled me into his office. "Okay, what did you do?"

I explained about the flowers wrapped in Rachel Levitas's image and the envelope under his door. Eric looked grim. "Why couldn't you just have gone by the book, for Christ's sake?"

"I didn't want him to enjoy another night of triumph."

"Well, you succeeded in that. Unfortunately, now you'll have to face the consequences, too. There's no way to keep your role hidden. The police will find the material in his room and figure out where it came from."

"I'm not ashamed of what I did. I didn't know he would kill himself." I decided not to mention my encounter with John Howard.

"There may be disciplinary measures. If you start to take a lot of heat, I won't be able to defend you. I've told you before, I will always protect the office and the mission above any individual."

"Yes, Eric, you've always been clear. What do you want me to do now? Am I suspended?"

"Are you kidding? This is the biggest story to hit this department for years, probably ever, and you're at the heart of it. The boss wants to see you right now."

Ten minutes later, I was sitting in the attorney general's suite, helping Eric brief the top brass. Eric did most of talking. As he spoke, I found myself reliving the experience as if it were a video clip looping in my head. The music ends. He bows. Arms out, right hand into pocket. The gun appears against his head. *Bam!*

"Mark, Mark . . ." I blinked and returned to the present. "Are you sure you're all right, young man?" the attorney general asked. "Perhaps you should see a doctor."

"No, sir, I'm fine."

"Well, get yourself together. You'll be appearing in a press conference here tomorrow morning. Apparently you're going to be the star of the show." Eric frowned in silence.

It took only a few minutes to craft a bland two-sentence statement for the press. "The Department of Justice Office of Special Investigations acknowledges it was conducting an ongoing investigation into the Nazi past of the late singer Roberto Delatrucha and was preparing to bring proceedings to revoke his U.S. citizenship. OSI director Eric Rosen and deputy director Marek Cain will hold a news conference at the department, Tuesday, February 21 at 11:00 A.M." Five minutes after we sent it out, it was on the AP wire. Five minutes after that, it was on CNN.

Eric and I prepared for the press briefing. At my suggestion, we decided to keep Sophie Reiner's name out of it. No point in muddying the waters with talk of murder in the streets of Washington. Delatrucha and what he had done at Belzec were the focus.

Eric turned on the TV, which was looping the video over and over. The footage abruptly cut off just as Delatrucha put the gun to his head, then resumed with his body on the ground. Our statement flashed along the bottom of the screen, along with another from Mitch Conroy expressing shock and regret.

"Now we have an enemy for life," Eric said.

"We're covered. I called Doneghan and sent over an envelope full of stuff. They'll be the ones on the defensive, not us."

"We'll see which angle the press wants to push."

"What do we want them to focus on?"

"From their point of view, this story has everything — sex, violence, and scandal. We want to downplay Conroy's involvement. If they ask why he wasn't informed in time, it was a simple breakdown in communications due to the snowstorm. I think the best angle for us and for the media is Rachel Levitas. Keep her at the center of the story. The press will lap it up. Keep the focus on Rachel, and they may not delve into how Delatrucha knew about the investigation."

"And if I'm asked about that?"

"I'll step in and say we're looking into it. This is the second leak we've had within a week, and obviously we need to do something about it."

Eric set Lynn to work on the press kits for the reporters next morning. When the print shop opened at eight, there would be enough time to make copies of extracts from Beck's diary in German and English, especially the passage where he described shooting Rachel, whose picture would be included in the dossier, along with the interview in *Diario ABC,* where Delatrucha admitted giving a recital in Berlin in 1944, as well as the notice George had found in the Nazi newspaper advertising the same recital.

Lynn had called in a couple of other aides to man the phones, which didn't stop ringing all night as reporters tried to scoop the story. George, even more grim-faced than usual, offered his services. At 5:00 A.M., the German Ministry of Justice called. It was Gunther Scharpf. "I have seen the news on TV," he said in his perfect Oxford English. "Quite a spectacular end to the story."

"It's not over yet. Is it big news over there?"

"Are you serious? With pictures like that? Everybody here is talking about it. There is some sympathy for Delatrucha. The morning news is emphasizing what a wonderful interpreter of German songs he was. They assume he was nothing more than a low-level Nazi collaborator. Nobody has any idea yet that he was in the SS and served at Belzec. It will be a sensation. I hope you realize you are going to be an international media personality. They plan to carry your press conference live in Germany and across Europe as well."

"Please don't say that. I'm not sure I can handle it."

"You can't avoid it. Just so you know, we will shortly be issuing a statement stating that we were aware of your investigation and assisted in it."

"That's fine. You did help."

"And one final thing: I tried to contact Herr Ruddiger, as you requested. I have to tell you that he died a week after our interview."

"Maybe he and Beck are comparing notes right now in the afterlife," I said.

"Indeed. The good news is you are free to use the videotape you shot of him, since he can no longer refuse his permission."

That was useful. I asked George to review the tape and transcribe the most dramatic part, where he described Franz Beck singing to terrified Jews as they came off the train.

At 5:30 A.M., the department's chief press officer came by to run through some of the anticipated questions. "Where did you get Delatrucha's diary?" he asked.

"It was sent to us by the daughter of Delatrucha's wartime lover after her death," Eric replied. "She asked to remain anonymous, and we are honoring her request."

The press officer asked a few more questions and seemed satisfied with our responses. By that time, the morning papers had arrived. All of them had dramatic pictures on the front page of Delatrucha with a gun to his head and Mitch Conroy covered with blood. "Star Singer Shoots Himself at Gala," said the *Washington Post*. The subheadline read: "Justice Dept. Probe Revealed Nazi Past." The article had no details on us, other than the statement we had issued, but plenty on Delatrucha's relationship with Mitch Conroy.

I was still wearing my black shirt and desperately needed to shower and change. Eric walked downstairs with me. "It's only a matter of time before the German press comes up with the Sophie Reiner connection. Once we give them his real name, people who knew him and his girlfriend when he was young will come out of the woodwork."

"Hopefully by that time the FBI will have solved her murder," I said.

"You really think he was behind it?"

"Who else? I think Sophie went down to Florida and introduced herself as his daughter. He was expecting her; he'd been tipped off by Susan Scott that she was coming. When he refused to acknowledge her and told her to leave, Sophie threatened to expose him by giving the documents to me. So he had her killed."

"Just like that?"

"You saw what he was capable of."

As I left the building, camera crews were already setting up outside. Media trucks with antennas and satellite dishes were congregating in the parking lot. A couple of reporters approached me, but I waved them away. Was this what my life was going to be like for the next few weeks? Lynn was waiting on the street with my car.

Washington was waking up as we drove through streets still piled high with heaps of snow. We went up to my apartment and collapsed on the bed. I kissed her deeply, hungrily. "You know what I said about you being my fiancée?" I murmured.

"Not now," she said, snuggling up to me.

"You know how I feel about you."

"I know, but you're really stressed out right now, and you have a big press conference ahead of you and days and days of interviews and publicity. You're not going to have time for me. Let's wait until things calm down, and then we'll figure out what we want to do."

The thought of all those cameras and reporters and questions made me queasy. "I'm not much good at TV," I said. "I tend to speak in long sentences instead of pithy sound bites."

"You'll be awesome. I know you will." She kissed me firmly, administering a dose of self-confidence, mouth-to-mouth.

"I hope you're right."

"It's just a question of finding the right tie to go with your spotless white shirt, and you'll knock 'em dead."

But I had done enough knocking people dead for one day.

At nine I returned to the department, which had been encircled by TV trucks. I parked in an underground garage several blocks away. Walking back, I felt more and more apprehensive. I wasn't made for all this exposure. This was Eric's scene, not mine. Lynn had forced me to eat some breakfast before leaving the apartment. "You can't do this on an empty stomach," she said. Now, I felt sick.

Reporters brandishing microphones stood outside the building, filling air time. I wove through a crowd of vehicles and people, trying to reach the entrance without being recognized. It was an amazing sight. All the major networks had sent mobile units the size of RVs, bristling with electronics, but there were also smaller vans representing local TV stations and radio outlets from all over the country parked in neat rows. It was a forest of antennas and logos. As I turned to go into the building, something caught my eye. Something was wrong; something didn't fit. At first it didn't register, but then it clicked.

There was a U-Haul in the parking lot.

28

I SWALLOWED THE URGE TO SHOUT OUT for everyone to run. That would set off a huge stampede and not help anyone inside. I walked back into the parking lot, edging closer to make sure. Perhaps it was a mistake or a coincidence. The world is full of U-Hauls. That hope died when I saw the side of the vehicle. A chartreuse T. rex roared at me, warning me to keep away. The caption read, "Move Yourself Safely." Fabrizio was right; the truck was from Utah. They were using the media frenzy as camouflage and had parked right against the side of the Department of Justice.

Two guys sat in the cab. The fat one was smoking a cigarette; I recognized him immediately. The other one was smaller and skinnier. He was eating a muffin. As long as they were sitting there, we weren't in immediate danger. They wouldn't blow themselves to smithereens along with the building. They would wait for the press conference to begin, so they could get the attorney general *and* all the media at the same time. What to do? Run to my office and call the FBI? I didn't want to let them out of my sight even for a minute. What if they spooked and decided not to wait any longer? They could just step out of the vehicle, set the charge, and walk away, and nobody would know to stop them.

Not knowing what else to do, I approached a reporter on the sidewalk, microphone in hand. He was chatting to his camera crew in German. I grabbed him by the shoulder and asked if he had a cell phone. "What?" He turned on me, angry at the interruption.

"Do you have a cell phone?" I said in German. "It's an emergency."

"Who the hell are you?" he asked.

"I'm Marek Cain, the guy giving the press conference," I said, shoving my security pass under his face. "I'll give you the biggest fucking scoop of your life if you just let me use your cell phone for a minute. It's a matter of life and death."

He looked at the pass, comparing the happily calm man in the photograph with the face of the man sweating nervously in front of him. Doubt and confusion flickered in his eyes. "Why?" he said.

"I'll tell you everything later. Just give me your phone. We're all in terrible danger."

"Danger?"

"I'll tell you in a second. *For the love of God*, give me your phone."

My desperation convinced him. He pulled out his cell. I punched in Fabrizio's number. *Pick up, pick up, pick up, pick up.*

After the sixth ring, she picked up. "Thank God," I gasped.

"Boy you've been busy. I really didn't—"

"Shut up and listen. I'm standing outside the Department of Justice looking at a U-Haul."

"Shit. The same one?"

"It has a T. rex on it. For Christ's sake, tell me what I'm supposed to do. I don't know what to do here!"

"Okay, don't panic. I need to alert our people. Is there anyone in the truck?"

"Two guys, the *same* guys!"

"Okay. Stay on the line. I'll be back with you in a second."

The German reporter was tugging at my arm. I tried to pull away, but he persisted. "What the hell's going on?"

"See that truck over there?"

"Which one?"

"The U-Haul. Those guys are neo-Nazis."

"What?!"

"And their truck is full of explosives."

He eyed me, trying to gauge if I was serious. When he saw that I was, he stepped back, eyes darting from side to side, searching for an escape route. "Explosives?"

"Keep your voice down. We don't want to set off a panic. The police will be here in a couple of minutes."

"O-okay." I knew what he was thinking. I was thinking the same thing. But to his credit, he turned to his cameraman, gesturing to him to start rolling film. "Ladies and gentlemen, urgent and dramatic news from Washington this morning, brought to you exclusively by Channel Three. We're standing outside the U.S. Justice Department here with Marek Cain, the renowned Nazi hunter. He says . . ."

Fabrizio came back on the line. "The police are on the way. You should hear sirens within a minute or two. Make sure those guys don't get out of the truck."

"How am I supposed to stop them?"

"Any way you can. They could detonate it electronically as soon as they get clear. They could either set a fuse from the cab or blow it up by remote control."

"How far away would they need to get to be safe?"

"I don't know, maybe a hundred yards."

The German correspondent thrust the mike into my face. "Herr Cain, would you please tell our viewers what's happening here?"

"Not now," I said, pushing the mike aside. I was listening for police sirens. Nothing . . . nothing . . . and then finally I heard one, faint at first, getting louder. A few seconds later, the guys in the truck heard it, too. I saw one nudge the other; I grabbed the reporter's arm. "Quick, get over there. You take that door, I'll take the other. Don't let those guys get out of that truck."

"What?"

I was already sprinting. I reached the door just as the fat guy in the driver's seat started pushing it open. He hadn't seen me coming. I shouldered it shut.

"What the fuck?" he shouted. The sirens were louder now. He

pushed hard and got it half open, but I held on tight, digging in my heels and leaning against it with my full weight. He started rolling down the window. Did he have a gun? I didn't want to find out, so I fished for the pepper spray out of my jacket pocket, turned, stuck the canister through the half-open window and gave him a five-second blast. He shrieked inside the cab as the spray took effect; he let go of the door, and I slammed it shut. The sirens were deafening, and there was confusion all around. Officers were fanning out through the parking lot, and cameras rolled as more reporters realized that a story was unfolding in front of their eyes, although they weren't sure what it was. The fat man lay writhing on the seat, hands clutching his eyes, racked with coughs. But his cohort had disappeared. The German reporter had let me down.

I circled the U-Haul and saw him earnestly yakking to his viewers back home. I grabbed him furiously by the lapels.

"Did you let him out? *Did you?*"

He tried to brush me off.

"Where'd he go?" I yelled, refusing to release him.

He pointed toward Pennsylvania Avenue. There, maybe thirty yards away, a skinny little man was jogging down the street, and he wasn't wearing a track suit. All he needed was sixty more yards to blow us all sky-high. He was almost halfway there.

I threw off my coat. He had a start, but he didn't know I was after him, which gave me a chance. I was flying, taking long, loping strides, keeping the heels of my dress shoes off the ground so as not to alert him. I didn't want him turning around and exercising his Second Amendment rights on me.

He jogged into a crosswalk. I sped up, desperate to catch him before the traffic light changed and cut me off. By the time he reached the opposite sidewalk I was only a couple of yards behind him. As I came closer, I could hear him breathing. I launched myself forward like a linebacker making an open-field tackle. My feet sailed behind me, and my shoulder cracked him squarely in the small of the back. My right arm wrapped around his torso while my left gripped the back of his head just below the hairline. He yelled as his knees crumpled. His head was careening toward the ground. A split second later, his nose and chin struck the pavement with an almighty thump. I was still driving forward, my upper body tight against his back. All the air went out of him with a whoosh, and he gurgled, fighting for breath against a rising fountain of blood. Half winded, I wrenched my right hand free, rolled away, and struggled to my feet, ready to kick him in the teeth if he stirred. But he was out cold. Pedestrians were staring at me, frozen where they stood. A minute later, the police arrived.

The rest of the day passed in a blur. Police evacuated the Department of Justice, the parking lot, and all surrounding buildings. Fabrizio had called in explosives experts to deal with the truck, which was loaded with ammonium nitrate and primed to explode. After a few hours, they towed the U-Haul, and the area was declared safe.

Both of the neo-Nazis were taken in shackles under armed guard to the emergency room for treatment. The one I tackled had a broken nose and multiple contusions to his ratty face, but he would live to stand trial. Police found a handwritten statement in his pocket, full of deranged ranting against the federal government, abortion, homosexuals, and Jews.

For the next couple of hours, federal agents and security types quizzed me on what I knew and how I knew it. Fabrizio helped me get through it. Eric rescheduled the press conference for 4:00 P.M. In the meantime, the cable networks were running two major stories: Delatrucha's suicide and an attempt to blow up the Justice Department. I was at the center of both.

Somehow I got through the news conference, though I'd never seen so many cameras and microphones in all my life. Lynn said I handled it well. The attorney general seemed pleased and clapped me on the back. Then an endless series of one-on-one interviews for different TV shows over the next few days. Eric was almost equally in demand. My picture even appeared on the front cover of a tabloid under the headline, "Nerd Who Hunted Nazis Saves the Government!" They ran my high school yearbook picture. I looked like a pimply young geek in thick glasses. "Why'd they do that? I complained to Lynn. "I haven't looked like that since 1976."

"No one reads that stuff anyway."

"Actually, millions of people do."

"Then I'm glad they called you a nerd. If they printed the truth, I'd be fighting off the competition," she said.

Delatrucha was buried quietly in Florida a week later. According to Fabrizio, who was there, only a few people showed up. One who did appear, and made sure she got herself photographed outside the cemetery, was Susan Scott, looking chic behind a black silk veil. Elissa, the grieving widow, kept her silence, refusing all requests for interviews. In a way, she was another of Delatrucha's victims.

As we had hoped, the press zeroed in on the Rachel Levitas story. Saying that Delatrucha had helped kill half a million people would have left people numb. The number was too vast to grasp, and he wasn't the one doing the gassing. Giving them the name and a picture of one pretty young girl made Belzec seem real. Soon, her face was everywhere, especially when Yitzhak Levitas, her brother who was still living in Israel, came forward. Now in his mid-seventies, he had survived the war as a refugee in the Soviet Union. On TV, he leafed through an old family photo album that contained several more pictures of Rachel and the rest of the family. One of the five-year-old Rachel holding a tiny violin pulled at my heart.

"Rachel was my beloved sister," Yitzhak told the TV interviewer. "I always wondered what happened to her. She never left my thoughts in all these years. She was the talented one in the family. She could have been a great violinist."

Eric decided we needed to publish Beck's complete diaries and letters as quickly as possible. George was named editor, with the task of writing an introduction explaining the significance of Operation Reinhard and Belzec and providing footnotes putting Delatrucha's comments into perspective. We hoped to have it in bookstores by April, with profits going to Holocaust education in the United States.

A week after the shooting, the McCready committee formally revoked Delatrucha's award. It was too little too late. The prizes would forever be linked with that horrific night.

Conroy seemed anxious to accept our unspoken offer of a truce. He wanted the story to go away as quickly as possible. Two days after the press conference, Doneghan called. "Mark — I can call you Mark, can't I?"

"Sure, Jack."

"The speaker doesn't blame you for that mix-up in communications we had that day. He knows, and I know, you tried to keep us in the picture, and we appreciate that. Of course, like I told you before and like I'm telling the press, we were one hundred and ten percent behind your investigation every step of the way. That's the message that needs to get out. If it hadn't been for the snow, your messages would have definitely arrived in time," he said.

"I'm glad you see it that way," I said.

"I do, and the speaker does, too. And he wants you to know the new Republican majority is fully behind the work y'all are doing for the American people. We looked at the figures, and every penny in your budget is well spent. We may even be looking to raise it a bit, seeing as how time is running out and there may be a few more of these Nazi types still hiding out and evading justice. And of course, we're going to look seriously at Eric Rosen's idea of expanding your mandate to deal with other crimes against humanity."

"Thank you, Jack," I said. "It's much appreciated."

After that, Conroy's folksy Texan drawl didn't pop up quite so much on TV and radio. He obviously felt the need to lower his profile, at least for a while. Political pundits reckoned his position as speaker was secure, but it was doubtful he would ever be able to run for president. The association with Delatrucha would forever hang over him.

John Howard quietly tendered his resignation. A week later, he was working for a Republican lobbyist on K Street.

One strange and unexpected outcome: sales of Schubert lieder soared at the record stores and garnered more air time on classical radio stations. It wouldn't be for long, but it was nice while it lasted. At least Mary Scott, the accompanist on most of Delatrucha's discs, would get a financial boost from the royalties.

Lynn and I decided not to get engaged. Actually, Lynn decided.

"I'm not ready," she told me a week after the press conference. "Ever since I've known you, you've been obsessed with Delatrucha." For a horrible moment, I thought she was breaking up with me, and my heart sank. "It's been awesome and exciting and all, but now I want to see what you're like when he's not there, buzzing around in your brain. I want to see what we're like together when it's normal." I heaved a silent sigh of relief. I could do normal as long as she was still around.

"And another thing — I'm starting my new job next week," she said. "You can woo me. I want to be wooed. We'll go to movies, concerts; we'll go out to dinner if we can afford it, and if you can find somewhere kosher. Maybe I'll come to shul with you. If you play your cards right, I may even stay to study the Mishna with you from time to time."

"What about weekends away? Sunset walks on the beach? Evenings in front of the log fire? Red roses for Valentine's Day?"

"Now you're talking!"

My father announced he was not quitting West Virginia to move to Washington after all. As soon as the snow melted, he planned to start rebuilding his cabin, with extra rooms for grandchildren. I told him not to hold his breath, but he just smiled and said he could wait.

Two weeks after Delatrucha's suicide, I received a letter from the Department of Justice inspector general advising me that an internal inquiry into my behavior was under way and that I might be required to testify at some point. I had the right to legal counsel if I so desired. I asked Eric if I was in danger of losing my job. He said it was highly unlikely after all that I'd done, but advised me to hire a lawyer, just in case. He also told me to see a shrink, muttering something about posttraumatic stress disorder. Oddly enough, I'd stopped having nightmares and was sleeping better than I had in years.

All this time, the Sophie Reiner case remained open. Fabrizio called me one day to say that the little guy who had tried to blow up the Department had confessed to the murder. He insisted he had been working alone. "Do you believe him?" I asked.

"No. He was definitely working for someone. Eventually we'll worm it out of him."

"Why did he do it?"

"He's borderline paranoid, I would say. He seems to have a personal fixation with you. He keeps swearing he's going to kill you and mount your head on his wall."

"What!?"

"Don't worry. He'll never see the outside of prison again. The attorney general's probably going for the death penalty."

"Even though his plan didn't succeed?"

"I forgot to mention — he's a serial killer. He's also confessed to shooting that jogger a few weeks ago and to pushing a young woman off the platform in the Metro."

"Jennifer? Oh, God!"

"Did you know her?"

"She was my ex-girlfriend. She was on her way home from my apartment. She'd just come to collect some stuff. Her family was told it was an accident. She would still be alive if she hadn't come that night."

"Don't be stupid. Of course it wasn't your fault."

"Why didn't he just kill me instead of her? And that jogger he killed — was that instead of me as well? He was killed where I go running almost every day."

"We'll have to go ask him."

As soon as she hung up, I called Jennifer's brother in California and explained what I'd just learned and how sorry I was. He was kind and told me not to blame myself. But I couldn't help it.

A few evenings later, I was sitting with Lynn watching TV when Susan Scott came on. NBC had been promoting an exclusive interview with her for days, promising that Delatrucha's daughter would make "shocking revelations." I wondered if she was planning to reveal the existence of Delatrucha's other, secret daughter, Sophie. But the interview took a different track.

"We've all heard about the ghastly crimes committed by Roberto Delatrucha as a young man," the stone-faced anchor began, as footage of his final performance at the Willard Hotel ran behind her on screen. "But what was he like as a man? What was it like to live with him, to grow up with him? What was it like to have a secret

Nazi as a father? Tonight, we speak with Delatrucha's daughter, Susan Scott, the only person who can answer these questions. Welcome, Susan, and thanks for having the courage to share what must be very painful memories."

"Barbara, I had to. I felt I had a duty," Susan replied. She was wearing a demure pink cashmere sweater, with a string of pearls around her neck. Her hair had grown since I had last seen her, framing her face and giving her a younger, more innocent look. Her lipstick and nails were a pale rose. Everything was calculated to produce a picture of softly understated elegance with a sort of bruised vulnerability just beneath the surface.

The interviewer asked her what she had known about her father's past and how she felt about his death. Susan said she had known nothing and was confused and devastated. Then the subject turned to her childhood and her own musical studies. Susan's memories flowed like a well-rehearsed sonata.

"I remember one time. I was sixteen and taking violin classes at Juilliard," she began. The screen cut to a picture of her as a teenager, holding her instrument. She was a gorgeous young woman, elegant and self-possessed even then.

"My teachers liked me. I had real talent; everybody said so," Susan continued. "Not that I would ever have been a big-time soloist. I didn't have the personality. Chamber music was my passion. My mother encouraged me. Everything was going well."

"And your father?" the interviewer asked.

"He encouraged me, too, at first, but less and less as time went on."

"Maybe he felt you were a threat to him."

"How? He was so great, such an enormous talent, such a towering personality. Everybody thinks of him now as this evil Nazi, and I guess he was. . . ." She dabbed at her eyes with a tissue. "But they forget what an incredible musician he was. I could never have rivaled him. Even if I had joined a chamber group or an orchestra, I would never have been famous like him." She paused. "Anyway, I recall this particular winter evening. I was at home in the music room, working on a piece. It was the *Trout Quintet*. I was working on the fourth movement, the theme and variations." She hummed a few bars of the now-familiar song in a pleasant soprano.

"I heard the door slam when my father arrived home," Susan went on. "He'd had a couple of drinks, maybe more than a couple. I could smell the liquor on his breath."

"Was your father a drinker?" Barbara asked in that quiet, understanding voice interviewers adopt with victims of trauma.

"Not really. He drank very rarely, but every six or eight months he would go on a big bender. He'd put away a whole bottle of whiskey. He must have been haunted by his past, but at the time neither my mother nor I could understand why he did it. This was one of those times. As soon as he came into the house, he started shouting at me from the hallway to stop playing. Of course, having read his diary, I know now what that theme must have meant for him — but I didn't know then. So I ignored him and carried on playing. He kicked the door open and burst into the room. I'll never forget it. He was screaming and yelling, 'How dare you defy me?' I'd never seen him like that. Never! He was almost incoherent."

A picture of Delatrucha in his SS uniform flashed on-screen as the announcer intoned, "When we come back, more dramatic revelations from Delatrucha's daughter."

A beer commercial came on, and Lynn muted the sound. "She's quite a piece of work," she said.

"Very illuminating."

"Like hell. Don't you see what she's trying to do?"

My own thoughts were beginning to crystallize, but I wanted Lynn's opinion.

"She's portraying herself as another of his victims, another Rachel. Of course, she just *happened* to be playing the *Trout Quintet* when he had his big tantrum. Don't you find that a bit far-fetched?"

"It could be true. What else would have made him blow up like that? Susan's always told us the truth. Why would she start lying now?"

"For a man of thirty-six, you —"

"Thirty-five until April 8."

"For a guy in his mid-thirties, you're still so naive. This interview

311

is totally bullshit, and it's pissing me off. I wonder how much they paid her for this sob story."

The commercials ended, and the program resumed. For the benefit of viewers just tuning in, Barbara gave a quick recap. "So you were practicing the *Trout Quintet,* and your father came in and started yelling at you. What happened next?"

Susan put her hands to her face, the same way she had when we had interviewed her in her office. Again, she struggled not to cry, gulping and turning her head away from the camera. The interviewer's face was a picture of sympathy and concern.

"It's been inside me for so long, for so many years," Susan said. "This hasn't been easy for me."

"But you feel you have to do it."

Susan nodded bravely. "I do, Barbara. I do."

"So you were playing, and he yelled at you to stop."

"That's right. And I remember looking up at him and saying, 'Why should I stop?' and I carried on playing. Then he . . ." She faltered. "He . . . He grabbed the violin out of my hands, and he . . . he smashed it to pieces over the piano. That violin was a birthday present from my mother. It was so beautiful, rosy-colored wood, almost golden — and now it was in splinters, the neck snapped and strings hanging everywhere."

"What happened then?" the interviewer asked.

"My mother came in and led him into the bedroom until he sobered up."

"And that was the end of it?"

"No. Later that night, when I was asleep, he came into my room to apologize and make it up to me. The best way he knew how." She was weeping, tears coursing down her cheeks.

"He abused you."

"I'm sorry, Barbara. I can't. That part of my life is over. It's over. I'll never speak of it."

The show ended with the accusation hanging in the air. A week later, the *New York Times* reported that Susan had signed a contract with a major publishing house for three million dollars to write her memoir.

"Big surprise," Lynn said when we met in the office. It was her last day. Eric was hosting good-bye drinks for her that night after work.

"Why do you say that?" I asked.

"That's Susan Scott's specialty, selling other peoples' stories of childhood abuse. This time it's her own story. It's big bucks for her."

"You've never liked her," I said, playing devil's advocate.

"Not true. I believed her in her office. Mostly. And I felt sorry for her. But now I see what she is. She's an operator, a player. Sometimes she'll tell the truth, and sometimes she'll stretch it. And sometimes she'll outright lie, if it suits her. Plus, she's a brilliant actress. They should give her an Emmy for that performance. You don't believe her, do you?"

"Not completely. The problem is sorting the truth from the lies."

"I don't believe a word of that interview. It's not enough her father was a Nazi. Now he's also a child molester, raping his own daughter. She said she'd never speak about it because it's so, so painful, but she's the one who brought it up! Excuse me while I dry my tears. She was jacking up the price of her book contract."

And the pieces of the puzzle fell into place. *That's it!*

"I need to call Fabrizio," I said, fumbling for the phone. "We're going on one more trip."

"When?" Lynn asked.

"Right now."

29

We reached Medford late that afternoon. The door to Susan's office was flanked with packing boxes. The waiting room was empty, no furniture, the posters and photographs gone from the walls. Susan was sitting behind her desk, feeding documents into a shredder. I knocked on the open door, and there was a momentary flash of shock on her face until she rearranged it into an expression of semi-welcome. She was back to the dark, metallic look — black turtleneck, black pants, silver chain around her neck, silver earrings, silver bracelet, silver nails. "What are you doing here?" she asked. "And Ms. Daniels, too. Why didn't you call to say you were coming?"

"Are you going out of business?" Lynn asked.

"No," she laughed. "Hardly, my dear. In fact, business has never been better. I've taken a new office on Beacon Hill. Much more appropriate for my needs. My clients didn't like having to trek out to boring old suburbia. This place was only temporary until things picked up. And of course, I need a more suitable place for writing my own book."

"Ah yes, your child abuse memoir," I said. "The memories so painful they couldn't be spoken of ever again. I can hardly wait to read it. Will it be shelved in the fiction or nonfiction section?"

She laughed again. "Now, now, Mark. No need to be jealous. You could write your own book if you wanted. *Memoirs of a Nazi Hunter.* Catchy title, great concept — I'm sure I could sell it for a tidy sum. I take a fifteen percent commission."

"I'll consider it," I said. "But surely you want to know how the story ends."

"What do you mean?"

"You want to know what happened to your half-sister, Sophie Reiner, and why she was killed. That's the heart of the mystery, isn't it?"

"That little guy confessed. Case closed, no?"

"He did, but that still leaves the question of who ordered him to."

"I take no pleasure in saying this, but it had to have been my father. He did it to keep her quiet."

"That's what I thought for a long time, too. But I think it was someone else."

"Really?" she said. "Who?"

"You, of course."

Her face registered surprise, fear, and outrage before settling on anger. She pointed a sharp, metallic finger at me. "You're crazy. Your case would never have gone anywhere without me. I helped make you world-famous."

"I know. At crucial moments, you supplied important snippets of information that kept the case going. That's why I was so slow to catch on. Lynn keeps calling me naive, and I guess I am. I was really naive about you."

"I have no idea what the hell you're talking about. And if you dare repeat in public what you just said, I will sue you for slander and defamation, and I will take you to the cleaners. By the time I'm done with you, you'll be lucky to own your own yarmulke."

"Nobody's going public. In fact, I'm your biggest fan. You deserve a lot more than three million dollars. Not only did you fool me, you fooled your father as well, to say nothing of the FBI. You ran rings around everybody. You were brilliant."

"You really are crazy."

"Maybe. But you might as well humor me and listen to what I

have to say. What have you got to lose? I can't prove a thing. At worst, you lose a few minutes of your precious shredding time. At best, you get a great final chapter to your book."

"Why are you here, Cain?"

"I want to offer my congratulations. Not many people get away with murder. You appear to be one of the exceptions. Like father, like daughter — although his was on a much grander scale. But even he paid the price eventually."

"You're wearing a wire. You're trying to trick me into saying something."

"You've been watching too many cop dramas. The FBI would laugh in my face if I went to them with my theory. They closed the case weeks ago. You can search me if you like. Do you want to check?"

She sunk down in her seat, a smug half-smile on her face. "No, it's not necessary, because I'm not going to admit anything. I'll listen to your crackpot ideas if it makes you happy, but I'm not confirming anything, I'm not accepting anything, and I'm not stipulating any-thing. If you say something and I'm silent, it doesn't mean I agree. Ms. Daniels here can be our witness, though she looks as surprised as I am. Did your geeky boyfriend keep it from you too, Lynn?"

"We don't have secrets," Lynn said.

"Ah, young love. How sweet. Go ahead, Mark. This is your Hercule Poirot moment. Give it your best shot."

"For the longest time, I was sure this case was about your father's attempt to cover up the truth. But it was really just about money. That's how it started, and that's how it will end."

"Good dramatic intro," Susan said, relaxing in her chair. "Do go on."

"When Sophie Reiner appeared in your life that day, you were in a deep hole. You have expensive tastes. You like designer clothes, jewelry — you stay in the swankiest hotels. A room at the Four Seasons goes for $350 a night, minimum. But your business was going down the tubes. And then Sophie came along. I think you told the truth when you said how shocked you were. Who wouldn't be?

But after she left, you got to thinking. That's when you called your father."

"None of this is new. I told you myself," she parried. "Come on, nerd boy. Surely you've got more than that."

"At some point, you and your father struck a deal. You'd take care of Sophie for him in exchange for a hefty payment. How much did he fork over? A hundred thousand? Two hundred thousand? How much was her death worth to him?"

"Don't be ridiculous. I'm a literary agent, for God's sake. You told me yourself you can't look up hit men under *H* in the yellow pages."

"True," I agreed. "But you have a very special friend. What was his book called?"

"From the Hood to the Joint and Back Again," Lynn chimed in.

For the first time, Susan looked rattled. She swallowed hard, and her fists clenched and unclenched. "Jimmy had nothing to do with this," she said. "Ask him yourselves. He'll be here in a few minutes. And he can be quite unfriendly when he's pissed off."

"I'm sure he can. That's what made him so valuable to you. Jimmy Williamson had the gangland and neo-Nazi connections you needed. I suppose you offered to split the money with him fifty-fifty or sixty-forty. He called one of his buddies to do the hit. But there was a wrinkle. You weren't interested in a onetime payment from Daddy Dearest. A hundred thousand, or whatever he paid you, wouldn't go very far in financing your lifestyle. Hell, it probably wouldn't even clear your debts. You needed him to keep on giving. That's where I came in."

"I was waiting for that," Susan said sardonically, looking at her watch.

"I was a little suspicious that first day when Sophie came to my office. She told me she'd come to me because she'd read my name in the German press. I've been quoted there a couple of times, but not for a long time. On the other hand, the *New York Times* had just run a profile of me a month before, which I saw lying right here." I slapped my hand on the desktop for emphasis. "You tried to hide it, which made me suspicious, although not until much later. My boss thought maybe that article had been translated into German. I checked, and it wasn't. All of which led me to conclude you suggested to Sophie that she come to see me."

"Why would I do that?" Susan asked. "Seems like a pretty dumb move to me, and I'm not dumb."

"You're not dumb, but even brilliant minds make mistakes. My guess is that after you got over the initial shock, your first thought was to blackmail your father. But Sophie wouldn't go along. She wasn't interested in money. She wanted love — the love of the father she'd never had."

"Drivel," said Susan.

"We'll see. Plan B would have been to get hold of Sophie's documents after you had her killed. Then you would have had your father over a barrel, and you could have collected regular monthly payments for as long as he lived. But Sophie had hidden the documents, and you didn't know where they were. You needed another way of squeezing him."

"Is there much more? This is getting tedious." She glanced again at her watch.

"Not that much. For it to work, you needed your father to believe he was still in danger of being exposed. That's where I came in." I had her full attention. "You knew Sophie had come to see me. Now you had to convince your father that I was actually investigating him. If he believed that, he might be persuaded to part with another chunk of money. To tweak my interest a bit more, you had someone plant that 6-6-6 on my car, which created a link to the 6-6-6 the police found in Sophie's pocket."

"Boy, I *was* smart, wasn't I? What did I do next?"

"You called your father again and told him how you learned that I was investigating him. You told him that I'd attended his master class at the University of Virginia, that I'd seen your mother splatter him with red ink, and that I'd even invited your mother to lunch to talk about him. That sends him into a total panic. He asks if you can arrange to have me silenced. The two of you agree on a price. Only you're much too smart to actually assassinate a U.S. government official, which would bring the whole system down on your head. You tell the two neo-Nazis who attacked me in my apartment lobby to make it look like an assassination attempt but not to kill me."

"You're getting nuttier and nuttier. Who'd believe such baloney?" Susan snorted.

"At the same time, Jimmy gives my name and Rosen's to a neo-Nazi newsletter. We're getting a flood of hate mail and threatening phone calls, which makes us even more scared and confused. We didn't know who was after us, and we certainly would never suspect it was you. If you'd stopped there, you would have gotten away with it."

"Have you thought of trying to write a thriller? You have a real talent for fiction. *The Nazi Hunter: A Novel.* I like it — I can hardly wait to hear what happens next."

"What happens next is that Lynn and I arrived here to interview you, catching you by surprise. You couldn't make up your mind how much to tell us, but then, as we spoke, you figured it was another golden opportunity to put the squeeze on Daddy. You asked me if I knew his real name, and stupidly I told you. At the same time, you let slip that your father had once hired an ex-con as his gardener. I passed the tip on to the FBI, just as you had hoped I would, and they started asking him questions. Now, he's totally freaked. You call him one more time and offer to try to get rid of me again — for another big fee, the biggest yet."

I smiled at her. She smiled back, a ghastly, joyless grimace.

"Arranging that attack on us in West Virginia was your biggest mistake. You got greedy. Before that, I didn't suspect you at all. But you were the only one who could have engineered it. Apart from my boss and the FBI, you were the only one who knew I was there."

"How could I have known that?" Susan protested.

"The day we arrived there, you called Eric Rosen and told him you needed to speak to me urgently. Eric gave you my dad's phone number, but you never called. Instead, you used it to get his address. A day later, your gaggle of amateur hit men showed up at the cabin. Unfortunately, it didn't go as planned. When it turned into a firefight, they lost their tempers and burned the house down."

"Absolute crap."

"Maybe I have some details wrong, but that's basically the way it went down. What complicated matters was that the skinny guy had his own agenda. He had a shitload of ammonium nitrate sitting in his truck, ready to blow up a government building. All of a sudden, he's forced underground. The FBI is on his trail. He decides to go ahead and carry out the big attack before he's caught."

"So that was my fault, too?"

"It may have been, indirectly. And now the most brilliant part of your scheme, the part I couldn't see until Lynn pointed it out yesterday. What had me confused through all this was the way you helped me along. Without those photocopies you gave me, and without telling me about Sophie being your half sister, we would never have gotten as far as we did. So I asked myself, Why would you help me?"

"Why?" Susan sighed.

"You wanted me to believe your father had a motive to get rid of Sophie, which of course he did. But the clever part came when you realized how much more money you could make if I actually succeeded in exposing your father as a Nazi. Like a lightbulb going off in your head. There was a limit to the number of fake assassination attempts he'd be willing to pay for, but, if my investigation were to succeed, you'd have something really good to sell."

"Which is?"

"Your story. You knew how much money a juicy memoir of child abuse could bring in. You'd already sold one. What was it called?"

"*Surviving Daddy: A Poet's Experience with Sexual Abuse*," Lynn offered with a smile.

"That was a big bestseller, wasn't it? But you had a much better version—a story about being molested by a Nazi war criminal. It doesn't get any juicer than that. When he won a McCready Award, he became a national figure. Soon, he'd be shaking hands with the president. What a great picture for the insert that would make! The market value of your memoir skyrocketed. You not only wanted me to succeed, you needed me to succeed. And when I did, it worked out better than you could ever have imagined. Daddy killed himself on national TV. Suddenly, the whole *world* is talking about him. And now you're three million dollars richer, and all your troubles are over."

"Well, this is all very ingenious, Mark, but as you say, you can't prove any of it," Susan said as she looked at her watch again.

"If you're waiting for Jimmy, he's been unavoidably detained," said Lynn. "I believe the FBI may be having a few words with him right now."

Susan hit back with her old defiance. "They're wasting their time. Jimmy won't talk. And without Jimmy, you can't prove a damn thing."

"Maybe Jimmy won't talk," I said. "On the other hand, if he's looking at the death penalty or life without parole, maybe he will. It'll be interesting to see."

"He won't talk," she said stubbornly.

"Even if he doesn't, something else will," I said. "I told you this case was all about money, and that's how it will be solved. The FBI will follow the money. Those checks your father sent you for killing Sophie and trying to kill me — they'll tell the story. The checks you wrote Jimmy, the money he transferred to his neo-Nazi buddy — it's all going to add up. Jimmy may not talk, but the money will."

We walked out, leaving the door open. I smiled at Agent Fabrizio and the three cops with her as we passed them on the stairs.

AUTHOR'S NOTE

This book is fiction, but Belzec is not. My grandparents, Adolf and Bertha Elsner, died there in 1942. All the chapter epigraphs about the extermination camp are authentic, as are the details of the camp itself and Operation Reinhard. Himmler really did witness gassings in Poland. The Nazis also organized small orchestras at extermination camps, including Belzec. According to Rudolf Reder, one of only two men to survive the camp, the orchestra at Belzec consisted of six musicians who usually played in the area between the gas chambers and the burial pits. The description of the camp memorial in chapter 21 is based on a visit I made there with my father in 1993. Fortunately, we were also privileged to attend the unveiling of a new, much more appropriate memorial in 2005, which finally honors the victims in a fitting way.

Give Schubert a try. You won't be disappointed.

ACKNOWLEDGMENTS

Many thanks are due.

Eli Rosenbaum, the real head of OSI, explained some of his bureau's investigative techniques to me. Mark Egan read an early draft of the manuscript and gave valuable suggestions. John Zogby made a crucial introduction, Cari Parven offered many positive editorial ideas, and Paul Holmes transferred me to a job where I finally had the motivation to write this novel. Paul Hamburger, Debbie Fox, and Justin Epner shared their thoughts on the experience and meaning of prayer. My rabbi and teacher, Stuart Weinblatt, has increased my love and appreciation of Judaism immeasurably.

I'd like to thank my agent, Fred Hill, for invaluable suggestions and constant support. Richard Seaver is a wonderful editor; he and his colleagues at Arcade worked hard to make this book the best it could be. Thanks to James Jayo for shepherding the book through to publication.

As always, I thank my wife Shulamit, who makes my life meaningful.